THE ASCENT

A TALE OF THE GREATEST PIRATE TO EVER LIVE

Y. HU

The Ascent

Print edition ISBN: 979-8-9985322-0-7
E-book edition ISBN: 979-8-9985322-1-4

Published by Y. Hu
www.yanahu.com

First edition: June 2025
10 9 8 7 6 5 4 3 2 1

DISCLAIMER: This is a work of fiction. All of the characters, organizations, ethnicities, cultures, and events portrayed in this novel are either products of the authors imagination or are used factiously. Any resemblance to actual persons, living or dead (except for satirical purposes), is entirely coincidental.

Cover design by Ayahna Hu
Cover images by Shutterstock
Author photograph by Ayahna Hu
Map curtesy of and copyrighted by Canva

This story is for the women who, despite all odds, refuse to drown.

Especially my mother.

THE GLACIAL PASS
HEAVENLY TEMPLE
FOREST OF DESPAIR
BASE 2
PINGSHEN
IMPERIAL TRAINING BASE
???
???
SUPREME TEMPLE
LANGCHENG
BASE 1
XIDAN
NINGBAO
IMPERIAL STRAIGHT
FORBIDDEN HALL
YUXI
POND OF REVERENCE
BEIFO
KWANGCHOW
SOUTH PINGSHEN SEA
THE OTHER
DIYÙ
YŬ XĪ
CELESTIAL TRENCH
BAHAN
CRIMSON OCEAN
FORMOSA
BASE 3
HEAVSO HEADQUARTERS
TEMPLE OF MAZU
BOH
JADE BAY
THE UNTAMED
GOISA
QUZ
SOUL SINGER'S COVE
CRIMSON OCEAN

TRIGGER WARNINGS

Abuse of Power
Child Abuse (Physical)
Death
Drug Addiction
Drug Use
Dubious Consent
Forced Prostitution
Forced Starvation
Genocide
Gore/Descriptive Injuries
Human Experimentation
Implied Child Prostitution (Non-descriptive)
Massacre
Non-consensual Drug Use
Period Typical Misogyny
Physical Abuse
Physical Violence
Poverty
Self-harm/Self-inflicted Injury
Suicide

GLOSSARY

Chinese Historical and Mythological titles/terms/items

Celestial Court – The high court of the Heavens
dao - sword
Dì Yù - Hell
egg boat - the floating dwellings of the Tanka, an ethnic group of Chinese boat people, who live around the ports cities along southeastern coastal line
good commoner – the highest class of civilian in Pingshen society
Huli – fox spirit
Jítóng – spirit medium for the Gods
junk - a type of Chinese sailing vessel, known for its distinctive flat-bottomed design, central rudder, and overhanging flat transom
mean commoner – the lowest class of civilian in Pingshen society
Mazu – Goddess of the Sea and Ocean
qì – the life force/energy within everything in the universe
shui gui – sea ghosts

Silver Bridge – the entrance to Hell
tien gow – gambling game played with dominos
Yán Luó – God of Death; ruler of Dì Yù

Created titles/terms/items

Astir world – a world of the spirits
beamlillies – a flower similar to a lily that reflects the moon's glow
blue moon – equivalent of 100 cycles
cycles – years
gale glass – a mirrored surfaced that allows one to look into both the past and future
Celestial World – the world of the Gods
Corporal World – the world of the mortals
Dì Yù Tǔ Xī – the island of Hell where Yán Luó resides; also known as 'Hell's Breath'
moons – months
Order of the Dragon – military order that believes in the emergence of the Zhì Gāo
sampan – similar to an egg boat
shoūsh – the Hokan curse word comparable to "shit", or "damn"
tâik-ing – the Hokan curse word comparable to "fucking"
tet – a Hokan greeting
The Untamed – mysterious foreign enemy to the West of Pingshen empire
The Other – mysterious foreign enemy to the South of Pingshen empire
Wave Kin – the collection of nomadic clans that share common affinity for the Goddess Mazu

Wielding – the ability to control and exchange energy of six elements (earth, wood, fire, water, metal, and air)
Zhì Gāo – the highest level Wielder; an entity that has the potential to Wield multiple, if not all elements including earth, wood, fire, water, metal, and air

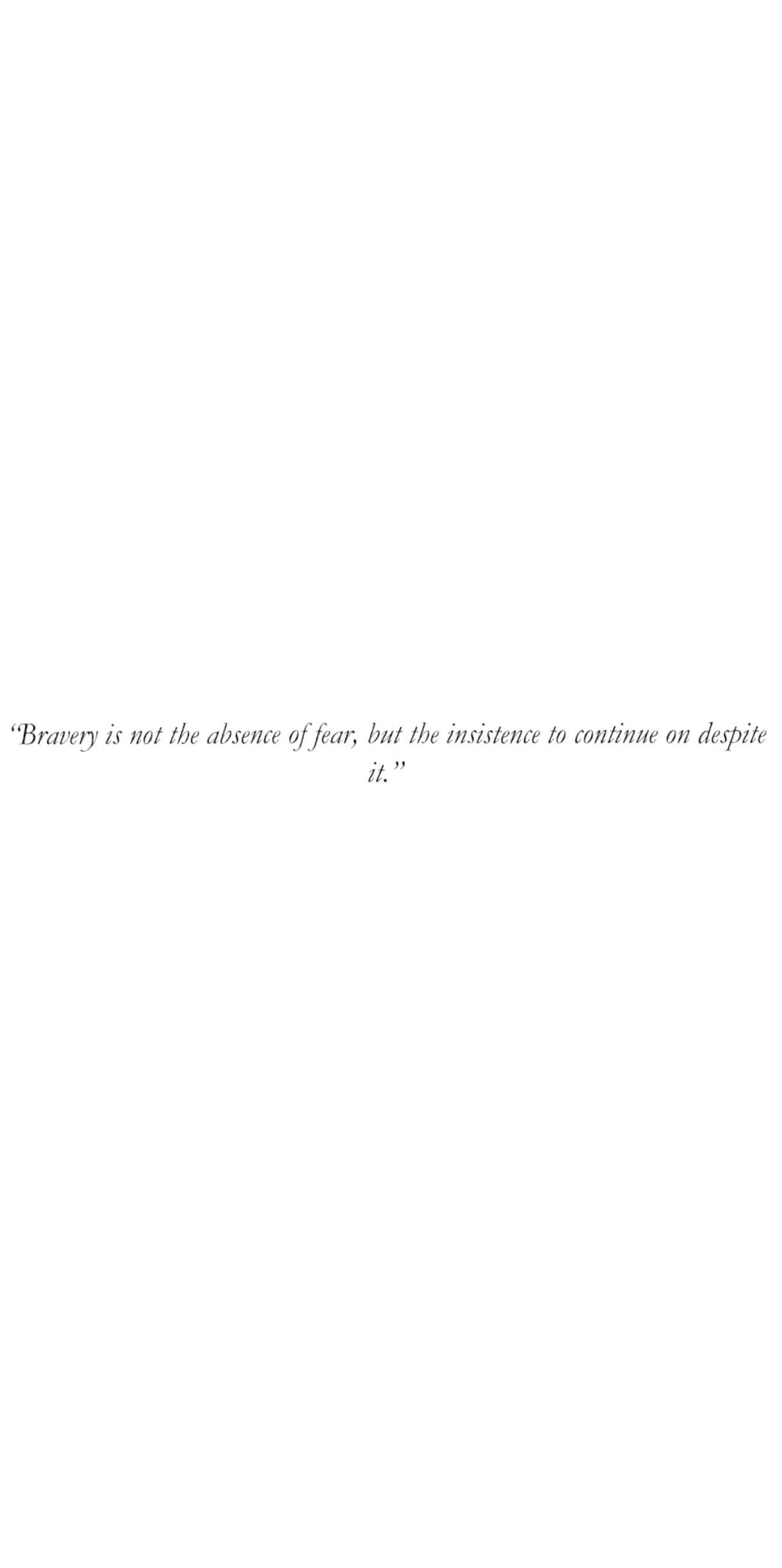

"Bravery is not the absence of fear, but the insistence to continue on despite it."

REBIRTH

I was there.

Deep in the soil

beneath the earth.

Watching from afar as

he plundered and torched.

As he ripped me from the air.

Suffocating me and leaving me to die.

Absorbed back into the ground which I lay.

I was there.

I carried this memory forever and retold it to you every

time you consumed me.

When I poured from the heavens, I wept for you to remember.

For it was me who hugged you in your moments of solitude.

Saturating deeper than your skin. Deeper than your bones.

From the beginning of your creation, I surrounded you.

I held you. I carried you.

I carry you.

PROLOGUE

THE NEW WORLD, 1814

I'd never truly believed in justice—until this very moment, with the weight of my heel pressed against the neck of a God. From above, I listen as his voice descends into a pathetic whimper, pleading for mercy like every other man I have broken before him.

Once, I might have pitied such a sound. I would've wondered, with a naive sense of urgency, what I could do to intervene, to shield someone from such degradation. But my journey here has taught me an undeniable truth: pity is a luxury stripped from those who have had their lives decimated by the whims of the powerful.

The version of myself that might have granted him reprieve was buried long ago. Deep within the land I formerly knew as home, alongside the one thing I'd once held most sacred. Never to return.

Much like the beasts made in his image, he has been nothing short of insatiable. Destruction and disaster are his sustenance;

the reliable path that always carried him to his deepest desire of death.

But this time, the path has betrayed him.

This time, it did not lead him to the indulgence he sought. It led him to something greater. Something far worse.

It led him to me.

He writhes beneath me, his breaths coming in shallow gasps. Around us, tinges of heat close in on all sides. The crescendo of war is dying, fading into a deafening silence. Falling ash and debris threaten to block my view of his defeat, but I force my gaze to steady.

I *will* see this.

Divine blood stains the ground in shades I do not recognize. In his groveling I see no grandeur, no majesty. Only desperation, only fragility. For all his power—for all his eternal divinity—he is not immune to fear. Not immune to pain.

His eyes, once glowing with hubris, flicker now with the dim light of realization. He knows there will be no forgiveness. Not from me.

"You bleed just like any man," I say, pressing my heel down harder. This draws a strangled cry from his lips. Sweat pours down my face, sliding into the open wounds littering my features. I revel in the sting of triumph.

His words tumble out of his mouth through chattering teeth. "W-what—are y-you?"

I watch, entranced, as a once-mighty form is reduced to a hallow shell wrecked by violent trembles.

And I feel it then.

A vindication so acute it cuts through the emptiness his destruction—his greed—left behind. It is not peace, nor solace, but something else. Something raw and primal.

For the first time, in all thirty-nine summers, I understand the true meaning of justice. It is not the noble ideal I once imagined in my youth, nor the blind, impartial scale preached by the divine and protected.

Justice is personal.

Justice is my heel on the neck of a God who dared to make me a pawn in a game I never wanted to play.

A God that dared to challenge my will.

I press down with all the strength within me and respond.

"I'm the worst decision you've ever made."

PART ONE:

MAGPIE

1
MID-MORNING
BEIFO PORT, 1799

A thick glob of my spit drops into the teacup with a muted *plop*, dissolving into the steaming liquid.

From the center of the room comes a voice, harsh as a whip. "Hurry with the tea, girl!"

I swirl the contents once, watching it settle before setting the cup alongside the others on the worn wooden tray. My fingers tighten around its edges as I move forward, careful not to let the silk pooling at my feet send me sprawling.

Wouldn't want their tea to spill before they've had the pleasure of tasting it.

"Quickly, now," Madam Lín snaps.

My jaw clenches.

The moment I come within reach, the stiff end of her quilted fan cracks against my foot. Pain sparks through my toes, but I dare not give her the satisfaction of seeing me flinch. Instead, I stifle a glower and slide the tea onto the table before its drinkers: Madam Lín at the head, and to her right, Pingshen Traders.

They are a hard-eyed duo—faces bronzed from the sun and bodies draped in fine but well-worn robes. Sellers who trade in everything from salted fish to human bodies.

Madam dismisses me with a flick of her gnarled fingers, but doesn't let me retreat far. "Stay near," she orders. "You will service them when business is finished."

My hands clench at my sides as I take a spot against the wall behind her.

She turns back to the Traders and adopts a smile as polished as the jade rings weighing down her fingers. "As I was saying, gentlemen, the Emperor's return to the Heavenly Liberation Festival is an opportunity like no other. The first in several decades! And such a moment calls for gifts befitting an august presence, don't you agree?"

The eldest of the Traders, a man with a wispy beard and calculating eyes, hums as he takes a slow sip of his tea.

A satisfied smirk twitches at the corner of my mouth.

"A fine gift indeed," he murmurs in traditional Pinesh. "But tell me, Madam Lín, what does an infamous flowerboat keeper seek from us that she does not already have in abundance?"

She laughs, a sound as saccharine as the perfume clinging to her sleeves. "Your finest wares, of course."

The youngest Trader—who has been idly spinning a chipped bronze tael between his fingers—tilts his head. "You seek concubines."

Madam's fan flutters as she waves at the thick, humid air. "Not merely concubines—prizes who will command desire with a glance, who will make even the most unyielding magistrates falter beneath the weight of their own hunger. Girls worthy of a place in the Emperor's retinue." Her gaze sharpens. "And if they are foreign, all the better."

A pause stretches between them, the air congested with the bitter scent of tea and perspiration from the autumn heat.

The eldest Trader strokes his beard. "Exotic girls are definitely a rarity." His eyes flick to me for the first time, dark and assessing. "But the Festival is in seven moons. We may have some options… but if they aren't up to your standards the costs of importing new ones alone—"

"Are of no concern," Madam interjects. "In three weeks' time, my coffers will be considerably fuller. Name your price—I will pay what is required."

The youngest Trader chuckles. "A generous offer."

Madam speaks again, adamant, "I have in mind at least a dozen beauties—girls plucked like blossoms for the Emperor's delight. All I require from you…" she pauses a beat, considering her words carefully, "…*reliable* men, is to make my garden bloom."

The room is quiet in the Traders' deliberation. The only sounds drift in from the docks—the rhythmic creak of moored ships, the occasional call of a dockhand. The men exchange glances, a silent conversation passing between them before the elder finally nods.

"Then let us discuss the price."

The younger claps his hands twice, the sound sharp. As if on cue, a group of their lackeys enter, and the trio go back to discussing business.

The men come dragging in a line of girls. At the sight, my stomach twists.

They are young—too young. Some barely past thirteen summers, their limbs thin, their faces still soft with childhood. Their wide eyes glisten with terror as they are dragged forward, ropes biting deep into their bound wrists. Others are older, their shoulders slumped, their gazes hollow. They do not struggle. They do not weep. Their fight has already been drained.

In them, I see myself.

But then—

A girl with matted hair and sun-darkened skin, her face gaunt but familiar. Features from another life, another shore.

The past collides with the present so violently that, for a moment, the room spins.

She is Hokan. Possibly the only other member left.

Her gaze flickers across the room, unfocused, lost in some distant horror. Yet, as if sensing me, our eyes meet. Recognition dawns, but it is not relief that I see. It is madness.

The captives stand in a line an arms-length in front of me, their forms taut and shaking as the lackeys pace back and forth. The Hokan girl is two bodies down from me. I wait, heart pounding, until the men reach the other end of the line. Carefully, I step closer.

My voice is barely a breath as I murmur in our native tongue. "Tet?"

Her eyes dart around as if the walls themselves are closing in. Then, she exhales—a tremulous, wrecked breath that shudders through her frail frame. "Tet-tet."

A lump rises in my throat. My knees nearly give out, my vision blurring with unshed tears.

The girl wets her chapped lips. "Do you know what they're saying? What are they planning to do with us?"

I relay to her the deal that is being struck. I have a thousand questions clawing at my mind, but only two escape. "W-what happened to you? Where did they find you?"

Where is everyone else?

A lackey passes by with a harsh shush, his beady eyes sweeping over the line. I press my lips together, head bowing to avoid notice. Across the room, Madam Lín glances up at the disruption, but the Traders quickly pull her attention back to the matter of coin.

When the eyes are off us once more, the girl exhales another ragged breath. "I ran," she whispers. "I hid. In the mountains. Where a fox spoke to me. Told me to come find you—to make sure you see me."

A fox? She came to see me?

She rambles on, not caring about being overheard now, "It said that this would help you make the right choice."

The words make no sense—no context, no explanation. A thread left dangling for me to pull. But before I can press further, her lips curl into something brittle, something broken.

"I'm so happy," she breathes, voice sounding suddenly consoled. "At least one of us will still be here. Even if it is *you*."

The slight stings, but I have no time to be affronted, because in a blink, she moves.

She twists, jerking her bound wrists over the nearest Trader's head. The rope of her shackles cinches tight against his throat, cutting off his startled cry. He flails, gurgles, but she holds fast, her wiry arms fueled by desperation.

Chaos erupts. The other men shout—scrambling for weapons. Their reactions are instinctual, but they are already too late. As the Trader staggers back, his balance thrown, she shifts with him. Twisting over his heaving body, she maneuvers her bound hands to the knife holstered against his chest underneath his tunic. The other Traders are merely a step away when she wrenches the blade free. But before anyone can stop her—before I can stop her—she drives it into her own neck.

The silence that follows is deafening.

She lets out a wet, gurgling gasp as a waterfall of blood spills over her hands. Then, her body crumples to the floor in a graceless heap.

The room swells with terrified shrieks and bewildered curses. And I—standing amidst the wreckage of this moment, breath caught in my chest—can only watch.

She got out before Madam could brand her, before she would be tied here forever.

She died free.

I wish I'd done the same.

Before I can mourn her for too long, a meaty hand clamps down on my shoulder and wrenches me back.

"Thought I heard a rat squeaking," a voice sneers.

Pain explodes through my ribs as a fist drives into my side. The force sends me stumbling, but another hand catches me before I hit the ground. I barely have a moment to breathe before my arm is twisted behind my back, forcing me upright. One of Madam's escort boys—broad-shouldered and eager to please.

"What did you say to her?" he growls.

Madam's fan snaps on the table with a sound like breaking bone. The sudden silence is more arresting than any shout. Her eyes burn with a quiet fury. "Take her to the back."

He doesn't wait for further instruction. I'm yanked through the back door—barely able to keep my footing as we stumble through the main hall chambers—to the dressing quarters.

He hurls me to the floorboards, the impact shuddering up my spine. The girls in the room shrink back, pressing themselves into the far corner like startled birds. I barely raise my arms in time to block the brutal kick aimed at my temple. My forearm absorbs the blow, the pain sharp and bright, but I seize his ankle and twist, sending him staggering.

I lurch to my feet, but my momentary triumph is short-lived. His fist drives into my stomach, knocking the breath from my lungs in a single, suffocating rush. I fall, gasping. The world narrows to the burn in my abdomen and the cold press of the floor beneath my knees.

How long has it been since I'd to fight like this?

He crouches, fingers digging into my chin. "What did you say to her?" he repeats. His words are softer now, as if we are sharing a secret.

I spit in his face.

Before he can react, I drive my fist into his groin. His scream is coarse. He collapses, writhing, and I'm on him in an instant, my knuckles splitting against his teeth, his nose, his cheekbone. Each strike sheds another layer of what I've pretended to be. The mask I've worn out of fear.

The blood on my hands is warm, sticky—real.

All I can see is the girl in the other room. The one with the now soulless eyes.

I don't even know her name.

"You're going to kill him!" a shrill voice, trembling with fear, cuts through the haze.

Good. People like him don't deserve to exist.

Footsteps thunder as other escorts rush in—hands seize my arms, my hair, dragging me back. I thrash, but there are too many.

"A week in solitude," one of the boys declares. "No food. No light."

They haul me up, my legs kicking uselessly as I'm propelled past the whispering girls, their faces a blur of pity and fright.

The boat's underbelly swallows me whole, the air thickened with damp and rot. The smallest room—hardly more than a coffin—yawns open. They throw me inside. The door slams, and the bolt rasps home. Darkness rushes in, absolute and suffocating. Only then, do I break.

I was raised to believe that one's water is too precious to be spilled, that tears are a gift from the ocean not meant to be wasted. But no matter how tightly I clench my jaw, no matter how fiercely I will them to stop, they come anyway.

They well and spill, rushing hot and unchecked down my cheeks, soaking into the front of my robe. My hands fly to my mouth, desperate to stifle the sobs, but it's useless—the screams tear from my throat, wild and unbidden. The walls seem to close in, pressing against my ribs, rattling the grief loose from my chest in heaving, erratic breaths. The rhythm is wild. Too fast, too shallow. I'm suffocating beneath the sheer weight of it.

I weep until the pain is unbearable. A splitting agony burrows behind my eyes, digging into the base of my skull. When there is no water left to give—when my body is wrung dry, hollowed out—I force myself to sit up.

Though I may not mourn the way she felt about me—the way almost all the clan did—she still deserves the Death Ritual.

I squeeze out the remnants of my tears that cling to my robe. My fingers press the dampness to the wooden planks beneath me. The gesture is crude, lacking the proper elements, but it is all I have.

I trace the sacred symbols in slow, deliberate strokes. They are imperfect in the dark, however, the meaning is the same.

A pair of zigzag horizontal lines.

May the tides carry you home.

A spiral enclosed in a square.

May the storm forget your name.

An arch underlined by a straight line.

May you find your way to still waters.

I lower my forehead to the cold, unyielding floor, letting its chill seep into my skin. My body is heavy, worn thin by woe and exhaustion. With a slow, shuddering breath, I close my eyes, surrendering to the darkness.

I let sleep take me where mercy will not.

2

THREE WEEKS LATER

BEIFO PORT, 1799

"Why aren't you naked yet, girl?"

The words sever through the heavy stillness of the dressing quarters, but my gaze remains fixed on the scene unfolding beyond the window.

In the distance, on the grime-streaked beach at the edge of the dock, stands a group of Pingshen Collectors. They are being administered by a magistrate and his Imperial guard. The men struggle to contain a mischief of magpies. The iridescent feathers flash like shards of night and light as they dart and weave through the air.

Most of the birds have already been captured; their freedom stolen as they are forced into a bamboo cage. But three others remain. Their wings beat furiously against the inevitable. They dip and dive in avoidance. One even lunges straight for the eye of its captor.

My fists clench involuntarily at my sides.

Come on. You can make it.

A pair manages to escape, but the third, too focused on exacting its revenge, is sliced down by the guard's steel. The tribe of magpies call after their fallen member—cries so loud I can hear whispers of it carried on the wind. The Collectors rattle the cage to silence them as the group turn back to the black-grey mosaic of village buildings behind them.

A small ache grips my heart.

Those birds will be in that cage until the day they die.

I shift my focus back to the unwanted presence in the room, where Madam Lín's demand hangs in the air, unanswered. From beyond the entryway, the air hums with laughter. Chimes of clinking wine cups, and the delicate notes of a guzheng coaxed by skilled fingers, accompany the sound.

Since that day three weeks ago, I have been kept under relentless watch. Every movement measured; every breath accounted for. Eyes linger on me—some wary, others expectant—but none meet mine. The other girls know better. Their silence is their shield, their way of distancing themselves from whatever fate awaits me.

Madam had to withhold me from my regular clients, unwilling to peddle damaged goods. She waited—waited for the bruises to fade, for the wounds to knit closed, for my body to be presentable once more. As if time could make me forget.

In the quiet, with nothing and no one, I have been left alone with my thoughts.

And I always think of *her*—of the reality she left me.

"Did you hear me?" Madam snaps, taking a step inside. The stench of her cheap perfume fills the cramped space. Her voice carries with the grinding of consonants common in the Pingshen accent. "You know I don't prefer to repeat myself."

I do not answer her threat. Instead, I let my fingers trail over the delicate silk of my robe—pale lilac, embroidered with cranes in flight, their wings forever suspended in elegant escape. A garment crafted to make me appear fragile, untouchable.

The irony is as sharp as the bone pin in my hair.

Her reflection looms in the tarnished bronze mirror in front of me, lips twisted in displeasure. I adjust the crude whittled pin, and for the span of a breath, I imagine driving it through the soft hollow of her throat. Once. Twice.

In her hand, she carries a lacquered tray where a small porcelain bowl filled with polluted liquid sits. Its contents are murky, swirling with something thicker than tea. When I turn to face her fully, the hulking silhouette of another escort boy steps into the doorway, his presence a silent warning. The fine hairs on my nape rise, but my face remains smooth, unreadable.

"You're wanted in the main chambers," she says.

I eye the dish warily. "What is that?"

Her lips curl into a thin smile displaying a row of teeth stained by repeated drug use. "What do you think it is?"

"I'm in no mood to play your vapid mind games," I retort.

The slap cracks through the air before I can brace for it. My cheek burns, the sting radiating down to my jaw. I lift a hand to the heat, fingers trembling—not with pain, but with the effort of restraint.

"Ai, you idiot!" Madam Lín's shrill voice cuts in as she strides forward. She strikes the boy's shin with the pointed toe of her slipper. "She needs to remain presentable for tonight. I won't have you ruining my sale!"

His eyes lock onto mine, smug, challenging. The dying evening light glints off the sweat at his temple, and I commit the curve of his grin to memory.

I will repay this.

But then, her words register. "Sale?"

She shuffles over to the vanity and sets the tray down with a clink of bracelets, her eyes cold as ice. "A tonic. Tonight's guest is important, and after your little stunt last moon, I want to make sure you will be… compliant."

"I'm not taking that," I say, voice clipped, "And what *sale* are you talking about?"

Again, she ignores me. "You *will* drink it."

Before I can respond, the flower-shaped mark on my right forearm burns with warning. I hiss, clutching it close to my abdomen.

It is a constant reminder of the grounded coal she Wields within the ink. A loophole she has exploited and perfected. One that slips past the greatest limitation of Wielding that prevents one from using the power against another person—from Wielding another's qì.

Under any other circumstance, such open use of Wielding would invite swift and brutal retribution. Imperial soldiers would descend upon her, dragging her lifeless body through the squalid, crumbling streets of the port village as warning. But, her act is not of rebellion. It threatens neither throne nor order. So, the magistrates and guards, ever pragmatic in their corruption, choose to simply look the other way.

Distracted by the pain, my arms are seized from behind, pinning me in place. I struggle violently, thrashing my head back hard. There's a crack, then the boy lets out a moan in pain.

The injury is not as severe as I would've liked, but it will have to do.

Madam's skeletal fingers, cold and unrelenting, take grip of my jaw. "Stay still!"

Then, my mouth is forced open. The liquid pours in, bitter and vile, sliding down my throat despite my attempts to spit it out. I gag, but it's futile. The swigs find their way down, my eyes burning with every swallow.

When she lets go of my face, her smile is triumphant. "Good girl. Now, to the chamber."

With the same brutish grip, Madam's boy drags me down the corridor behind her, cursing me for the broken nose.

However, I cannot revel in the retribution. My body already feels strange—a faint warmth spreads through my veins, my pulse louder than usual. The tonic's residue lingers on my tongue, igniting like a mouthful of raw ginger root—sharp, searing, and impossible to ignore. I clench my fists, digging fingernails into my palm, forcing the sensations aside. I do not know what awaits in the main hall, but I must keep my wits about me.

The space is a cacophony of lantern light and sound when we enter. Merchant Fang sprawls on a cushion, already half-drunk and naked. His plump face glistens with sweat. Girls hover around him—giving him massages, unauthentically giggling at his perverse jokes. As one of the only regulars who does not find thrill in abusing a Flower, they must figure they owe him that much.

When he sees me, his bleary eyes light up, and he waves me over. "Shi Yang! Blessed be the Emperor. Come, come!"

I receive a shove that has me stumbling into the room. Then, Madam and the boy are already off toward the front of the boat to terrorize the next girl.

Steadying myself as much as I can in my current state, I make my way toward Fang, my steps unhurried. The silk of my robe falls from my shoulders, pooling at my feet, baring my skin to the cutting night air. My chin sits high despite the fading redness on my cheek.

The cushion at his side is warm as I lower myself onto it, a stark contrast to the chill that has tightened my nipples. "Blessed be the Emperor," I murmur, inclining my head in practiced reverence. Pouring wine into his now empty cup, I continue with the routine. "Merchant Fang," I say smoothly, "you honor us with your presence."

The lie dances of my tongue and into the air easily. However, we both know the truth. His presence here is not a luxury he can afford, not without the arrangement he has brokered with Beifo's officials. He trades information—whispers of foreign ships skimming our waters, names of our own country's traders with cargo worth seizing—and in return, they grant him access to indulgences usually reserved for their own ranks. The pleasantries we exchange are nothing more than ceremony, a veil draped over the understanding between us.

He grins. "Shi Yang, you're too lovely for this place. If you were not so dark, and I were not an old man, I would keep you for myself."

I bristle at the thinly veiled insult. The thought of choking him to death is appealing, but the faint stinging of the brand on my arm restrains me.

Relaxing, I let out a low hum, sharp and cutting. "And if I weren't bound here, Merchant Fang, I'd tell you exactly what I truly think of such flattery."

The girls around us freeze, their laughter dying on their lips. But Fang only roars with delight. "Ah, you've got such spirit! That is why I like you." He caresses my shoulder, his fingers running down the length of my arm. "I have much on my mind today, dear Shi Yang. Let us laze and converse."

The hour stretches endlessly, each moment drawn out into an unbearable crawl.

Thankfully, the man's loneliness manifests only in ceaseless prattle. His need for companionship demands nothing more than the occasional nod or murmured reply when necessary. My only effort is to sustain the illusion of conversation.

Not that I could manage much more—not after that tonic. I feel as though my body is sinking through the cushion, past the wooden boards of this boat, and into the cold, black depths of Jade Bay. My mind drifts, expanding into an endless void where I exist in silence, untethered, alone. Yet even through the haze, I can still register the rising cadence of Merchant Fang's voice, the ragged edges of his rant cutting through the fog that attempts to swallow me whole.

He slurs as he raises his cup, wine sloshing over the rim. "To the Serpent Emperor!" He drains it in one gulp before continuing, his voice thick with mockery. "Ah, yes. Our magnificent leader. Descendent of the *Chosen* Jade bloodline that brought us aetherbloom and carried out The Great Ascent." He lets out a sardonic wheezing laugh that rattles in his chest.

The girls around him exchange anxious laughs.

Any mention of that war—of the time before—is strictly forbidden. If any of his Imperial contacts were within earshot, we'd all be hanging from the docks by morning, punished not only for his words but for the crime of having heard them.

Ignorant to the precipice he teeters on, Fang continues. "The Emperor," he burps, "is a clever bastard, isn't he? Bans Wielding—tells us it is for our own good. That we must not provoke the Gods with the power we've spent centuries honing since their departure from our world."

One of the girls leans in to refill his cup, but before she can finish, he yanks it back, sloshing wine onto my thigh.

Fang barrels on, his words growing looser and louder. "Then, he proclaims the aetherbloom edict to the Heavens—making Pingshen an enemy to the world!"

The girls have long since abandoned the pretense of amusement.

"'No more aetherbloom,' he says. 'For the prosperity of Pingshen's society.' Bah! As if he cares for the fishermen or the merchants—the beggars that become Bloomers." He jabs a stubby finger at no one in particular.

A dull twinge of resentment flares through my chest at the term. Flashes of vanishing egg boats and a dwindling sea village emerge in my mind. The man continues to rant on.

"You think the trade is gone? That foreign dignitaries give a Godsdamn?" He lets out a bitter bark of laughter. "Hah! The best aetherbloom, the purest resin—it doesn't simply vanish, no, no…"

I strain to catch the rest, but the words dissolve into drunken slurs, his consonants sheared off at the edges. A foreign country given the name of *The Untamed* swirls through my mind, billowing like smoke before dissipating. The breeze sweeping in through the windows steals what little sense remains of his secret, carrying it out to sea.

My head swims, frustration curling tight in my chest.

I have so many questions.

"Bah, never mind," Fang mutters, waving a clumsy hand as if brushing away his own thoughts. "None of it will matter after the Heavenly Liberation Festival anyway."

Then, with a sudden, deliberate shift, he leans into my space, breath thick with alcohol. His eyes dart about, searching for Imperial guards who might materialize from the shadows, or from the very air itself.

Even through the sluggish thrum in my ears, I hear the shift in his tone—the implication in his next words.

"They would all rather see this country burn, than to rid the world of aetherbloom. Pingshen's reckoning is upon us," he breathes. "I do hope you are prepared."

And with that, he slumps backward, the weight of his own tirade dragging him under. His words dissolve into drunken snores. The silence left behind throbs with unanswered questions, and the distant hush of waves beyond the window.

Though my curiosity begs for me to shake him awake to interrogate him for more answers, the heat in my veins only grows stronger. Colors burn too brightly; sounds scrape against my ears. The room spins as I excuse myself with unsteady grace.

Back in the dressing quarters, I grip the vanity table, my knuckles taut. My blood feels like waves crashing against unseen barriers, surging with a force I can't control. My breath comes in short bursts as I stare at my trembling hands.

What had that old cow put in the tonic?

As if having summoned her with my thought alone, Madam Lín's footsteps approach.

"Shi Yang," her tone ominous, "I need to speak with you."

I straighten, wiping the sweat from my brow. "What do you want?" I ask curtly.

"You and those manners," she grumbles. She slides fully into the space and closes the bamboo divider behind her. It's just the two of us. "You've caught the interest of someone important. He's an officer from the Southern Imperial Navy, with money and influence," she says, her gaze unyielding.

If he's that important, what is he doing this far from the Imperial Bases or the Forbidden Hall?

"He's offered to buy you outright."

My breath catches, but I keep my face neutral. "Surely, you are mistaken."

"He's coming in an hour's time to try you out, but you *will* be leaving with him tomorrow morning," she concludes. The arrogance with which she speaks is as if the matter is already settled. "His name is Captain Zhào. He paid handsomely."

My world tilts slightly as the nausea from both the tonic and the news takes over. I have heard whispers among the girls aboard—of victims from other ports sold to this man before. None survive longer than a season. They're always found the same way: floating stomach-up in the port, their bodies bloated, and faces battered beyond recognition. The only identifier of their former life: an Aether flower branded into their skin. A final cruel reminder of the flowerboat they were once bound to, and how their lives were never their own.

My jaw clenches, and my heart hammers against my ribs.

A desperate bird in a shrinking cage.

"No."

Madam Lín's eyes narrow. "You will do as you're told." She points a gnarled finger at me. "Remember your place, Shi Yang! Your life belongs to this boat—to *me.* I decide whether you remain on it..." her lips curl into a wicked smile, "or vanish forever."

I step closer—close enough to see the patches of powder caking in the wrinkles around her mouth.

"For eight summers, I have chosen my battles on this boat. I have let you and your boys think that I'm someone you can break." My voice drops lower, steadier. "But every assault, every threat—I've gathered them all. Stored them away. And one day," I whisper, letting each word bury itself into the space around us, "One day, I will make you atone. And when that day comes, your power over this boat will not save you. Your Wielding will not save you. Nothing will."

Her smile falters for just a moment, a crack in her painted mask. The hand bearing her jade bracelets trembles slightly before she can still it. Quickly, she regains her composure, straightening her posture.

"Good luck carrying out that justice of yours when you're dead."

With that, she turns on her heel, her silk robes whispering against the floor as she sweeps out of the room. When silence finally envelopes me, I stand rooted in place, trembling. A sting of acute pain makes me glance down at my palms. They are blooded, littered with crescent cuts in the shape of my nails.

I squeeze my eyes shut. The tonic's lingering claws still tangle in my mind. I force myself to take a slow breath, the stale scent of the room filling my lungs. My thoughts whirl with schemes of escape.

First, I need to break the bind. Then, I need money—enough to disappear, to slip through the veins of this country and resurface in a city far from here. Perhaps, in time, I'll find myself donning the identifier of an Untamed or an Other, shedding this nation like a snake abandons its skin.

Pushing stray curls from my face, I exhale sharply, willing clarity to come.

Then I pause.

Reaching back, my fingers brush against the whittled bone pin securing my bun. I let my hair loose and turn the pin over in my palm, considering its potential for violence. It is a simple, unassuming thing.

The raw heat within cools into sharp, focused determination.

A plan forms slowly, urgent and incomplete.

Tonight, I will lay with Captain Zhào. But tomorrow, I will not be leaving with him. That I'm sure of.

Clutching the pin tightly, I sink into the corner of the room. I steady my resolve, tucking the weapon back into the thick tresses of my hair.

And I wait.

3

MIDNIGHT

BEIFO PORT, 1799

When Captain Zhào finally boards the flowerboat an hour later, I'm told to meet him at the main entrance. I immediately catch the telltale flaw in his stride. The slight irregularity in his gait is subtle, but to a practiced observer, it is impossible to miss.

He marches toward Madam Lín without preamble, voice gruff as he demands to see me. The command is carried by the weight of someone acquainted with the power of fear.

But even with my inebriated state, fear is not something I feel—not now.

I watch him approach from afar, studying him as an owl might watch a mouse. His face is riddled with wrinkles and scars from cycles at sea. The front half of his head is bald, with the back half tied into a long ponytail—an expected appearance of the state mandated queue. His skin is leathery, decorated with sunspots. Up close, a thought lodges into my brain; the infamous Captain Zhào, a man dreaded across the ports and rivers and seas, is nothing more than flesh and bone.

Flesh that can be pierced, and bones that can be broken.

The shift of his shoulders causes his Magua to sit unevenly, and that imbalance reveals what he is trying so carefully to conceal: a silk belt beaded with porcelain ornament. It is an accessory that will easily go for more than five silver taels.

When he stops in front of me, I hold my composure, though every nerve in my body hums with anticipation. He looks me over with a critical eye, his gaze raking across my tawny-brown skin as though appraising livestock. His lip curls in a scowl. It is more than disgust that weaves itself through his features—it is contempt. The kind of deep-seated loathing I'm all too familiar with. It may beg the question of why he would even bother to purchase me in the first place, but whatever reasons he has are irrelevant now.

What truly matters is the key to my freedom, concealed beneath his Magua—a secret he hadn't intended for lesser eyes to see.

But lesser, I'm not.

Panting, I lie motionless—my limbs ache, and my head still feels slightly laden. Every breath I take is stifled beneath the oppressive weight of the body pinning me down. The man above me exhales a foul, heavy sigh that turns my stomach. The stench curls in my nostrils.

He pulls himself away, before hocking a load of spit in the direction of the waste basket in the corner of the room. He does not care that it lands on the threaded crane on my robe.

Every second of the last half hour confirms what the rumors have warned: he is a beast masquerading as a man.

A harsh snort and a muttered insult cuts through my thoughts.

"Lazy bitch," Zhào sneers.

He has switched tongues to address me in traditional Pinesh. Likely under the assumption that I cannot understand. But he underestimates the environment he's in. The cycles I've spent among officials has taught me to trace the subtle threads that bind their dialect to the simplified Pinesh I have learned well.

He turns away, reaching for his aetherbloom pipe with a casual arrogance that makes my skin crawl.

As he prepares to indulge, he speaks again, his tone laced with cruel amusement. "You'll be put to work on the ship until we get to the Master. The men need something to keep them entertained at sea."

The Master.

The words lodge in my mind, like the barb of a fishhook catching flesh.

That night. The attack. The blood soaking the dirt as if it were tasked with blooming death.

He must know.

Know what became of the Hokans dragged away like cattle. Know the identity of orchestrator; the one who turned our lives into ash. Turned *my* life to… this.

Pushing through the waning effects of the relaxant, the whirlwind within me hardens into a single, unwavering resolve.

With his back toward me, I see my opening.

Rising from the floor, my eyes stay locked on his back while my right hand silently moves to my hair. My movements are prudent, every step slow. I glide behind him without a sound. One hand positions the pin just below his ribcage, the other holds my balled-up robe, ready at the height of his mouth. I'm careful to keep it just beyond his peripheral vision.

I draw a deep, silent breath.

Then, with a surge of force, I drive the bone into him. The sickening crunch of flesh and sinew punctuates the act.

An agonized scream is ripped from his throat before I cut it off with the garment. The fabric stifles his voice, leaving only the faintest echo of his agony hanging in the air.

Leaning in close, my voice is a venomous whisper, low and seething. "What became of the sea nomads of Kwangchow port?" I demand. "Where were they taken?"

Like a wild boar being drained of its blood, his body attempts to revolt and pull away simultaneously. But I'm braced for the instinctual defense. I retch the bone out, and then drive it in again, this time on the side of his torso.

"Tell me!"

A muffled curse erupts from him, strained and furious. I duck, narrowly avoiding the pointed backward swing of his elbow. He may be more than 20 summers my senior, but I'm no match for his military training. Twisting around with a fluid, predatory grace, he lands a brutal punch across my face. The force of it sends me sprawling backward, my body slamming into the unforgiving wall of the boat. Pain radiates through my skull, and I taste the metallic tang of blood as it wells at the corner of my split lip. The iron-like flavor floods my senses, mingling with the dizziness that clouds my vision. Stars burst and swirl before my eyes.

Then, I see it—before I can even process the pain, before I can steady myself. A black form, thick and sinuous, begins to curl out from his body like a living, breathing entity. It writhes in the air, twisting and coiling with a malevolence that chills me to my core.

My breath catches, eyes widening in horrified recognition. The dark haze surrounding him is a haunting, unmistakable signature. One I've seen before, etched into the memories of my past. It's the same shadowy essence that clung to the pirates who once tore my world apart.

He's one of them.

Suddenly, my body freezes, locked in place by a force that grips me from the inside out. It is as if invisible chains bind my limbs, and my will is no longer my own. His power bears down on my mind with an oppressive, crushing weight that should not be possible.

His gaze burns into mine, and I can feel the command radiating from him—a demand for me to stop breathing.

My throat begins to close, and lungs constrict painfully. For a moment, I'm certain this is the end.

But then, deep within me, something stirs.

A flicker of heat blooms in my chest, spreading like fire through my veins. My body, teetering on the edge of collapse, responds instinctively. All at once, I sense it—a pull, an unseen thread tethering me to him.

A siphoning force courses through me, dark and relentless, drawing his essence into a void within my body. His qì, heavy with malice and raw power, floods my senses, thick and suffocating. The ink-like tendrils recoiling from his body falter, withering as his life force ebbs away. He staggers, his frame caught in a futile battle against the inescapable.

Crimson spreads beneath him, seeping from the open punctures in his abdomen. His wild eyes begin to flicker with disbelief as they drop to the bone hairpin poking out of him. A brutal testament to his unraveling mortality.

"You… sea demon," he rasps, his voice barely audible over the roar of my heartbeat.

He lunges, a desperate, final attempt to end me. But before he can reach me, the last of his strength evaporates.

His body freezes mid-motion. I watch, transfixed, as his energy is torn free. A luminous wisp that twists and floats before it is drawn into me. A brilliant flash of light bursts behind my eyes, blinding and all-consuming.

And then it's over.

He collapses, his form crumpling lifelessly at my feet. The shadow that once surrounded him dissipates into the air, vanishing into nothingness.

The invisible hold restricting my body and mind fades, and I'm free once more. A shuddering breath escapes me, breaking the silence of the room. My chest heaves as I struggle to steady myself, yet beneath the fatigue, something hums. A low, insistent vibration pulses through my skin—his power, his essence, now woven into mine.

Now more conscious, I gather enough strength in my legs to kick his head over and over. I do this until I hear something crack. I'm not sure if it is the sound of his skull or neck, but I kick him one last time for good measure. I do not leave any possibility of him coming back.

The cubicles at the back of the boat are far too close for the scuffle to have gone completely unnoticed. I've done my deed, and now I need to flee.

I must rid of this skin seal first.

Looking around, my mind races for a cure. I'm not a Wielder, so countering the binding energy is not an option. I have to remove it physically. My eyes land on the lantern.

I scramble over to it and tear off the shade covering the flame. Grabbing my robe once more, in a brutal moment of irony, I stuff it in my own mouth. With a trembling grip, I forcefully lower my forearm to the fire.

The pain is excruciating. My vision blackens for a several moments. When I look down to my violently shaking arm, all that looks back at me is muddled, bubbled flesh where the brand used to be.

Tears streaming down my face, I quickly shuffle over to the bucket of water left in the corner for clients after a session. I dunk my arm in without hesitation. Immediately, the liquid soothes the lancination.

As I balm my self-inflicted injury, my eyes search for the key to my escape.

Where is that Godsdamned belt?

Quickly, I stumble to my feet. As I steady myself against the wall, I realize that my forearm has lessened to a subtle throbbing. My brow furrows when I'm greeted with a shocking sight.

My wound is completely scarred over. As if it was incurred seasons ago…

Puzzlement fills me, but I cannot afford to deviate from the course I have set myself on.

My eyes continue to frantically roam the space for his garments. I spot them by the sliding door and step around the body to make my way over to the pile. I immediately begin to pat down the cloth in search of the accessory. Twisting the fabric side to side, I feel nothing.

Just then, several feet belonging to Madam's escort boys echo in the distance.

Usually, I'd be relieved to hear them coming, knowing that they'll take a troublesome client off my hands, but this time, the sound fills me with dread. The moment they see the body they will surely amputate my limbs or castrate me. Both, if they're feeling particularly starved for entertainment.

My pulse begins to swell. I glance around the space, feeling the familiar speed of my breaths increase.

This can't have been for nothing. I won't allow it to be so.

Out of options, I close my eyes and inhale deeply. I silently send a prayer to the Goddess I have long abandoned.

Mazu, if you were ever watching over us, I seek you now.

I can feel sweat accumulating on my brow. The voices are gaining in numbers and getting closer.

Suddenly, the boat rocks as if nudged by an abrupt, yet steady wave. Then, a dull scraping sound of an object sliding across the floor caresses my ears. I peek my eyes open, expecting to see the belt. But instead, a step away, something far more intriguing catches my gaze. A token the man must have tucked away deep in the folds of his dress.

It is a silver compass—a far greater bounty.

I waste not a second more.

Barefoot, exposed, and my nerves frayed, I slide open the divider and break into a full sprint towards the back of the boat. If the cubicles had windows, I would've thrown myself out of mine without hesitation—but Madam is far too cunning for that. Not the sort of person kind enough to dangle death in the face of girls who yearn for its embrace.

As I weave through the labyrinth of cramped rooms, I fumble to pull my robe back on, hastily tying it. I'm steps away from the outer deck when I feel something stirring, something strange. A faint pulsing, not from within, but pressed against my skin, emanating from the metal in my grasp. A pull, subtle yet insistent, like an invisible current weaving through the air, seeking direction. The warmth it radiates contrasts sharply with the night's biting chill, seeping into my hand and spreading up my arm like a whispered command.

Gods. What now?

A feminine voice cuts through the cloud of my thoughts, "There! She went that way!"

A knot tightens in my stomach, coiling with anger and despair. Of course, one of the other girls gave me away.

I push my legs to carry me faster.

The compass pulses again. I glance down, just for a heartbeat. The needle isn't pointing north. It's spinning, slow and measured, like it's searching for something.

Wonderful. I killed a man for a broken trinket. One that likely won't be enough to convince even a cabbage farmer to lend me a ride on his cart.

Another shout rings closer this time. I clutch the compass tighter, its warmth spreading across my chest like a fever. There's no time to figure it out. Not here.

Reaching the end of the boat, I race up the stairs that follow the upturned slope of its back. I shoulder past a few girls coming from the upper deck. They shout indignantly at me for my shoving, but I cannot spare a second to apologize to people I'll never see again.

I burst onto the balcony at full speed. I slam into the railing with enough force to drive the breath from my lungs. Gasping desperately, I struggle to steady my racing heart. However, stopping is not an option—not with their voices drawing nearer.

Hunched over the railing, I stare down into an abyss of pitch black below. I know that water is down there—I can feel her whisper.

The compass jerks in my hand once more. Using the dim light from the boat's lanterns, I can see the needle locking in place. It points out ahead of me to the sea. The reflection of the moon on the waves acts as a pathway to freedom.

"Ya! Stop right there!"

"We've got a runner!"

No time to think. No time to question.

The compass goes in my mouth, clenched between my teeth.

I climb over the banister and jump.

4

EIGHT CYCLES AGO

KWANGCHOW PORT, 1791

The shouts rise behind me like thunder. Each bellow striking closer, driving me onward through the twisting, decaying paths of the marketplace.

My heart hammers against my ribs as I clutch the stolen bundle beneath my arm—dried fish and two precious rolls of cloth. It will be enough to keep me fed and mended for weeks. If I could just lose the merchant, just slip back into the labyrinth of docks and boats, none of these Pingshens would be the wiser.

The vendor's voice claws through air, echoing off stone and wooden stalls. "Stop, thief!"

His booming footsteps have multiplied. Others must have joined in from the crowd; their collective hate for Hokans acting as a unifier.

In my sixteen summers, it has always been an unspoken rule that we are forbidden from setting foot on *their* soil. Even with the establishment of the Hebosuo—the Imperial bureau tasked with governing riverine affairs, meant to grant us some fragile semblance of citizenship—the land folk make certain we are never truly welcomed. Their laws may tolerate our existence, but their hearts do not.

They cling to their disdain as tightly as a drowning man to driftwood, ensuring that no matter how many cycles pass, we remain exiles in the only home we have ever known.

But what choice do I have?

The waters have been barren for weeks. Our nets yield nothing but tangles of seaweed and the never-ending land waste from the shores. With no catch to trade, the amount of tael in my possession is laughably sparse.

The festering wound on my arm burns with each shift of my stride. It is a stark reminder of my desperation.

The marketplace blurs as I dodge between stalls. The summer sun is particularly sweltering today. My garment has plastered itself to the perspiration on my back. Spices and steamed vegetables mingle with the odor of sweat and grime.

As I sprint away from the bustling heart of the port and toward the outskirts of the village, away from the well-trodden main path reserved for foreign trade, the transformation is stark.

The polished veneer of a thriving port city dissolves into rows of dwellings with sagging rooftops and weather-beaten walls. Here, the illusion crumbles entirely, revealing the stark canvas of deprivation that lies beneath the Pingshen empire's façade.

Behind me, I can hear the coins in my pursuers' pouches jingle closer with each step.

I skid past a cart of watermelons, nearly losing my footing on the uneven dirt. I duck under a hanging banner advertising a seemingly abandoned stall's ware. My chest burns, but I do not dare to slow.

I rush through the shack too sharply and crash into something solid—or someone, rather.

The impact nearly sends me sprawling, but I catch myself. The man's curse rolls out in an unfamiliar tongue, guttural and harsh. When his fingers clamp around my arm, I twist from his grasp with a fluid motion born from cycles of necessity.

Then comes another voice. A warning sneered in the same strange dialect.

The realization hits me then: there's three men. Two of them standing out from ordinary sailors. Their garments are weathered by the sun and salt, but there are snares—cuts in them that are born only from a confrontation with a blade. The looks on their faces are ones of men who have led harsh lives, with an even harsher hand.

Behind them, another figure stands in a black cloak of linen.

I have seen him before.

I do not know his name, but I know his kind. He and others like him had once made a habit of slinking into the docks after dark, looking for Hokans susceptible to bribes.

He says something to the men in high Pinesh. My forehead creases.

That language is only reserved for Imperial officials and guards. How could he or either of these men speak or understand—

"Where is that filthy sea barbarian?" snarls a voice just beyond the partition of the stall.

My breath catches, my stomach knotting like a tangled fishing line. The slur churns the air, heavy and venomous, sinking into my chest. My eyes dart to the entrance, the fragile sheet fluttering with the breeze. Its meager protection offers little solace.

I step back cautiously, my heartbeat drumming in my ears. The men outside feel like wolves on the scent, their presence seeping through the thin barrier. But it's not only them I sense.

Inside the stall, the three strange men stand silent. Their eyes follow me, sharp and assessing. But they do not alert the merchant.

Cold unease slides down my spine, its fingers curling around my ribs. These men are wrong… wrong in a way that feels far too dangerous.

Still, I force the fear down, shoving it into the dark corners of my mind. My arm clutches closer to my side covering the bounty I lifted from the vendor.

The growls outside rise in urgency, the merchant's voice joining them with shouts and accusations.

Not wasting another moment, I turn, heading out the back, continuing my escape.

The narrow pathway opens suddenly onto the docks, and I race toward the murky water where the Hokan boats sit clustered like a floating village. I hear the vendor's shouts growing fainter, my lead widening.

Relief surges through me as I reach the shallow waters and begin to wade waist deep to our egg boat. I do not feel a sense of calm until I'm hauling my drenched body up into the foredeck. The familiar creak of the planks beneath my weight and the aroma of seaweed are a welcomed comfort.

But the feeling is short-lived.

As I slip onto Ba's sampan, I catch a flicker of movement out of the corner of my eye. Turning, I see them again—the three men from the stall. They are watching from the shore. The one in the cloak raises a hand in a slow, harrowing motion, pointing directly at me. At our village.

I glance left and right, scanning for any sign of others nearby. No matter how the clan feels about me, they would not let hostile land folk wander into our community uncontested. A couple of boats away, I spot some of the men and boys fishing, and a flicker of relief steadies me. But when I turn back to where the men had stood, they are gone.

My stomach twists uneasily.

I duck beneath the linen sheet draped over the sheltered dome that conceals our living quarters. Moving swiftly, I crouch near the uneven floorboards and shove the stolen goods beneath a loose plank, pressing it down to ensure it looks undisturbed. I murmur a silent prayer that Ba will not go looking around where he shouldn't. If he does, another altercation between us is inevitable.

And I would've to kill him this time.

Not daring to tempt Fate any further, I settle near the bow. Folding my legs beneath me, I feign focus on mending my arm. The pretense feels thin, but I maintain it for some time.

As the sun kisses the sea at the horizon, blue and purple clashing with yellow and orange, the unrest I felt earlier refuses to fade. It coils tighter with every passing moment.

Who were those men? Why did they follow me? What did they want?

These questions plague my mind so fiercely I begin to grow a headache. I decide to divert my attention to the task at hand. Ba has ordered me to accompany him while he collects fish. Any other day, I would've ignored the command—it's not like he will share any haul with me. *But*, I desperately need the distraction.

We float between the open waters and the sea village. The egg boat mildly rocks back and forth as he sourly resets his empty net. It will take him a while since he's only got one hand. Without a catch tonight, he'll go hungry. I *would* offer to help, but—

Actually…

No, I wouldn't.

While he grumbles on about how the sea Goddess Mazu has forsaken him once again, I turn my focus to the water beneath us.

Most days, the constant lapping of the waves against the hull is enough to lull me to sleep. But tonight, it does nothing to balm the growing tension in my chest. The faces of those men linger in my mind.

Something tells me I have not seen the last of them.

"Are you listening to me, girl? This is your fault, too, y'know!" Ba spits.

His accusations are no stranger to my ears. There was a time I burned to prove him wrong, to earn some scrap of his respect. But that desire has long since gone cold. Now, I find a dark satisfaction in his misery. It is a vindictive thrill I look forward to.

When I only turn and stare in response, the fury drains from his posture as quickly as it came. He wilts beneath the weight of my silence, then turns away, grumbling as he fumbles back to whatever menial task he pretended to care about.

Satisfied with having sent the message that I want to be left alone, I lift my eyes to the sky, where the fading light stretches like the last breath of a dying fire. In a few minutes, it will be completely dark. Then, we can go back to village and tuck in for the night. By dawn, I will leave this unsettlement behind. A nightmare I'll forget by tomorrow afternoon.

Ba pushes his luck until night has fully claimed the waters, the inky black stretching endlessly around us. The only light comes from the dim lantern on the floor, its feeble glow flickering between us. It does little to help, casting more shadows than clarity.

With a frustrated sigh, Ba finally relents. "Oh, forget it!" he moans, yanking the net onto the boat with impatient tugs. The water sloshes against the hull as he works, his irritation palpable in the jerky movements of his hands.

Relief unfurls in my chest. Seizing the chance to return, I reach for the oar, eager for this day to end.

Suddenly—

A sound echoes from the waves around us.

Paddles dipping into water, faint but steady, and far too many for it to be our own clan returning from their nightly fishing.

I sit upright, every muscle taut.

Chaos erupts onshore.

Shouts, raw with alarm, collide with the piercing cries of fear. The sounds are quickly followed by screams of terror and the splintering of wood.

Suddenly, clusters of fire roar to life on the Hokan boats and on land. Ba quickly grabs the steering oar from me with a trembling hand. The air surrounds me with the tension of unspoken dread.

I'm sure this is my doing.

"We must get back," Ba mutters, his voice hoarse. "Back to the others." He rows with frantic determination, calling out warnings to nearby boats to retreat. All around us, panic ripples through the darkness like a stone dropped into still water.

As we draw closer to shore, we pass a silhouette looming at the dock. A large junk boat, dark and hulking. Its menace is unmistakable even under the veil of night. Figures pour from its deck, body after body, sword in hand.

Pirates.

I glance at Ba, his gaze fixed on the top of ship with a terror that hinders his rowing for a moment. Following his eyes, I see it; the dragon and phoenix emblem of the Southern Sea Raiders. Flickering light from the flames illuminate the onyx flag as it twists in the night wind like the mark of death itself.

A merciless bunch of outlawed bandits; these pirates have carved a bloody path through the southern coasts since the New World Order commenced. Yet until now, Hokans—and other similar clans—always managed to slip away, like minnows darting through the fingers of a careless hand.

Our lives, adrift on the endless expanse of water, have granted us a peculiar freedom—one that lends clarity to their movements. We understand the rhythm of the sea, the ebb and flow that guides their marauding vessels.

While those on land fall prey to the sudden crash of their assaults, we have always anticipated their storms and sailed beyond their reach.

But we did not sense them coming this time.

A terrible certainty takes root in my chest. Something about this night echoing finality.

I fear we have outrun them for the last time.

"Go!" Ba shouts as we finally touch shore. "Nothing we have is worth our lives. Take nothing with you!" He jumps out into the shallow waters, and I closely follow suit. As soon as we hit compact sand, we part ways, as he heads over to evacuate Hokan boats on fire. I sprint down the dirt road into town.

How had they gotten past us? It was like they appeared out of nowhere.

The questions race through my thoughts as I dodge through flames. I pass several local Pingshen men engaging the attackers in combat. They are brave, but certainly no match for pirates that pillage for a living. The hot air begins to smell of seared flesh. As I look around, there are slain, mutilated bodies already lining the streets. Violence rages in every direction, but all I can focus on is my own heartbeat thundering in my ears.

The panicked crowd surges around me like a human tide, shoulders and elbows battering against me as they flee the violence erupting through the streets. Something whistles past my head, and I dive behind an abandoned market stall. Behind the barrier, there's a whimpering Pingshen woman clutching her child to her chest. Her eyes are wild, face covered in soot.

I lift my own shaking finger to my mouth. She does not respond to the plea, but her noises cease.

Cautiously, I peer around the stall's wooden support. The sight that greets me is of the merchant I robbed earlier locked in combat with a pirate. I don't plan on helping him, but something about the confrontation gives me pause. I squint my eyes to see clearer through the smoke and ash polluting the air.

Something's wrong.

His arm raised with a dagger to strike, the merchant stands frozen, knife glinting in the firelight. Only his eyes move, darting wildly with terror. And across from him, a dark essence coils around the pirate like a living shadow. One of his tendril's grips onto the man's arm as he watches with a grin.

My mind reels.

What in the…

Before I can process what I'm seeing, the merchant's arm is jerked unnaturally. And he is forced to plunge the knife into his own chest. Again. And again.

I clamp my hand over my mouth to stifle a gasp. His chest becomes a ravaged cavity of bone and gore, but his body remains upright, mouth stretched in a silent scream.

A piercing wail cuts through the chaos—high-pitched, terrified. It is the woman from beside me who has just seen what I have.

I rush to cover her mouth, but she is hysterical.

When I glance back around the stall to see if we have been spotted, the pirate turns to look over his shoulder.

Directly at me.

I burst from my hiding place, my feet pounding against the scorched earth, hoping the woman has the sense to run as well. But I can't look back. Not now. Survival is all that matters.

The clash of steel and crack of gunfire grows too close. I push myself harder, lungs burning.

The town's women and children will be fleeing inland, away from the water. I have never ventured that far from the coast, but now I have no choice.

Then—pain.

A rough fist snatches my tunic, wrenching me mid-stride. The world tilts violently as I'm thrown back, my body colliding against the charred remains of a shop. The impact sends embers cascading from the half-collapsed roof. Searing heat licks at my skin. I hiss, jerking away, but before I can regain my footing, I see my attacker—another pirate.

He looms over me, his face twisted in cruel amusement as I scramble backward. The flickering firelight casts grotesque shadows across his features. Sweat pours down my temples in the heat that surrounds us. He mutters something in that same foreign tongue I'd heard earlier, his hands moving to untie his trousers. My heart begins to thunder.

Panic claws at my throat as I scan for an escape, my gaze locking onto a butcher shop across the path. A meat cleaver glints on the counter, its blade half-buried in the worn wood.

If I can just get around him—

The man watches with sick pleasure as he gets closer. Steadying my resolve, I wait. I let him think he has me. Let him come within reach.

Then, with every ounce of willpower, I snatch a handful of still-burning embers from the fallen roof. Agony explodes through my palm, but I grit my teeth and hurl the embers into his face.

His scream splits the air, raw and guttural. He claws at his blistering flesh, his agony twisting his body. The rancid stench of charred skin makes me gag, but I don't stop. I stumble to my feet and bolt for the butcher shop.

The moment I reach the stall, I lunge, fingers curling around the cleaver's worn handle.

Immediately, muscle memory from cycles ago stirs—a skill shaped by a boy I once knew, his hands guiding mine through shadows of the past.

The weight, the balance, the motion—my body remembers what my grief has tried to forget.

I turn, swift as the wind over restless waters.

And I let the blade fly.

The cleaver arcs through the air, the God of Fate guiding its path. It buries itself deep in the pirate's spine with a sickening thud.

He pitches forward, collapsing into the flames. Fire hungrily consumes his body, but then that same mysterious black smoke I'd witnessed earlier begins to curl from his burning corpse. I watch in a stupor, swaying from the pain and the inhalation of smoke.

What manner of men are these? Can they even be called such?

Pain pulses through my burned palm, but there's no time to dwell on it.

A second pirate—farther away—spins to face me, pistol raised, but I'm already in motion heading toward escape. I stumble into the side paths of the village, refusing to look back.

When I reach the outskirts of town, I find the locals gathering before retreating to the mountains en masse. The pirates haven't made it this far, but there is no guarantee they won't venture further.

As I make my way through the crowd, I overhear plans to exit. With lit torches guiding the way, making it to Beifo—the next closest port village—won't be more than two weeks' trip if we start the journey now.

I let go of a tense, shaky breath I did not know I'd been holding.

Suddenly, more gunshots crack through the night, closer this time, sparking a fresh wave of panic. The crowd surges, feet pounding against the dirt road as a stampede erupts toward the dark path out of town. I turn to flee with them when, through the chaos, I hear a shout from back at the village.

A voice I know.

I whip around, my breath catching in my throat. Through the thick smoke and the flickering flames licking at the remains of shops and homes, I see Hokan people—I see Ba—being rounded up.

Hands up above their heads. Their knees are kicked from beneath them, sending them sprawling like livestock being herded for slaughter. On instinct, I make a move back toward them, but I stop short.

Memories rush in, quick and visceral. I remember the days when the sea itself felt like the only thing that understood me—the only thing that would take me without question.

I remember the looks, the whispers, the resentment I never earned but bore all the same. Their blame and their intolerance wrapping around me like a net, tightening, suffocating. I was a burden they never wished to carry.

They raised me. They gave me food and shelter.

But never love. Never happiness. I should not thank them.

Do I not owe them at least the kinship of dying by their side?

The war inside my mind lasts only seconds. But it is a costly hesitation.

A sharp crack explodes against the side of my skull, and my vision lurches. Pain flares hot and blinding. My knees buckle, the ground tilting beneath me as I crumple forward.

A rough hand seizes my tunic, wrenching me upright. My head pounds, the taste of iron thick on my tongue.

"Thought you could run, huh?" the pirate chuckles.

I'm unprepared for the harsh tug and grip of my hair in his meaty fist. He drags me towards the corralled Hokans.

I scramble on my knees after him, digging my nails into his arm and wrist deep enough to draw blood. However, the struggle is futile. My vision is still filled with bright dots and patterns from the blow.

"Ouch! Knock it off, you little bitch!" he snarls. I wince as he grips harder. "Got another one trying to get away, Cap'n."

I'm tossed the distance between him and his superior. My scalp burns as though on fire.

The captain takes a calculated glance at my appearance. He chuckles, "An exotic one."

I lift my head up at him and say nothing. As he studies my glare, I'm sure he gets the message: *If I had it my way, you would be bleeding out.*

He only delivers an ominous smile in response to my silence.

"What should we do with them, Captain?" one of the pirates asks.

The clan members begin to cry and beg for mercy. However, that sways nothing.

"We do as we were told. Deliver them to The Master," he says indifferently.

Master? Who would the likes of these men answer to?

"But someone killed my brother!" another pirate outcries. "I know it was one of these animals!"

The captain contemplates for a split second. "You're right. Since I lost one of my men, it's only fair they lose one theirs, is it not?"

A wicked smirk spreads across his face as black outgrowth begins to coil around him. Panic spreads like wildfire, and yet, amidst the chaos, one voice pierces through.

"Take *her*!" Ba shouts.

The black tendrils that had been coiling outward hesitate, writhing in the air like wounded serpents before retreating into his flesh. The captain stares at Ba with a sharp, calculating gaze—amusement flickering behind his eyes, tempered by something colder. Disdain. A predator sizing up the weakest in the herd, weighing the worth of an unexpected offering.

He glances at Ba, then back at me.

I do not look Ba's way.

I can feel the pounding of my heart in my ears. I'm angry and heartbroken enough to shed a tear—my own sacred water. But I refrain.

I should've left them to die.

I don't think I could've lived with myself if I had.

"Why just this one?" he challenges, "What's wrong with her other than her hue?"

"I don't know!" Ba heaves hysterically, "I tried drowning her in the sea, and it spit her back out! Cost me my entire hand, but believe me, I tried!" Spittle flies from his mouth as he bargains their lives—really just his—for mine. "Sh-she's done nothing but terrorize us for the last few years! Pummeling her way through the clan. If you spare us, you can have her."

As the captain weighs this, one of his crew scoffs, "You expect us to believe that?" He gestures to me lazily, a sneer set on his face. "This *girl* is lethal enough to cause you 'terror'. Please! *All* you water barbarians are the same. You will sly your way out of anything. You didn't fight during the war, and you still won't even fight *now*."

"Not to mention that abomination will make no good to use to us. Captain, we should just kill it now and put it out of its misery," another one laminates. As he does, he swiftly lifts his gun to my forehead awaiting the order to put me down like a diseased stray.

I move my head forward until the warm metal meets my skin. "If you are going to shoot me," I press harder, "then do it."

Heat licks at my skin, but I feel nothing—not the warmth, not the fear, not even the weight of the moment. This is the first time anyone in my clan has ever heard my voice. And it carries no emotion, no tremor, no trace of the person I was before tonight.

It is empty. As empty as I feel now.

Just as the pirate begins to curl his finger around the trigger, the captain's hand shoots out, gripping his forearm with unsettling calm.

"Captain?" the man's voice wavers, confusion lacing his words.

"Wait," the captain murmurs, crouching down to my level. He seizes my chin in a rough grip, tilting my head side to side. With eyes devoid of empathy, he dissects my features as if I were a trinket under inspection. "If you look past her skin," he squints slightly, "she's not too hard on the eyes."

The other pirate snorts, the sound acute and derisive, as though the very notion of finding someone like me desirable is a joke too absurd to entertain.

"I'm sure there's some fool out there who'd take a liking to this," the captain continues, his tone calculating. "And if she's pure, we could fetch twice the silver selling her to a flower house."

The words hang in the air, chilling and predatory.

The other man falls silent, the weight of the suggestion settling heavily over him. After a pause, he steps back dropping his weapon.

My jaw clinches so hard I'm sure my veins pulse at my temples. To keep my mind from unraveling, I turn my focus to the pirate before me, studying every detail of his face. Committing it to memory.

His features are forgettable—another vulture among many. But there is one thing that stands out. A jagged, ugly scar slashes horizontally across his forehead, the skin uneven and warped. It looks like it had festered once, ravaged by infection, leaving behind a mark that refuses to heal cleanly.

If I make it out of this alive, I will see this face again. And he will come to know wrath.

The captain rises to his full height, towering above the captive crowd. His voice cuts through the tension like a blade. "Fine. I'll take her." He turns to his crew, his gaze sweeping across them with deliberate intensity. "What the Master does not know shall not hinder our contract, hm?"

His words are both decree and warning, a thinly veiled threat wrapped in a veneer of camaraderie. The crew exchanges uneasy glances, understanding the consequences of disobedience without needing further explanation.

Relief ripples through half the clan, a muted tide of selfish gratitude. The others, though, wear their guilt like a shroud, their gazes heavy with pity as they glance my way.

None of them give voice to a protest.

The captain turns, steps purposeful, to a stop before Ba. The older man crumples under the weight of his shadow, trembling as though the ground itself threatens to swallow him whole. For a heartbeat, time seems to freeze. The air thickens, pregnant with unspoken dread, as the world holds its breath.

Then, with a swift and seamless motion, a tendril of darkness unfurls from the pirate's body like a viper striking. The obsidian blade arcs through the air, exact and unforgiving, and Ba's head separates from his body in an instant. The severed skull falls with a muted thud, followed closely by the lifeless body collapsing to the ground.

The silence that follows is more deafening than any scream, a void filled only by the echo of the act itself. The darkness lingers for a moment longer, writhing and alive, before returning to its owner, as though sated by the sacrifice.

The crowd erupts into screams, a deafening symphony of shock, grief, and prayers to a Goddess who does not seem interested in receiving them.

I'm silent, rooted in place. The world feels distant, muffled.

The captain turns, dispassionate, and strides toward the shore where his ship awaits. He doesn't look back as he speaks, his tone cold. "Flog any that resist you. As for that black one—" he waves a dismissive hand, "—Madam Lín will break her in. That is all."

A fresh wave of hysteria sweeps through the air, a commotion of desperate cries and wails. My lips tremble, my fists clench, but no sound escapes.

Rough hands seize me, lifting me from the ground as if I weigh nothing. I do not struggle. I only allow myself one last look at the clan I will never see again.

They were never family, but they were home. Now I have none.

And it is all my fault.

5
PRESENT DAY
BEIFO PORT, 1799

I've held my breath to the very edge of my limits. Breaking the surface, I spit the compass into my palm and cough violently. Saltwater stings my throat and lip. Its brine mingles with the taste of blood. My chest heaves as I fight to steady my breathing. Whatever substance Madam Lín gave me has finally worn off.

I glance back toward the boat. It is no more than a tiny speck near land, its inhabitants reduced to ants scrambling in chaos.

My brows furrow.

How long have I been swimming? How had I not passed out?

Rubbing the saltwater out of my eyes, I attempt to clear my thoughts. Answers—if they exist—can wait until I'm no longer on the verge of freezing to death.

I tread water, my gaze cutting through the suffocating darkness of the semi-open port. The inky blackness of the night feels oppressive, but I scan relentlessly. A glimmer of light catches my eye. In close breadth, a couple of torches flickering aboard a nearby trade ship, its silhouette anchored and still.

It is certainly a gamble. But it is my only chance.

Kicking forward, I force my body into motion, each stroke mechanical. Focusing on the monotony of cutting through waves allows me to ignore the concerning autumn chill settling into my bones.

I just need to make it to the boat.

Nothing else but that matters.

As I near the vessel, the weight of my crime settles over me.

There is no undoing what I have done. Once word spreads, the mainland will become a specter of the past—an untouchable memory.

It is a thought that soothes the raw edges of my mind.

Now, there is no other choice for me than to leave this part of my life behind. Whatever fate awaits me, lies beyond the horizon I have watched for eight long summers. A horizon where the Heavens meet the endless blue, and whispers of something more.

When I reach the base of the boat, my limbs feel leaden. The burst of adrenaline from before has depleted. I need to get onboard soon or else I may give myself up to the sea. For the briefest of moments, I wade softly and consider doing so.

It wouldn't be a horrible way to go. This water has carried me time and time again. Perhaps, I should let it carry me one last time to my final resting place…

Voices, and a shuffle of feet above, break my concentration. There are two of them, and they're carrying torches. I quickly pull closer to the vessel to avoid being spotted.

"I'll tell you one thing, brother, the best brothels are always in this port," one of them tells the other.

I roll my eyes as they shuffle past.

"You would be the one to know all about that, wouldn't you?" the other retorts, mirth lacing his words.

The conversation continues as their voices fade out in the direction of the front of the boat.

I linger in my hiding place, heart pounding. Slowly, I edge back to survey the ship more clearly, scanning its dark mass for a way atop.

There must be something—anything—that can get me up there.

My eyes settle on the thick twists of a rope anchored to the depths below. I begin paddling toward it, careful to avoid even the faintest splash that might betray my presence.

Once beside the cord, I pause. My ears strain for any sign of movement—footsteps, murmurs, anything. The silence persists. Tentatively, I give the rope a tug, testing its strength. The fibers are firm beneath my hands, and nothing creaks or shifts above. Emboldened, I pull harder. Each breath is shallow as I listen for the faintest hint of danger. Still, all remains quiet.

Deeming it safe, I bite down on the compass as before. Its cold metal reverberates through my mouth, creating an ache in my teeth. I freeze at the sensation.

The compass is humming anew.

The resonance feels like it's urging me forward, guiding me toward this ship.

I have no option but to listen to it.

A moment passes to gather my body's rapidly dwindling strength. Then, I steel myself. Adjusting my grip higher, the crisp night air is like a thousand needles against my exposed forearms. I push the discomfort to the back of my mind, bringing my knees to my chest. The weight of my drenched clothes clings to me like a cloak, turning each pull into an agonizing strain on muscles already pushed to their limits. My fingers ache and tremble. Progress is agonizingly slow—every inch gained feeling like a mile. The climb becomes a quiet war.

One breath.

One pull.

One moment at a time.

Several excruciating moments stretch into eternity before my fingers brush the beam at the top. The reach to grip the rough wood is equal parts terrifying and nauseating. A drop from here, even with a boat of this smaller height, would surely shatter a few bones.

I manage to attain a solid grip and bring my body to the banister. Before my arms give out, I quickly haul myself over.

Once aboard, I pry the compass from my mouth. Its surface resembles ice in my trembling palm. Slumping against the side wall of the steering helm, I let out a shaky breath.

Just one moment to steady myself.

One moment to push back the tremor in my limbs and the fire in my lungs.

That is all I need.

That moment is abruptly shortened by the sound of footsteps—and the same two voices from earlier—ambling closer. Panic snaps me upright. My gaze darts around, frenzied. To my right, against the back mast, looms a large bamboo barrel. Without hesitation I rush toward it, lift the lid, and climb inside.

The pungent stench of decay envelops me instantly. Dead fish, packed deep enough to hide me, fill the barrel—likely the crew's catch for sustenance. I bite down on my tongue to stifle a gag. Lowering the lid above me, my heart races in the suffocating dark. I place my free hand over my mouth to mute my labored breathing. Dim torch light grows brighter as they come closer.

"I heard we head out tomorrow morning at sunrise," says one of the sailors. The man spits out phlegm from his throat onto the deck. "We have a few more rounds to make before heading to Ningbao for the Festival," he says, voice gruff and low.

My forehead puckers at the mention of the event.

But Heavenly Liberation Day isn't celebrated for another six moons... Why would they need to start any preparation so soon? And hadn't Merchant Fang mentioned something about it, too? What was it he said again—

His partner responds in a higher tenor. "Yeah? Good. Let's get the hell out of the port before the Emperor's watchdogs poke their noses into what we have below—"

They both stop abruptly right outside the barrel.

My heart hammers hard enough to break my ribs. A silence stretches for a beat.

If they find me, there will be no choice. I will fight them both.

One of the men raps the barrel lightly with the butt of his torch. The hollow sound vibrates through my very bones; each knock a heartbeat closer to discovery. My breath catches as I press myself tighter into the rancid embrace of the dead fish.

"Thought I heard something," the gruff one mutters, his tone uneasy.

"Your ears are sharper than your blade," the other replies with a laugh. "What did you think—a stowaway snuck aboard to nap with the catch?"

"I don't like it," the first insists, his voice dropping to a dangerous bass. There is a pause, and then the barrel shifts slightly. The weight of his hand presses against it. My heart lurches, the stillness within me turning brittle.

But then, as if the God of Fate was watching, the pressure relents.

"Enough. If anyone's skulking about, they'll be wishing for death if we catch them," the tenor voice says. "Come on. We have more rounds to finish before dawn."

Their footsteps fade, and the compass in my hand continues its quiet, but steady, thrum.

I remain curled in the filth for what feels like hours, my body stiff, my breath shallow. Only now, as the night settles into uneasy stillness, do I dare exhale fully. Though, even that feels like a risk.

My limbs have long since gone numb, swallowed by the cold and grime, but I fight to stay awake. Breathing it in is nauseating, but it is a small price to pay for staying alive.

I force my mind away from the slick filth beneath me, and from the sting in my muscles. Instead, I focus on my next move.

I have been counting.

Each round of the on-duty crewmates lasts roughly four hundred and eighty heartbeats. When they pass this next time, I will have fewer than four hundred to find another place to hide. But where?

I swallow back frustration, pressing my fingers to my temples in a futile attempt to ease the growing ache. I cannot afford panic. Not now.

But then, through the muffled sound of approaching voices, something new cuts through the air.

A faint splash.

I go rigid, ears straining.

Silence.

Then, another.

Not the aimless ebb of the port's tide, but something much more deliberate. Purposeful. Someone—or something—is moving stealthily alongside the ship.

Through the small hole of the barrel, I catch a glimmer of movement. It looks like mere shadows. My heart picks up.

Not again.

However, as my eyes adjust, I realize they aren't shadows at all. Multiple moonlit outlines of men climb aboard like flies swarming a carcass. I count three, then five, then more. All of them with blades at their sides. The air changes, thickening with a tension that prickles at my skin. Before I can process the impending doom, a loud cry pierces the night.

"Pirates!"

The shout rends the air, jagged and desperate. A bell tolls, its clangs rising in panicked rhythm.

My senses are ablaze as I push the barrel's lid aside and climb out. Torches flare to life as crewmen rush to arms, but chaos descends faster than they can draw their swords.

It appears my long night of running has not yet ended.

I must get out of here.

My mind races for a solution. This boat is not floating near the port, but I consider returning to it. If I go back, I'll only trade one danger for another. I'm bound to be caught by Imperial guards prowling about the shore like wolves—waiting. Retribution for a slain captain would be merciless. The thought is dismissed as quickly as it comes.

I look to the sea. That option is no better. I would surely freeze to death this time. Or, if my luck continued to go the way this night has, I would drown from exhaustion before I ever reached safety.

Around me, the deck is a storm of commotion. The pirates' blades sing as they clash with the ship's defenders. Crates splinter underfoot. Torches fall and gutter, their embers scattering like fireflies in the summer.

Abruptly, I remember the two Traders from earlier remarking the importance of something below deck. That suggests another opportune place of hiding.

I will take my chances.

It takes three steps before I have some feeling in my legs. I look for the stairs or hatch door leading below, but—

At the heart of the fight is a man who moves like a warrior. There is no chaos in his maneuvers, no wasted energy. His blade arcs with deadly precision. It is as though the fray bends to his will, and not the other way around.

"Captain Zhèng," a pirate calls, his voice cutting through the discordance, "The cargo is ours!"

The name echoes through the biting air, carrying with it a force of more than a hundred men.

Zhèng Yī.

Tales of this man have reached every corner of the coast—of a pirate king whose mastery of Pingshen's surrounding waters has made him both a legend and a scourge.

He stands tall amid the melee, his presence commanding despite the simplicity of his garb. He is not draped in the finery one might expect of a man who commands a fleet. Instead, his garments are practical. There are no embroidered robes, no ostentatious displays of wealth to proclaim his power. Instead, his attire is pragmatic. Built for movement—for battle.

Beside him, a second figure emerges from the shadows—a man of slightly leaner build. It can only be one person—his elusive and rumored second-in-command, Luo Jinhai.

Unlike Zhèng's quiet command, he radiates a restless energy. His arrows soar out with practiced ease even as a grin plays across his lips. The man is no less imposing, but… a lot more naked.

He's got nothing adorning his tan upper body but the bow and arrow sleeve strapped to his back. Thankfully, linen pants cover his undesirables.

Zhèng's movements suddenly slow as his gaze sweeps across the deck. "Enough bloodshed," he announces, his voice loud and imbued with authority. "Subdue the remaining crew. Kill only if necessary."

Luo lets loose one last arrow, striking an injured crewmate clawing at his feet with a dagger in hand. Only then does he lower his weapon.

"Do tell, captain, what awaits us next on the itinerary," his voice is light and mocking as he leisurely wipes a smear of blood from the carved grip of his bow.

Zhèng Yī does not reply to Luo's remark. Instead, his dark gaze continues its assessment of the boat—calculating—before it settles… on me.

"Shōush." The Hokan curse slips from my mouth before I can apprehend it. I step back instinctively, but it is too late. One of his men, eager to please, has already begun rushing to me.

I make a break for the back of the ship.

Perhaps jumping overboard isn't too bad of an idea.

I run though the labyrinth of stacked cargo, but my legs are still lacking the strength reserved for urging my stride quicker.

The pirate catches my left arm, yanking me backward, "Got you!"

The momentum alone feels like it's going to pull my arm out of its socket. To thank him for the assault, I spin, punching him squarely in his nose. He yelps in pain but does not release me. Instead, a death grip encases my other arm. Exploiting his brute strength, he hauls me over back towards Zhèng.

I'm tossed two steps away from his feet, but my grip remains firm on the compass. Which, in disastrous timing begins to vibrate itself, and my hand, violently.

The world seems to tilt as Zhèng strides toward me. Luo follows close behind, his expression alight with curiosity, as though approaching an unexpected prize.

They stop before me, and the captain regards me with a gaze that is neither harsh nor kind. It's piercing, as though he is attempting to make sense of my appearance.

"And who," he says, his voice a low sound that resonates through the air, "might you be?"

His face, framed by a tangle of coarse facial hair, bears the unmistakable cut of a man shaped by cycles at sea. His hair, long and thick, is pulled back with care. The intentional choice in appearance is an unspoken defiance of the crown. An obvious declaration that he yields to no Emperor, no law.

The co-captain tilts his head, his grin widening. "A stowaway, perhaps?" He looks me over with more intent, "Or something more interesting?" In the torch light, his skin glistens a shade of warmth. Not as dark as mine, but certainly not as fair as Pingshen people often are.

Blood roars in my ears, but I refuse to speak, explain, or defend myself. I owe them nothing. More than that—I do not know what lurks beneath their skin, what monsters they might be hiding within.

I have had my fill of shadowed horrors today.

Around us, the battle has waned, the cries of the defeated crew fading into tense silence. The pirates have easily claimed the ship. I realize then, with growing disdain, that my fate now rests in the hands of these men.

As Zhèng's eyes glide around my person, I become hyperaware of the robe clinging to my skin and reeking of fish. His gaze snags upon my scarred forearm.

I flip it facing inward. I do not want to invite any questions that might land me back in the bindings of the flowerboat. Or worse.

Thankfully, he does not probe. Instead, his eyes settle on my shaking, clenched fist. He bends down slowly, and I shift backwards. Unfortunately, his men are right there to hold me still. Without a word, he gestures for one of them to apprehend my trembling forearm. They do so and bring it up to face level with the captain.

Though most of the compass is hidden in my grip, he must recognize it immediately. His eyes widen and dance with thinly veiled wonder, before shuttering. His role of a leader regains priority.

He glances at the device's shaking form, then looks at me. "How did you come about this, woman?"

"I took it off one of the crew you just butchered," I lie, letting the crisp mainland accent I have worn for nearly a decade slip away like a discarded mask. Something tells me these men would grow even more belligerent if they suspected an official was out there, eager to pay for the return of their concubine.

My voice is dry, but bitterness alone cannot mask the flicker of unease creeping beneath my ribs. It coils there, tight and persistent, a quiet warning that I may have already mis-stepped.

The corner of his lips lifts at the end slightly, though the gesture is devoid of warmth. "Sure, you did."

He sends a look over his shoulder at his co-captain. In silence, they share an exchange of glances that betrays their attempt at a hidden conversation. It is abundantly clear they know something about the compass that the rest of us do not.

Turning his attention back to me, his dark eyes do not leave mine as he pries my fingers off the object.

"Curious thing, this," the co-captain muses, his eyes on the object. "It's been in many hands over the cycles. None of them alive now," his tone is almost conversational.

I know he means to unsettle me, to carve fear into the spaces between his words, but I do not give him the satisfaction of a reaction.

Zhèng lifts the compass, angling it slightly for his crew to see, no doubt intending to demonstrate its power. But something changes.

Now in his hand, the vibration has come to a stop.

He tilts and turns the device for a few moments before turning its face to me. The needle remains utterly still, lifeless as a stone. His expression darkens, suspicion brewing behind his eyes.

"What did you do to it?" he demands, his voice low and dangerous. "Are you Wielding it?"

I scoff at the accusation.

"If I were a Wielder of metals' energy," I say, my voice edged with hostility, "do you truly think I'd be here, listening to you ramble on incessantly? Or would I have already bent the very composition of your blades to my will and cut you all down where you stand?"

I stifle a pleased smirk as the crew stirs uneasily.

Let him wonder—let them all wonder—if there is even a sliver of truth to it.

I hold his gaze, unflinching, but the captain does not seem deterred by the possibility of a Wielder being in their midst.

"Then why isn't the relic working?" Zhèng challenges, pointing to the compass. "Why's the needle gone still?"

The murmurs of the crew grow louder.

Before I can answer, Luo moves from his spot. His gait is unhurried as he orbits me slowly. His eyes gleam with the focus of a predator circling its quarry.

"A relic?" I echo, skepticism curling through my tone.

The co-captain stops beside the captain once more, his grin widening. He addresses the crowd like a showman on stage. "They say it points the way to something beyond mortal understanding. Endless treasure, perhaps," He pauses, reveling in the murmurs of awe rippling through his underlings. Then his expression shifts, his gaze cutting back to me with an assessing edge. His voice turns pensive. "Or power."

I glare at him, refusing to betray the confusion swirling within me.

Power? Treasure? The compass I'd stolen—on impulse, no less—had seemed nothing more than an ornate bauble to be sold. A means to an end.

But this revelation could change everything…

Zhèng's fleet sails beyond the reach of the law, beyond the grasp of those who would see me dead.

If I can earn his trust, bend his ambitions to align with my own, then perhaps I can use his power and resources to secure my escape—and the truth.

"I didn't know," I say carefully, my voice steady.

Luo tilts his head. "No?" His tone dances gleefully with a dare, as if trying to trip me up in a web of falsehood I'm not privy to.

I stare him down with a glower that could set fire to an Aether bush.

Honestly, what is his problem?

The captain frowns, holding up the compass again, his grip tightening as though the force of his will alone might compel the needle to move. But judging by his expression, it remains still—its defiance a silent rebuke. He is truthfully perturbed now.

"Enough games," he mutters as he stands, his patience dwindling. "What do you know of this compass? Speak, or I'll see you thrown to the sea."

"I *said* I know nothing," I insist, voice rising in frustration. "I took it because I needed coin, not because I thought it was some... some cursed artifact!"

The crew stirs at the word 'cursed', their restlessness growing louder.

Luo raises a hand to silence them, his grin fading as his expression turns thoughtful.

"Perhaps she speaks the truth," he ponders.

Zhèng steps closer, his gaze boring into mine from above. "You're coming aboard," he says, voice leaving no room for argument. "Until we understand why the compass responds to you, you will remain under our watch."

"And if I refuse?"

I know I have little choice in the matter, but I must maintain the appearance that this is not the outcome I'd hoped for.

"Then you'll find out how long a person can tread freezing water," Luo replies lightly. The reinstated smile that accompanies his words is anything but kind.

They have no idea the distance I have just swam, but I keep my secrets to myself. They need not know what I'm capable of before I even understand it myself.

I concede, begrudgingly nodding my head once.

The captain's expression remains unreadable, though I catch a flicker of relish in his eyes.

Nearby, a younger man—his wiry frame tense and his eyes shifting nervously—steps forward. "Cap'n, we can't take her aboard!" he exclaims, his voice shrill with fear and superstition. "Don't you know a woman is bad luck?"

Bad luck.

All my life, I've been labeled as such, as though my very existence were an affront to the natural order. I have grown *incredibly* wary of hearing it.

Zhèng turns to the crewman, his gaze cutting through the man's protestations with the efficiency of a serrated blade. "If misfortune courts you because of your proximity to a woman," he says, voice calm yet filled with menace, "it is safe to assume you were never lucky to begin with."

The young man falters, his mouth opening and closing as though he might argue further, but no words come.

The captain turns to the rest of his crew, raising his deep voice above the din. "Onto the small boats, and back to the main ship. We've wasted enough time."

As the pirates move to obey, Luo lingers, fixation still on me. "Welcome to the crew," he says, his tone dripping with irony.

As I'm dragged to my feet, someone comes behind me to tie my hands in rope. When I'm brought to the edge of the side of the boat, I see multiple small sampans floating below. This will be the first one I step foot on in eight cycles.

As I'm forced on the small boat with a handful of the crew, I contemplate in secret.

I'm still not free, but that will change soon.

6

AT DWAN

SOUTH PINGSHEN SEA, 1799

We paddle until the sun slowly begins to rise, and the sky is a myriad of yellow, orange, and soft blue.

The moment I'm brought off the sampan, and my feet touch the deck of the pirate junk ship, I'm struck by the vessel's imposing presence.

It feels alive, breathing with the sigh of the waves. The hull, broad and sturdy, is painted a piercing black, its lacquer chipped in places to reveal weathered teak wood beneath—scars that tell of its long and violent history.

The sails, billowing high above, are unlike any I have seen before. They are massive, ribbed with bamboo slats that stretch the crimson canvas taut, their edges fraying. The masts rise skyward, gnarled and darkened by salt and sun.

Above me, the sterncastle looms, its structure decorated yet fearsome, adorned with carved dragons whose open mouths seem ready to spew their rage. Lanterns hang from the railings, their red paper exteriors glowing faintly in the dim light of dawn. The air is thick with the mingled scents of brine, tar, and something acrid. Perhaps it's the faint metallic tang of blood that clings to the ship's planks.

Having been on the last boat to arrive, the deck is already flooded with noise and movement. Around me, the crew bustles with practiced efficiency, their voices raised in commands and curses, preparing to set sail.

I'm shoved forward, nearly stumbling over a coil of rope lying carelessly on the deck. One of the pirates—broad-shouldered and leering—grabs my arm to steady me, though the grip he uses is more bruising than helpful.

"Careful, girl," he says. His breath is foul with the stench of salted fish and stale grained cereal wine. "Wouldn't want you tripping and falling overboard now, would we?"

His laughter is coarse and it grates against my ears like the screech of gulls. A Pingshen. In one of his lobes hangs an earring made of small twine and tiny bird bones.

I already dislike him the most.

I tear my arm from his grip, my glare lethal. He only laughs harder before turning back to his work.

Luo strides ahead of me, clusters of crewmates parting on instinct to let him through. He pauses at the base of the sterncastle's stairs before turning back to cast me a sly smile. "Welcome to the Red Dragon. She's a beauty, isn't she?"

I say nothing, though my eyes flicker over the ship once more.

Beauty is not the word I would choose.

The Red Dragon is magnificent, yes, but it is a… dark magnificence, a thing of power and menace rather than grace.

"The captain awaits you," he says, tone laced with mockery. He stretches his arm out in the direction of the upper deck.

The two men flanking me prod me up the stairs, but I do not stumble. I square my shoulders, determined not to give them the satisfaction of seeing me falter.

The crew below murmurs among themselves, their voices low and gritty. I catch words like "trouble," "black," and "unlucky," but I force my head high, refusing to let their words bother me.

When we reach the top of the sterncastle's stairs, we are met with the captain's quarters. I eye the door warily. The co-captain senses my trepidation which only causes him to grin harder as he pushes his way inside.

The cabin door groans as it swings inward, revealing a space far removed from the chaos of the deck. It's smaller than I'd expected but far more lavish.

Painted wooden walls gleam in the portlight coming in from the far side. Their surfaces are inlaid with intricate patterns of pearls. Dragons and phoenixes writhe across the panels, locked in eternal combat. The air is heavy with the mingling aroma of incense—burnt and heavy—struggling to mask an underlying tang of vinegar and sweat.

The sheer opulence stuns me. The carvings alone could fund a lifetime of comfort, yet Zhèng scours the waters still grasping for more.

At the center of the room's back wall stands a low table, where the captain's hulking figure looms in stillness.

A firm nudge from behind propels me forward until I stand on the opposite side, facing him. The silence is heavy, fraught with unspoken tension. I use the time to truly take in his appearance.

There's a nick of a scar on the left of his face, nestled in the hallow of his cheek bone. His ears are pierced, but only one plain metal earring dangles from his right. He wears a dark tunic, simple but well-made. It is cinched at the waist with a sash of crimson silk—the only indulgence, if it could be called that. He looks ridiculously out of place in contrast to the room he calls home.

He does not acknowledge me at first, his focus entirely consumed by his hand and what's in it—the compass.

Its silver casing gleams softly, catching the flicker of daylight. The needle inside remains stubbornly fixed, pointing toward an unseen horizon. For a moment, I wonder what thoughts twist behind his impassive gaze as he studies the device, his brow faintly creased.

"The compass," he begins, "has not moved once since it left your hands hours ago."

I force myself to straighten my posture, refusing to shrink under the weight of his presence. My eyes narrow, irritation prickling beneath my skin. "And what am I to do with this information?"

Zhèng's lips quirk into a faint smile. I doubt it is from amusement or understanding.

When he finally looks up, his gaze is unrelenting.

He turns the piece in his hand. "This," he says, holding the device out between us, "points to something many would kill for. Something many men *have* killed for."

"And you're one of them," I assume bluntly.

If he has a point, I would like for him to get to it.

The captain inclines his head slightly, the admission sliding from him without shame, "I am."

I arch a brow but say nothing.

A pause stretches between us, thick with unspoken weight. When he speaks again, his voice is measured.

"It's a token said to belong to a Founding God."

My forehead puckers at the confession. "*The* Founding Gods?" Disbelief weaves itself throughout my words. "As in the ones we banished to the Heavens almost one hundred cycles ago?"

He gives a silent nod.

I glance at Luo for further confirmation, but all he offers is a slight shrug.

I do not even know why I bothered.

I exhale sharply. "Then, why is it here? Why is it in the Corporeal World and not in their own?"

Zhèng's fingers trace the edge of the compass as though it might speak to him. "We don't understand the full breadth of its power or purpose yet, but one thing is certain—it's shown up now, on the eve cycle of the first blue moon since our Worlds were split. That is not a coincidence. If it has chosen you as its keeper, then you are bound to it, whether you wish to be or not."

The shiver that creeps down my spine is one I cannot fight. Doom sinks into my chest like an anchor dragging me under.

Using the compass as leverage was not supposed to be this Godsdamned complicated.

"I surely did not ask to be," I retort, my annoyance rising to the surface.

"No one asks for destiny," Zhèng replies. "But it finds us all the same."

For a moment, silence falls over the cabin, broken only by the creak of the ship and the distant crash of waves.

"How do you even know all of this?" I cannot contain the accusation in my tone.

Maybe he's just making all of this up. Why should I trust anything a pirate says?

"I have spent a long time accumulating *friends* that know things. Things even the Serpent Emperor himself doesn't know."

With that, he straightens to his full height, the conversation seemingly concluded. He tucks the compass deep into the folds of his tunic, hiding it away as if the very sight of it might summon more questions he has no interest in answering.

He turns to his co-captain. "Take her to the crew's quarters to change. She'll earn her keep or be cast into the sea."

I snort softly, daring to test the limits of whatever punishment he imagines lies in store for me. "I thought you needed me?"

His attention snaps back to mine. "You presume much," he says, voice calculated. "Need and necessity are not the same thing. If you think yourself indispensable, you overestimate your worth."

His delivery is cold. But it is a show.

I meet his stare brazenly, unwilling to flinch under his scrutiny. "Then throw me overboard," I counter, feigning indifference. "I'm sure the compass will guide your way just as well without me."

His jaw twitches ever so slightly. "If it were only that simple," he murmurs. Then, louder with a wave of his hand: "We'll see how vital you prove to be, woman."

When I make no move to exit, his eyes cut to me once more.

"You *are* aware I was bestowed a name at birth just as you were, correct?" I ask.

One brow arches, but he does not dignify my remark with a response. Instead, his obsidian eyes slide deliberately back to Luo, his head tilting toward the door in a silent dismissal.

But the man hesitates.

For the first time, I see his sardonic mask truly wane. His brow crinkles deeply. "Captain, she's a woman—"

Zhèng interrupts, his voice impatient and resolute. "A woman the compass favors. For now. If she is bad luck, then let adversity come. We'll meet it head-on, as we always have."

"That's not what I meant," Luo says, tone laden with an unspoken warning.

I study his expression.

What? Is he concerned for my safety among pirates?

These men know nothing about me or what awaits a man foolish enough to try forcing himself upon me.

"Fine," I say flatly, cutting off whatever concern Luo might voice.

I need no pity from him or anyone else.

The captain's unreadable gaze shifts back to me, lingering for a beat. Then, he nods toward Luo. "You heard her."

Luo nods, though his lips press into a thin line. He grabs my arm, pulling me toward the door.

As I'm dragged away, I look back over my shoulder.

Zhèng's hands rests on the desk, his face indecipherable. I cannot tell whether he is a man driven by greed, ambition, or something more dangerous.

Moments later, I find myself in the bowels of the boat. The room is cramped, lined with hammocks swaying gently with the ship's movement. Crates carrying the crews' sparse belongings are stacked haphazardly in the corners.

"This way," Luo beckons.

He does not bother to look back as he strides to a wooden chest near the far wall. When he opens it, he pulls out a bundle of clothes, tossing them onto the nearest hammock.

"Change," he orders.

I stare at him expressionless. "Well, I will likely need my hands to do that, won't I?"

His high cheeks flush a soft rouge in embarrassment at the oversight. As he loosens the rope, some strands of his ink black tresses fall into his face. His hair, like Zhèng's, is outgrown. It sits in lax waves atop his head, flowing down to his shoulders.

"Okay, now change," he says once my wrists are free. "Unless you'd rather do it on deck in front of the crew."

I do not move. "Turn around or get out."

His mouth parts slightly with incredulity at being ordered around, but I do not care.

After a stretch of tense silence, he complies, pushing past me back to wait at the cabin's door. "Don't take too long. You've got work to do."

I approach the hammock, my fingers brushing against the rough fabric of the clothes. With one last look over my shoulder to ensure the man's eyes aren't wandering, I slip out of my dirty robe. The cool sea air against my skin makes me shiver as I pull on the light-colored garments.

I'd once dressed in the loose banana hemp textile of a Hokan woman, the fabric soft and fluid; forgiving. A nod to the waves my clan called home.

Now, the scratch of cheap linen against my skin feels like an insult.

As I firmly tie the strings on the pants taut, my teeth clatter. The adrenaline has subsided, but I still haven't fully shaken the cold that set in hours ago after swimming.

It does not help that my arms are bare—save for several scars earned over cycles of survival. The tunic and trousers drape stiffly on my frame, but they allow for movement. I cinch the sash around my waist, adjusting it until the top feels secure.

It will have to suffice.

"Done," I inform, voice hard.

The co-captain turns, arms folded across his chest. His gaze sweeps over me before giving a curt nod. "This'll do."

Luo's broad frame blocks the entrance. As I glance over his stature, I consider, if I had to fight him off, what weapon it would take to end him.

"Are you at all inclined to wear a top?" I ask, hoping my disdain is palpable.

He offers a tight-lipped grimace. "Let's go," he says curtly.

I glance down at my bare feet, wrinkling my nose at the dampness seeping through the planks. Pointing, I ask, "Do I at least get slippers?"

"No." The single word is clipped, daring me to offer a complaint or some excuse.

Glaring, I say nothing.

With that he gives a stiff nod. "On deck. Now."

The ship is active with movement as I re-emerge onto the deck. Crew members swarm like insects. The captain stands at the stern, his hands resting lightly on the steering wheel as he barks orders.

"She's all yours," Luo calls, gesturing toward me with a wave of his hand.

Zhèng's attention lands on me. "Good. She can start with the ropes."

The casual way they speak about me—as though I'm not even here—stokes a simmering burn in my chest. I plant my feet. This visibly provokes Zhèng, as I see the faintest flicker of irritation flash in his eyes.

"Did you not hear me?" he demands angrily.

"I have a name, and you *will* call me by it."

Zhèng's expression doesn't waver, but there's a dangerous stillness in his demeanor now, as though weighing how far he'll let all of my challenging go.

"Then, do tell," he says, his words disgruntled, "what is your name?"

"Shi Yang," I say brashly, the syllables hanging heavy in the air.

For a moment, only the shuffling sounds of the crew around me fills the silence.

A quirk pulls at the corner of Zhèng's lips, though his eyes remain cold as steel. "Well, Shi Yang, we'll see if you can keep that attitude when your hands are raw, and your muscles are screaming."

His words are meant to provoke, but I find them unworthy of a response. Instead, I turn on my heel and head toward the masts, whose shadows fall across the deck like the bars of a cage in the now climbing sun.

My first task is hauling lines to secure the battened sails. It pains me to admit it, but the work *is* excruciating. The rough fibers of the ropes dig into my palms until they bleed.

Regardless, I grit my teeth and keep going.

With every passing second, my Hokan instincts—long dormant—stir to life. I remember the sea village, our boats light as feathers on the waves. This armed junk ship is larger, its movements heavier and more demanding, but the rhythm is not so different.

"You move like you've been on one of these before," quips a crewman hauling another line beside me.

I spare him a glance.

He is young, but likely not much younger than I. His hair, nearly void of color, is so pale it seems to glow in the rays of sunlight. Both sets of eyebrows and lashes are similarly colorless, blending into his starkly pale skin.

His complexion bears the angry red flush of prolonged sun exposure, the burns noticeable against his skin. However, whatever pain it causes does not seem to bother him.

I return my focus back to the task at hand.

"Because I have," I lie. I do not want my inexperience to be an invitation for further conversation.

He laughs. "Not bad for a woman!"

Just like the captain's comment earlier, I do not deem a reply worth the breath wasted. Unfortunately, that does not seem to deter him in the slightest.

"My name is Hé Chūnqiū, but you can just call me Hé," he huffs between strained hauls. His voice is far too casual for someone pulling such a heavy load. The taut stretch of his irritated skin reveals lean forearms and narrow shoulders, his movements quick and practiced.

How does he have the endurance to talk while doing this?

"I don't care," I snap, each word punctuated by my struggle to catch my breath. My frustration only seems to entertain him more, and the simmering annoyance drags my native tongue to the surface.

"Tâik-ing mouthy pirate"

He lets out a hearty laugh, finishing his haul and securing his rope to the base of the mast with infuriating ease. The absence of his haul adds even more weight to my unfinished line.

Lovely.

"Well, aren't you just a flower," he quips sarcastically as he strides off toward his next task.

The word stops me cold.

Flower.

My mind lurches backward, unbidden, to the brothel.

I'm no one's flower.

Something ignites deep in my chest—a slow-burning ember fed by snide remarks and unbearable men, now roaring a head. A surge of indignation so visceral it feels like a second heartbeat.

In an instant, I remember the Hokan girl, and the look in her eyes when she had that Trader at her mercy. How the room feared her.

Sails be Godsdamned.

I cease my efforts. With a sudden strength I hadn't possessed a moment ago, I seize the length of the rope and loop the coarse fiber around Hé's neck. His airway cuts off, and his body jerks in panic, arms flailing wildly. The commotion draws the attention of the crew. I fully expect them to rush in—to tear me away and defend their comrade. But they don't.

Instead, they form a loose circle around us. Jeers and jesting comments erupt from every direction, their voices a chaotic, raucous symphony.

"Place your bets!" someone calls out.

"She's got spirit, I'll give her that!"

"I bet 2 silver taels that she kills him!"

This is sport to them. Amusement shines in their eyes as if they'd bet their entire fortunes on the outcome.

They are ridiculous.

I'm no executioner. At least, not for their pleasure. I simply seek to send Hé—and everyone watching—a very clear message: I will *not* be an easy target.

The scrimmage does not last for long, as the noise brings Zhèng out of his cabin. He storms to the sterncastle railing, his expression thunderous. Eyes scanning the scene below, he roars, "What in Dì Yù's name is going on?"

At this, everyone quiets.

Sensing that I have proven my point, I loosen the rope, quickly dropping my hands as if nothing is amiss.

Immediately, Hé is coughing and heaving air. As he leans on the side of the boat's railing, Luo breaks through the crowd. I expect the look on his face to be stern or condemning. But instead, to my confusion, he's grinning.

Zhèng, on the other hand, is not.

"Shi Yang to the brig!" He cuts his glare across the others surrounding me. "Anyone else want to join her?"

He receives complete silence as a resounding denial of the offer.

"I presumed so. The next person to create a problem is getting strung up from the mast by their feet. Get back to work!"

With that, the pirates scramble. Everyone but the co-captain disperses; even Hé, who gives me an impish evil eye as he staggers away.

When it's just the two us, I'm roughly grasped by the collar of the rags they call clothing.

"Off we go," Luo quips in a derisively cheerful tone.

7

LATER

SOUTH PINGSHEN SEA, 1799

The air is thick—dust mingles into something almost tangible. It clings to my skin. Overhead, a dim lantern sways in time with the ship's slow, groaning movements. Each flicker distorts their shapes, twisting them into figures that stretch and shrink in endless contortions.

For hours, I have done little but watch them dance. Well, that, and wrangle my matted curls into something resembling a braid. An effort that has proven to be more frustration than success.

With a quiet exhale, I push myself upright. My palms throb where the rope has bitten deep, leaving raw, burning grooves against my flesh. I glance down, flexing my fingers experimentally. I snort softly.

I suppose my grip was tighter than I thought.

The cold planks are unforgiving beneath my bare soles as I pace the narrow confines of the cell. I'm sure the sun has set, and dinner is being prepared given the faint echo of laughter and bawdy songs drifting down from above. I have no intention of paying them any mind, but a fragment of conversation snags my attention.

"And just like that, the captain has secured another chest of Dì Yù's own Aether," one pirate remarks, his voice muffled through the walls.

"Let's raise our glasses to that!" another chimes in. A muted clink of metal cups filters through the floorboards above, followed by the low rumble of laughter.

"The third ship raided in two days," someone else muses. "I sure hope this mysterious 'interested party' the captain is working with rewards us generously for the effort."

The rest of the conversation dissolves into the cadenced lapping of the ocean against the hull, the murmurs of men reduced to a distant hum beneath the night sky. But I have heard enough.

I had been wondering what these pirates were after on that trading ship. Their opposition to the empire was expected—inevitable, even. However, Aether smuggling? And not just for their own gain, but for a hidden benefactor?

The revelation twists in my mind. My curiosity flares, even as something uneasy settles beneath it. The knowledge leaves a bitter taste on my tongue.

Involuntarily, my thoughts drift back to the bustling port of Kwangchow—to the labyrinth of egg-boats and junks. The way Hokans had lived for over nine hundred cycles—before the Pingshen empire even existed.

From the moment aetherbloom emerged, its use had been tightly controlled. One of the first laws set in stone forbade 'illegitimate' Pingshen-born ethnicities from consuming it. It remained that way until the war. Then they had made some concessions. But not for Hokans.

That is, until disguised emissaries found their way into the floating village, slipping between the narrow sampans under cover of darkness.

They traded bronze taels for secrets about ships in the port and aetherbloom for loyalty. What developed as timid experimentation born of curiosity, soon gave way to dependence in their wake.

A pipe passed among neighbors to dull the ache of backbreaking labor, then another to ease the restless nights. A fire that spread faster than it could be extinguished. And before long, those who indulged too often began to change.

Whispers circulated of strange visions—phantoms of the sea, of divine figures calling from the depths. Some swore they heard Mazu herself in their dreams, her voice a song beckoning them home. Yet when they awoke, they were no closer to divinity. Instead, they were left only hollow, brittle, and more desperately entwined in the bloom's grasp.

Then, one day, the emissaries stopped coming.

And the Hokans began to vanish.

The village dwindled to a ghost of what we had once been. And then, when we were at our most vulnerable, the pirates came.

More accurately, I led them to us.

I squeeze my eyes hard, trying to wrestle with the guilt—an emotion so full, it blocks my airway, making me choke on it.

Fragments of a singular memory—of one particular boy—rush to the front of my thoughts, unchecked. One with patient eyes, and a bright laugh. The sound of wood clashing with wood, and the smell of rain…

Breath in, breath out. Breath in, breathe out.

Focus.

I stop pacing. A vow takes root deep in my chest.

Even if all that remains of them are only ashes, I will gather them and bring them here, to the ocean, where they belong. As the sole survivor, I should…

And Mazu *will* accept them.

She *must.*

Regardless of the war Pingshen waged on the Founding Gods, we still prayed to her. We kept her shrines full. We kept her *name* alive. Some still exalted her, even when they knew it would be their last breath.

Her silence throughout it all demands recompense. And the sea will not deny its children their proper rest…

Right?

The hatch above suddenly creaks.

Though there is very little light to see with, I can tell that it is Luo who descends the ladder. He bores a simple clay bowl in one hand and slippers in the other.

Crouching before the bars, he slides both toward me before rising to his full height. "Eat."

I do not deign to move. My gaze remains fixed on the bowl, my mind dissecting every possibility. I do not know if I can trust any of these men. They could've drugged the food—just like that old heifer had the tea. My brows fold slightly.

She'd given me aetherbloom, hadn't she?

The pungent smell of pickled greens atop stale rice curls into the air, cutting through my revelation. My stomach betrays me with a low, drawn-out gurgle. I grit my teeth. Hunger claws at my insides, but it does nothing to shake my caution.

"No."

His brow arches, a flicker of intrigue crossing his otherwise nonchalant face. "You'd starve yourself, then?"

"If it meant that I did not leave my life in the hands of men who have no regard for it, then… yes," I retort.

A smirk plays at the corner of his mouth, "That's fair." He crosses his bare arms, settling into a stance that suggests entertainment rather than offense. "But how do you know what kind of men we are?"

"Only morally corrupt men would willingly procure and sell Aether."

For a long moment, he merely watches me, his dark eyes shining with quiet interest. Then, he exhales a soft chuckle, as though my words entertain him more than they should. "You speak of matters you scarcely understand," he says at length.

"Do I?" I step forward, closing the distance between myself and the bars. "I know well what aetherbloom does. I've seen it—how it reduces men to beasts, tears whole communities asunder. And you—all of you—could not care any less. So long as your pockets are lined, correct?"

The subtle quirk of his lip vanishes, replaced by a rigid stillness that betrays the cracks in his composure. His jaw tightens, but he offers no rebuttal. In the heavy quiet that follows, I refuse to look away.

With a low scoff, he turns on his heel.

"Enjoy your righteous indignation," he says over his shoulder as he ascends the stairs. "I'm sure it will keep you warm and full."

The hatch closes, the echoes of its weighty thud lingering in the damp air. My gaze moves back to the bowl, and my stomach growls a second time.

But still, I do not reach for it.

Instead, I exhale slowly and retreat to the center of the cell, lowering myself to the uneven floor. The boards are ruthless beneath my back, pressing their splinters through the linen, into my skin like punishments.

I shift, finding the least uncomfortable position, before letting my eyelids slide shut.

They may think I will not survive. I have endured worse.

PART TWO:
CRICKET

8

TWO DAYS LATER

SOUTH PINGSHEN SEA, 1799

Each moment of solitude is spent turning over the same determination: how to find the answers I want, how to escape this ship, and how to survive after.

I have no sense of where we are, no inkling of our next port of call.

I don't even know our current destination.

And even if I did—what then? Stealing a lifeboat and casting myself adrift would be a death sentence. We are likely far out into the South Pingshen Sea by now. The open ocean is merciless, and even if I stripped the ship of every last provision, hunger would find me eventually. My strength would dwindle. The sea would swallow me whole. I let my head fall back against the cell wall with a quiet thump. The dull ache is welcomed.

I should probably focus on not being thrown overboard, first.

Looking for a change of thought, I glance down at my forearm, the memory of its miraculous healing still unsettling. A wound that should've festered, closed within minutes, mended by nothing more than a salve of seawater. I don't understand it—just as there are countless other things beyond my grasp. The compass, the mysteries of my own body, the forces that bind me to both…

A yawn forces its way out, my exhaustion finally breaking through the storm brewing inside my mind. It is impossible to tell how many hours have passed since my last visit from the co-captain. There is no sun, no moon, no measure of time in this suffocating space.

The stench of the waste bucket has thickened, clinging to the stagnant air like rot. The planks beneath me press into my bones with none of the begrudging softness of the dead fish barrel I hid in. My limbs are sore, my muscles aching for relief, yet there is none to be found.

Still, my eyelids grow heavy.

And when sleep takes me, it does so swiftly, without mercy.

My body remains in the dark belly of this ship, but my mind is pulled elsewhere—into the depths of a dream.

⨯⨯

I stand on a shoreline, my feet sinking into wet sand. The world around me is bathed in an eerie haze of gold and crimson light. Before me, the sea roils. A dark, seething expanse capped with foaming waves, restless under the influence of some unseen force.

I do not recognize this beach, but something about this place breeds familiarity. The air hums with energy, crackling and alive, as though the world itself holds its breath.

Then, a gust of heat presses against my back, hot and oppressive. The power of it pushes me a step forward, sending my curls whipping in wild disarray. It is the kind of heat born only from destruction, consuming everything in its wake. I turn toward the warmth—then freeze. Every muscle seizes as my breath catches in my throat.

The sight before me is carnage.

Suddenly the environment shifts, and I'm no longer on the beach. Instead, my body has transported to the battlefield.

The ground is scorched and broken. Piles of rubble and bodies stretch across the land—human forms interspersed with grotesque creatures I cannot name. Their shapes are monstrous, nightmarish, unlike anything I've seen in my twenty-four summers.

Smoke rises in thick plumes from distant temples engulfed in flames. Ash drifts through the wind like ghostly snow, blanketing the ruins. Yet, there is one structure that still towers above the rest. Its silhouette is unmistakable even through the haze.

The Forbidden Hall.

I've only seen it in ink paintings, but the grand edifice bears an undeniable resemblance.

What happened here?

Behind me arises chants of war. When I turn, before me is what is left of an army of mortals—Wielders? They manipulate and contort the water from the sea. Suddenly, their gazes are turned upward to the sky where thunder rumbles, and lightning forks in violent arcs.

It fractures, revealing glimpses of a realm far beyond my understanding. From it, figures—larger than the average man—descend geared for battle.

Gods.

Then, an ear-splitting, discordant roar cuts through the storm.

I whip around to its source and feel my heart plummet. A dragon, vast and otherworldly, materializes from the smoke that had consumed the temples. Its body is a slithering mass of black vapor, its glowing yellow eyes burning with malevolent intent. I should feel awe, but all I can manage is dread.

Beneath the dragon, men of shadows gather—familiar, horrifying forms. Tendrils of black circle around them, just as they have every time I've crossed paths with them. I stumble backward, my heartbeat ricocheting.

How do these nightmarish things continue to find me?

Before I can think further, the dragon's roar shatters the air. The deafening blare sends me sprawling. My body is paralyzed as it plummets toward me, its maw gaping wide to consume me entirely. Then, in a last attempt of survival, I scramble back, breath failing me.

Just as the dragon's jaws close in, the scene shifts into nothing, dissolving like mist.

⨳

I snap awake, heart pounding, to the sound of heavy steps descending the ladder.

I force myself to inhale slowly, but each breath feels thin, as though I'm still suffocating in the heat of that other place.

It felt so real—less a dream and more like slipping between worlds, into something vast and inescapable.

A shudder racks through me.

Having slumped over in my sleep, I sit up slowly. My limbs heavy from days without a meal. The effect of the nightmare lingers—its grip still tight around my throat—when I croak out, "Do not bother."

I'm fully expecting another unfulfilling visit from Luo. But the silence I'm met with makes me peer through the dimness. My breath holts when I see it is Zhèng.

His looming presence commands attention even in the cramped confines of the brig. His gaze sweeps over me, assessing my weakened state, before he speaks.

"Two days," his voice deep and edged with reproach. "And still, you persist in this foolishness."

"If you were me," I rasp, "would *you* trust you? Or any other man onboard for that matter?"

His jaw tightens, the muscle feathering beneath his skin, but he does not speak. Instead, he steps closer, his approach making the floor beneath us groan in protest. The sound is deceptively ordinary, but down at this height, where I'm forced to look up at him, I notice something that sets my nerves on edge.

His boots.

Not the practical shoes of a sailor, nor the polished, high-reaching silk worn by Pingshen officials. These are different. Shorter, cut off at the shin, molded from hardened leather darkened with wear. The soles are embedded with iron studs—cruel little fangs designed for one thing alone. Not stability, not protection, but injury. Shoes meant for combat and war.

I've seen these before.

Imperial soldiers wear them when they march through the streets, grinding their heels into dirt and bodies alike. The guards at the dock, the enforcers who patrol the beaches, the ones who have never needed a reason to crack bone beneath their tread.

Interesting.

His shadow falls over me like a storm cloud.

"You will eat," he commands, producing a small bundle wrapped in cloth. He unwraps it to reveal a clumped ball of rice and a strip of dried fish. The sight, though modest, is enough to twist my empty stomach into painful knots.

I send him an apprehensive look. "You eat it first," I say hoarsely, my voice rasping from disuse.

His thick fingers collect a bit of rice and fish as he crouches before the bars. The next words out of his mouth are calm, but there is a dangerous undertone in the narrowing of his eyes. "Do not mistake me for a man of infinite patience."

Before I can muster a reply, he reaches through the bars with surprising swiftness, catching my chin in a tight grip. His touch is not crushing, but there is no denying the strength behind it.

My hands snap up to claw at his, but my strength is spent. I try to spit at him in a final attempt to maintain dignity, but the hold he has pushes my cheeks together so hard the drool dribbles down my chin. It is as humiliating as it is infuriating.

The action only makes him grip harder.

Holding the food to my lips, his expression accepts no argument.

"Eat," he says again. "Or I will make you."

My pride wars with my body's desperate starvation, but in the end, necessity prevails. I take the rice and fish onto my tongue, the taste of them both a balm and a torment as I swallow reluctantly. He watches until I have finished the meager offering, then rises to his full height.

"You're doing an excellent job at making me regret not having you walk the plank."

Swallowing dryly, I sarcastically respond, "Then why didn't you? Huh? Oh, that's right. Because you *need* me."

"Yes," he concedes, almost amused. "Which is why you can't die. Yet." With an air of indifference, he drops the bundle between the bars, letting it fall unceremoniously to the floor. I refuse to give him the satisfaction of watching me scramble for it like some starving rodent.

I lift my chin, gaze burning. "When you reach the Silver Bridge and are cast into Dì Yù, may the Judges damn you to all ten levels of torment—for eternity."

He hums, unmoved. "I'll be sure to pass along your regards."

I roll my eyes.

I'm sure he will.

"You will return to the deck," his definitive tone hints at the conclusion of our parley. "And you will *not* try to kill anyone else."

I do not agree to the terms, but he unlocks the cell anyways. Then, he turns to leave without checking if I will follow.

My legs tremble as I stand. The days of confinement and famishment are certainly exacting their toll. I press a hand against the wall for balance, swallowing down the dizziness that threatens to pull me under.

Before I exit the cell, I look to the slippers Luo left nights ago. They sit untouched in the corner, a silent offering. The part of me that abhors the idea of owing anyone *anything*, recoils at the thought of wearing them. But… my soles are raw, a patchwork of callouses and broken skin.

I hesitate, then curse under my breath.

Swallowing my pride, I slide them on, the worn fabric rough against my battered feet. They are obviously meant for larger feet, the width of them gapping around my arch. I stumble as I climb the ladder, but I grit my teeth and press on.

The sunlight that greets me above deck is blinding, and the sea air feels almost foreign after my days below.

Zhèng waits for me to orient myself before nodding to a small, stocky old man standing beside him. The ship's chief steward.

"You'll answer to him." Then, he sweeps away toward the front of the ship. I watch him go with disdain before a mop and bucket are thrust into my hands with little ceremony.

"To the bow with you," the old man says. "It will not scrub itself."

As I resentfully trudge toward the weathered planks, my gaze falls upon a familiar figure already at work, his wiry frame bent over his own mop. Hé.

I stop short, a simmering irritation giving way to disbelief.

All this time, I'd assumed he had escaped punishment. Yet here he is, his hands as red and raw as mine will surely be by day's end.

He glances up, his deep brown eyes meeting mine. There is no malice in his gaze, only a soft wariness. He offers a small, almost apologetic smile. A brief flicker of contemplation dances across his face before he walks over to me meekly.

"So… I think we got off on the wrong foot. Let's start over, yea?" He sticks out his pink sweaty hand for me to take. "My name is Hé Chūnqiū. I'm sorry for whatever I said back there that made you want to strangle the life out of my body. Please don't do it again."

There's a faint lisp that hangs on the 's' of his words. An attribute I had not noticed prior. It is disarming in a way.

I look back and forth from his face to his palm a couple of times. The hand confuses me. I'm not sure what he wants me to do with it.

"I won't," I reply instead. I pause, "That is, if you do not *give* me another reason to."

His smile does not drop as his hand hangs in the air. "Sounds like a deal."

It couldn't hurt to have an ally aboard. Perhaps, he could be of use later.

Puzzlement still lingers on my face as I stare down at his hand.

Hé suddenly wears an expression of realization. "You're supposed to grab my hand and shake."

My raised eyebrow communicates what goes unsaid.

I do not believe him.

"I promise I'm not lying. It how we pirates make a deal with each other that we will both honor," he says. "I know that men and women don't do it where you're from, but you're one of us now."

I contemplate for a moment, then hesitantly reach to shake his hand, "I am Shi Yang."

Hé only smiles wider—the gap sitting in the middle of his top teeth taking center stage—and goes back to mopping, leaving me be.

With a resigned sigh, I plunge the mop into the bucket and set to work.

The day stretches long, folding into the cadence of monotonous labor. I try to anchor myself in the tangible—the salty spray that clings to my skin, the burn of exertion in my limbs, the undercurrent of chill in the wind that speaks of the changing season. But my mind refuses to heel.

It turns over the fragments of my dream, trying to piece together the horror that still resides in my bones. Trying to make sense of shadows I cannot seem to shake.

It was just a nightmare.

A nightmare that felt too much like reality. Too much like I'd *lived* it.

9

TEN DAYS LATER

SOUTH PINGSHEN SEA, 1799

Time passes in a series of restless nights, and invariable days. I wake up to the stench of the crew's cabin, get my tasks from the chief steward—who I have been told to refer to as 'Old Chou'—then, I work until even the hairs on my head ache. After that, I go back to sleep. Repeat.

I've given up the pretense of not needing sustenance. Since we ran out of rice a day ago, I have begrudgingly succumbed to the monotonous meal of pickled eggs, cabbage, and dried fish. Eloquently chased down by in-house fruit wine.

It is all positively awful.

I will never admit it, but I spend hours waiting for the captains to finally call me to help guide us through the waters. Anything that would allow me to escape the tireless routine. But the two men haven't spared me so much as a glance since the day I was let out of the brig.

This morning, the chill of winter has finally begun to set on the waters. The sun rises clear over the sea, gilding the deck in hues of burnished yellow, but it offers little warmth.

Old Chou, ever practical, has adjusted accordingly—upping the number of chores to keep our blood moving, our limbs from stiffening. Still, even the most grueling labor allows for brief respites, an hour or two granted in between the grind of duty.

Preferring to take mine alone, I retreat to the ship's banister where the horizon stretches endlessly, an unbroken divide of sky and sea.

As I stand watching the waves roll in their ceaseless pulsing, I come to a realization: I'm entirely too familiar with an environment I don't plan to be in any longer than necessary. The infinite expanse of water, the creak of timber, and the clatter of shoes against the deck. Some part of me finds solace in the predictability.

That cannot stand.

A collection of roaring laughter booms through the air. Near the starboard side, a cluster of the crew have gathered. Curiosity carries my feet in their direction. When I draw closer, I linger against a barrel of coiled rope, observing in silence.

It is obvious the crew has been together for quite some time. They share a comradery that I must *begrudgingly* admit is admirable. Despite my distaste for them and their choices, I do wonder how they all came to join this notorious legion of piracy.

I *would* ask, but besides the occasional cordialities with Hé, the communication between them and I has been thankfully sparse.

Bits of conversation drift over—snatches of tales from distant ports, exaggerated feats of bravery, and crude jokes punctuated by coarse laughter. I scoff softly.

These men would not have lasted a single day in the brothel.

"What about you, Shi Yang?"

I'm taken aback by the sudden acknowledgement.

What was even asked?

My eyes roam the group seeking the voice that called out. I find a large-shouldered man staring directly at me. His jaw is strong and wide, as are the rest of the features on his face. He is the ship's cook. "Ah Fei", I have heard him be called. To my confusion, his tone is more curious than mocking.

As he waits for my response, he lifts the huge, tanned hand holding his cup to take a swig of its contents. "What's your story, eh? Where did you come from 'fore all of this?"

The others turn their heads like owls, their gazes brimmed with interest. It is the kind of question that invites danger if answered poorly. So, I take my time to formulate a response.

I learned long ago how to navigate treacherous waters—literal and otherwise. This is no different.

"From the rivers and seas, same as you, I assume," I respond cautiously. Embedded within, is a highlight to the Weiman accent, a subtle drawl of vowels, I hear threaded in his words. A conspicuous display of my nomad knowledge, and a warning.

I see you.

This drags a grin from his lips. "Ah, yes. You've guessed right," he says, raising his cup into the air. "A proud member of the Weiman clan, that I'm! It would make us two Wave Kin then, no?" He winks at me, his amber eyes sparkling with mirth. "The way of the sea is in our blood!" He stomps to emphasize his point. "And thanks to my ancestor's knowledge of Wielding water, we are fed every day, are we not? Here, here!"

The crew responds, "here, here," back to him, laughter lacing the chorus.

None of the other men seem to be stunned by this admission. However, my mind races.

Hokans aren't the only indigenous peoples scattered across the empire. Nomadic ways of life—rooted in oral tradition, ancestral worship, and seasonal migration—stretch far beyond our southern coasts. Though some nomads break away, venturing alone and crossing paths with others, most remain within the clans they were born into, bound by bloodlines, customs, and centuries of memory.

During the Great Ascent, the then-Eldermother had made it abundantly clear that our people would not participate. Our clan too unwilling to betray the spiritual compacts passed down through generations. But the other clans, the Weiman and Humic, did not share the same sentiment. They stood alongside the empire.

In return, the Emperor granted them access to aetherbloom. Those chosen within their clans became Wielders. Their allegiance bought them not just some semblance of power, but elevation. They were given the façade of inclusion in the New World Order.

And so, a rift opened among the nomads.

Where once we were kin, we became stratified—some exalted by Imperial favor, others left behind to preserve our fading ways. A caste formed in the ashes of our unity, one that has only deepened with each passing cycle. A wound still festering, still dividing.

It is the cost of refusing war—and the punishment for surviving it.

I peer at Ah Fei with renewed scrutiny.

Huh.

I have only ever met one Wielder, and she used her skills to chain me and hundreds of other girls to a life of misery for profit. I would expect the same selfishness from him. Yet, he uses ability to manipulate the ocean to ensure we all do not go hungry.

That kind of communal care is a relic of a past long abandoned—a duty to one another beaten out of the land Pingshen has seized for itself.

It stirs something in me, a distant echo of what used to be. What could be…

I stomp it out before it takes hold—before it can grow into something dangerous, something that might tether me further to this ship.

"Wave Kin", huh? Perhaps getting closer to him wouldn't be such a terrible thing. If he proves worthy of knowing the truth—I might yet uncover the missing pieces.

Readjusting my posture, I relax my shoulders.

I'll be nice… for now.

Ah Fei takes a generous gulp of his wine before turning his attention back to me. "You still haven't answered my question, Shi."

I offer a measured, conciliatory smile, one that reveals nothing. "Does it matter where a fish was born if it moves with the current all the same?"

Ah Fei lets out a bark of laughter. Another sailor, by the name of Huò, I've learned, nods appreciatively. "Oh, that's fine way to say nothing at all. She's slippery, this one!"

"Or just dull," says a voice from the back.

A man steps forward from where he has been perched atop a crate, his frame is wide, but his limbs scrawny. His aura is that of a stray, wild dog's. I immediately recognize him as the first pirate I encountered when I boarded this boat. I remember the disturbing feeling I'd felt in just that brief moment of interaction.

"Do not be a condescending bastard, Kāng," Huò says, smile fading.

Kāng's eyes glint, not with humor but with something meaner, more jagged. "A slippery one," he mocks, his voice pitched just loud enough to carry.

The mood shifts, subtle as a change in the wind.

"Words can be as pretty as you want to make them, but out here, they're worth less than the shit under my boot. Fancy 'lil quips will not halt a blade from opening your throat. Strength will, and you've got *none*," he spits out.

Ah Fei's smile abates, and a few of the men exchange uneasy glances.

Kāng evidently has a talent of souring the air around him.

"Strength," I say evenly, "takes many forms. Not just the ones that make you feel more like a man." I make sure to enunciate my next words slowly, as if communicating with a child. "Even someone with your limited capacity of… *mental strength* could understand that much." I emphasize the insult with a smile.

His face darkens, a muscle in his jaw jumping. The embarrassment from having his intelligence questioned in front of an audience brings a burnished color to his neck and ears. A growl rumbles low in his throat as he steps toward me, shoulders squared, fists curling.

I do not flinch.

"Oh, believe me, I understand plenty of things," he shoots back, his smirk humorless. "Understand what happens to women who think they are equal with men. Women who think they are anything more than holes of pleasure. They get put in their place. *Sooner* rather than later."

An uncomfortable hush washes over. My veneer falls. Without thinking my fingers reach for the barrel beside me. They tighten around a coil of rope, though I keep my face neutral.

"Perhaps," I say, stepping forward, voice mild, "you mistake me for someone who needs to be kept in her place." The length of rope now trails behind me, my grip on it severe.

Kāng's smirk deepens, his posture shifting as though preparing for a fight. "I don't mistake anything, *girl.* I know exactly what you are." His eyes flick down to the scar on my forearm where the faded, mangled Aether flower brand resides.

Of course *he* would be familiar with the mark of a flowerboat.

I'm sure the girls that have serviced him have seen his ghastly face more than his unfortunate mother.

I subtly turn my arm inward to hide the mark from any other wandering glances.

Seeing this, his eyes alight with sadistic pleasure, "Nothing more than a sea barbarian whore."

"Ya! Watch your fuckin' gab, Kāng!" Ah Fei shouts, rising from his seat. His voice no longer holds the amicable tone from minutes ago.

I feel fire. Bleeding from the cavity of my chest to the tips of my fingers. Without another word, I bring the rope from behind, poising it to get ready to wrap around his neck. To hang him from over the side of the ship.

Once again, it seems as there is a message to be sent.

And this time I will finish the job. If I get thrown overboard with him as punishment so be it.

Just as I take a step to close the distance between Kāng and I, a hand grips my elbow. It's firm… but also gentle? I turn to bark at the offender, when I'm confronted with a warm, weathered face. Old Chou.

I jerk my arm to free myself, but the grip only tightens. I send him a glare, but falter when I see his hazy grey eyes reflect up. They are… kind.

Though his gaze is unable to focus on my face, the crinkled skin surrounding it softens in compassion. A gesture I'm not familiar with.

Still wanting to make Kāng pay for the insult in blood, I try to remove my arm once more. But Old Chou simply shakes his head lightly as if to tell me '*He is not worth it.*'

A moment passes. And another. Then, I release a tense breath. Raw heat slips away into a dull simmer as I drop the rope. He delivers a quiet smile and then turns in the direction of the group.

At the arrival of the chief steward, everyone has shot to their feet. His face has hardened into the expression of the superior we are familiar with.

"And what do we have here, hm?" He wonders closer to the cluster of men, wooden stick leading his path. "It seems as though I have not been handing out enough work to keep you lot busy," he muses. "I want the ship scrubbed top to bottom—twice."

The crew lets out a chorus of groans. He wears a pleasured smile.

"Off you go to your stations. No one eats, sleeps, shits, or pisses until this big beauty is spotless. If I feel a spec of grime, you'll answer to the captain!"

The group disperses slowly with a loud final tap of his staff against the planks—letting loose a round of grumbles and curses. Still annoyed, I turn leave as well.

Kāng steps in front of me.

"Thanks a lot, bitch."

I swing my elbow back as far as possible. Before anyone can stop me, my fist sails through the air and connects loudly with Kāng's eye. A resounding thud echoes through the still ocean air.

My knuckles throb, but I don't care. My voice drops. "Keep talking, Kāng. Keep trying my patience. I do not have much of it left."

The crew has stopped once again to watch.

The words and assault hang between us, and for a moment, I think he might lash out. I steady my stance, muscles taut.

May he bring his best strike. He will not have another chance to do so.

But to my surprise, he only straightens himself and smiles—thin and wolfish. A stretch of lips that promises trouble yet to come.

"You just wait," he says, stepping back at last.

Old Chou speaks from beside me. "Oh, and Kāng, I forgot to tell you that you'll be on waste bucket disposal for the rest of the week."

Several of the group snicker quietly behind their hands.

Kāng, obviously irate with the display of power used to humiliate him further, clenches his fist and sends us both a scathing sneer. But he does not pick the battle. Instead, he walks away, covering his quickly bruising eye.

I exhale slowly, releasing the coiled energy from my limbs, though the anger still churns beneath my skin.

Old Chou steps back into view. He stares in my direction for a moment before nodding his head and walking away.

I hope he did not punish Kāng for me. I do not want to owe any of these men any more favors.

"Don't mind him," Ah Fei interrupts, his voice back to its light cadence. However, his expression remains pinched. The slur has obviously left him vexed as well. "Kāng's got a mean streak, but he's all bark."

I arch a brow. "Sure."

I know what goes unspoken in Ah's comment.

Kāng's reluctance to engage in confrontation likely stems from his hesitation to challenge other men—especially those who are stronger and more capable than himself. He craves dominance, yet only where he feels assured of victory.

But now, with a woman aboard? There is no doubt he sees this as an opportunity granted by the God of Fate himself.

"Just don't show your back to 'im. He's an alright pirate—" he turns to head to his station, "—but a deeply troubled man."

I nod, filing the warning away.

Trouble, indeed.

But if Kāng thinks he can break me, he will soon find himself sorely mistaken.

10

THE NEXT MORNING

JADE BAY, 1799

I wake to the clang of urgency—shouts from above deck slicing through the early haze of sleep. The lookout's call to arms.

Around me, the crew erupts into motion, springing from their hammocks like sparks from dry tinder. Half-dressed and wild-eyed, they grab their weapons. Their shoes hit the wood with the heavy rhythm of instinct before pouring out onto the deck like a bubbling land fissure.

It's a frantic, practiced chaos—an entire atmosphere shifting into battle stance in seconds.

I, on the other hand, am less quick to follow.

I have no weapon to wield. No loyalty binding me to this vessel. And if I'm honest, despite my ulterior motives, there is still a part of me that has no burning urge to defend it.

So, I rise slowly, stretching the sleep from my limbs. My steps are measured as I climb the narrow stairs leading topside.

When I reach the deck, the sky has already soured. The air hums with restlessness. From the south, heavy clouds roll across the sky like bruises spreading over skin, swollen with rain. The wind cracks at the sails. Below us, the ocean churns, each tide slamming into the hull with increasing force.

I brace against the railing, fingers gripping the slick wood as a burst of salt spray stings my face.

We were bound to run into a storm eventually.

As if summoned by the thought, the first raindrops begin to fall—fat and cold, striking with the weight of stone. The crew shouts over the rising wind, securing lines and giving orders. The ship creaks and groans beneath our feet.

Their movements are swift and precise. Honed by cycles of repetition and necessity. There is no room for hesitation, no space for an outsider to stumble through their well-worn routine.

So, I stay where I am, watching as they work, seamless and efficient, a machine built from muscle and intuition.

The rain intensifies, transforming the deck into a slick battlefield. Waves swell, lifting the ship higher before dropping it hard again. Lightning forks across the sky, illuminating the horizon in a stark, blinding flash. For a moment, the world is painted in silver and black.

And then, what the lookout had spotted comes into view.

A shape—vague at first—etched into the curtain of rain.

Another ship.

Smaller, sleeker. It closes fast, carried by the violent winds. A banner dances above it—stark and blue. It draws closer with each passing moment. And the sea, as if on purpose, places it directly on a path toward us.

"They've spotted us," Luo calls from the helm, voice loud over the deafening gale.

"Good," Zhèng shouts back.

Through the onslaught of downpour, I can see a smirk curling at the corner of his mouth. It is written all over his face that he enjoys this; the prospect of acquiring another ship as his own. I imagine that drive is what has awarded him the loyalty and reputation he has.

He stands at the bow, loose strands of hair clinging to his wet neck. The confidence that radiates off him is as if he's greeting an old friend. "Let's see if they have the sense to turn tail."

They don't.

The smaller ship cuts through the waves, cannons gleaming in the muted light. The men around me bristle, hands tightening on swords and matchlock muskets, eyes darting to the captain for orders.

"Battle stations!" he roars. "Let's give them a proper welcome. Hoist the banners!"

The command is met with swift obedience. Crew members rush to the mast, and within moments, the crimson banner of Zhèng's fleet unfurls into the storm. It twists and turns with fierce animation.

I freeze at the sight of the emblem. A dragon and phoenix.

My forehead creases, and the steady beat of my heart skips, then quickens.

How had I not noticed it before?

The intricately carved walls in the captain's quarters flicker through my mind. A dragon and phoenix. Interwoven with the images are fragments of the same emblem—only black—illuminated by the glow of the burning town of Kwangchow.

But… it can't be. He doesn't bare the slash across his forehead.

I squint through the rain, studying the man. He is cycles older than me, surely, but no more than ten. His jaw is chiseled, his nose long and wide. A beard cloaks the lower half of his face, but not enough to obscure his identity if he were the man I remember. The man I vowed to kill.

But then, why… why do they fly the same mark?

Around me, pirates scramble to their positions, loading cannons and readying grappling hooks. I push off the railing, striding to confront Zhèng.

But before I can take another step, Luo intercepts me. His bow and arrow are already prepped for battle. The usual glint of mirth that riddles his face is nowhere to be found. What remains is cold focus. He places a rough, stilling hand on my shoulder. "You," he barks, "need to stay out of the way—"

I swipe his hand off my person, sending him a lethal glare. Just past his shoulder, the captain has turned his attention to our interaction. From a distance, I can feel his gaze roaming over me, as if he can sense my suspicions mounting.

Answers will have to wait.

I let out an irritated sigh. "Give me a weapon to help or throw me in the brig and be done with it—just spare me the lecture," I clip. I peer over my shoulder out into the sea where the rival ship is closing in. "I truly do not care which decision you choose, but I suggest you do so quickly."

His eyes narrow, but there's a glimmer of amusement there too. Rain clings to his lashes, sliding down his angular face as he weighs his options. Tilting his head quickly, he relents. "Suit yourself. Just don't get killed." He unfastens a dagger from his belt and tosses it my way before striding off.

I scramble to catch the blade with both hands, hoping it does not slice them open in the process.

Bastard.

Once secured, I turn the weapon over in my hands. It is unlike any I have seen before—even during my cycles at the flowerboat. There were many times men arrived drunk on tael and ego, flashing steel they thought would impress. Some brought blades with ornate hilts, inlaid with gems or carved from bone. Others carried curved daggers of foreign origin, each one whispering of distant wars and conquests. Those weapons were meant to be shown, not used. Men playing with their toys; symbols of power.

But this…this is not ornamental.

The handle is thick, weighty, its shape rounded to fit snugly into a clenched fist. Gold gilding catches what little light remains, dull and aged, not polished for display. Strange symbols—runes, maybe?—wind along its hilt in a script I don't recognize. Not Pinesh… not *any* language I'm familiar with.

What in the Gods names…

I'm almost too hesitant to use this, but there are no other weapons laying around. I adjust my grip, feeling the balance, the weight.

How hard can maneuvering it be?

The enemy ship fires first.

A cannonball rips through the air, slamming into the water just shy of our hull. The splash soaks the deck further, and the crew lets out a collective howl of defiance.

"Return fire!" Zhèng commands.

The cannons thunder, the recoil shaking the ship. Smoke and fire erupt from our side. The deafening blasts make my ears ring. The smaller ship wavers under the onslaught, its crew scrambling to recover.

Through the haze of the onslaught, I see them: boys, slightly younger than me. They have seen at most nineteen summers. Most of their faces are pale, movements jerky with panic. They lack the discipline and grit of seasoned pirates that I'd expected. Instead, they are more like fishermen's sons who picked up blades too early.

"Practically children," I whisper under my breath, a bitter note twisting in my throat.

"You've got sharp eyes, Shi Yang."

The voice comes directly over my shoulder. I jolt, instinctively stepping back, feet slipping slightly on the slick deck. I catch myself just before I fall. Zhèng.

His long, ink black hair is no longer tied up. It spills around his face in dark, sodden strands. The ends cling to his shoulders like seaweed.

The storm may be loud, but I hadn't even heard him get that close. That worries me.

Zhèng must not sense my discomfort—or chooses to ignore it—because he continues without preamble. "Watch closely," he says. He speaks as though we are simply observing a training exercise. "This is how you take a ship without sinking it. Now, Luo!"

My head whips around to the man at the stern railing. He draws a deep breath, steady and practiced, as he raises his bow high. The arrow nocked is unlike the others—its head wrapped in oil-soaked cloth, already burning.

He lets out the breath. And the arrow sings.

The rain has softened just enough that the fire holds. It arcs beautifully, almost lazily, before it lands—dead center—in the rival ship's mainsail.

Flames erupt.

The rival crew stares upward, horror-stricken, as orange fire races through the fabric. Their rigging crackles. Shouts rise into the wind, ragged with disbelief.

It is now clear they are goners to the most infamous pirate captain in the country.

Grappling hooks fly, latching onto the other ship with a series of dull thuds. Zhèng's crew pulls hard, heaving in synchronized beats, drawing the ships together. All at once, the pirates from our side hop onto the opposition's deck.

I expect it to be a swift defeat, but—to my surprise—the band of young pirates do not cower. Instead, they fight for their lives. They meet their aggressors head on. The sounds of blades clanging together fills the air.

Some of their crew manage to jump aboard ours in the havoc. One of them—a gangly boy with trembling hands—lunges toward me, a rusty dao raised high. My body moves before my mind catches up. I duck under the swing and swipe the dagger, nicking his side. He crumples, clutching his abdomen.

He'll live. Probably.

"Stay alert, you prat!" Luo's voice cuts through the din as he sends an arrow streaking pass me. I whirl around just in time to see one of the rival crew stagger backward, clutching his arm. The shaft of Luo's arrow juts from his bicep, buried deep. The crude axe the boy had been raising—no doubt meant for me—clatters uselessly to the deck at his feet.

I exhale sharply through my nose, jaw tight with irritation.

Perfect. Now I owe Luo a debt.

Another attacker comes at me, and this time he brandishes a sword sharper than his fellow crewmen. He is focused, more agile. He swings his blade with an experienced ease that overwhelms me.

He slashes down in front of me. I barely manage to block it from cutting my face in half. I'm forced back a step, heels slipping slightly on the drenched wood. Without pause, he slashes again, quick and low, and I pivot just in time to avoid it slicing open my stomach.

Our blades lock again, but this time he uses the length of his sword to twist under mine, a flourish of movement that throws my balance off. My stance breaks, and in that instant, he crouches lower and swings his blade along the outside of my thigh.

Pain blooms fast. I stagger with a short, involuntary cry.

The cut isn't deep, but it sears like fire. Blood begins to wet the fabric of my trousers, warmth spreading even in the cold of the storm. I force my weight to the opposite leg, eyes narrowed.

He arcs his sword upward toward my ribs, expecting me to retreat. But instead—

A whisper of memory flows through my limbs. A ghost of a boy's grip guiding my arms, steadying my stance, teaching me how to move with momentum rather than against it. I can almost feel the familiar weight of a bamboo practice sword in my hand instead of this foreign dagger.

My torso turns instinctively, shifting into a diagonal line that slides me just outside his direct reach. My shoulder tucks low. I become a smaller target.

I strike.

My dagger slices up in a tight, controlled arc, catching him off guard. The tip of the blade grazes his face, leaving a clean, red line across his cheek. He flinches back, blood trickling from the cut along his jawline.

Before he can raise his sword again, a click echoes loud and final through the noise.

A musket barrel presses to the side of his head.

"That's enough, boy," Zhèng warns. "Look around you."

The young man hesitates, breathing hard, his gaze flicking left and right. Around us, his comrades are bested—some already disarmed, others bleeding or down. The sails of his ship burn high behind him, a fiery beacon in the mist.

He lowers his sword slowly.

My thigh throbs, hot and angry, but I keep my dagger raised a second longer—just in case.

Deeming it a surrender, Zhèng lowers the musket with the same calm precision he used to raise it. With a single nod, he summons a pair of his men forward. They move swiftly, seizing the trembling youth by both arms. The boy doesn't resist—his sword slips from his fingers and clatters to the floor, a hollow sound swallowed by the wind.

As he is dragged toward the center of the ship, I catch the slight tremor in his right hand—the one that had gripped the blade. Barely steady.

Practically. Children.

I exhale through my nose.

Zhèng steps in front of me then, blocking my line of sight with infuriating ease. His eyes sweep over me looking for wounds. The probing gaze lingers for a split second at the blood soaking my pantleg. Then, he turns on his heel toward the center of the deck without another word.

I watch his retreating back, left standing breathless and annoyed. Again.

Now I owe them both. Marvelous.

I push through the slick chaos of the deck, careful with my steps. The pain in my thigh flares, but I force myself forward, weaving past fallen rigging and wounded men until I reach the edges of the gathered crew.

The boy—my attacker—is on his knees now, his soaked clothes clinging to a frame that looks even slighter without the sword in his hand. His head remains bowed. Around him, the rest of his crew are hauled aboard one by one, wrists bound tight with rough rope.

They stumble past jeering pirates who watch them with a blend of disinterest and amusement. Zhèng stands over the kneeling boy like a judge before a prisoner.

"I assume you're the captain," he asserts. "What is your name?"

The boy says nothing. His jaw clenches, and he keeps his eyes fixed on the wet boards beneath him.

Zhèng's tone hardens, slicing cleanly through the air. "Now is not the time for pride. You're no good to your crew dead. Speak, or I'll feed the bunch of you to the sea serpents and sleep soundly afterward."

At that, a visible flinch ripples through the kneeling boy and his mates. The threat lands.

"What's your name, boy?" Zhèng asks again. His voice is quieter this time, yet there's a heaviness behind his words that was not there before.

The boy hesitates, and then mutters, "I go by Rabbit."

The crew explodes into laughter.

A nickname like that sounds like something torn from a child's bedtime tale. *Rabbit,* of all things. The pirates revel in it—hearty, barking mockery that echoes under the gray sky.

But Zhèng doesn't laugh.

He raises one hand, and the crew falls silent with startling obedience.

He studies the boy for a beat longer, then speaks. "Well, Rabbit, you fought bravely. Foolishly. But bravely."

Rabbit lifts his eyes. His deeply tanned face is smeared with grime and his reddish-brown hair is matted from saltwater. Cautious awe dances in his expression.

He looks so… kind and unassuming now. All aggression I experienced earlier has dissipated, as if I encountered an entirely different person.

"However," Zhèng continues, "do not confuse my acknowledgement for condonation. Bravery without a plan—without discipline and wisdom—gets men killed. How many summers have you seen? Fifteen? Sixteen?"

Rabbits chin juts forward petulantly. "Nineteen, for myself. Eighteen for the rest of m' crew."

A whisper of mirth laces the captain's words when he responds. "Nineteen. And already trying to captain a ship," he nods his head. "Ambitious."

He takes a slow and deliberate step forward. Rabbit's lips tremble, but he holds Zhèng's gaze.

"Crusading through my waters, attacking my ship… tell me, Rabbit, what made you so bold?"

Rabbit's brows furrow. "It wasn't boldness. It—it was desperation! We weren't setting out ta' attack; we were fleein'.

We thought you were reinforcements for the scout crew we escaped."

Now that the storm has passed, the murmurs of the crew rise clearly through the thinning air, heavy with unease.

"A week and a half ago. Pirates in Goisa port," Rabbit continues, his voice trembling as if trying to make sense of it. "They… they were different."

I wipe the residual rivulets of rain from my face as my eyes squint.

Different how?

The crew shifts restlessly, and several groan in disbelief, exchanging wary glances. It's not uncommon for foreign pirates to dock at Goisa.

Goisa—along with its twin, Formosa—marks the furthest reach of Pingshen's territorial grip. Both serve as the only outposts for foreign trade, a thin edge of civility carved out of an archipelago that once belonged to another world entirely.

It was the then-Phoenix Emperor, ahead of the war, who laid claim to the islands—conquering not just the land, but the lives already rooted there. Now, they serve as the empire's shield and buffer, a defensive line drawn between the familiar and the foreign.

The chain of islets stand like sentinels before the yawning chasm of The Untamed. A land whispered about in stories, filled with people—or beings that only *look* like people—I have never met. Cultures I'm sure Pingshens never bothered to understand.

Some of them have dared to venture further than the islands, but not often. Pingshen keeps its mainland tightly guarded. To the court, for decades, foreign lands are useful only as a means to an end: they are the largest exporters of Aether, and nothing more.

Well, at least, they were, until the Emperor issued his edict.

Now, trade has slowed, and tensions have risen. I doubt any nation—The Untamed or otherwise—would not grow resentful waiting on an empire that sits between them and their profit.

And when that patience runs dry, it will not be the Imperial heartland that falls first—it will be Goisa and Formosa.

Maybe one already has.

"You don' understand! They… they came at night. Raided the shore village—set fire to everythin'. We barely made it out alive." His voice trembles as if still trying to make sense of whatever he saw.

His Pinesh is halting, words cut short. As if though the unfamiliar shape of the language sits awkwardly on his tongue. Something he was forced to learn, not inherited. In addition to the hue of his skin, it is evident his linage belongs to those that are island-born.

The knowledge ignites a twinge in my chest, a sense of understanding. But before I can contemplate further, his voice breaks through again, urgent and unraveling.

"They were strange. Wieldin' shadows that come alive."

The words ripple through the crew, unsettling even the more seasoned among them.

Blood rushes in my ears.

This can't be chance—it feels as though Fate is baiting me.

Zhèng's expression remains still, almost impassive, but his eyes gleam with calculation.

"Did they pursue you?" Luo asks, his tone firm.

Rabbit shakes his head fervently. "We lost them coming aroun' Quz." His eyes go distant for a moment, caught in a memory. "Back at the port… they were looking for something. I… I don' know what."

Zhèng exchanges a glance with Luo. "What do you think?" he asks, voice low.

They exchanged a weighted glance, eyes dancing with a conversation the rest of us do not hear. Then the co-captain responds.

"I say we go."

Zhèng stalls a beat before nodding small.

"Are you going ta' kill us?" Rabbit dares to ask.

"No," Zhèng says, turning his attention back to the boy. "Killing you would be a waste. You and your crew are coming with us. Serve under me, and I'll shape you into formidable men. You'll learn the ways of the Southern Pingshen Sea."

The younger pirates trade nervous looks, likely unsure whether to thank him or not.

They have about as much of a choice as I did.

Rabbit hesitates, then nods, his shoulders slumping. Just another soul swept up in Zhèng's growing fleet.

The captain turns to Ah Fei, "We got enough room in the rations for a couple extra mouths?"

Ah Fei nods, with a welcoming smile. "Sure do, captain." Sweeping his arms out he announces, "Welcome to the crew, boys!"

With that, Rabbit's crew are shuffled away.

Old Chou takes the uninjured to delegate tasks for clean-up, whilst Huò—who I now know is the ship's medic—tends to their wounded.

As the pirates shift around me, barking orders and falling back into rhythm, I ease the weight off my right leg. The moment my hand brushes the torn fabric of my pants, I hiss through my teeth. Blood, soot, and the dull ache of a clean slice greet me. I grimace, pressing into the skin just enough to assess the damage.

A deep, rueful chuckle escapes me—unexpected and unbidden.

That little bastard. This genuinely hurts.

It stings more than I would like to admit, both physically and otherwise. The wound is not too severe, but it's enough to need tending. I utter another curse under my breath and start limping toward Huò, only to catch movement from the edge of my vision.

Luo stands there, calm as ever, one brow raised and a hand held out expectantly.

With an exaggerated roll of my eyes, I limp my way over to him, slapping his dagger into his palm.

"You look like a street beggar," I snip.

He does not rise to the bait. I watch as his gaze, too, lingers on my leg. But just like the captain, he says nothing of it.

Of course he doesn't. That would require an admission of concern.

Instead, he sheathes the blade with precise efficiency and says flatly, "Your knife skills are atrocious."

I feel my cheeks heat up to an indignant flush, embarrassed at the reminder of having been bested by a boy five cycles my junior. It has been well over a decade since I trained with such weapon—not that I owe him even the slightest explanation.

"Your existence is atrocious," I snap back, voice piqued and juvenile. Without waiting for a reply, I pivot and limp away, heading toward Huò. Behind me, Luo's laughter follows. Dry. Derisive. Infuriatingly amused.

And just because of that, I will not be thanking him for earlier.

The ship groans beneath my feet as it veers with purpose, navigating cleanly through the waves.

A shift in course. A new heading.

11

TWO DAYS LATER

JADE BAY, 1799

Hé finds me coiling excess rope near the prow, the sea air tousling strands of hair that have slipped free from the rows of braids against my scalp.

Though winter has fully arrived, the sun still hangs high and harsh throughout the day. Keeping my hair this way reduces my sweating significantly.

"Beautiful morning, isn't it, Shi Yang?" His voice breaks through the rhythm of my work—cheerful, almost singsong.

I glance up at him, blinking into the brightness. The glare makes it hard to see much past the silhouette of his frame. Still, I catch the glint of a grin and the white choppy ends of his self-cut hair sticking out in stubborn tufts.

His lisp reminds me, absurdly, of spring songbirds back home—the ones that used to land on Ba's sampan as we drifted just beyond shore. I would sit there, as a child, watching them take flight again and again. Spiraling upward until they disappeared into the sky, far above the weight of everything.

I used to wonder what it would feel like to join them. To look down on the world until it became nothing but a speck.

I'm still caught in that thought when Hé abruptly pitches his voice up in an exaggerated mimicry:

"*It sure is, Hé! I'm so glad you pointed it out so I could stop and take it all in!*"

He blinks at me, waiting for a laugh that never comes. I meet his eyes with a flat stare, unimpressed and unamused, brow arched.

Was that supposed to be me?

When I don't respond, he lets out an exasperated sigh, but continues his one-sided conversation.

"Looks like you've been over here for ages." He shifts his weight from one foot to the other like he's trying to linger without making it obvious. "If you're preparing more rope to choke another victim, should I be worried?"

The corner of my mouth twitches, despite myself. He lets the dead air hang a beat, then presses a hand to his chest in mock indignation.

"What, no mean retort? No eye roll? You wound me," he says dramatically, feigning a stagger as if my quiet is an actual blow.

"You talk a lot," I say at last, wiping my dripping forehead with the back of my hand.

"Only to fill the silence you leave behind," he quips easily, the teasing softened by something gentler in his tone. "But fine, I'll spare you the dramatics."

He gives me a small, conspiratorial smile, like we're in on a joke no one else knows. Then, he jerks his chin toward the sterncastle deck.

"The captain's asking for you. Said to send you up."

I rise with a sigh, brushing rope fibers from my hands and trousers. The bandaged leg beneath my clothes gives a throb, but

I don't let it show.

"Thanks," I say, nodding once.

That seems to take him by pleasant surprise. His grin brightens—genuine now, almost boyish. He reaches out, gives my shoulder a light, friendly pat.

"Anytime," he says. "And if you need rescuing from whatever terrifying meeting you're about to walk into, I'll be down here pretending to work."

I shake my head and turn to go, catching the tickled glint in his eye just before I leave him behind.

My steps are slow as I climb the steps toward the stern, the creaking boards muffled by the wind. When I reach the captain's door, I hesitate.

I still have not confronted him about the flag. Is this the time to do so? Or should I wait to find out more? If I reveal something I shouldn't too early, my whole plan will be unsalvageable.

Multiple voices from inside the cabin cause my thoughts to stumble. My brows crease. Then, I abandon thought altogether and push the door open.

Inside, the scent of parchment and lamplight greets me, along with the abrupt end of conversation.

A map sprawls across the desk—oceans inked in sweeping arcs, territorial lines like veins across the surface. And at its heart, resting in eerie stillness, lies the silver compass.

It had sounded like three people were speaking when I stepped in—low, overlapping, threaded with tension. But when my eyes adjust to the muted sunlight of the cabin, I see only the two: Zhèng hunched over the map, and Luo standing off to the side, arms crossed, his gaze fixed on the device.

And yet… there's something else. A thin curl of white smoke

lingers in the air between them, ghosting upward before unraveling into nothing.

My forehead knits faintly.

Huh.

"You summoned me," I say cautiously, letting the door click shut behind me.

"Yes. Come."

I bristle slightly at the command, but shuffle my way to the center of the room regardless.

When I reach the desk, the captain rises to his full height, a heads length taller than me. "What I'm about to tell you is not to leave this room, do you understand?"

My brow arches. "And here I thought your pride would keep you from asking for my help."

Zhèng, to his credit, lets the jab pass. His eyes pierce mine as he waits for my acknowledgement.

I nod.

He gestures to the map. "The route we planned—down through the southern arc of the Foreign Trade Route—it's compromised. Naval ships are patrolling further and heavier than expected. Our informant… *underestimated* their presence."

"Or lied," Luo says coldly.

Zhèng's jaw flexes, but he does not argue.

One of the 'friends' he had mentioned the first day on the ship, then? Is that who was just in here? Where did they go?

He taps the map again. "Now we are left with fewer options."

"And you want me to get the compass to find a new one," I say.

He nods. "It *is* tethered to you."

Letting out a reluctant sigh, I hesitate a moment before

reaching forward. The compass vibrates faintly as I draw close, as if it recognizes me. There is something odd in the way it hums, almost sentient beneath my hand.

When I place my fingers on its face, the needle jolts violently, then spins once before fixing its point—due west. It aims at a narrow sliver on the map through two of the four collected islands.

Luo inhales. "Fenghua Pass."

A silence falls heavy between us.

"What is that?" I ask.

"Fenghua is legend. A treacherous channel of treacherous shoals and spiraling fog banks. It's said the spirits of those who drowned—Shui Gui—lurk in its body of water. Their primary objective is to lure mortals to their deaths. To possess their bodies so that they may be freed, and the victim takes their place, continuing the cycle. Many ships have vanished between the rocks and waves without a trace," Zhèng says, voice contemplative.

I tear my gaze from the compass, my thoughts churning with what I have just heard. "Spirits?" I ask, incredulous. "I thought they all returned to the Astir World just before the war began?"

The captain's expression shifts—his mouth opens, then closes again, as if the truth catches on the edge of his tongue. When he finally speaks, his voice is tight and cautious, almost reluctant.

"A lot of them stayed."

He does not elaborate.

I narrow my eyes, further suspicion blooming in my gut.

And how exactly does he know that?

I'm about to press him when Luo interjects, his tone harsher than usual, as if eager to steer the conversation back to more practical dangers.

"No one in their right mind sails through Fenghua," Luo states. "That's suicide."

Zhèng does not flinch. His eyes remain trained on the map spread before him, strong jaw taut with calculation. "It's the fastest way to cut past the patrols," he murmurs.

"The fastest way to Dì Yù, more like," Luo grumbles, arms still crossed.

Zhèng shoots him a look—a quiet but pointed warning—and their eyes lock. There is heat in their gazes. Not just disagreement. History.

I feel the tension spiking between them, sudden like a struck match. I raise a hand, interceding before it burns any hotter.

"So, let me get this straight," I say, tone edged with disbelief. "You'd rather gamble with a stretch of sea known for drowning men and swallowing ships *whole*—than risk running into the Navy?"

Zhèng finally looks at me. His expression is hard, but not unreadable. His eyes gleam with grim rationale.

"I'd rather not be caught in open waters by three Imperial warships armed with broadside cannons and a grudge," he says. "Fenghua Pass may be cursed. But we've sailed through worse."

Silence again. The kind that reeks of doubt.

I glance at the compass. The needle has not budged. Whatever force guides it—divine or other—seems certain.

"I don't like it," I say. "But I think we are meant to go through it."

Zhèng looks at me. "Meant to?"

I shrug. "That is how this compass works, is it not? It obviously does not point to safety. It points to destiny."

The comment hangs in the air.

Then, with the deliberation of a man who has already made peace with the situation, he pulls the chart toward him and begins adjusting the heading.

"We sail at dawn. Into the Pass."

I observe his movements quietly.

This man hides more than I can probably imagine. I plan to figure out just how much.

Luo does not move. He watches me a moment longer than he should—like he wants to say something but doesn't.

The atmosphere in the cabin seems to grow tense, and the distant sound of waves against the hull feels obnoxiously loud. The compass in my hand feels warmer and more unsettling than ever.

Hours later, with the cruel certainty that we are sailing toward our doom by weeks' end, I descend into the crew's quarters.

The air inside is thick with anxious energy, and whatever conversations had been buzzing cease the moment I appear.

That seems to be a reoccurring theme around here.

Dozens of eyes track my every move as I make my way to my cot.

I do not care for these men—not their loyalty, their trust, nor their lives. But… there is an unfortunate weight in knowing they've been condemned to a watery grave without their consent.

Kāng, ever eager to antagonize, is the first to break the stillness. "What'd the captain say?" he grunts, his tone dripping with suspicion and jealousy.

If he wants to be in my position, he is more than welcome to it.

Ignoring him, I sink onto the creaking hammock.

Their stares burn into me, waiting for answers. I know I'd agreed to keeping my mouth shut, but there is no use in withholding the truth. They are likely to find out soon anyways.

"Our course has changed," I say flatly. "We will navigate through Fenghua Pass."

The room collectively inhales, the kind of breathless reaction reserved for tales of ghosts and spirits.

One of Rabbit's boys crosses himself—a gesture I have seen sailors use when they are clinging to superstition in the face of something beyond their comprehension.

"No one's ever made it through," Ah Fei utters, his hands trembling as he rolls some dice idly between his fingers. It is a nervous habit that betrays his fear.

"You're correct," I reply, lying back against the cot and staring at the ceiling. "But the compass seems to believe that we will."

Heckles erupt. It is the sound of despair that comes when people begin to realize they are already dead.

"A compass," Kāng spits, voice loaded with accusation, "doesn't navigate one of the most dangerous areas in the South Pingshen Sea. Something *else* is leading us to our deaths."

It is evident that he is fishing for a fight, hoping to turn the crew against me, but I can't muster the energy to care.

What festers beneath my skin is something far more enduring: the gnawing truth that I'm still no closer to uncovering what happened to my clan.

And now I'm probably going to die alongside these men—these strangers—before I ever find out.

"Well?" Kāng shouts, voice rising. "Say something, you wench!"

I turn my head slightly, meeting his scrutiny with all the disinterest I can summon. "What would you like me to say, Kāng? That I somehow tricked the captain into this decision? Well, I didn't. He saw what the compass said, and he made his choice."

"The captain's gone mad," Kāng mutters bitterly, his anger simmering beneath the surface. He glares around the room, desperate for someone to reciprocate his sentiment, but the other men are too lost in their own dread to care.

"Just be quiet, Kāng," I sigh, rolling onto my side to face the wall. The coarse linen scratches my skin, but I close my eyes and let the swaying of the vessel lull me to sleep.

Waves splash incessantly against the body of the ship now that it is properly out to sea. Dark and endless, the chill night air carries the tang of salt that is palpable every time I open my mouth for a yawn.

My doze had lasted longer than expected. Supper is nearly over, the deck scattered with pirates nursing their bowls and conversing in low voices. The men move like ghosts themselves, now. They shuffle around deck eyes downcast, minds adrift in the awaiting adversity of Fenghua Pass.

I sit apart from them, near the rail, where the lanterns' glow barely reaches.

My mind wanders. I cannot stop thinking about the nightmare I had. Even now, weeks later, it haunts me in intervals. It clings to the corners of my mind like cobwebs that refuse to be brushed away. I think about what it could mean. About being stuck on this ship with men—a captain—I cannot trust. I think about the path I set out on, the promises I made to myself, and what happens if I drift too far from them.

The quiet scrape of shoes pulls my attention.

I glance over my shoulder. Luo approaches with a steaming bowl in hand, his gait easy, unbothered. That unbothered, infuriating manner hangs off him like a second skin, and for some reason, it needles at me more than it should.

He lowers himself down a few steps away, folding into a cross-legged position. He plans to stay a while.

Shōush.

"You missed supper," he says, holding the bowl out toward me. "Thought you might be hungry."

I don't take it. "I suppose this is your idea of recompense for starving me in the brig for two days."

I'd already planned to lift my share of provisions from the food storage later when everyone was sleep, but he does not need to know that. I want him to feel chastised.

But he does not budge.

"Well, to be fair," he says, a smirk tugging at the corner of his mouth, "I did offer you food, but you denied it—like you're doing now." He tilts his head slightly. "Look, I'm all for letting you dine exclusively on your own pride if that's what gets you through the day, but we can't find the treasure if you're no more than skin and bones. So…" He extends the bowl closer.

I shoot him a look of annoyance. "No, thank you."

"Fine." He shrugs, setting it between us. Then, he just sits there.

We stay like that for a while.

In the intermission, I turn my gaze to the sky. Studying it—imagining the Heavens opening like I'd seen in my dream.

The stars are brighter here than they were at any of the ports I've lived. They sit scattered like spilled pearls across the black velvet sky. In them, I'm reminded of home, of nights spent on the water with only the moon and its children of dotted light to guide us.

The thought tightens my chest.

"So, you're from a port city?" Luo asks abruptly. His tone is conversational.

I stiffen, but don't look at him. "Why are you asking?"

"Curiosity," he says. "You're brash, difficult, violent—"

I heave an exasperated sigh hoping he will leave.

He does not.

"—insubordinate, demanding… did I already say difficult?"

I waive a response.

A few seconds pass before he speaks again, tone no longer mocking.

"You carry yourself differently. You acclimated quickly to the ship. Like someone who's spent more time with the sea than on land. Your words carry an accent of a mean commoner, which tells me that is how you grew up. Yet," he pauses, tone considering, "your speech is formal. Careful. The kind of careful that comes from being around people who'd punish you for anything less. And underneath that…" he halts, as if searching for the right word, "There's a Pingshen cadence. The kind you pick up from spending time around merchants, Imperial guards, and the like. Maybe even officials."

At the end of the comment, his eyes drift down to my scarred forearm.

I tuck it in toward my stomach as quickly as possible, heart picking up speed. He holds up a hand in surrender.

He won't probe, but he has noticed.

For a moment, I consider ignoring him. But there's no point in keeping it a secret out here tides away from land.

"I'm Hokan," I say finally, voice firm.

He's quiet for a moment too long.

When I glance at him, I see it—the flicker of tension in his jaw, the way his hand stills against his knee. He recovers quickly, nodding as if the word means nothing to him. "The sea people," he murmurs.

I narrow my eyes. "You've heard of us, then."

"I have… encountered some of your Kin before," he says. His tone is neutral, but his gaze flutters, betraying a guardedness he cannot quite hide. "Fishing folk, mostly. Believers of the Old-World order—of Founding Gods."

"And doomed Bloomers," I say bitterly. "The ones everyone agreed were expendable once the empire decided who was worthy of Wielding."

It hadn't been a secret, our disappearance. In fact, many of the land-dwellers had jeered from the shore about how much better the port looked without our boats cluttering the docks.

The memory of it strikes like salt in an open wound. My chest tightens with a heat that is half-grief, half-fury. I think of the ones—*the boy*—who vanished first. Of the way no one on land cared to figure out why.

He doesn't respond immediately, his gaze dropping to the bowl between us.

His reservation mirrors the deafening indifference of a society that watched us be cast aside. Ostracized, marginalized, and reduced to mere thoughts on the edges of its vision. I understand, on some level, that he alone is not to blame. The weight of centuries, of systems designed to forget us, cannot rest on his shoulders solely. Yet, when I face him, the fury I have tried so long to swallow rises regardless.

The ache of abandonment, the corrosive grief of being unseen—it spills out in biting words. I lash out, not because he deserves it, but because I have no one else to give this pain to. It's not fair. But I cannot force myself to care.

Leaning forward, my voice drops to something mean. "How many of your fellow pirates have grown fat on the silver and bronze of the addicted, huh? How many lives have you destroyed with your greed?"

It is obvious that he does not revel in his connection to Aether trade. However, it does not stop him, so I will not let it stop me.

He meets my ire. "Do you think I've had a choice in every order I've followed?"

"Choice? You want to preach to me about choices?" I turn fully toward him. "Everyone has a choice. You and Zhèng choose to peddle a flower that can destroy lives. You do not get to pretend otherwise," I say, my voice raising. "That blood will *always* be on your hands!"

My final words are meant to cut him—but it is me who bleeds. The sting of truth pierces deep. I'm crumbling beneath the weight of my own guilt.

Maybe if I'd spoken up—told the Elders about the hooded figures slipping between the boats under the cover of darkness, placing the drug into waiting hands—maybe things would've been different. Maybe the addictions could've been stopped before it took root. Before…

My breath stutters, chest tightening like a noose drawn too fast.

It wouldn't have changed anything. Even if I'd raised the alarm, there would've only been more of us gathered that night. More fates for me to uncover, one tragedy at a time.

I can feel my shoulders shake with the effort to hold myself together.

The space between us becomes overwhelming. The sounds from the crew can no longer be heard—the scrape of bowls and conversations gone completely. They are surely listening to my outburst.

But Luo just peers at me.

Dark brown eyes flicker back and forth between mine. The intensity of the stare makes me freeze momentarily.

When he speaks again, his voice is measured, expression carefully blank. "I'm not here to argue. Just make sure you eat the Godsdamned food."

He rises smoothly to his feet, brushes off his trousers, and walks away without another word.

The bowl of food remains untouched.

The murmur of the crew rises and falls again in the background, but it feels distant, muted. I stay where I am, staring out at the stars, watching as they blur, before they collect in the single tear that falls down my cheek.

12

THE NEXT DAY

JADE BAY, 1799

After granting myself one night to wallow, I wake with clarity hardening in my chest like cooled iron. The new recruits have proven unexpectedly adept at shipboard tasks, easing the workload for the rest of us. By the time I finish my few morning tasks, I have a scheme formulating.

Zhèng had made his announcement to the crew at dawn, only to be met with a wall of knowing shrugs and grumbles. If the fire in his eyes when they cut to me was any indication, he is certainly furious. Angry that I broke our agreement; angry that I undermined him in front of the crew.

However, his fury is a storm I have no time to weather. If I'm to continue operating as if we *will* survive Fenghua Pass, I have more pressing concerns at hand.

It's said the journey to Fenghua Pass will take two days—two long, uneasy days weighed down with the tension of what awaits. I plan to use them wisely. I need to talk to Ah Fei. I need to understand who he is, what he knows.

Maybe I can even learn something about his Wielding…

When I finally seek him out, I find him in the heart of disruption.

A fight ring has been hastily assembled on the main deck. The pirates, ever resourceful in their pursuit of distraction, have abandoned the rigging for revelry. The deck pulses with the noise and sweat of barely contained mayhem. Coins clink, dice rattle against the planks, and the occasional cheer erupts as fortunes shift with each roll. A barrel of watered-down liquor in the corner keeps spirits buoyant and tongues unbridled.

They mask their fear with debauchery, drown it in cheap spirits and broken knuckles.

At the center, two sailors grapple, one of them Ah Fei. Their shirts are discarded, muscles flexed under the strain of contest.

Leaned up against a mast, I watch with detached interest. Even Zhèng has reemerged from his cabin, standing at the circle's edge with a look of idle bemusement.

A couple of moments of struggle pass before Ah Fei flips his opponent on his back. He holds the man there as the group of pirates count down to his victory. When the match is finished, Ah Fei stands tall, rippled chest heaving.

"Next up! Who shall dare face Ah Fei?" bellows one of the sailors, pointing to the burly man. Ah Fei cracks his knuckles with casual ease. His grin is wide and cocky as he wipes sweat from his brow. The crew roars in encouragement, their voices blending into a chaotic chorus as they goad new challengers forward.

I guess I will have to wait until he's tired himself out.

I turn to leave, weaving through the bodies crowding the makeshift arena—when my eyes catch on a familiar figure at the edge of the fray. Luo. He sits perched on a crate nearby—face slightly softened by the faintest trace of a smirk.

A pang ricochets through my chest. My outburst from last night flashes through my mind.

I have already angered the captain. It's unwise to find myself at odds with both men at once. I cannot afford to stack enemies among those I sail beside.

More than that, he didn't deserve of my wrath—well, at least not all of it. He was simply the nearest target, and I… I let my bitterness spill over, misplaced.

Before I can reason with myself, my feet have already begun moving. I'm halfway to him when a sneering voice slices through the noise.

"And where do you think you're going, girl?"

I turn slightly to find Kāng, his perpetual snarl marring his face. He swaggers closer, the crowd parting to create a direct path from him to me. "What's the matter? Afraid we'd break ya?"

I remain motionless, my gaze stone. In an instant, my defenses are up, and my mind is alert.

A round of exaggerated "oohs" ripples through the assembly. I can see that even Luo raises an eyebrow, though his expression betrays the cold assessment he's giving Kāng. His eyes follow him closely.

My lips press into a thin line.

I harbor no wish to prove myself to these men, but Kāng's taunts are persistent. And aggravating.

"I told you my patience is scarce, Kāng," I say calmly, slipping off my slippers.

The circle erupts in cheers, sensing the brawl brewing.

Kāng leers, clearly pleased with his handiwork. "That sounds like a challenge to me. What'd you say, men? Shall we see what the little stowaway is made of?"

The crew shouts their approval as Ah Fei steps out of the ring, and I step in. I pause at the edge of the crowd and gather my hair, dark curls coiling around my fingers. I twist them into a low, tight bun at the nape of my neck. A man like Kāng does not fight with honor—he fights to win. I will not give him the advantage of a single exposed strand.

When I finish, I spin around slowly to take in the audience. As I pull on my tunic's knot to make sure its secure, my gaze briefly catch Zhèng's. His stare is flat, yet intense. However, I can sense his interest is peaked.

Kāng bounces lightly upon his toes, confidence exuding from every sinew.

"Don't say I didn't warn ya," he quips, smirking.

I make no reply. I spent cycles fighting off the other kids in the floating village. I can spot a coward when I see one. Kāng is no different than them. Just louder. And far too used to being cheered for.

I exhale slowly and raise my hands, palms open, fingers relaxed, stance low and fluid. My weight shifts evenly across the balls of my feet, knees bent, spine lengthened. Every muscle coils, waiting.

In the blink of an eye, a memory breaks through. Guided movements from cycles ago, recalled for this fight. As the world fades in the background, I hear a voice, boyish and firm. One that reminds me of rain.

"If it is between you or them, do not hesitate. Choose yourself. Again and again."

The world quiets for a second.

Then Kāng strikes first, his frame a blur of motion.

He lunges for my shoulders, fingers curled like claws. But I move as though I'm water itself. Shifting my weight onto my back leg and pivoting smoothly, his grasp finds nothing but empty air. Seizing the opportunity, my foot sweeps in an arc to catch his ankle.

Kāng falters, the deck shifting beneath him, but his reflexes save him from a complete fall.

As he reorients himself, my eyes follow his every twitch. The tension between us is heightened.

Kāng feints left, his feet gliding across the planks in a deceptive shuffle, before his fist lashes out from the right, aiming for my ribs. I twist, torso folding in smaller. My forearm comes down to deflect his blow. In the same breath, I counter—my fist striking upward in a quick jab to his shoulder. The impact sends Kāng stumbling back, his balance shaken.

Our spectators erupt in cheers, bets being exchanged and recalculated with every blow.

He lunges, faster now, driven by ego and the sting of wounded pride. He ducks, and before I can spin away, his shoulder slams into my midsection. He lifts me with a grunt, then drives my body into the deck. The impact explodes up my spine robbing the breath from my lungs. For a second, the world becomes fractured sound and blurry motion.

He takes full advantage of my stagger. A fist cracks against my nose—white light bursting behind my eyes. A lightning strike of pain. My head rings, but no blood runs, and I take small comfort in that.

Kāng presses his advantage, hands like iron as he pins my

arms, leveraging his weight. I thrash beneath him, ire surging with every failed attempt. Then—clarity. Memory.

I dig my heels into the deck, grit my teeth, and thrust upward with violent force. Kāng was not expecting a counter. His body jerks forward just enough.

My arms shoot up, wrapping around his waist. Then, I maneuver my left arm up and around his, breaking his balance. I twist with everything I have—hips, shoulders, momentum—until gravity finishes what I started.

He crashes beneath me.

Pain hums through every inch of my body, but I push it aside.

Still gripping his arm, I shift my weight and swing my legs upward, locking them tightly around his head. My thighs constrict until I can feel the wound smart once more.

I feel him tense—his muffled grunt of resistance lost beneath the jeers.

Kāng taps the ground in a yield. But there is one thing he does not consider with me: I'm not a pirate. I do not have to play by their rules.

So, I take his arrested arm and twist it until I hear a sickening pop.

Kāng screams, a raw, visceral sound. Around us, the crowd recoils with a collective groan, hands flying to their own shoulders as if feeling a phantom pain.

In one seamless movement, I flip him onto his stomach, drive my knee between his shoulder blades, and wrench his damaged arm back between my thighs, locking it in place.

My voice is cold. Detached. "Bother me again, and you *will* die."

Kāng thrashes once, twice, his pride warring against reality. I pull his arm back farther, and he shouts in agony once more. Then, he slams his free hand against the floor harder, his voice bitter with defeat.

"Fine," he spats. "Now get off!"

I release him and rise slowly, chest heaving. The sun glints off my dark, sweat-slick skin. Stepping back, my eyes never leave Kāng as he is brought to his feet by nearby mates.

Huò gingerly comes over to help shuffle him away down below deck to be aided to. As they disappear through the crowd, the medic throws a wink at me over his shoulder.

A buzz lingers over the audience as my victory over Kāng hangs in the air.

Luo stands now, fixated on me. The expression on his face is indecipherable, his gaze is weighted. Eyes round and tortured like he is looking at something his right mind cannot comprehend.

Suddenly, Zhèng steps forward. "Impressive," he says. "But skill against a sailor blinded by his own pride is not the same as true combat."

My eyes narrow.

What is his objective here?

"Is that a challenge?" I ask, tone empty.

A ripple of skittish murmurs passes through the pirates. They shift, reforming a wide berth around the captain and me.

Zhèng smiles, but it does not reach his eyes. "No, not a challenge." He sheds his robe, bearing a tanned, toned chest. "A lesson."

I bristle viciously. He is irater than I initially assumed.

Fine. If he wants to fight, then so be it.

This time, I move first.

I launch forward with a jab aimed at his ribs, but he twists away, sidestepping it. He moves in close, and before I can adjust, he hooks my arm, twisting me off balance. I stumble, but recover swiftly, sliding my feet into a wide stance.

He glides forward, his palm cutting through the air toward my temple. I crouch, his hand missing by inches. I counter with an elbow strike, aiming for his side, hoping to hit an organ or two.

He absorbs the blow with a subtle movement of his torso. Then, he lowers and delivers a calculated hit to my outer thigh, causing the suture to tear open.

I let out tight groan as I stumble back slightly, hand flying down to my wet pantleg to clutch at the throbbing flesh.

"Your energy is scattered," he remarks coolly, almost instructive.

I clench my jaw, ignoring the taunt.

I get it now.

He's testing me, measuring my resolve.

I shift tactics, feinting a punch and spinning into a kick aimed high at his head. For a split second, I think it might land—but his arm rises in a smooth arc, deflecting the blow as if swatting away a fly. The force of his redirection sends me skidding back across the planks.

My back hits the wood hard. The ache from the previous match triples.

"Stay down," Zhèng says. He speaks as though he is offering advice.

Indignation burns in my chest at being talked down to. I roll to my feet. This time, I throw myself at him with everything I have—a whirlwind of punches and kicks, refusing to cower. But the man does not stumble. He meets my fury with precision, rebounding each swing. When I press forward, he treads back. When I hesitate, he closes in, his strikes measured and patient.

The final exchange comes too quickly.

He steps into my guard, catches my wrist—twisting it just enough to sap my strength—then sweeps his leg low. My ankle buckles, and I hit the deck again, the impact jarring every bone in my body.

I'm done.

Zhèng squats beside me, his expression indecipherable. "You have skill," he says quietly. "But skill without discipline is wasted potential."

I force myself to meet his blank gaze, as I lay facing the sky catching my breath. My silence is the only acknowledgment I'll give him. My pride burns hotter than any ache in my body.

I'm never thanking him for saving me the other day. Ever.

Luo approaches, his attention flickering between us two, offering a water skin. Zhèng waves him off, instead extending his hand to me.

I stare at it, a moment of decision hanging between us. Slowly—reluctantly—I grasp it.

As he pulls me to my feet, the crew watches, the air filled with tension. Then, he turns away, collecting his robe, before heading up the sterncastle to his cabin. When he turns his back to me, I find myself frozen in disbelief.

Tattoos.

They cover almost the entirety of his skin. The biggest of them runs down the middle of his spine. A depiction of a black dragon, its body coiled and eyes darkened. Surrounded by billows of clouds. Of shadow.

It reminds me of the dragon from my nightmare.

My shock is interrupted by Luo offering *me* the water skin now. I shake my head silently. He lingers a beat before following closely behind Zhèng.

As I watch them go, my thoughts scatter.

I have too many questions, and not nearly enough answers.

Unable to ignore the sting of my reopened thigh wound, I head to the infirmary in the crew's cabin before meeting Zhèng. Each step sends a jolt of pain radiating through my leg. By the time I reach below, I'm clenching my teeth to keep from wincing aloud.

The air is teeming with the mingled smells of sweat and dried blood. The earlier contestants who lost their brawls are laid out on the lower hammocks, nursing their injuries with damp cloths and scraps of linen. Some groan softly, while others sit brooding, their egos likely wounded as much as their flesh.

I scan the room, looking for Huò. My eyes land on him toward the back, where he's bent over Kāng, still tending to the man's arm. As I make my way over, my slippers scuffing against the creaking planks, Kāng locks onto me.

His face twists into a snarl. "You—" he growls, struggling to push himself up from the hammock. His eyes are wild with malice.

Before he can do anything, Huò places a rough, calloused hand on Kāng's chest and shoves him firmly back down onto the hammock.

"Would you give it up?" he snaps with exasperation. "You lost. Get over it!"

Kāng bristles but stays down, though his glare burns holes into me. It is lethal, full of promises of revenge. I meet it with a roll of my eyes.

Turning to Huò, I pull up the legs of my pants. When I move aside the blood-soaked cloth tied around my thigh, it reveals the sluggishly bleeding wound.

"I just wanted to know if you have any leftover linen wraps," I say, tone clipped with irritation. "Your bastard of a captain reopened my wound, and now my leg is leaking all over the place."

Huò straightens, wiping his hands on a rag that's seen far better days. His eyes flick down to my wound, expression obscure. "You fought Zhèng?" he asks, though it sounds more like a statement than a question.

I shrug, the motion casual and bitter. "More like he used me to make a point."

Huò lets out a low whistle and shakes his head. "You're lucky you're still walking."

"Lucky," I scoff, "yeah, sure." I lean my weight onto my uninjured leg as the pain in the other begins to throb overwhelmingly.

Huò thinks for a moment. "It's very rare that the captain does something unjustified."

I stare at him, face blank.

Noticing that the conversation will not continue, Huò gestures for me to sit on the edge of an empty hammock. I lower myself carefully, wincing as the movement pulls at the cut. He rummages through a small chest nearby. Then, he pulls out a roll of linen and a jar of something that smells alcoholic and medicinal.

"This is going to sting," he warns, unscrewing the lid of the jar.

"Just get on with it," I say, bracing myself.

He chuckles softly, shaking his head again. "Tough one, aren't you?"

As he starts to clean and rewrap the wound, I glance over at Kāng, who's still watching me with murder in his eyes. I offer him a smirk, more out of spite than amusement, and he growls under his breath, turning his head away.

"You'd better keep an eye on him," Huò tells me, jerking his chin toward Kāng. "He's got revenge written all over his face."

I let out a snort, wincing slightly as he tightens the bandage around my leg. "Let him try. You'll just end up patching him up again."

The exchange brings a small, wry smile to my lips. It's a rare moment of levity in a place where it's scarce.

He finishes binding the injury, pats my leg once and rises without ceremony, already moving on to the next man awaiting his care.

I take it as my cue to leave.

As I limp my way back up to the deck there's only one thought on my mind:

It's time to get some answers.

13

LATER THAT NIGHT

JADE BAY, 1799

I find Ah Fei at supper. The rations have already been passed around, and he sits nestled among the other crewmates, laughter rising from their circle like smoke. They're deep in animated recollections of the day's skirmishes, their voices loud and unrestrained.

"Ah Fei," I say, threading my voice through the noise. "Would you mind if we talked?"

He looks up, eyes glinting with the thrill of leftover adrenaline. "For the woman who floored Kāng?" He grins broadly. "I'd be a fool to say no."

A ripple of amused agreement follows from the others. I wait while he untangles himself from their midst, slapping shoulders and exchanging quick farewells. Then, he guides me across the deck, his gait relaxed.

As we exit, I catch Zhèng's attention. His face is illuminated by the glow of the makeshift clay firepit at the center of the ship. Steady, brown eyes follow us as we reach the side rail. Though it is likely too dark to see the severity of it, I send him a scathing glare.

Ah Fei stops at the far side of the ship, where the churn of the ocean supersedes the sounds of the crew. He leans one large arm on the railing, posture open and friendly.

"So, what can I do for you," he asks. The warmth of his smile is a welcomed gesture.

I exhale a short laugh, dry and transparent. "Can't a woman want to get to know a friend?" I let my formal verbiage drop slightly, allowing bits of Hokan flare to resurface within my speech.

His discerning eyes stay on mine. The smile does not falter, but I can tell he sees through me. He tilts his head ever so slightly, an action that suggests he is patient, not passive. "Sure, she can," he says lightly, "but that's not why you want to talk now, is it?"

My breath catches, before a soft puff of air leaves my nose. "No, it's not." I look over the rail, down to the abyss. I do not know what kind of man Ah Fei is beneath the amicable surface. Regardless, I steady myself, hoping that he proves to be a worthy investment. "I would like to know more about Wielding."

Ah Fei does not answer right away. He watches me for a moment, then quietly sets his bowl aside. He unlatches the waterskin from his belt—simple leather, worn smooth with use—and unscrews the cap.

Then he tips it.

A single droplet escapes, round and silver-black in the moonlight.

It doesn't fall.

It *hangs*, suspended between us, trembling with a faint internal pulse. Vibrating with energy, the drop is caught somewhere between form and will.

Breath does not come.

I have seen Wielding before—felt its sting more than once. But always as a blunt force, a demonstration of control meant to humble, hurt, or bind. I have never seen it used like this.

Never seen its elegance.

He lifts two fingers, and the droplet begins to stretch. Not downward, but outward—elongating in the air, unfurling like some strange, weightless fern. It grows in size as water is pulled from the atmosphere around it. It spirals into a serpentine ribbon midair, gleaming as it spins.

Then, it falls like rain.

And before they can reach the deck, the drops vanish, dissolving into vapor.

Ah Fei caps the flask. "That," he says simply, "is Wielding."

I stare at the space where the water had been. Stunned.

I lean forward, not bothering to hide the hunger in my voice. "What did you *do* to it?"

He raises an eyebrow. "What do *you* think I did to it?"

I pause. The question is real—not rhetorical, not mocking. He genuinely wants to know what I see.

"I…" My thoughts stumble. "You didn't control the water. You controlled the qì."

He tilts his head, but says nothing else. I hesitate.

"Is there something I'm missing?"

His mouth tugs back into a grin. "Closer." He shifts to fully face me now. "What did Hokans know of Wielding? Of the Great Ascent?"

The chain of questions is abrupt. I don't answer immediately, too busy sorting through the rubble of what we were allowed to remember. Though the New World Order had left us behind, Hokans had been there at the beginning of the Old World's end.

"Stories, passed from one generation to the next, spoke of the first Harvester ships," I begin. "Ominous silhouettes coming from the west, hulls full from their visits on Dì Yù Tǔ Xī—the only known source of Aether.

"The Untamed had managed to slip under the watchful eye of the Founding Gods who, at the time, had walked the earth amongst mortals on mainland Pingshen. Their relationship to the Gods was entirely different. Or at least, it was rumored to be so," I say.

He nods his head for me to continue.

"There had been an established stratification in which Gods, who held divine power, were the overseers, and mortals the flock.

"But that order shifted with a single accord—the trade agreement brokered by the then-Phoenix Emperor and The Untamed. The foreign country had monopolized Aether sourcing through their geographic proximity to the island. They had found no use for the flower," I pause briefly, distaste coating my words. "and the Emperor had intended to keep it that way. He wanted this power only for the Pingshen empire—Pingshen people."

Ah Fei shifts beside me. I do not look at him, but I can feel the discomfort radiating off the man like heat from a sunbaked stone. The strained relationship Wave Kin have as a result of his clan's access to the drug hangs heavy in the air.

Nevertheless, I push on.

"The Harvester's hulls had glistened with promise as they reached Goisa and Formosa. It was there, beneath the scrutiny of town officials and merchants alike, that Aether was introduced. But not merely as a flower. Instead, as the seed of a greater ambition—one that would birth a new dynasty unlike any before it.

"The refinement of Aether into an ingestible form was heralded as a miracle. The Phoenix Emperor believed it a key to unlocking the potential buried within mortals. Not only could it elevate the mind beyond its ordinary limitations, but more importantly, it could unearth an ancient ability. Stirring forces long thought dormant in those nature had deemed worthy. A rare few, scattered among the many," I recite.

At my port, land-children learned this history seated cross-legged on town floors, sun high overhead, their midday lessons drilled into them like scripture. For me, it had been attained through stolen moments—narratives overheard as I loitered near open doors just long enough to pretend I belonged.

My brow tightens as the memories drift away, replaced by the story itself. "How he knew the potential of the drug was never explained," I murmur. "Perhaps, he'd seen it in a vision. I suppose it didn't matter. Pingshen had planned to go to war, and he'd brought them the singular thing that could liberate the Corporeal World from under the heel of the Gods," I shrug. "Blindly believing him was only natural."

Once again, the man says nothing. I'm sure the undertone of bitterness in my voice does not escape him.

"In the wake of the first consumption, the Wielders emerged. Men and women who could manipulate inanimate qì in the world around us. Conjurors that could control the energy that lies dormant in bedrock and in sea.

"The war took more than one hundred cycles, but mortals eventually achieved liberation, banishing the Gods to the Celestial World," I voice, though it feels almost uncomfortable to say so.

I'm not sure why. I have not revered in a God in cycles.

Praying in a moment of extreme duress does not count. Or at least I don't think it does.

I release a heavy sigh, coming to the end of my knowledge. "But that victory came at a cost. The Corporeal World never truly recovered. The Phoenix Emperor, once exalted as a liberator, was overthrown for failing to rebuild what had been broken. And in his place, the Serpent Emperor rose, his claim to power uncontested."

"And in the decades since, he has turned his back on the very force that secured his throne," Ah Fei finishes for me. He is solemn for a long time. Then, he nods.

"You know more than most. Very impressive," he provides. He folds his arms across his chest, deep in thought. "Still, there are gaps. Understandable ones. I'll tell you what I can."

I duck my head in return, grateful, though I do not trust myself to say so aloud.

"When aetherbloom first birthed the Wielders, they were split by inclination," he begins, voice steady. "Two disciplines emerged: those who leaned toward Enkindling, and those who embraced Entropy."

He turns slightly, focus drifting toward the stars as though drawing from them.

"Everyone is born with a combination of stable and chaotic qì within them, but people usually have an affinity for one over the other. Enkindlers tap into their own stable inner qì, marrying it with an element's chaotic qì—be it from water, fire, or air. Entrops, on the other hand, draw on *their* disorderly inner qì and espouse it with an element's stable qì—which can be from wood, metal, or earth."

I angle myself closer, hanging onto the drawn-out vowels within his words as they embed themselves in the space between us.

"When one Wields, the power only enhances your natural tendency. If you prioritize order, you construct it from chaos. If you harbor ruin, you destroy stability."

That explains much of the war then.

When the Great Ascent began, it was the Entrops who fought, Wielding chaotic energy like an artist's brush upon the battlefield. And the Enkindlers were left to mend the fractures—to forge a New World Order from the wreckage of war. A task that was thwarted by the Serpent Emperor's usurpation.

Ah Fei's light chuckle catches my ears.

"Perhaps that's why the universe did not grant us the ability to Wield another person's qì," he says off-handedly.

"Why can't they?" I ask.

"Because, if the two strands of qì within yourself meet another person's the volatility of that much energy is too great. It will destroy the both of you."

My mind churns for a moment.

Then what about the shadows of the living?

"Both disciplines have tiers. Wielders are classified as high or low-level depending on the depth of their power." His brow creases. "But high-levels are rare—one in one hundred, maybe even less. And among those, fewer still have mastery. Very few people will ever fully control more than one element within their respective discipline," he continues. "Mastering both disciplines is unheard of."

I give a small hum as I try to absorb all this new information.

"That covers the history," he says at last. "Now we move to the act of Wielding itself." His eyes narrow slightly. "You truly know nothing more?"

"Obviously not," I snap, irritation slipping out before I can stop it. "No offense, but the Wave Kin who *did* gain power didn't exactly hold demonstrations for Hokans. And they surely didn't explain it to people like *me*."

He flinches—just slightly—but it's enough. The sting of my words hits its mark, and for a moment, I feel a tinge of guilt. But I shove it down.

Some truths are not meant to be palatable.

He nods slowly, chastened. "Fair enough," he murmurs. "I can only speak to the way *I* Wield, though."

My head nods in understanding.

"I listen to its qì," he says introspectively. "Water always wants to transform. It carries the memory of rain, tides, fog. Its qì is restless. Just now, I simply gave it guidance."

That makes something stir in me—something tight and strange. "You gave water permission to… become mist?"

"Not exactly." He glances at me. "I reminded it that it *could.* Despite what Pingshen has taught its Wielders to believe, Wielding isn't really about domination. It's an exchange."

I let that sink in.

He's obviously an Enkindler.

"So... when you Wield to catch fish?" I press, curious now.

"I negotiate. I offer my qì to balance the water's disorderly qì. And in that moment of harmony, Yīn and Yàng is complete. I become a part of the ocean. I can feel the fish, sense the shape of them in the current. Then I guide just enough water to the surface, and they come with it." He pauses, chuckling at himself. "It sounds more complicated than it is. Maybe you'll come watch sometime. It'll make more sense when you see it."

"Yeah," I murmur, my mind already far from the deck. "Maybe."

Now I understand Merchant Fang. Banning Wielding was never about not provoking the Gods. It was preemptive defense. *The Emperor understands the threat it poses, not to the Heavens, but to his throne.*

"How many times—" I shift uncomfortably, bracing for the unpleasant air that is bound to come, "—how many times did you have to take aetherbloom before you began to Wield?"

As expected, his expression tightens considerably.

He knows what I mean.

There's a hunger that lives in people—the kind that hollows them out in search of power. Some chase Wielding so desperately they will drive themselves to addiction to gain it. That is how the empire ended up with the Bloomer epidemic.

How so many *Hokans* ended up lost to it.

His next words are small, half-claimed by the wind skimming across the sea. "More than I'd like to admit." He shifts slightly. "There isn't an exact amount, but there's never been a Wielder born just after one dose or hit. Ever."

This knocks the wind out of my chest.

Then, what does that mean for me? I'd never had aetherbloom before Madam Lín had slipped me some without my knowledge. That one dose should not have been enough to trigger Wielding. And even if it was, why was my Wielding so different? I was able to take a person's qì! What I did… shouldn't be possible—

A quiet yawn from Ah Fei pulls me from the spiral. He stretches, his body relaxing as fatigue sets in.

"I did enjoy this little chat," he says with a vague smile. "But I think it's time we both got some rest." Then, he turns to me, eyes heavy with meaning. "I can only show you so much, Shi Yang. If you want to truly understand Wielding, you'll need to do more than *observe.* You'll need to *listen*—to the qì inside the world. And inside yourself."

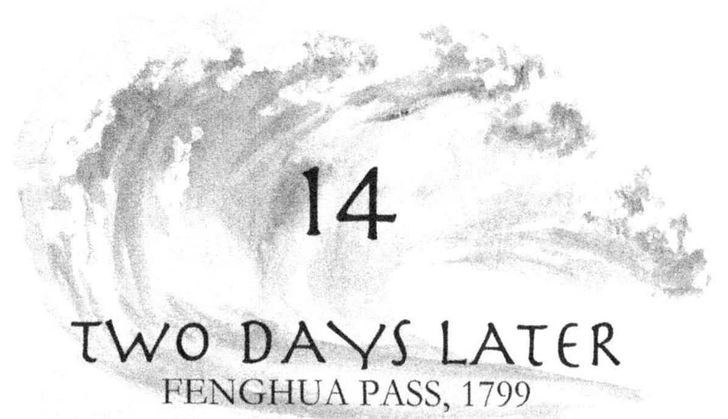

14

TWO DAYS LATER

FENGHUA PASS, 1799

What I learned from Ah Fei sticks with me throughout the rest of the journey to Fenghua Pass. In-between tasks, I try spending some time watching him fish. And he was right, it *was* much more understandable seeing Wielding in person.

Whilst with him, we talk of nomad life, of the sea and its moods, of the things we miss. We skirt around clan politics, carefully, deliberately. The tension still simmers under the surface—mostly mine—but neither of us pushes. We build a nice rapport as I help him clean and skin the fish for the crew.

I'm tipping the last bucket of fish innards overboard, watching the slick trail spiral into the waves, when the ship creaks to a halt. The sails groan, and the anchor drops with a deep, echoing splash.

We have reached the gorge.

Then, Zhèng's voice cuts through the air. "Gather up, crew!"

The bellow of his voice reverberates in the valley that now cradles us.

The ship comes alive with the shuffle of boots, men rousing from hammocks or dropping what they were doing to make their way to the main deck. I wipe my hands on a rag and follow.

Zhèng stands above us, his dark tunic catching the breeze, the storm-colored sky casting him in silhouette. His gaze drifts slowly across the gathered crew like he's memorizing each of their faces in case some do not make it through. Luo stands off to his right, once again, shirtless.

I mean, honestly.

His gaze, too, sweeps across the group, before landing on me. His face is solemn, but as if some irreverent thread in him just can't help itself, he tips his head the slightest inch and throws me an obnoxious wink. Then he's looking away, and the moment's gone, swallowed by the sea mist and the weight of what's coming.

I roll my eyes, though a sliver of an amused exhale escapes my lips despite myself.

It seems he's forgiven me for the outburst a few days ago—or at least decided to pretend it never happened. Back to his usual self.

"Time to rally the men," Ah Fei whispers over my shoulder, tone failing to remain light.

Analyzing the men around us, I see that their faces are grim. Shoulders are stiff. Eyes cast down. Hands tremble on hilts or clench too tightly at their sides.

I turn back to Ah Fei, my tone dry. "Yeah. Good luck to him with that."

Zhèng's voice breaks through the murmurs again.

"Men," he begins. Then his eyes shift. "And Shi Yang."

A few heads turn toward me, but my expression remains unmoved, unimpressed.

Let him have his dramatics.

"I'm sure you've heard the stories. The myths about Fenghua Pass."

His voice carries across the deck like a slow drumbeat. Around me, the crew leans in slightly.

"Rumors that the water's cursed," he shouts. "That there are voices that reach up to drag you under."

A few men glance at each other. One utters a prayer. Zhèng does not stop.

"I'm not going to stand here and tell you it's all fallacy. I do not truly know," he states. "However, if the tales *are* true. They are spirits. Shui Gui."

This causes a rising hum of complaints to roll through the men. They have the same disbelief I had. As far as we knew, spirits were supposed to be in their own world.

Zhèng silences the din with a single raise of his hand. When the pirates quiet, he continues. "What they want is not your death—but your flesh. Your bones. They want to wear your skin back to shore and breathe your air. They want to be Rerisen.

"They don't speak with mouths. They speak with guilt. With desire. With the voices of the ones you couldn't save. If you listen, you're already halfway overboard. So, if you hear a voice calling your name—*don't* stop." Zhèng steps back and points toward the narrowing channel ahead. "You want to live? Watch out for each other. And when the dead come crawling—you make *sure* they don't leave with the living. Am I understood?"

A resounding chorus comes from around me. "Yes, sir!"

"Set the oars. Ready the fire oil. We pass in an hour's time."

The men scatter like a colony of ants.

I stay where I am. The wind brushes my face, carrying the foul breath of the Pass. I take a deep breath, smelling nothing but decay. Then, I head below to get a weapon.

When we enter, the cliffs that frame the channel stand steep and spiked like dragon spines. The rocks are weathered black by centuries of storms. As we slip between them, the crew goes quiet. The sails are lowered, oars drawn. The fog is unnatural—dense, cloying, sweet with rot. The reddish glow of the lanterns stands out against it, but doesn't provide much clarity in the haze entrapping us.

Zhèng's arms are folded over the rail near the prow, watching the pass ahead with narrowed eyes. His posture is rigid, shoulders squared like he's bracing for impact that hasn't come yet. The light here is strange—anemic and fractured, too dim for this hour—and it casts his face in half-shadow.

Luo is at the helm, hands steady on the tiller, but his shoulders are tight. His bow hangs on his shoulder blade, the string pressing into the muscle there. Any levity the man had earlier, is replaced by a stone expression.

Even he is not immune to the sinister pressure of this place.

We keep drifting, the air so thick it could be chewed. Time stretches. An hour passes, maybe more. It's impossible to tell in this half-world where sky and water have blurred into one cold, breathless veil. The only sound is the rhythmic dip of oars cutting water—but even that starts to subside.

Then, the vessel slows.

Not naturally. Not gradually. It's like the water itself begins to resist us—dragging at the hull like invisible hands pulling us back. Oars creak in their locks, the men straining harder now, teeth bared, muscles contracted. Despite their efforts, we're moving at a crawl.

And then, nothing. The ship shudders once. Not from impact, but from stillness.

We are floating.

"We have to keep moving," Zhèng barks. "Faster!"

"The current's dead." Luo replies, voice tight.

The captain turns his focus to the main deck. "Ah Fei! We need you now." The command thunders.

Beside me, the man in question straightens, already lifting his hands in answer. "On it, captain."

I assume Zhèng wants him to push us forward—manipulate the water to cut through the dead sea. I step back instinctively, giving him room. Ah Fei shifts his stance. The air around him vibrates.

Then, a scream rips through the silence. All heads whip around to its source.

One of the deckhands drops his oar and stumbles backward. His eyes are locked on the water beside the ship.

"I heard her," he whispers. "My sister."

The blood drains from my face.

"It's her," he says again, louder this time, voice breaking. "She needs me."

"No, wait!" someone yells.

But it's already too late; he vaults the rail.

The splash echoes unnaturally loud in the dead stillness. No thrashing. Not even bubbles.

I bolt forward, heart hammering, to the edge of the railing. I lean over, scanning the dark void of water below.

Just when I think he's gone—a hand slams against the hull.

Relief catches in my throat, but it dies there. Because the hand is *wrong*. The skin is wrinkled and peeling in sheets. The nails are molded and long. The fingers twitch in a grotesque way.

He pulls himself halfway up the side.

His face follows—gaze blank, mouth slack. His greenish-white skin sags off his bones, water-logged. Whatever wears that body now is *not* human.

I stagger back, spine colliding with the mast. Pain blossoms through my shoulder, but it barely registers. My lungs seize. I breathe hard, harder than I should.

The man is gone. All that remains is the spirit that has taken his body as its own.

Another voice erupts from the starboard side. Then another. And another. A choir of laughter and sighs, voices calling names.

"Yang," someone breathes behind me. It's Rabbit. His face is ashen. "Look…"

Through the fog, come shapes—figures. They are dozens of them all around us. Rotting bodies controlled by spirits who have already claimed their prize. Some look fresh, bloated like they drowned only last week. Others are little more than bones wrapped in sea-wet tunics.

They climbed the ship before we even knew they were here.

"Attack!" Zhèng's voice booms across the ship.

What follows is nothing short of mayhem.

The men let out bellows of war as they clash violently with the Rerisen.

Zhèng jumps from the upper deck into the fray without a second thought. His blades sing, cutting down and through the onslaught of distorted figures. He carries two long swords, wielding them in concert with one another. When one slashes high cutting off a head, the other arcs low disemboweling a torso. He is taking on three bodies at once when I hear a screech from above.

My head whips around. Luo is no longer at the helm. Or rather—he *is*, but not steering. He is turned fully, bow lifted, loosing arrow after arrow into the horde clawing their way up toward him. Each shot is precise, merciless—through sockets, through jaws, pinning decaying limbs to the deck. He has abandoned maneuvering the ship altogether to hold the line at the stern.

Why would so many go directly to him? Think, think…

It clicks.

They are going to try and crash the ship—to drag this entire vessel down with them into the abyss.

"Fire oil!" I shout, throat raw, praying someone hears me. Suddenly, something brushes my ankle.

I look down.

A hand.

A limb of gray fog, rising through the slats of the deck. I jerk back, and the thing retreats. But more hands come. Several of them. Clawing upward through the ship's very bones, grasping, scraping. They reach blindly—*hungrily*—for anything warm.

I sneer and rip free the short sword strapped to my side. The blade whistles as I slash down, hacking through hand after hand. They fall away, dissolving into water vapor.

The moment I clear the last of them, I bolt toward the sterncastle. Luo needs backup.

If they take the helm, we're dead.

Across the chaos of the deck, I catch sight of Ah Fei. His arms are lifted, fingers curled as he Wields water into vicious streams. The sea responds like an animal unleashed. Snarling ropes of saltwater twist upward, lashing out like whips. Each strike sends spirits hurtling backward. Their borrowed bodies fling into the depths like a child's discarded cloth tiger doll.

Near the mast, Hé lets out a guttural roar and hurls his axe straight into the chest of an approaching Rerisen. The momentum does not stop there—it cleaves through one spirit and crashes into a second behind it, pinning both down. He doesn't wait to retrieve it. He draws a dagger and throws himself into another.

I reach the helm just in time.

A Rerisen has made it to the wheel—its rotting fingers clawing around the wood, inches from control. I swing my sword hard, severing its hands at the wrist. It screams. A raw, high-pitched wail sends a ripple of nausea through my chest. Another one hears it. It hurls itself at me from the side. I barely register the blur before it's on top of me.

It is far heavier than a living man, its form inflated with water from days, maybe even cycles, in the sea. We slam into the deck with a dull, wet thud that knocks the wind out of me. My shortsword skitters across the planks, out of reach.

I grit my teeth and drive my elbow into its face. The blow lands with a satisfying crunch. Its jaw dislocates, hinging off to the side in a deformed angle. The spirit shows little care. Its nails drive into my shoulders, pointed and yellowed, and I cry out as pain flares bright and hot—

Two large hands grab either side of the spirit's skull. *Snap.* The sound is clean and final. Like a branch breaking underfoot.

The Rerisen goes limp on top of me, collapsing with the dead weight of something truly empty now. I shove it off with a grunt, chest heaving, and look up.

Luo stands over me. His chest rises and falls like he has run the length of a single village. Grime streaks his neck and arms. There is a thin gash across his temple, bleeding down into his brow. But his eyes are locked on mine, focused, urgent.

He does not waste a second. "To the hull—now!"

I scramble up as he yanks me to my feet. My muscles scream in protest, but I grab my fallen blade and take off without a word. My slippers pound against slick wood.

The battle is everywhere. Figures locked in combat, weapons flashing in the fog. Arrows fly past me in rapid succession clearing the path ahead.

Luo.

To my left, there's a splash—another crewman leaping overboard in madness. I hear Zhèng shouting behind me, but the words are drowned by the chaos.

I slam into the stairs leading down to the weapons hold. I miss the last two steps—my foot slips—and I hit the landing hard, my ribs knocking against the planking. Pain radiates, but there's no time to dwell. I catch myself, right my balance, and shove the door open with the full weight of my body. And I come face to face with four Rerisen.

I move to retreat, but it's too late.

From the gaps between the floorboards, more gray hands surge up—liquid mist-made flesh. One curls tight around my ankle like a vice. I grunt, trying to wrench free, but I'm locked in place. The cold of it creeps up my leg, and for the first time, fear pulses vividly in my throat.

They rush me.

I let muscle memory take the reins.

My sword is already swinging—first high, catching the rake of claws meant for my eyes. The impact sends sparks from steel-on-bone. I parry down at chest height, and my blade pierces the sternum of the closest one, where a heart once beat. I wrench it free with a ruthless twist, then maneuver into my next swing. The blade is buried into the face of another. It shrieks and crumples, leaking rancid fluid.

I slash down, severing the gray limb at the wrist. It dissipates with a hiss. Pivot. Spin. I try to cleave through the third spirit, but another hand catches my foot mid-turn. My body wrenches off-balance, and I hit the ground hard.

The breath rushes out of me.

And then more gray hands are on me. Grabbing, dragging, pressing me into the deck. I'm pinned. My sword arm strains against the weight, muscles screaming, teeth clenched. I writhe. Thrash.

They do not relent.

I open my mouth and scream for help, but a sinking feeling takes hold in my chest. I'm preparing to die alone when—

A long sword plunges clean through the throat of the spirit looming above me. It lets out a strangled moan and collapses backwards, lifeless once more.

Then another sword carves through the misted hands binding my arm. The pressure releases instantly.

I don't stall.

With a growl, I lurch to my knees and swing up, my blade arcing fast through the last spirit's abdomen. The cut is clean. Its insides spill out in a wet cascade—half-rotted, half-fluid—before it collapses in a disgusting heap beside me.

My lungs burn. My body shakes. When I turn to offer my

gratitude, the words catch in my throat. Zhèng.

His tunic hangs torn off one shoulder, exposing three long claw marks carved across his chest. Blood streaks down in rivulets, already soaking the waist of his trousers. It's too much. He should be down. But his adrenaline prevents him from registering the pain.

He doesn't wait for appreciation.

"Let's go," he says moving past me to the containers.

I will thank him later.

He sheathes the two swords, then hefts two large jugs on his shoulders. One of the wounds on his chest pulls open wider under the weight. He winces, just once, but keeps moving.

I spring forward and grab a jug of my own. It's heavier than I expect—nearly the weight of a few sacks of rice. My arms struggle, but I force them steady. I huff as I match his pace up the stairs and back into the fight above.

The deck is still havoc. There are less Rerisen, but the rest of the Shui Gui still surround us in the water. Zhèng commands any available bodies to retrieve the rest of the jars as we weave through the disarray.

I glimpse Huò and Old Chou back-to-back, defending each other with everything they have. Ah Fei sends another lash of water across the deck, knocking two more spirits into the depths. Hé's axe flies overhead, cleaving one ghost in two before boomeranging back toward his waiting hand.

I will not let their fighting be in vain.

Zhèng reaches the railing first, and I follow half a heartbeat after. We toss the oil jugs out as far as we can. Almost instantly, arrows blaze through the haze. They sail from the sterncastle in elegant arcs—lit at the tip and hissing through the air. They hit the water, and the sea explodes.

A roar of fire consumes the surface. Heat lashes outward. Orange and gold leap into the fog, a wall of light so sudden, it renders the shadows into fleeing shapes.

I hadn't understood Zhèng's plan before, but now it's clear.

They cannot stand the light.

Zhèng grabs me suddenly, one strong arm pulling me back into his chest. His other hand curls around my head and presses it to his collarbone as he shields me from the heat. I hear the fabric of his clothes crackle from the rising temperature. He grunts as the flames flare higher, licking dangerously close. His body is between me and the inferno. His back takes the brunt of it.

I want to tell him not to, but it all happens too fast.

The fire spreads quickly. The oil-fed blaze coats the water in ruthless flame. Spirits shriek and hiss as they boil beneath the surface. Some vanish into steam. Others sink, their moans echoing into silence. The sea calms. Slowly. Reluctantly.

And then—it is done.

The *Shui Gui* are gone.

Fog parts in shreds, revealing the narrow mouth of the Pass—and beyond it, the blue expanse of the Crimson Ocean.

Zhèng releases me.

I take a breath, blinking through smoke and ash. The hush that follows is surreal. When I turn back toward the captain, my stomach drops.

He sways on his feet. The entirety of his chest is red now. There is an unmistakable smell of burning skin clinging to his tunic, to the air around us, to *me*.

"Oh no…" I whisper, stepping toward him.

But he is already tipping forward. I barely manage to catch him, stumbling under his weight. His body is bulky and slack, a man who has reached the edge of what he can endure. My legs tremble with the effort to hold him up.

My voice tears through the quiet. "Luo! Huò! Anybody—Zhèng's injured!"

Within seconds, footsteps thunder. The co-captain appears first, wild-eyed, followed by Huò. Without question, Luo throws one of Zhèng's arms over his shoulder. Huò mirrors the motion on the other side.

"We got it. It's okay," Luo says.

They carry Zhèng off toward the captain's cabin, his legs dragging slightly. I watch them go, the imprint of him still in my arms.

I think the world is shaking. However, it is not until I feel a hand on my shoulder—Ah Fei's—that I realize it is just me.

We don't begin tending to the wounded or the dead until we're clear of the gorge—more than an hour later. The crew operates with caution as if the shadow of that valley still clings to our heels.

We cannot escape that tâik-ing place fast enough.

I do not breathe freely until the gorge is nothing more than a tiny notch on the horizon, no larger than my thumb held at arm's length. Only then do I feel the tightness in my chest ease.

I throw myself into cleaning alongside the others, sweeping what remains of the oil fires' filth and ash. But the smarting pain in my shoulder grows harder to ignore with every passing moment. When the ache can no longer be ignored, I pass my broom to Old Chou, who accepts it wordlessly. His silence says everything.

As I set out for Huò down below, I pass the crew still scrubbing the main deck of blood. The ones tasked with corpse removal pray over the names of the dead. Others work solemnly, their faces gray with exhaustion and grief.

In the crew's quarters, the air is hot and close. Huò has conscripted Rabbit and a handful of the younger boys as his makeshift assistants. They move franticly, sleeves rolled up, hands stained red. I settle into my hammock, waiting. Rabbit passes by and slows when he sees me. He pauses a few steps away, unsure of himself.

"Need help?" he offers, but I wave him off gently, nodding toward Huò, still busy with another pirate.

Rabbit lingers. As I wait for him to speak, I notice the cut I gave him on his cheek has healed nicely. The boy shifts from foot to foot, biting his lip. Something is obviously on his mind.

I raise an eyebrow. "Can I help you?"

"Oh! No, I…" his teeth pinch his bottom lip, "I jus' wanted to tell you that I saw you. Take out those spirits when they were goin' for the steer," he says. "I couldn't reach you, but… I saw."

He does not elaborate further. Instead, his lips pucker awkwardly before he scampers off, back to providing aid.

Just then, Huò comes over to me. His face is lined with sorrow, his eyes dim with fatigue. The crew lost at least seven men today. Death clings to him like the fog we've only just escaped—unshakable and omnipresent.

He works in silence, humming something old beneath his breath—something I half-recognize from the docks in

Kwangchow, a lullaby often sung by widows who discovered their husbands had been lost at sea.

"You'll scar," he mumbles, tying off the linen.

I shrug. "Just another to add to the collection." I aim for light-heartedness, but the pained look he gives tells me that the attempt falls flat.

When Huò finishes dressing my wounds, I ease my top back over my shoulders. The fabric is stiff with dried blood, sweat, and the lingering stench of smoke. It scrapes uncomfortably against raw skin, but I say nothing.

I open my mouth to ask about Zhèng—if he's conscious—but the words fade before they can form. Suddenly, they feel too personal, too revealing.

Would it be distasteful? To only worry about the captain in the midst of so many casualties?

My throat tightens with hesitation. Before I can decide, Huò speaks.

"His cabin," he says, without looking at me. "He's awake."

The heat rises to my cheeks, a flush rushing to the tips of my ears. I curse my own transparency—how easily he read the question I didn't ask.

A dozen deflective responses crowd my mind.

'Good for him'. 'I don't care'. 'So, what?'

But none make it past my lips. Instead, I dip my head once, because the excuses, if there are any, don't need to be spoken. Huò already knows.

15

SAME DAY

FOREIGN TRADE ROUTE, 1800

When I reach the captain's cabin, the door is slightly ajar. Voices drift through the heavy wood, muffled. I pause, hand resting on the frame, and gently nudge the door just wide enough to see inside.

Zhèng is on the pillowed mat in the corner of the room, propped halfway upright. His posture keeps pressure off his back while leaving his chest exposed—clearly an attempt at minimizing pain, though his clenched jaw betrays him.

Kneeling beside him is Luo, a small blade glinting in his hand. He slides it carefully beneath the torn hem of Zhèng's tunic, slicing the ruined cloth away in one clean motion. His touch is deft, but careful. Intimate.

Zhèng's head is tipped slightly toward him. Not speaking. Just watching.

I stay quiet in the doorway.

Luo's voice is edged with dry humor. "You nearly made me captain today." He pours a splash of wheat liquor onto a rag. The smell hits the air, sharp and clean. "I'd appreciate it if you didn't get my hopes up." Without warning, he presses the soaked cloth against Zhèng's wounds.

The injured man hisses out through his nose. "Seems as though you seek to finish the job right now."

Luo doesn't miss a beat. "Perhaps, I might," he replies, pressing harder. It's not enough to harm—but enough to make a point.

Zhèng's hand moves swiftly, fingers locking around Luo's wrist. "Don't make promises we both know you won't keep."

For a breathless moment, they lock eyes. Luo is the first to look away.

"Turn," he says quietly.

Zhèng's eyes linger a moment, before shifting, his muscles moving with pained precision. He turns until his back is laid bare.

I bring a hand to my mouth, barely stopping a gasp.

His back is in ruin. The sand-hued skin boasts several raw and blistered patches where the fire kissed him. Burn marks cut through the ink of his tattoos, warping old scars with new. Every twitch of his shoulders is a tremor of restrained pain.

Lead settles in my stomach.

That would've been me.

My eyes drift to the memory of fire etched into my own skin: the burn that stretches across my forearm, puckered and pale brown.

Would water help heal him as it did me?

Suddenly, Zhèng speaks, voice soft but urgent. "They were right. They told us spirits were returning. You know what this means," he pauses, "The cargo… it unquestionably has to reach Ningbao now," his voice rumbles.

"And we're sure about this?" Luo's tone is tightly wound. "The risks are high. If any Imperials suspect—"

"They won't," Zhèng interrupts firmly. "We've come too far. Our duty is nearly fulfilled. And now that we have the compass…" he trails off, the meaning heavy between them. "It will see us through."

I frown, my heart thudding against my ribs.

Cargo. Risks. Duty. Ningbao.

The words slam against my skull in an unstoppable fashion. My mind jumps to Merchant Fang's strange warning: "*None of it will matter after the Heavenly Liberation Festival anyway.*"

Everyone seems to be moving toward something I don't yet understand—but can feel it looming. The presence of it is growing day by day… And more interestingly, who is this 'they' the captain speaks of?

I press closer to the door, eager to catch more.

"It's her," Luo says. His volume is so low that I almost miss it. "I think she's…"

Something about his tone is off… is *sad.*

Zhèng's voice is reserved, more so than I have ever heard it, when he replies. "I know."

I pull back abruptly, the blood pounding in my ears.

Are they talking about me?

The wooden door creaks beneath my shifting weight. I go rigid, breath catching. Luo hears it. His guarded eyes snap to mine. He doesn't flinch, doesn't move—just studies me for a moment before offering a single, measured nod. Zhèng notices the shift in attention and turns to follow Luo's gaze.

"Come in," he says. His voice is rough, worn thin, but he raises it enough to carry.

I step through the threshold slowly, swallowing hard against the dryness in my throat.

Do they suspect my eavesdropping? What happens if they believe I've heard too much?

"I didn't mean to interrupt," I say carefully. I can't tell if my tone is meant to reassure or defuse.

Luo studies me for a moment, past my eyes, through bone and memory, searching for something beneath the surface. Whatever he sees—or doesn't—seems to satisfy him. Or perhaps he simply stops looking.

"You didn't," he says at last. His hands return to cleaning the wound.

Neither man offers further conversation. Neither looks up again. I remain near the desk, observing. I want to ask a thousand questions—need to—but I can't bring myself to interrogate them just yet. Not before I settle what I owe.

"I came to say thank you," I blurt, the words rushing out before I lose my nerve. "To both of you."

Zhèng tilts his head slightly. "For what?"

I swallow, heat rising in my neck.

Of course he won't make this easy.

My jaw twitches. "For having my back during the fight," I say slowly. "For helping me get the jars. For blocking me from the heat of the flames. Take your pick."

"You saved us and the ship," Luo replies, not looking up. "Seems we're even."

A frown creeps across my face before I can stop it. "But I—"

"We're even." Zhèng concludes, voice final.

My mouth opens, then closes again. I must look like a fish gasping for breath. I do not know what this means for our…

Relationship? Absolutely not. Collaboration? I guess that is more fitting.

I nod once, brisk and impersonal, then turn on my heel to leave.

"Actually," the captain calls after me, stopping me mid-step. "If you want to repay us—" he shifts onto his knees with a pained grunt, "—you can start by guiding us with the compass."

Both men are now focused on the cypress desk. I watch as Zhèng leans forward, bracing his weight against the table. The large map from my first visit is still spread across it, curling at the corners like it's trying to escape the humid air.

He slowly circles to the drawer on the far side, pulling a key from his pocket. He unlocks the top drawer and withdraws the compass.

I say nothing, but my eyes track every movement. I memorize the details—his motions, the drawer, the placement of the key—filing it away. It's information that might be needed later.

When he hands me the compass, I take it carefully. As soon as it contacts my skin, it creates that familiar pulse I had felt more than a moon ago. Its surface is warm in a way metal should not be. I lift my chin.

"I thought we were heading toward Goisa?" I inquire. Suspicion tingles in my gut.

They have tolerated me up until this point—saved my life even—because of my connection to this compass. If I overstep too many times, or look too closely, who's to say they won't lock me in the brig for good? I plan to tread lightly, but… I still want answers.

"We are," Zhèng replies, tone measured. He diverts his attention to the map. "Despite the…" he pauses as if considering his words carefully, "*complications* we have encountered. We do have business elsewhere. We need to know if the compass will lead us in that same direction."

He emphasizes on the word 'complications' like it's a euphemism. Like *I* might be the complication in question.

I hum with forced nonchalance. "And where is this *business*, might I ask?"

A tick pulls at the corners of his eyes, subtle but telling. "Let's just see where the compass takes us, yeah?" he says, dodging the question.

I expected such answer, but his vagueness only fuels my irritation. "You know," I snap, "all these quiet conversations and roundabout answers are becoming more than *a little* vexing!"

Shōush.

I regret the slip immediately. My mouth opens to begin backtracking when—as if instigated by my surge of emotion—the needle begins to spin wildly. It lets off a blur of motion that sends a hum through the space. The artifact pulses, its sensation intensifying before the needle lands in a precise direction.

Zhèng leans forward, wincing as the position bites into his wounded back. His fingers move across the map, tracking the compass's line. It cuts across the collections of islands, and the Jade Bay, to an unnamed city in the northwest snowcapped mountains of the mainland. The only pathway will force us to ride along the Pingshen Territory Border into a clearing of the Crimson Ocean marked with an inked skull and crossbones.

Dread falls over the room like a shroud.

"Well," I murmur, throat tight as I force the words out. "That route looks *perfectly* safe—nothing even remotely life-threatening about it."

Neither Zhèng nor Luo cracks a smile.

The captain continues to study the map. His hand rests just above the course the compass has laid bare, fingers curling slightly, as if resisting the urge to ball into a fist. Then, he straightens—or rather, attempts to.

A twinge of pain crosses his face, but he does not concede to it. "We'll need supplies, a discreet route through the border, and… a convincing story if anyone asks questions," he says, voice hoarse.

He is clearly addressing Luo, not me, but the mounting hysteria bubbling in my chest breaks loose before I can bite it back. "You mean something *more* believable than 'Oh, we're just transporting barrels of contraband across national lines for the thrill of it'?" I ask dryly. "Surely, *that's* enough to dissuade Imperial warships from blasting us straight to Dì Yù."

"Shi Yang," Luo warns.

My laugh comes hollow and humorless. Less at their predicament, more at the growing difficulty of my own.

This is what I asked for, isn't it? A way out of the country. An escape. I just hadn't imagined it might involve drowning at sea. Not to mention possibly dying in battle before ever reaching the answers I left my previous life behind to chase. Not that it could be considered much a life to begin with…

I let out a slow breath, the taste of irony bitter on my tongue. "Is it too late for you both to consider a less treasonous vocation? Tea trading, perhaps?"

Zhèng does not so much as glance up. "Wherever the compass leads, we follow." His words are absolute. A dismissal.

My jaw tightens. I drop the compass onto the desk with intentional laxity, the clang of metal on wood banging harshly in the otherwise quiet cabin.

I make for the door. My fingers are nearly on the handle when Zhèng's voice stops me cold once more.

"And Shi Yang," he calls, "this conversation *does not* leave this room."

His eyes burn with a severity that leaves no space for misunderstanding. A slow churn rises in my gut. It's a reminder: I may have the compass, but he commands the ship. The narrative.

So, I was right. Our dual was a display to show that my insubordination was not going unchecked.

"Compass or not," he continues, "I won't be so lenient the next time you decide to undermine my station or sow seeds of doubt among my crew."

Luo doesn't add on, but his stare speaks volumes: *Take the warning.*

My tongue presses against my cheek as I wrestle with the heat crawling up my neck—part embarrassment, part defiance. Still, I nod tersely. No apology.

Just before I cross the threshold, I pause, casting one last glance over my shoulder. "What if the compass doesn't lead us back?" I ask, voice tense. "If this journey ends with no return—what will you tell your men?"

I hadn't thought I cared about the crew. And truthfully, for most of them, I still don't. But my mind drifts to Ah Fei, to Hé, to Old Chou. To Huò with his quiet humming. Even Rabbit and the other young boys.

Do they not deserve to choose whether they lay down their lives for a captain who speaks of destiny only in concept, but nothing of its cost?

The question hangs in the air like the ring of a tolling bell.

But Zhèng does not answer.

Unexpected disappointment lingers in my mind, but I swallow it down.

Why, of all things, do I even care?

I scoff softly before slamming the door behind me.

16

TWO DAYS LATER

FOREIGN TRADE ROUTE, 1800

The next two days pass without incident. We held a quiet funeral for the fallen crewmates the evening after my conversation with the captains. There were no grand speeches—just some whispered prayers, and the sound of the sea taking what was left of the dead as they were tossed over the railing.

Since then, I have made a deliberate effort to avoid the lead men, which does not prove to be difficult. Zhèng has barely left his quarters, choosing to recover in seclusion. Luo surfaces now and then. Sometimes to relay orders or adjust our course, but overall, he too remains behind the teak door. Both stay locked away in whatever strategy they're nursing.

Unlike before the encounter with the Shui Gui, I do not seek out Ah Fei. It's easier that way. I find it difficult to meet the eyes of any crew member, knowing what I know about the uncertain path ahead. Especially him.

So, I retreat inward.

Discipline becomes a sanctuary, a tether. If recent conflicts have revealed anything, it's that survival is not won by fortitude alone.

As much as it pains me to admit it—especially if it means conceding even an inch of ground to Kāng—physical strength does, in fact, matter. And mine leaves much to be desired.

Skill on its own is no longer enough. Technique may offer dexterity, but when the body cannot meet the demands of the moment, it becomes a hollow thing. My arms, in particular, have betrayed me time and again—easily overpowered. More than one opponent has noticed. More than one has exploited it.

So, I train. Simply because I must.

That vow is front and center in my mind now as I finish my second round of pushups near the ship's stern, tucked out of the way. My muscles tremble with effort, each repetition more agonizing than the last, until finally—

"One… hundred," I rasp, collapsing onto my back, lungs heaving.

I lie still, letting my breath even out, the familiar pulse of the ship humming beneath me. The atmosphere thrums—the groan of wood, the taut snap of sails, the cry of gulls overhead. The pirates are loud again today. Voices drift from the main deck: shouts, laughter, the occasional barked command.

Yesterday, the mood had been starkly different. The usual boisterous spirit of the crew had been smothered, replaced by a muted shuffling of feet and fragmented conversations.

But pirates don't mourn long. Not openly. And today, the sorrow has lifted, or at least been masked beneath noise and motion. Cackles ricochet across the deck, rough and raucous. They're back to their natural state—unruly and unbothered.

Sweat drips down my face in steady streams, soaking into the linen of my tunic. The winter wind, while not freezing, is biting enough that my damp skin prickles with chill. It has been days since I've had a proper wash. Usually, I wait until the dead of night to bathe, when most of the crew is asleep. But the grit and sweat clinging to me have long passed the point of tolerable.

I push myself up and make my way to the bucket I hauled out earlier. Grasping the rope tied around its rim, I lean over the railing, lowering it. Once full, I heft it back aboard and begin the trek below to the waste cabin. Ah Fei insists it's called a 'head', however, I will *not* be calling it anything of the sort.

As my feet carry me through the hull, memories of fetching water for Ba and the egg boat flood my mind. Snippets of mocking words and shoving hands.

I shake my head, refocusing.

The bucket is dropped off in the waste room before I quickly duck into the weaponry. I snatch a small oar and a dagger. Both come with me as I return to the cramped cabin. There's no place for someone to hide in here, just two simple wooden boxes built over holes that empty into the ocean. Still, I check.

Satisfied I'm alone, I wedge the oar against the door to keep it blocked. When I'm sure it won't budge, I grab the communal soap powder, and I make quick work of cleaning my body, hair, and clothes. The dagger stays within reach.

Once finished, I dump the dirty water down the holes, return the borrowed tools, and make my way back to the main deck to dry off. My damp clothing causes the wind to cling to my frame like a second skin. I try not to shiver, biting down on the click of my teeth as I walk toward the front.

It is then, as I near the others, that the words being traded among the crew start to separate into distinct phrases. Bits of gossip and arguments are among them.

"Ah Fei, you filthy liar!" one man bellows, slamming a weathered dice cup onto a barrel. "You're cheating again, aren't you?"

They must be playing a game of tien gow.

Ah Fei's grin is as cutting as the blades he keeps tucked at his hip. "Cheating?" he teases. "You're just sore because I know how to roll better than you!"

"Go back to cooking, why don't you!"

Another cluster is sparring with wooden practice swords, their movements more showboating than actual technique. Each parry punctuated by exaggerated groans and dramatic flourishes when someone scores a hit. Even a glaring Kāng, still tending his wounded pride and broken arm, looks somewhat pleasant enough to be around for once.

I lean against the foremast, arms crossed, watching it all with a mix of intrigue and mild disdain. It is remarkable, really, how quickly pirates—*men*—bury their fear beneath a veneer of bravado and aggression. They drink, they gamble, they spar, throwing themselves into distractions with reckless abandon.

It is as if they believe, with enough noise and movement, they can drown out the truths of their past or outrun the uncertainty of their future.

A familiar judgment begins to stir within me, instinctive at first, before settling in my chest uncomfortably. My thoughts tighten into knots I can't easily unravel.

But…am I honestly so different in that regard? My methods may be dissimilar, but the end goal is shared. Avoidance.

The realization is distasteful. I grimace, not from pain, but from the unpleasant clarity of self-awareness.

The thread of reflection snaps as a fresh wave of rowdy shouting erupts nearby. A couple of steps away, a group of men bicker over a knife trick that's somehow turned into a contest of egos. Among them is Hé, who—when spotting me—stands to make his way over.

I heave a pre-irritated sigh.

The wiry man eyes me cautiously. When I don't tell him off, he takes it as a tacit invitation, leaning one pale arm against the mast just above my head. He plants himself far too close, studying me with a peculiar blend of awe and apprehension.

"So…" he begins, drawing out the vowel with theatrical flair.

It reminds me of the way girls on the flowerboat would speak when exchanging succulent gossip about a client.

"I've been meaning to talk to you about the other day. And—" he pauses dramatically, "—I have a question." His voice lilts, almost sing-song. He's like a child restless from boredom and in search of entertainment.

"What do you want, Hé?" I ask, voice flat and laced with fatigue.

"Despite the demonstration you used me for," he jokes, "I hadn't expected you to fight like you came into the world already swinging those arms of yours."

My eyes flick to his, and I snort. "Did you not see me lose to both Zhèng *and* Rabbit-boy?"

He waves a dismissive hand. "Please. Those don't count. Zhèng's a walking scroll on hand-to-hand combat, and you only had a dagger when you faced Rab. Completely unfair matches."

My expression contorts at the nickname, and Hé, ever observant, catches it instantly.

"That's what I'm calling him now, by the way. You're welcome to borrow it."

Before I can retort, he barrels on, words tumbling over each other like loose cargo in a storm.

"Anyway, like I was saying—you did well, both times. Very well, actually." A pale finger taps thoughtfully against his chin, eyes narrowing in mock scrutiny. "Unless, of course, you're secretly a master of close combat and blade work. In which case, frankly, you should be ashamed of yourself," he grins, gap tooth on full display.

My eyebrow raises. "You have exactly five seconds to ask a question before I walk away."

"Okay, okay!" he blurts, throwing up his hands in mock surrender. "So strict." His bottom lip sticks out in exaggerated sulk before he straightens, tone softening with genuine curiosity. "But seriously…where'd you learn to fight like that?"

The question gives me pause. I know what he—what *they*—see when they look at me. A woman, first and foremost, in a world that does not expect us to wield anything more than our allure. And then the rest of me—skin a different shade, voice carrying unfamiliar rhythms.

I'm sure I challenge all notions of what they think a woman should be.

My eyes move to the endless stretch of the sea surrounding us. For a moment, the question drifts unanswered, caught in the wind. I contemplate whether I should divulge any truths about myself, but ultimately, loneliness triumphs.

I suppose it's best at least one other person know my past. Anyone else that could attest to it is already gone.

"When I was young," I begin, "the other children in my clan used to call me a 'demon child'. They'd sneer at my skin, darker than even theirs, and say it was a mark of something cursed." I pause, the old sting dull but not gone. "At first, I thought I could endure it. That if I stayed quiet, kept to myself, they'd grow bored. But cruelty, *hatred*, is like fire—it does not simply burn itself out. It feeds until there's nothing left."

A whisper of a frown touches Hé's lips in what could be empathy. I don't bother to ask and find out. Instead, I focus on the pulsing of the veins at my temples born from the memories of jeering and torment. It feels like a different lifetime. I look back at it almost utterly detached.

"And then there was my father—if he could be called that," I chortle mirthlessly. "A fisherman by trade, but his hands were rougher on me than they ever were on his nets. There is a kind of violence that has no purpose but to remind you of your place. And my place, as far as he was concerned, was beneath his heel."

A heat takes root in my chest. "But eventually, I grew to know the truth. He feared me," I say evenly. "They all did."

The man shifts uneasily, glancing at the others in the group he'd come from. I hadn't realized that their conversations went quiet.

So much for it staying between me and him.

The men remain silent, so I press on.

"But," my voice takes on a softer tone, "there was one boy in the village." The words are touched by something that feels like fondness. "His father instructed him how to fight—small things at first, how to grip a stick, how to parry. Eventually, he taught him how to truly handle a sword; how to defend himself in combat. And I watched them every day, in secret. Hiding behind the boats or crouched among the reeds. I didn't know why I was drawn to their lessons, only that it stirred something in me. A need to understand."

Hé listens closely, nodding his head to communicate he wants to know more.

The crisp breeze of the seawater wraps around me as a singular recollection brings about goosebumps. "One day, the boy caught me watching," I say. "I thought he would beat me like the others, or worse—run to tell my father so he could do it himself. But, he just handed me a stick and said, '*Show me what you've learned.*'"

I see Hé's lips stretch in a small smile before my eyes close at the memory. Disbelief trickles into my next words, the emotion still fresh after all these cycles.

"I was awful. Clumsy. I swung too wide, tripped over my own feet. Fully expected him to laugh like everyone else. But he didn't. He just… corrected me. Patiently. Again and again. Every misstep, every failed strike—he'd stop, adjust my stance, show me how to move. For weeks, he taught me everything his father had taught him."

"Sounds like he was a good friend," Hé says quietly, the mischief drained from his features.

Words catch in my throat. I swallow hard, trying to force them down, but the ache doesn't leave.

Was he my friend?

I shake my head, as if that might scatter the grief. I shove it aside, making room for something easier to hold. My fingers curl around the railing until my knuckles go light.

"The first time I landed a blow on the ones who tormented me," I pivot, "it was like breaking the surface after being held underwater. After that, I stopped waiting—for insults, for beatings, for permission. I sought *them.* I found the worst bastard in the village and made him bleed." A cruel tilt curls at the corner of my mouth. "And that was the last time my father ever laid a hand on me."

The air becomes still.

I wonder if they'll come to fear me too.

One of the younger boys hesitates before asking, "What came of the boy?"

My breath catches, and the tightness returns, squeezing until there is barely space to breathe. "He…" The word fractures. I let out a rough cough, forcing myself to continue, tone clipped and flat. "He disappeared." I turn away, unwilling to show them the water that wells at my lashes. "I don't want to talk about this anymore."

What follows is awkward, laden with things left unsaid. The others squirm where they stand, unsure how to move past what I have given them—or what I refuse to. Then, a slow, deliberate clap cuts through the strain, its sound drawing every gaze upward.

From his perch atop the sterncastle, Luo leans over the railing.

"Spoken like someone who's seen the worst of man," he says. His tone is laced with both admiration and something more—whatever it is makes my skin prickle.

I discreetly dab at my lower lid, rising my internal guard up to shield my moment of vulnerability.

Luo follows the movement.

"What do you want, Luo?" I ask impatiently.

Then, as if donning his usual sly personality like a mask, his smirk widens, the corner of his mouth tilting upward in a way that feels almost antagonistic. "Just appreciating the view," he replies, words embedded with double meaning.

I scoff with disinterest. I turn without another word, striding toward the chief steward with brisk, purposeful steps.

Anything—scrubbing decks, inventory, grease work—would be more tolerable than indulging whatever game he thinks he's playing.

"Yeah, you enjoy that," I mutter coldly over my shoulder.

His laughter follows me as I walk away, but there's an itching cadence to it. One that causes a brief disruption in my stride. Still, I march forward. Because the only thing louder in my head than his laughter is one thought:

Whatever this is between me and these captains—I hope to the Gods it ends soon.

Long after supper has been served, and the men are below deck, I find myself sharing the night-watch alongside Old Chou. I sit at the bow with him, our forms hunched over a torn sail that bears testament to previous weeks' squall with Rabbit's crew.

The light from the lantern situated between us casts distorted shapes across the sagging canvas, making the worn fabric appear severely aged beneath our threads. My stiff fingers are struggling with the bone needle, when Old Chou breaches the quietness we've established.

"And how are you coming along," he asks, his weathered hands never ceasing their steady work.

I pause, studying my tight-knuckled grip. Even after many moons aboard the ship, my body remains wound up tight unconsciously.

I flex my appendages to counter the ache. "I think I'm managing," I say, though my voice betrays my uncertainty. We both understand that I'm not solely talking about the task at hand.

He leans over, unfocused gray eyes roaming around the black veil surrounding us. A soft, wrinkled touch falls on my hands, feeling their position. Then, he lets out an amused puff of laughter.

"Everything isn't a weapon, child."

Heat blooms in my cheeks. "It is…a difficult habit to unlearn," I confess.

He says nothing in return. Instead, he slowly readjusts my grip to mirror his own. Then, he turns back to his own work, humming a tune I don't recognize. Something slow and melancholic.

I watch in awe as his fingers move in seasoned motions. Before each stitch, he presses into the fabric with his pads, reading its weaknesses through caress alone. He commits the tactile feedback to memory—the resistance, the wear, the slight give of fiber under pressure. Then he sews. Repeat.

I try to mimic him, and gradually, the silence folds around us once more like a blanket.

"My daughter was like you," he says eventually, the words catching me off guard. There is a gentleness to his voice now, like he's opening a door that has been shut for years. "Always ready to wage war with the world before it could wage war with her."

His words land too close. I feel a tightness rise in my throat, and something hotter stir just beneath it. There's shame in being analyzed so blatantly—and irritation, too.

"The world and I have been at odds from the moment I was born. I'm this way because it refuses to leave me be," I say curtly. The grate in my tone is unintentional, but honest.

All the man does is hum.

The sail's rough canvas feels suddenly heavier in my lap. Another pause passes before *I* decide to break it this time, changing the subject.

"You said *was*," I murmur, eyes still on my stitching. "Your daughter…"

"Fever took her. Ten winters ago, now." His needle doesn't stall in its rhythm, though something in his voice catches. "She would've been about your age, had Sīmìng been kinder."

The mention of the God of Fate sends a shiver through me. I press my lips together, swallowing the anger that stirs. A deity with the power to lengthen or shorten the thread of a human life—and yet, those who bring the most ruin seem to walk untouched, cycle after cycle.

Sympathy feels as hollow as a gutted fish, and pity would be an insult to us both. So, I say nothing. Instead, I focus on my stitches, trying to match his careful pattern while the ship rocks steadily. I fixate on this moment, on learning something that isn't merely about survival, from someone who doesn't seem to want anything from me.

"Tell me about her," I say, surprising myself with the boldness of the request.

Old Chou's face softens, cycles falling away as his mind searches for memories.

"She loved the sea with a passion that would've made Mazu weep."

At the mention of the Goddess's name, something breaks open behind my eyes—a flash of vision, golden, blooming like spilled ink across my mind. I'm no longer seated on the ship.

Instead, I find myself standing at the edge of an underwater precipice, poised above a fathomless abyss. The water around me glows with ethereal light. Shifting, fractured by the shimmering veins of rays from the surface far above.

Beside me must be none other than Mazu.

A towering figure draped in flowing white robes, her form half-concealed by ribbons of seaweed and current that wrap around her like living sashes. Her eyes burn with divine white fire, without iris or pupil, as though the heavens peer out from within her skull. Her lips do not move, but still I hear: *'Summon them.'*

I do not understand the command until several roars come from the black depths below. I look down and see yellow orbs pop up in pairs. There's one, three, eight. Too many to count before the vision tears itself away from me, vanishing as swiftly as it came.

I gasp as reality rushes back in.

My chest feels too small for my lungs. I can feel the pounding of my heart in the back of my throat. I blink hard as the man across from me comes back into clarity. He is still reminiscing as if nothing is amiss, still lost in his memory.

I cling to the sound of his voice, grounding myself in its evenness. I watch his lips part and close, follow the cadence of each word, using them like rope to haul myself back from buoying out at sea—back into my body, back into the now.

"She used to sneak aboard my fishing boat when she was supposed to be helping her mother at the market," he says. "Couldn't keep her away from the water any more than you could tame a tide." He chuckles, the sound is rich. I grasp onto it. "Stubborn as a barnacle, that one. Much like another young woman I know."

I let out a hollow exhale, my breath finally calm. "I can't possibly think of the person you're referring to," I tease gently. My voice is small, weak to my own ears. But he pays no mind as his warm laugh follows.

"Ah, so the little dragon has a tongue for jest after all. Not just claws." He reaches into his salt-stained tunic and pulls out a small flask wrought in beaten copper. "Here. Best cure ever created by mortal men for midnight ramblings and thoughts that take our breath away."

So, he had noticed the change in my mannerisms.

The cereal wine burns going down.

I expect him to continue talking about his daughter, but he seems content with what little he has shared. Instead, he switches to another topic.

"The crew speaks of your fighting style," he says carefully as though testing thin ice. "All quick attacks and survival moves. Effective, but..." he pauses, weighing his next words, "I could teach you some defense techniques I learned long ago. If you've a mind to learn."

It is more than just an offer of combat training—we both know that truth. It's a hand being held out, a connection I haven't allowed myself since... well, ever.

"I…" I swallow roughly, spit caught in the back of my throat. "I'd like that," I say finally, the words feeling foreign.

He nods, satisfied. "Good. You just let me know when you're ready. But first—" he points in the direction of where he'd felt my crooked stitching, "—you're going to learn to mend a sail properly. Can't have my pupil looking like she picked the craft from a drunken monkey in a Formosa tavern."

I chuckle, and for once it doesn't feel like betrayal of some sort.

Though, I will probably deny it in the morning, I allow myself to sit in this moment of peace with someone who looks at me and sees something worth teaching, worth knowing.

"Thank you," I say quietly, not specifying for what exactly.

Old Chou just nods, understanding anyway.

We work together until dawn paints the sky in red and gold, and Goisa emerges from the horizon.

17

DAWN

GOISA PORT, 1800

Instead of the bustling activity expected of a harbor at daybreak, a graveyard of charred ruins expands before us. Blackened skeletons of stalls and houses lean precariously against each other, their bones still smoldering. Wisps of smoke curl upward, dissipating into the sky, while the faint scent of burnt wood and scorched flesh hangs in the breeze.

It had been weeks since Rabbit and his crew escaped, but the sight looks as if the attack had happened merely days ago.

The docks, once lined with vibrant trade ships and lively workers, are nothing more than splintered planks jutting out over the water. And at the center of it all, a singular foreign ship—its sleek, unfamiliar designs stark against the devastation—sits ominously at anchor. The strange flag it bears flaps in the wind. Solid black.

A tangible unease settles over the crew.

Now in good enough condition to walk, Zhèng surveys the scene from the stern deck. His face hardens, the muscles in his jaw flexing as he takes in the destruction and the audacious positioning of the vessel.

"Only one ship," he says aloud. "Heavily armed."

Luo stands beside me, hovering by the bow railing among the rest of the crew as we approach. "They're sending a message," he calls back, tone edged with suspicion. "Burn the town, occupy the port, and let anyone who comes near see what they're capable of."

The captain descends the stairs briskly, crossing the deck in seconds. The gathering of pirates part ways to let him through to the front. "They're daring someone to retaliate," he says coldly. His next words are heavy with promise. "Something they will now regret."

As the ship eases to a stop just outside the harbor, the unnatural silence of the port presses against us. The side of the hull is now facing the foreign ship wading out in the open. Without further preamble, Zhèng lifts his hand in the air before bringing it down swiftly, shouting, "Fire!"

Then, booms of cannon rip through the still air. They smash and break and tear the other ship apart.

Everyone tenses waiting for returning fire, but none comes. Zhèng does not stop the onslaught until the other vessel begins to take on water. We watch with bated breath for any crew jumping ship, but the boat sinks and floods unceremoniously. This makes the pirates even *more* uneasy.

Once satisfied with removing any possibility of escape, Zhèng ceases the attack.

"They must be on land." Luo says.

Zhèng nods. "No matter. They have nowhere to run. Either they flee to the mountains or hide long enough for us to find them." He turns, addressing the crew. "We'll send several small parties ashore," he says, voice calm but commanding. "Luo, Ah Fei, each of you take a handful of others. I will take another. We will find out who these men are and why they're here. Old Chou, you go with Huò. Check if there are any survivors in the town who need aid, anyone who can provide us with more information."

"And if we encounter them?" the co-captain asks. The twinkling of anticipation in his eyes is similar to that of a child given a new toy to play with.

Zhèng's jaw sets. "Then we remind them where they are and who they're dealing with," he responds in a steely grumble.

The crew murmurs their agreement before breaking into their parties. Their vigilance is heightened as they prepare for the mission.

The captain turns to me. "You're staying here."

"Fine by me," I say brazenly. "I had no interest in going."

Normally, I would argue on principle. However, I'm in no mood to die today. *And* I have other plans.

For the past few nights, I've been watching, waiting—timing the perfect moment to slip into the captain's quarters. While fleeing at this port is no longer viable, another chance may present itself soon. And when it does, the compass will be coming with me.

With the captains and most of the crew gone, I can focus on figuring out how to open that drawer without its key.

Possibly with a chopstick… or a knife?

"You didn't let me finish," Zhèng cuts in. "You're staying here—in the brig."

Indignation immediately takes over. "For exactly *what* reason?" I bark.

"Let's just say I can't have you running off or wondering around," he responds. His expression is firm, but in his eyes is thinly veiled mockery.

Shōush. Had he seen me eyeing his movements the other day?

The uneven edges of my fingernails carve moons into my palms. I open my mouth to retort, only to be silenced by a sharp lift of his brow. The warning is clear.

I breathe in slowly, counting to ten. My voice, when it emerges, drips with contempt. "Will anyone *else* be here, or must I defend the boat from the cell *myself*?"

The man gestures over to Rabbit and his crew. Unlike the other mates, they are standing awkwardly, rooted to their initial positions on the deck. It's obvious that they have been left out from any of the other parties.

"You boys stay here and guard the ship," he says. "You've already weathered the wrath of these men. I won't make you face them again if you don't have to."

The boys—and I, though I would never admit it—are taken off guard by the unexpected mercy. But, before Rabbit can respond, the captain pushes past the moment, turning to the waiting search parties. "Make ready," he commands. "The hunt begins."

As they all prepare themselves to disembark, the ship creaks and groans, its timbers sounding almost like a bad omen. A chill runs down my spine, when I'm led away from the group. Something about the stillness feels wrong. The hair on the back of my neck stand on end.

Hours pass by with the search parties off to shore.

I sit cross-legged on the cold, damp floor, tracing patterns in the grime with my fingertip, trying to distract from the gnawing hunger in my stomach.

Ah Fei had better not get himself killed. I was actually looking forward to that fish stew he promised.

Idle chatter from the boys drifts down through the slats. For a moment, I consider calling one of them down—Rabbit, most likely. He'd be the easiest to sway. As he escorted me down here I could tell guilt still clings to him. After all, this cramped brig was also his and his crew's sleeping quarters when they were first captured and forced into mates.

He might just let sentiment get the better of him.

Suddenly—

Muffled sounds of a scuffle break my concentration. I freeze, ears straining. The soft murmurs have stopped abruptly, replaced by heavy, hurried footsteps on the deck. There's a flurry of metal clashing with metal, before an unrecognizable, muffled voice speaks.

"Give us the compass!"

Oh no.

"What compass?" one of the boys shouts shrilly. "We don't know what you're talking about!"

And it's true. These poor boys weren't here when it was confiscated from me. I feel an unbearable pang of fault rip through me.

They don't deserve to die.

"We know that the compass ended up in a port. Hand it over or prepare to cross the Silver Bridge!"

Without thinking, I shout loud and urgent. "Down here, you bastards!"

There's a brief silence. Then, a couple of thuds. My pulse quickens, and my heart fills with dread.

The hatch to the hull swings opens with a creak.

The steady sound of boots descending the stairs fill the brig. Moments later, three men appear, their silhouettes stark against the dim lantern light.

The rival band of pirates I assume. Their weapons are drawn but not splattered with fresh blood. I spare a second to feel relief. Perhaps, the boys aren't dead.

The leader, a tall man with tattoos scattered across his face, leers when he spots me.

"Well, well, well," he taunts. "What do we have here? Looks like we've got ourselves a prize."

My spine goes ridged like an iron blade. I back against the wall of my cell. "I'm nothing special," I rush out. "Just a prisoner looking for a fight apparently." Disbelief wraps around the words, thick with irony. My senses are only now catching up to the weight of my own idiocy.

Godsdamn that pirate, Zhèng. If I die right now, I'm going to haunt him for the rest of his miserable days.

Tattoo-face tilts his head, his leer widening. "A prisoner on Zhèng Yī's ship? I doubt that. What's he hiding with you, eh?" He gestures to his men. "Open it up."

One of the pirates moves to cut down the lock. When the cell is open, Tattoo-face's hand extends toward me, the air around him shifts. Shadows seeps from his fingertips, curling unnaturally. The tendrils slither toward me, and I feel an invisible force wrapping around my body, freezing me in place.

I knew it.

My throat closes as panic surges. Just like every time before, I can't move. Not even blink.

Tattoo-face lets out a vicious chuckle. "Deliciously perverse, isn't it? I could do whatever I wanted to you right now, and you wouldn't be able to do a thing about it."

The shadow tightens its grip, and I feel my thoughts slipping away, my vision clouding.

But then, deep within, the feeling stirs again.

A flicker of heat rises from my core. The briny scent of the sea fills my nostrils, and a distant roar, like waves crashing against a cliff, echo in my ears.

Through my eyes, all I can see is blinding light. But, somewhere in my mind, the scene is projected from afar, as if I'm watching from above.

The hold of the black essence weakens.

"What—" Tattoo-face mutters, his smirk vanishing.

The atmosphere around me begins to crackle and pulse. A surge of power and light bursts from me, a tidal wave unleashed. The shadow disintegrates with a hiss, and the man staggers back, clutching his head.

The lanterns swing wildly as the ship shakes violently. A deafening crack splits the brig's wooden wall allowing seawater to gush through the breach. Currents of it rush into the cell and begin to surround me in a sphere, as if creating a barrier of protection.

Outside the cell, the other pirates stumble, shouting in confusion. One tries to grab me, but the water rushing into the brig lashes out, as if sentient, slamming him into the far wall with a fatal crack of his spine. The third man tries to escape but is tugged down by a tendril of water wrapping around his leg. He is dragged beneath the depths and held there until he drowns.

Tattoo-face screams as the energy overwhelms him, his body convulsing and contorting grotesquely before he crumples beneath the waves, lifeless.

Above deck, the shouts of returning crew echoes.

In seconds, Zhèng and Luo drop down into the brig, water up to their waists with swords drawn. They stop short at the sight of me.

"Gods…" Zhèng rasps, voice barely audible above the roar in my ears.

My gaze follows the sound, and then the light fades.

As if sensing the threat has passed, the water begins to recede, draining slowly back to sea. I collapse into it, the protective barrier that had held firm around me finally giving way. My clothes cling wetly to my skin as tremors seize my limbs, my body betraying the fear I'd kept at bay.

Luo wades forward with deliberate care. "Shi Yang," he says softly, "what… happened?"

"I—I don't know," I whisper, voice fraying. "They were looking for it. They were going to kill the boys. Maybe they already have." The words stumble out, disjointed and frantic. My thoughts are knotted, fighting to find order. Pain throbs at my temples as I try to make sense of it all. "I couldn't stop it. It—it just…" I look up at them, my head suddenly heavy. "What is happening to me?"

Neither man has an answer for me. I don't expect them to, but still… a part of me wishes that they did.

Zhèng lowers his sword, the metal sliding quietly into its sheath. He steps toward me, slowly.

I flinch back. “Don’t come any closer. I don’t know if I can control—”

I don’t get to finish the warning.

He kneels beside me, then slips one arm beneath my knees, the other around my back. I tense instinctively, but he remains silent—just lifts me as though I weigh nothing at all and begins wading through the water with determination. The rush drains from my body like the sea water from the brig. My limbs go numb, my vision blurs at the edges. I barely register the motion as we move through the half-flooded chamber, and up toward the light.

By the time we reach the deck, exhaustion has claimed me.

PART THREE:
MANTIS

18

TEN CYCLES AGO

KWANGCHOW PORT, 1790

Another one of us has vanished. I wonder who will be next.

I tighten the bandage around my ribs, wincing as the fabric presses against an aching bruise. The pain is dull but persistent, pulsing with each breath. My knuckles fare no better—split, bloodied, and raw from the scuffle. Every flex sends a fresh wave of heat through my hand.

I reach for the strip of cloth, soaking it in the harsh local spirit I lifted earlier.

The vendor hadn't taken kindly to the theft. Neither had I to him.

I got lucky. Any bigger man would've surely been an issue.

I wince again.

I took what I needed. That's all that matters.

A sigh leaves my lips as I press the cloth to my hand, teeth clenched against the sting. My thoughts drift—inevitably—back to the disappearances.

When the first of us went missing, majority of the villagers were certain it was the doing of land-dwellers. A belief that, ostensibly, makes sense.

The hostility toward nomadic lives has long simmered beneath a fragile surface. Their resentment for us breeds from many things out of our control. Mostly the widening chasm between the mean and good populace.

The promises of Pingshen's prosperity have proven as hollow as the bellies of the Bloomers now slumped along the alleys. And yet, it is we—those relegated to the water—who find ourselves at the receiving end of the townsfolk's growing discontent. We try to keep to ourselves, as we always have, but the decay has made boundaries porous.

Still, despite all their contempt—despite the whispers, the slurs, the beatings—their hatred has never crossed the threshold of the shore. Whatever holds them back, be it fear, superstition, or shame, it is a force stronger than their derision. And I find it hard to believe they would abandon that restraint without grave provocation.

Or at least I think.

"Come on! It's almost time!"

The sound of feet shifting on wood snaps me out of thought. Voices rise across the water as younger Hokans begin steering their sampans to the center of the beach. At the end of their destination lies one of the larger vessels in the floating village, one that houses the clan's Elders. Its worn wood is stained dark brown by both the sea's grime and the weight of generations. On its deck, basked in the glowing light of burning candles, sits our Eldermother.

Once, the stories she spun beneath the stars were tales of the past—of tempests, of spirits, and seasons we could barely imagine. Lately, however, the clan gathers not for comfort, but for answers. Hoping that somewhere in those ancient narratives lies a reason for the disappearances… or a way to stop them.

A low grunt draws my attention back to our egg boat. Ba shifts upright, still groggy, his bronzed face creased with suspicion. I tense, preparing myself for whatever his next move may be.

He does not speak right away. Just glares at me then clicks his tongue. "Well, don't just sit there," he mutters. "Take us to the meeting."

For a moment, I consider ignoring the demand. Forgo attending all together, forcing him to steep in his *ripe* bitterness while the community gathers without us. But… curiosity claws at my insides. The Elders may not have the answers we seek—but if they don't, who, or *what*, does?

My gaze drifts briefly to the open water behind us.

The sea has always been more than a home; it is a living force—sacred, beautiful, and unpredictable. Perhaps Mazu has taken the vanished for some slight or another.

I think back to *that* night cycles ago. A conversation not intended for my ears.

Perhaps she'd heard the hurried words spoken amongst some members, filled with regret. Comments that questioned whether turning away from the Great Ascent was a mistake. Whether we had dishonored our place in the world by choosing to stay buoyed. Tethered. Small.

Ba clears his throat. It's pointed. Antagonizing.

I turn to him once more, studying the lines on his face—the way they tighten under my scrutiny. I hold his stare just a moment past what's comfortable, until his posture wilts. The illusion of authority fractures.

He tries, sometimes, to act as if nothing has changed. That I still fear the clench of his fists. That his words still carry weight.

But he knows better.

He remembers.

His *body* remembers.

My hands made sure of that.

He only speaks to me the way he does because I allow it. And he knows this, too.

Still, I move to the rudder, inquisitiveness outweighing spite, just this once.

The boat rocks gently beneath us as I set our course toward the great vessel where everyone gathers. Behind me, I hear Ba release a quiet breath of relief. Despite the weight in my chest, and the ache in my fingers and abdomen, a dark amusement tugs at the corner of my mouth.

By the time we reach the meeting, the others have already anchored their sampans and boarded the larger ship. I bring our boat to a gentle stop at the edge of the cluster, letting the sandbag drop to hold us in place. From this distance, I can just make out the low murmur of conversation drifting across the water.

It's understood—without needing to be said aloud—that I'm not welcome any closer. Some believe I'm not Hokan. That my mother was a foreigner from a faraway land, maybe a slave woman brought here by Traders from the west. Somewhere farther than The Untamed. The others, who do not care about me much at all… well, they see no point in challenging them. Either way, the mystery surrounding my appearance has convinced just about everyone that I carry ill fortune.

On the deck, they sit close together, circled around small clay bowls of fire. The scent of charred fish permeates the air as the Eldermother begins to speak, her voice rising and falling like the tidal flow.

Once, like the rest of the young, I clung to her words as something sacred. A tether to something ancient and enduring.

But now, they just sound like hollow fables.

"In the beginning," she intones, "the Gods walked among us. They moved through the world as we do now." She lifts her gaze to the darkening sky, face aglow with reverence. "Mazu, our great sea goddess, watched over her people. Her hair was a curtain of black silk, her hands clear as the purest water. She stilled storms, led lost sailors home, and blessed the faithful with calm seas." She motions toward the waves with her gnarled fingers. "The ocean was her cradle, and we—her children."

A timid voice, almost uncertain, breaks through the din. "Are we not still her children?"

A few cycles ago, interrupting an Elder would be met with censure. However, this time, all gazes fix their eyes on the Eldermother expectantly.

We have all heard these stories more times than we can count. But, with the world collapsing around us, the old tales no longer feel like enough. We *need* answers—something more tangible than legend. A reason to believe that Mazu even cares at all.

Does she still watch over us, or has she turned away in our hour of greatest need? Can we hope for salvation, or is the fading of our people as certain—and as indifferent—as the rising and setting of the sun?

The Eldermother squirms under the scrutiny, unfamiliar with not being defended immediately. But she recovers, peering through the curling smoke to find the source of the heckler.

"The Gods have grown weary of us," she says clipped, "or perhaps we grow too *bold*."

I can feel her reproach even from a distance. However, it does nothing to quell the other speaker's discontent.

"So, that's it?" the same voice asks. "We are left on our own with no sign from her? No explanation to go on past what you conjure up?"

The speaker steps forward—a man roughly twenty cycles older than me, one of our seasoned fishers. His boat is usually moored three vessels from Ba's. He's also one of many to have lost a member of their family.

His challenge ignites a ripple of dissent. Voices multiply, layered and chaotic. A storm of fear and desperation builds, swelling with every word.

Thwack, thwack, thwack!

Three sharp cracks of the Eldermother's cane against the deck cut through the noise. She stands tall despite the tremble in her limbs, her eyes burning fiercely.

"Silence, all of you!" she roars. "Serving Mazu is the reason you weren't slaughtered in the war that devoured the mainland! That is the only reason you're even alive to complain! You would do well to remember that!"

The rebuke doesn't fully extinguish the fire in the crowd. Before the unrest can boil over again, another nameless Elder in the Council raises a hand. As he stands, I recognize him as one of the more reserved members—his two sweeping white eyebrows the only ostentatious thing about him.

The Council of Elders is composed of four enigmatic figures, with the Eldermother presiding at their head. Their names have long been forgotten—or perhaps deliberately cast aside. When they pledged themselves to the sacred duty of guiding the community, they relinquished all personal identity. To serve the whole, they became no one.

Their role is not to lead in the way Ba and the other men in the clan do. Rather, they oversee those leaders—guarding the balance, interpreting omens, and ensuring that the old ways and knowledge are neither lost nor misused.

They have never truly stepped off the deck of the Council ship, even when consulting with the Hebosuo or Imperial guards. No. They stay rooted upon that boat as it drifts at the center of the floating village like a beating heart—part shrine, part courtroom, part tomb.

"I hear your pain," he says, voice steadier than the Eldermother's. "We have long told you that prayer is the only way to reach Mazu. But that… was not the entire truth."

Puzzlement ripples through the assembly. The Eldermother makes a high pitched noise in protest.

"What do you think you're doin—"

The Elder looks to her, his expression stone. "It is time they know the history we refused to tell."

A shiver passes through the crowd. We know what this means. The lines that are being crossed.

The secrets of our people—the ones never written, only spoken—reside with the Council. They are the keepers of the forbidden stories, the forgotten rites, and the true histories buried beneath generations of suppression. By sacred custom, these truths aren't ours to know. The Elders are sworn to secrecy, and we are expected to obey without question. That is the balance our way of life rests upon. At the end of the day, their word is not debated. It is law.

But... what is law in the face of uncertainty, chaos, and grief?

Nothing.

"It is true that the Gods withdrew long ago," he continues. "They left their temples and vanished into the heavens or the mountains, into the depths. Into silence." He closes his eyes and breathes deeply. "But they did not depart before leaving...*marks* on the world."

This incites a chorus of confusion in the group. I sit upright in my boat.

"What kind of marks?" another voice asks.

The Eldermother's lips pull into a withering line, stretched thin with bearing unwelcome truths. "The divining children," she starts.

The group falls silent. Faces turn toward her like plants to the sun.

"They are referred to as Jítóng. They are chosen by the Gods, born with a thread of the divine in their veins. Thin as spider silk, but unbreakable. Because of the war, when the Gods have something to say, they do not appear in glory or descend from the Heavens. They speak through the Jítóng—borrowing the mortal body."

Some of the children aboard let out a soft chorus of gasps and "oohs" in amazement. But the Eldermother cuts their imagination short with a raised hand.

"Do not be mistaken, it is not a gift of any sort," she adds quietly. "It is a burden few survive."

"Why now?" comes an abrupt question from a young adult. Betrayal bleeds from his words. "Why speak of this only when our future darkens? Why did you not tell us before?"

She turns to him, regret awash across her face. Moments pass before she clasps her hands before her.

"It was not my secret to tell," she says in resolution. "The knowledge of the Jítóng has been carefully branched and guarded for generations, passed down through the Wave Kin clans. It is entrusted only to the Elders, each bound by an ancient oath sworn to Mazu herself. They are secret weapons no mortal was supposed to know of. A pact between the Gods that Mazu broke for *us*."

Threads of this new information loop and tangle in my mind.

Why would Mazu reveal this? What could we possibly do with this information? Wouldn't just knowing this put us in harm's way?

"Such truths are like pearls hidden deep within the sea—not to be retrieved until the tides demand their surfacing," she continues. "To speak of them without just cause risks more than curiosity. It risks the wrath of Founding Gods themselves, their ire falling not just upon the bearer of the truth, but upon all our people. That is why no single clan holds all the pieces of this information. Knowledge divided is knowledge preserved, a shield against those who would wield it for ruin."

Then, her eyes flick with to the other Elder man who brought this confession about. He only nods unflinchingly in return. That small gesture drains the rest of her resolve.

"But…" she exhales. "I fear that the Jítóng are being summoned."

Even more confusion and fear sweeps through the group.

"So, what? Everyone who has disappeared is a Jítóng for Mazu? *That* many of us are divining children?" a girl my age asks.

Eldermother shakes her head, a grim expression marring her face. "I do not know, child. The amount of Jítóngs that still walk the earth is information not left with our clan." Her eyes sweep over the group, taking in anxious faces. "However, something within my qì tells me that what is happening to us is not Mazu's doing. No, whoever is calling them—whoever is *taking* them—does not know exactly *who* the divining children are, but they know of their existence. They are being sought, and our members are becoming collateral."

My thoughts are drawn back to that hidden hushed conversation from the past once more. The head of the Lo family who had organized the meeting had mentioned a war coming to the nomads, of a supposed army building in the shadows.

Had this been what he meant? Were we being drafted into something we were not prepared for thanks to the Elders? Or, are we being punished for knowing what we shouldn't?

Sweat collects on my palms as panicked voices begin to surface, and children begin to whimper.

The Eldermother does not wait for the noise to settle before speaking again. "For many cycles," she calls out, "I hoped this day would never come. I'd hoped that my intuition was wrong, that our lives might remain simple, untouched by divine intervention. But the omens have grown too strong to ignore."

The young adult from earlier shakes his head, his voice broken and raw. "But surely you knew the risks of waiting. What if—what if we needed this knowledge sooner? What if we knew the signs to look for and could've escaped elsewhere before they disappeared?"

Under the chastisement, the Eldermother's small shoulders sag. "I asked myself the same questions, over and over, for cycles. With every instance of disappearance, I wondered if the time had come. But the Gods do not speak plainly, and I dared not act until the signs were unmistakable. I could not risk the wrath they would unleash if I was wrong."

A heavy quiet settles over the assembly, suffocating all attempts at conversation. It isn't until another young child speaks, that the quiet of the group is broken.

"How do we know if someone is a Jítóng?" the boy asks, voice wavering as if he half-expects to be named.

The Eldermother's expression softens slightly. "The signs are not always clear, but I will tell you what I know," she says cautiously.

I lean closer unconsciously, rocking the sampan without care.

"It is said that it begins with dreams—visions that feel too vivid to be your own. A voice that speaks to the Jítóng in the silence. Not from the world around you, but from the tie to the divine within," she shares. "And when the God is ready to speak through the Jítóng, it is not their own actions but those of the Heavens itself that flows through."

I swallow hard, my chest tightening as my eyes fixate on the shifting flames at the center of the deck.

A Jítóng.

A child chosen by the Gods.

The idea feels almost too big, too strange, to fit inside my head. I try to picture it—a man or woman. A body that commands storms, moves mountains, or brings the dead to heel.

A person turned into a vessel without having a single say in whether they wanted to become one. It sounds like a nightmare dressed as divinity. How is that fair to them? To any of us?

I can feel my hands trembling with the first cracks of fury. The raw rage building in my chest is dampened when the distraction of Ba's voice breaks though the hush.

"What happens to them?" he shouts loud enough to cover the distance.

Yes. What happens after they've been hollowed out and used like kindling for a God's will? What becomes of the body once the divine no longer needs it? I would love to know.

The others shift where they sit, turning their heads toward us from across the water. The Elders' faces darken when they catch sight of me. For a heartbeat, I think the Eldermother might refuse to answer simply because the question came from Ba—and by extension, from me.

But she does.

"I—I do not know," she admits at last, voice breaking.

I can see her lip quiver, firelight carving deep shadows into her weathered features.

Nothing more is said. Eventually, the fires burn low. One by one, the others slip back to their egg boats, their shadows folding into the dark.

Ba doesn't bark at me to row us back to our usual spot. The meeting has soured his temper. Instead, he drinks more wine from his chipped jug, then slumps into a deep slumber, snoring soon after.

Torches go out as nightfall reclaims the sky. The waves lap gently at the hulls, soft and endless, as everyone tucks away for bedtime. However, I stay seated, eyes fixed upward. The stars move slowly, as if indifferent to the mess unfolding beneath them.

I think. I seethe.

Do I believe the Eldermother? No. She's lying. She has to be. Also, why would I trust any of the Elders? Their inabilities to make the right decisions when needed have damned us to this reality.

I let out a harsh puff of air through my nose.

And yet—even if they are lying or telling truths, it's not like knowing for certain would make our situation any less unfortunate.

I lean back until the cold of the planks seeps into my shoulders.

I need to find out what happened the Lo family. What the head knew and how. What happened to his son…

These thoughts gnaw at me for hours, however, one in particular truly takes root.

The Gods must be out there watching. Doing nothing. Or worse—doing it all. Either way, it is something I don't think I will ever forgive.

19

PRESENT DAY

GOISA PORT, 1800

The first thing that registers is that I'm lying down. Next, is the mat beneath me. It does little to cushion the hardness of what I assume is a wooden floor. My head pounds as though it's been smashed with a rock ten times over. I want to grip my head or massage my temples, but just the thought of the slightest movement is enough to make me nauseous. Slowly, the aroma of incense fills my nostrils, overflowing with traces of tea leaves.

I know that smell.

My eyes, heavier than they have been in a long time, open gingerly. The sight to greet me is one I would not usually be happy to see.

Zhèng leans against the front of his desk, arms and ankles crossed. A snuff pipe dangles from his lips, smoke wafting up toward the ceiling. Though his expression lacks its usual intensity, there's still that calculation that never quite rests in his eyes.

Behind him, lounging in the captain's chair with one leg propped and crossed at the ankle, sits Luo. He toys idly with the dagger he lent me weeks ago, letting it turn between long fingers. The blue glass marbling of the handle glints in the dim lantern light. When his gaze finds mine, a small, unguarded smile tugs at the corner of his mouth.

"Ah, and she's back with the living, I see," he says lightly.

I roll my eyes instinctively and instantly regret it. A bolt of pain sears through my skull, forcing a low groan from my throat. I decide to take the risk and bring my fingers up to my temple to ease the pain.

If I vomit, at least it's in Zhèng's bed and not my own. Small victories. And speaking of that…

"What am I doing here?" I rasp, voice dry and rough-edged.

Zhèng doesn't answer immediately. He exhales a slow stream of smoke, then removes the pipe with practiced ease.

"How are you feeling?" he asks instead.

"Like I took a round-trip visit to all eighteen levels of Dì Yù itself."

He nods, unsurprised. "Thought so."

He taps out the remainder of the snuff into a copper ashtray and lets out a quiet cough, more from habit than discomfort. When he turns back to me, his expression sharpens.

"Do you remember anything that happened before you woke up?"

The moment he asks, it all rushes back—the blinding light, the waves, the surge of power. The memory strikes like a thunderclap, leaving phantom echoes rippling through my limbs. My hands squeeze the blanket. I look between them both, my brow drawn tight.

"I remember," I say slowly. "But… I don't know how."

I try to sit up, hoping movement might settle the chaos in my mind, but it only stirs more unease. The room tilts slightly. There's a war unfurling in my head—between wonder and dread.

These powers saved my life. Twice now. That should be a comfort. But it isn't.

A sinking feeling settles in the bottom of my stomach.

Because having them means possessing the one thing I have never wanted.

The captain must sense it—the impending spiral.

"Settle," he says, voice gentler than expected. "We are just going to talk, okay?" He uncrosses his arms and gestures to the room like it's neutral ground. "Start from the beginning. Tell us everything you remember."

Giving a small nod, I recite my memory. My voice stays steady until I reach the moment the pirate began Wielding his shadow. Then, Zhèng cuts in.

"Describe the Wielding. Exactly as it happened." His eyes are fixed entirely on me.

I hesitate—the recollection of the moment unenjoyable—before responding.

"He was cloaked in black smoke," I say finally. "It moved like it was sentient. And when he grabbed me, I couldn't move. Not even to breathe. It was as if he was *inside* of me, wearing my body like a garment, forcing it to obey."

Zhèng straightens.

My eyes narrow in accusation. "You know what it is, don't you?"

Luo sighs, dropping his feet to the floor. "Are you familiar with shadow puppetry?"

The question jars me. My forehead creases. "You mean the paper opera shows? With the cut-outs and the strings?"

I think back to Heavenly Liberation celebrations in the past. I used to sneak ashore to see them, pressed into the alleyways out of sight. Much of the entertainment consisted of opera, often in the form of local puppet troupes. The art form always included music, song, ritual, marital arts. Anything you could think of. Most of the time, it told cautionary tales of Heaven and its Gods, or re-enacted the Great Ascent, retelling mortals' victory to children. Other times, they were little more than propaganda for the Emperor's favor. *Those* shows weren't nearly as interesting.

"Sometimes they use rods," the co-captain adds off-handedly.

I level him with a dispassionate stare. "Who cares? I know of them. What does that have to do with *anything*?"

"Well, they aren't just about entertainment. To many, they reflect the belief in a liminal world: shadows are attached to the natural, but only visible because of Heavens' light. Thus, they prove there is a space between the Corporal World and the Astir one. A world of shadows that directly reflects reality. And someone," he hesitates, "or *something*, has figured out how to breach that space. To control it. And apparently, to drag others into it. These pirates… someone has given them the ability to Wield shadows. To control another's movement, bending their will, and consequently, their qì."

"Like puppets," I say in a daze.

Luo nods once. "Like puppets."

My pulse picks up a beat as the information registers. I eye both men suddenly cautious.

Why do they know so much? Do they possess the skill? No. They couldn't possibly. If they did, I'm sure they would've used it on me weeks ago. However, one could never truly know for sure…

Before I can voice the suspicion, Luo raises his hands in mock surrender. "Before you go trying to kill us all in our sleep—*no*. Neither of us Wields shadows. No one aboard does."

If I feel even a flicker of relief, I bury it.

"This shouldn't be possible," I murmur. "You can't Wield someone else's qì." But even as I say it, my thoughts stray—back to Madam Lín. The flowerboat.

There are always loopholes. And people who know how to use them.

"Why didn't you say anything before now?" I press.

Zhèng shifts, the line of his jaw tightening. "It's… complicated. Those pirates had ties to… forces I'm sure you're not familiar with."

"Well, what *kind* of forces?" I ask, losing patience. "Because I think it's connected to all of this—my powers, the compass, everything. And if that's true, we can't afford to keep sailing carelessly. Not if we're following that thing to Gods know where."

Zhèng opens his mouth, hesitates, then looks to Luo. The co-captain gives the barest shake of his head.

That's it.

"If I'm supposed to trust you," I snap, "then you need to trust me. Or do you still think this is some kind of game? Is my life that disposable to you?"

Luo's gaze intensifies. "Of course, we don't think that," he says flatly. But beneath the statements is something apprehensive. "You have to understand… we're speaking of powers that don't just corrupt—they consume. Once you're revealed to them, there's no hiding."

"Well, I think it's far too late for that," I bite back. "They've already found me. Twice!"

I'm getting closer to understanding what happened to my clan. What happened to the Lo family. I will not let them stand in the way of that retribution if they have information I need.

Zhèng steps closer to me. "Twice?"

Shōush.

I take a breath, preparing myself for what comes next.

"The night you found me stowed away on that trade ship… I had killed a man. A captain of the Imperial Navy," I confess.

A quiet settles in the cabin. The sound of the wind keening against the hull sounds almost too loud.

"That's where I found the compass," I continue. "It was on his person. He was no pirate, but he was just like the men I encountered. Wielding his shadow. And mine."

When I look at Luo, he is bewildered. Zhèng, however, seems like he's just heard a ghost story.

When he regains his composure, his face is steadfast. He stands up from his position, rounding the table. Once he reaches Luo, he signals him to vacate the seat.

"Up."

However, he does not wait for the co-captain to fully remove himself before his hands gravitate to his waist, lifting, then shifting him out of the way.

Interesting.

Like a man on a mission, he hefts the heavy wood chair and marches over to the cabin door. He then wedges it beneath the doorknob. Once he deems it secure, he makes his way back over to me, taking a seat on the mat. I shift back, slightly thrown off by the flurry of movement.

He takes a deep breath before speaking.

"I'm going to tell you something that no one but the people in this room know. You will not repeat it to anyone unless explicitly told to do so, understand?"

It's a statement, and not at all a question, but I answer anyways.

"Yes, under one stipulation. No more secrets or hiding."

Zhèng nods his head. "You have my word."

I study his expression, but it only reads as sincere.

I'll have to just believe that I suppose.

Luo only responds with an empty smile. Not a yes or a no.

I roll my eyes before I turn back to the captain, gesturing him to begin.

"I wasn't always a pirate," he starts. His gaze is fixated somewhere in the past. Scarred knuckles rest on his knees, tracing invisible patterns into the worn tunic.

He seems tormented, and I'm not *entirely* a sadist.

"You don't have to tell me," I say, though the curiosity in my chest burns.

He ignores the out.

"I was always meant to command a fleet. That was my father's plan." He exhales deeply, like the thought itself is a burden pressing down on his ribs. "I… grew up in the Imperial Navy. Stationed at the Base 3 fortress," he swallows, "I was surrounded by men who only saw the world in orders and punishments. My father was a decorated general, and he made sure I would follow in his shadow. I wasn't given a choice."

I knew I had recognized his military boots that time in the brig.

My eyes dance around his face. I've never seen this side of him… it is fascinating just as much as it is off-putting. The confession makes him look cycles older than what I think he is.

The man who cuts through enemies with a sword and a glint in his eye seems a world apart from the man before me.

"By the time I was thirteen, I could take down any man in hand-to-hand combat. My instructors called me a prodigy. They taught me how to fight with a blade, spear, anything I could get my hands on. And when I wasn't fighting, I was learning strategy—how to command, how to win. They weren't raising a boy; they were forging a weapon."

"And you were good at it," I supplement. He doesn't strike me as someone who's ever failed at much.

"Too good," he replies.

His eyes return to mine, and for the first time, I notice that there are flecks of amber in the pools of dark brown. More than that, there's something else in there—regret, maybe, or shame.

"By the time I reached twenty summers, I had my own fleet. I thought I'd made it, that the sacrifices of my childhood, of my happiness, meant something. But then... I saw what the Navy really was."

I lean forward. "What do you mean?"

Zhèng pauses as if saying the words will summon him back to the past. "Once you reach a certain rank, you are inducted into a secret military order. The Order of the Dragon." He begins to shrug off his top, exposing his broad chest.

"What are you doing…" I ask, voice dying off as he turns his torso to show me the scarred tattoo on his back. The fire from the oil jars had seared the skin, but most of the design can still be made out. My eyes roam over every detail.

"I've seen this dragon before," I breathe, "in a dream I had the second day I was on this ship."

The look on his face is grim as he secures his top. "What was it doing? Where was it?"

I close my eyes trying to recall the dream as clearly as I can. "I was on a beach and then a battlefield," I relay, voice still hoarse. "On one side, people—Wielders. They bent the ocean to their will," I hesitate, "similar to what I did earlier."

Without a word Luo holds out a water skin in front of me. I hadn't even noticed that he got up. I take it from him gingerly, and down its contents.

I whisper a small gratitude before continuing. "But on the other side, it was carnage; an inferno. The army that emerged from the disaster were shadow Wielders and creatures much more monstruous." My face contorts in disgust at the memory. "Just like the pirates at the port and the naval captain, their shadows sprouted from them like branches on trees. They followed the command of a shadowed dragon in the sky. And above the creature the Heavens fractured, displaying Founding Gods in confrontation as well. It ended with the shadow dragon attempting to swallow me whole."

When I open my eyes again, the men before me wear unreadable expressions. Zhèng rubs his eyes as if a sudden, vicious ache makes home in his mind. But he continues to share what he knows.

"The tattoo is what you must receive to be initiated. That dragon is the symbol of the Zhì Gāo, a personification of what The Order believes will be the highest-level Wielder. It's what they worship. A deity to be shaped by mortal desires, tasked with channeling power even greater than that of the Gods for their own will.

"With foreign enemies like The Other taking interest in the awakening power of aetherbloom, their territorial ambitions grow stronger. And it doesn't help that the Emperor's edict against trade and usage of aetherbloom has only incited further hostility with The Untamed. The country is unstable and on the brink of war. We are beyond vulnerable. Furthermore, any attack that comes *will* do so from the sea. The members of The Order have convinced themselves that the only defense we have against multiple foreign adversaries lies in the Zhì Gāo." Suddenly, his eyes shift downward. "But The Order couldn't wait around for the being to reveal itself. So, they began to take matters into their own hands as they established a shadow Wielding army."

He looks like he's about to be sick with the memory. There is an uncomfortable churn in my stomach as well.

"It started with rumors—whispers of prisoners vanishing after being captured during raids. Pirates, dissidents to the Emperor, and the like. No trials, no executions. At first, I dismissed it as idle gossip. But then, one night, I saw it with my own eyes."

A chill snakes down my spine. "What happened to them?"

"I'd spotted a group of officers escorting prisoners toward a secluded section of the fortress. Their faces were hollow, eyes shimmering with the glaze of aetherbloom withdrawal. So, I followed. At first, there was nothing but muffled voices," he says, shaking his head. "But then came the screams. Raw, inhuman."

Dread settles in my stomach.

"I remember a dark figure moving through an ominous haze. Prisoners writhed on the floor, their shadows twisting unnaturally. Many died in the process. But… the ones that survived… those men were swallowed by darkness, their bodies contorting into deformed shapes before emerging as something else entirely—like puppets controlled by a master."

Master.

My mind races back to the pirate during the raid in Kwangchow and the naval captain in Beifo. Both of them spoke of a Master.

A puppet master.

Zhèng continues. "They made them into something unnatural. Something unstoppable. The prisoners were just a test. The higher officers were surely next. So, I told my father what I had seen. We knew we couldn't stay. But they don't let commanders or generals just walk away—not with what we'd seen and knew."

"So, you ran."

"We defected," he corrects. "I took my fleet with me, every man I could convince. Most didn't follow, too scared of what the empire would do to them. But I wouldn't stay. Not for that."

"And your father?" I ask.

"He pirated for a while," he says. "Then, he took another route."

He doesn't elaborate further. A hush falls between us as I process this information. The more my mind churns, the angrier I get.

So, these shadowed soldiers eradicated my clan on the order of this Master. But why? Could it be true that it was in search of Jítóngs? Could they have been taken to Base 3? I need to find a way to make Zhèng take me there. And soon.

"I intend to find this *Master*," I whisper, the words tasting bitter on my tongue, "and kill him."

Zhèng's irises flitter between mine. Whatever he sees seems to satisfy him.

"I would expect nothing less of you."

He gets up, retrieving the chair from the door. When he heads back to his desk, he passes Luo on the way. The other man looks like he's at war with himself. I don't have enough care within me to push him to speak, so I let him stew silently.

"Get some rest," Zhèng says, his tone transforming him back to the persona I'm used to—calm, commanding, and distant.

I bristle at the demand, but lie down nonetheless. Everything I've just learned has only exacerbated the throbs in my skull.

Perhaps laying down isn't such a bad idea.

Before I allow my body to relax into slumber, I find myself asking, "What did I look like? When you came to the brig?"

"The brig was destroyed, flooding. And yet, there you were encased in water, unharmed, curls swirling around you like a concentrated tempest." There's a tinge of awe laced in the anecdote. "Your eyes and hands glowed with a yellow light so bright I thought we'd lose our sight. When you looked at us, it was like you were seeing *through* us."

I take the description in.

"I couldn't see you," I say. "I only saw light until it faded. It was like I was blind." I shuffle uncomfortably. "And the energy within seemed like it had a mind of its own. I couldn't contain it or control it." I grimace thinking about the hole I left in the brig. "I felt like a monster."

At this, Luo finally snaps out of whatever trance he's in. He looks me straight in the eyes, and says, "You were ethereal."

Then, he stalks out the cabin, door whining closed behind him.

I sleep in the captain's quarters for two days.

I'm not sure where he goes in the meantime, but I only catch glimpses of him in between bouts of sleep, when he occasionally comes in to bring me food or grab a fresh tunic. The solitude is nice. Being left alone with my thoughts allows me to re-evaluate some things.

Zhèng and his ilk are no longer a priority of mine. At least not as much I'd initially considered. There's little reason to believe any of them are part of this illusive shadow legion. But I'm still plagued by why they would be collecting and transporting aetherbloom given Zhèng's knowledge of what it could lead to if in the wrong hands. If his objective was to destroy every trace of it, we would've been ordered to dump it overboard a moon ago.

He needs it for something. But, for what? Who?

I let my mind wander back to the conversation I overheard several days ago.

Zhèng had said that the 'cargo' needed to reach Ningbao port. The Heavenly Liberation Festival is now only four moons away. And we are nowhere near the Imperial Straight that leads to the city.

My mind tampers with the ambiguity of the 'cargo' he could be talking about. It could be anything; the drug, the compass, or…

Me?

There's a knock at the door.

I wipe at my eyes to rid of any sleep left in the corners and tug a quick hand through my mess of ringlets. I haven't washed up since I was transferred here. I hope whoever's visiting doesn't think I smell as much as I do.

"Come in," I shout.

The door creaks open to reveal Huò. As he steps into the cabin, a faint scent of herbs and seawater cling to his person. His thick frame is cloaked in a threadbare robe, and his hands carry a wooden box marked with strange, flowing script.

"Captain's orders," he says friendly. "Let's make sure you're recovering properly."

I oblige, pulling my knees close to my chest on the edge of the mat. He kneels beside me, opening his box to reveal an assortment of tinctures, bandages, and odd tools. With expertise, he takes my wrist and presses two fingers against my pulse.

"You've been through a lot," Huò says, his gaze softening as he studies my face. "But you're strong. You'll be fine, as long as you keep—"

"I feel fine now." I cut in. And honestly, I do. Yes, all that energy consuming my body at once *was* draining, but I notice nothing now. All I want to do is make sure that this boat makes it to Base 3. Quickly.

He looks at me with disbelief, before his face slides into a soft chuckle.

"Of course you are." He shakes his head. "Just let me make sure, you impossible woman."

He examines my hands and checks my breathing. When he hands me a small vial of bitter liquid, he offers an encouraging wave of his hand. "Drink this. It will help with your strength."

I take it without protest. The bitterness lingers on my tongue as he packs up his kit and rises to his feet. "If you need anything," he says, "just ask. Don't hesitate, alright?"

For a moment, his kindness leaves me speechless. I nod, and he gives me a reciprocating one before stepping out, his footfalls light against the planks.

Not long after, my second visitor arrives. Old Chou enters. In his left hand he lugs two metal buckets—one filled with clean water that's stacked in an empty one. In the other rests a bundle of fresh bed and clothing linens. His aged face lifts into a warm smile when he hears my greeting.

"Ah, there you are," he says. "Figured you might appreciate a clean bucket and some fresh linens."

I flush.

I knew they would be able to smell me.

I sit up straighter as he sets the buckets down near the door and places the linens at the foot of the mat. His movements are slow and careful, as if he's looking out for a wayward child.

"The captain's been keeping an eye on you, but it doesn't hurt to have a little extra comfort," he adds with a smirk. "Now, let's make sure you're settled."

He busies himself swapping out the soiled bucket and arranging the linens neatly. As he works, he chats in an easy, familiar tone. "The brig's fixed now," he says, almost as an afterthought. "Set the crew to immediately patch it up that night," he hesitates a moment before continuing, "not that we'll be needing it anymore."

It is a timid truce; possibly an invitation to become a permanent fixture in the canvas of this unruly crew. I do not know if I want to accept it.

I reply with a grimace before I can control my expression. One I'm sure would put a damper on his mood if he could see it. "I felt us moving in the early hours of the morning, where are we heading?" I ask instead, trying to sound casual.

Old Chou pauses, looking my way with an expression that's equal parts tender and knowing. He gives me the out, and changes topic. "We set a course for Formosa last night," he replies. "We should be reaching there two days from now at dusk. Don't you worry about that, though. You just focus on getting your strength back."

His concern is… touching, but I plan on staying at Zhèng's side until I find out what I want to know.

Noticing that I probably won't be adhering to his advice, he takes it as his cue to leave. He pats my knee gently, then exits. His presence lingers like a soft summer breeze.

The cabin is quiet for all of ten minutes before Hé appears.

He doesn't knock. Just waltzes in with a lopsided grin plastered across his luminescent face and a jug of something suspiciously alcoholic in hand.

I groan long and loud.

"Thought you might be bored after two days of being by yourself," he says, plopping down on the stack of quilts, cloth, and fine silks the captain has surrounding his kip like a cradle. "Figured I'd keep you company."

"I didn't ask for company," I reply dryly, eyeing him exhaustedly.

"No, but you've got it anyway." He leans back, propping his feet on a nearby crate. "You're welcome, by the way."

Despite myself, I can't help but crack a tiny smile. He might be obnoxious, but there's an interesting charm to him, the kind that makes you forget—if only for a moment—the grim realities of life aboard a pirate ship.

He tells me stories of past adventures, embellishing every detail until it's impossible to tell where truth ends, and falsehood begins. But I find that I don't mind. His voice is warm, his laughter infectious, and for a little while, the weight on my chest feels a bit lighter.

When he finally leaves two hours later, I hate to admit that the cabin feels emptier than before. With my back on the bed, I stare at the ceiling contemplating as we sail along.

Formosa.

It's not the destination I had been hoping for, but I have a gut feeling that something important waits for me there.

20

TWO DAYS LATER
OUTSIDE FORMOSA PORT, 1800

I cannot bear the stench of myself any longer. The layers of sweat and grime on my skin feels unendurable, like a second, suffocating layer of clothing.

Getting up after not having stood on my feet for a period proves to be more of a hassle than I would like. My legs shake at first, but the numbness begins to ease as I shuffle behind the desk.

I grab the chair, dragging it across the cabin floor with a soft scrape. Just as Zhèng had done before, I wedge it under the doorknob.

No more surprise visits.

A minute sense of relief sweeps over me as I ensure the barrier is secure. They are tolerable pirates, but there's only so much conversation held with a man a woman can take.

As I begin to peel my clothing off my body, the pungent smell rises, making me gag. A dire wash-up is needed.

When I reach for the hem of my trousers and push them down, the sight stops me cold. My thigh, where an injury should be—a gash still healing from fighting Rabbit—is nothing more than a scarred expanse of skin. The blemish runs diagonally across the muscle. My fingers hover above the mark, quivering as I trace its length. It looks old, as if it had healed cycles ago rather than days.

My heart races, and my breath quickens.

How can it be gone?

I shift my focus to my forearm, where a similar scar resides from a different time. A different moment of survival. They match. Two wounds that shouldn't have healed this way.

I sit down heavily on the edge of the desk, the trousers forgotten at my ankles. My thoughts spin—an uneasy feeling creeping through me.

This is the water's doing But…how? Why?

Shaking my head, I rise again, the discomfort of my musty body pulling me back to the task at hand. Curiosity will have to wait.

I strip off the rest of the linen, letting the soiled garments fall to the floor in a heap.

After cleaning up, I finally step out of the captain's quarters. The fresh air is a much needed change. As I descend to the main deck, I see that the sun is sitting high in the sky.

I slowly make my way to the prow of the ship where Zhèng and Luo are conversing. As I pass by the others, I briefly see the boys that had been guarding the boat at Goisa port. They have bandages upon their heads and linen arm casts tied around their necks. I let out a sigh I didn't know I was holding.

I'm glad they're alive.

They look back at me in awe. The rest of the crew's gazes, leery yet intrigued, follow me until my destination. When I close in on the two leading men, both turn to greet me with small nods.

"We're nearing the Formosa port," Zhèng informs. There's a tinge of caution throughout his words. He leans in slightly, lowering his voice before continuing. "If what you told us was true, I'm sure your likeness will be plastered on bounty posters all over the town." He eyes me intently. "It won't be long before the Imperial officials catch wind of us. We're taking a risk docking here."

I squint. "Then, *why* are we docking here?"

Hé had told me that we'd somehow managed to skirt past any patrolling Imperial ships at the territory border. But now, we're certainly pushing our luck.

My eyes dart between the men as I probe, "Is there some Aether you mean to steal again? To replenish what had been in the brig?"

Zhèng's lips twinge slightly. "No," he says flatly. "Surprisingly, the Aether in the brig survived… *you*. We have no need for more at the moment."

"Then, please share what it is we're doing here if docking in the port is just a precursor to my execution," I press, crossly.

"We don't have a choice," Luo replies. His eyes scan the port city in the distance, vibrant with activity. "The crew needs supplies, and you…" he says, drifting off. "There's someone we want to take you to." He pauses for a beat. "If we can find them, that is. They can help make sense of… *things*."

Help make sense of me is what he really means.

I'd braced myself for awkward tension between us, but the firm set of Luo's jaw and the determined look of focus on his face tell me otherwise. He's too preoccupied—too serious—to dwell on my reaction to his "ethereal" comment from the other day.

Fine by me.

"If you say so," I drawl slowly, studying him. There's something in his mannerisms—a tick in his left brow. A telltale sign of nerves. He looks like he wants to say more but ultimately decides against it.

"We're going to head out first, scout the places where we think the individual might be. It could take a couple of days. Once we have a solid lead, we'll come back for you," Zhèng says, his tone all business.

"I'm not staying on this boat while you all go off again." My words come out hard, leaving no room for negotiation.

Zhèng exhales, already resigned to the argument. "Fine," he relents, but then adds, "but you're going with a keeper."

He barely finishes before turning to the crew still bustling across the deck. He lifts two fingers to his lips and whistles a smooth, bouncing note. The sound penetrates the air, halting the crew's movements. For a moment, no one speaks. Then, as if the whistle was meant for him alone, Ah Fei steps forward.

I watch as he makes his way toward us. When he reaches our trio, his eyes are filled with intrigue. They dance between us, reading the rigidity in the air before settling on Zhèng fully.

"You called, captain?" he asks, arms folding across his chest.

Zhèng gestures at me with the tip of his chin. "You're with her today."

Ah Fei breathes through his nose, not quite a snort, but close. "Guard duty? What'd she do now?"

"I'm standing right here," I say dryly, leveling him with a glare.

Ah Fei's lips twitch upward in the ghost of a smile, but there's something assessing in his usually amicable gaze. Like he's reevaluating a familiar piece now recast in an unfamiliar role.

We've spent time together over the past few weeks—shared stories, meals, laughter. But that was before. Before he knew what I could do. Before *I* knew.

I wonder if that changes how he sees me.

My posture straightens without thinking, shoulders pulling back, feet subtly grounding. My defenses raise internally. Just in case.

Zhèng cuts in before I can push back further. "She's not staying on the ship, so, you're making sure she doesn't get caught or killed." His tone is clipped, impatient.

Ah Fei tilts his head slightly. "Seems to me that she's proven she can handle herself, captain."

Zhèng doesn't blink. "I'm not asking."

A beat of silence passes before Ah Fei sighs, rolling his meaty shoulders. He turns to me. "Fine. But if you run off, I'm not chasing you."

"Good," I shoot back. "I don't need a lug like you slowing me down."

This makes Ah Fei bark out a quiet laugh. "This is going to be fun."

Zhèng, visibly done with our back-and-forth, steps away without another word, Luo following closely behind. I watch them disappear into the throng of sailors, leaving me alone with my newly appointed guardian.

Ah Fei doesn't speak right away. Instead, he observes me, his amusement still lingering, but not unkind. Finally, he shifts his weight and, with all the seriousness of a man about to discuss battle strategy, asks, "So, what do you know about the art of cooking?"

I arch a brow, crossing my arms. "That I could probably do better than you."

A deep, hearty chuckle rumbles from Ah Fei's chest, full and warm, as if I've just said something truly outrageous. The sound is disarming, and despite myself, I feel the smallest sliver of my defenses slip. It's a reminder that, for all his size and strength, Ah Fei has never been the type to brandish intimidation like a weapon.

"Is that so?" he grins, eyes crinkling at the corners. "Guess we'll have to put that to the test." He claps his hands together, the force of it making a few nearby sailors startle. "Come on then. Off to the galley to prepare for our market run. Later tonight we'll see if you can back up that big talk."

I shake my head but still find myself mirroring his enthusiasm. "Hope you're ready to lose."

Ah Fei gestures grandly toward the other side of the boat. "Hope *you're* ready to be humbled."

And just like that, the tension eases, replaced by the kind of camaraderie I've reluctantly come to welcome.

The midday heat is vicious as the ship glides into the harbor, threading between merchant junks and warships. The air is pregnant with fish gutted and left too long in the sun, the sour musk of sweat, and the pungent spice of fermenting pickles.

Beneath the folds of my heavy robe, sweat trails down my back in thin rivulets. The fabric is stifling, but necessary. My hood casts my face in darkness, shielding me from wandering eyes. This place thrives on attention, and the less of it I draw, the better.

As I disembark down the gangplank—and onto land for the first time in what I realize is weeks—my legs wobble as if still expecting the ground to weave and ebb like water. My companion glances at me, chuckling slightly.

"You'll get used to it," Ah Fei quips.

"I hope so. It will prove to be quite disadvantageous if I have to run for my life again."

That brings a wider grin to his lips.

The large port town of Formosa is alight in a way that cities built solely on land aren't. A portion of it exists on the water. Its streets are narrow and winding, a tangled mess of stone alleys and wooden walkways built atop the sea, shifting with the tide. Part floating city, part traditional city.

I guess that is to be expected of the biggest trade port in the empire.

Lanterns swing from sagging eaves. The people move in currents—foreign sailors with hard-set expressions and even harder words, merchants with rings on every finger, street children quick as silverfish, their hands darting between folds of silk and weaved pouches.

I've never seen anything like it. It is almost too much to handle.

Ah Fei nudges me forward, his casual demeanor a stark contrast to my own anxiousness. He moves with the easy confidence of someone who belongs in places like these. His twin daggers rest at his hips, gleaming in the sunlight. It's a warning to anyone who might consider us an easy target. His tunic is loose, open at the throat, the fabric worn. I can feel the way he scans through crowd, locating the dangers before they have a chance to reach us.

"Steady now," he murmurs, his voice a thin thread between us. "Try not to look like you're expecting a knife in the back."

"I wouldn't have to if this place didn't seem like *just* the place for something like that to happen."

His smirk is pointed. "That's what makes it fun."

A boy—no older than ten summers—brushes against Ah Fei, nimble fingers reaching for the coin purse at his belt. Before he even realizes his mistake, Ah Fei's hand closes around his wrist. The child freezes, tiny eyes going wide. For a moment, there is no movement, no sound save for the dull roar of the crowd around us. Then, Ah Fei clicks his tongue.

"Too slow," he muses, releasing the boy with an almost lazy shrug. "Try again when you've learned to use both hands."

The child bolts, disappearing into the throng. I watch him go, half expecting a second wave of thieves to follow.

"You're generous," I remark.

The man lets out a soft laugh. "No need to cut the wings of a bird that's still learning how to fly."

We move deeper into the port, onto land, weaving through alleys where the scent of charred meat and spilled liquor permeates the air.

The market sprawls across the harbor like a beast that has outgrown its cage, its arteries twisting and digging into every available space. Stalls press against buildings, the awnings stretched wide in a desperate attempt to offer shade. Silk merchants call out in rapid, rhythmic voices, their hands smoothing over bright bolts of fabric. Fishmongers haggle, their tables heavy with the day's catch: silver-scaled mackerel, eels still writhing, and the occasional hideous grouper with a mouth gaping wide in permanent surprise.

I keep my head down, letting Ah Fei guide the way. The further we walk, the richer the aroma of food grows—cinnamon and star anise curling together from simmering clay pots, the sizzle of meat hitting a hot iron pan, and the unmistakable sweetness of caramelized sugar.

Ah Fei pauses beside a vendor frying skewers of squid over a charcoal brazier. "Blessed be the Emperor. How much?" he asks, tapping the counter with two fingers.

"Blessed be the Emperor…" the vendor drawls slowly. He eyes us both, lingering on me a moment too long. I tighten my grip on the folds of my robe, willing myself to be still. "Two bronze coins per stick."

Ah Fei flashes a tight smile before he tosses eight coins onto the counter. "Four sticks, then."

The vendor hands them over, and Ah Fei passes me two without question. The heat of the skewers seeps through my fingers, the glaze of oil glistening in the sunlight. I hesitate before taking a bite, the rich, smoky-sweet taste blooming across my tongue.

We eat in silence for a few minutes as I watch passersby. I am just about to ask Ah Fei more about his background when a commotion rises ahead.

Shouts rise, there's a scrape of wooden carts against stone, and then the unmistakable crunch of a fist meeting flesh. The marketplace, already a storm of constant movement, seems to recoil. Conversations dull, merchants duck their heads, and the usual echoing calls of sellers hawking their goods waver.

Ah Fei tenses beside me, his steps slowing. His fingers flex at his sides, as if itching to reach for the hilt of his blades.

"What is it?" I whisper.

He doesn't reply, so, I follow his gaze. A man is on his knees in the middle of the street, his face bruised and swollen, blood trickling from his nose. But it is not just one man who looms over him—it is a squadron, and they wear the scaled black armor plates of Imperial guards. Their uniforms gleam in the afternoon light, lacquered plates dark as wet ink, marked by the silver insignia of the Serpent Emperor.

My heart hammers.

One of them has a hand wrapped around the victim's collar, lifting him just high enough that his knees barely touch the ground. The man sputters, blood speckling the dirt, but his captor's grip does not loosen. Another soldier stands with his arms folded, his expression one of sheer boredom. The third draws his blade—its steel polished and well-kept, meant for swift executions rather than battlefield combat.

The Serpent Emperor doesn't rely on conquest alone to keep his dominion intact. Intimidation is his weapon of choice, and the best way to exercise it is onto those who already suffer.

"Thought you could run to a different island to escape your debt, huh? Where is the rest?" the soldier with the sword asks, tapping the flat of the blade against his own palm. "You were short by five taels. The tax does not change simply because you lack the coin."

The kneeling man coughs. "Please—my fishing boat was wrecked by foreign pirates I—"

Me and Ah Fei share a weighted look.

The soldier sighs as though he has heard it all before. "Not my concern." He turns to the gathered crowd, whose eyes dodge his scrutiny. "Tell me," he continues, voice mean, "if we do not punish thieves of the empire, what happens to order?"

No one answers. No one moves.

Ah Fei shifts beside me, his jaw locked.

The soldier crouches to meet the fisherman's gaze. "The law is clear. A man who fails to pay what is owed forfeits something of equal value. If not taels—" He grips the fisherman's face hard, turning it toward a woman huddled near the edge of the crowd, a child clutched tightly to her chest. His smirk is slow, cruel. "—then perhaps something else can be arranged?"

The man jerks violently, twisting against the soldier's hold. "No! Please, I-I'll find the coin—"

The soldier sighs, unimpressed. He straightens and raises his blade. "Too late."

I don't realize I have moved until Ah Fei's fingers clamp around my wrist. "No," he says under his breath.

I glare at him. "They're going to kill him."

"And if you interfere, you'll be next." His grip tightens. "We cannot fight the entire empire here in the middle of the street."

The kneeling man gasps sharply as the blade presses against his throat. My nails bite into my palms as the executioner lifts his blade in the air. The woman in the crowd stifles a sob. Then—

An arrow whistles through the air and lodges itself into the soldier's eye socket. His body jerks and topples backward with the momentum, dropping his blade. The kneeling man scrambles away, gasping for breath as chaos explodes in the marketplace.

Shouts ring out as more arrows rain down, striking the Imperial guards with uncanny precision. I expect to see Luo suddenly reveal himself.

A figure jumps down from behind a tower of barrels stacked in an alleyway across the square from us. It moves from the crowd. My skin prickles in anticipation but is quickly subdued when the shadow steps into the glaring beam of the sun.

I couldn't have been more wrong in my guess.

Through the havoc, a woman, dressed in harshly worn, black linen, steps toward the soldiers. Her face is half-covered by a dark crimson scarf, and the environment around us slows as I take in her appearance.

What truly mesmerizes me is not the defiance and contempt scorched across her features. No, it is her eyes and the way they burn with molten gold.

At the sight of her, color drains from the captain of the Imperial soldier's face. "It's the Atzu Rebels!" he bellows. "Seize them!"

She moves like a dancer, fluid and purposeful. In one hand, she holds a curved dagger, in the other, a short bow; smaller than a soldier's longbow but just as deadly. Before the Imperials can react, she fires again, this time aiming directly for the captain. He lifts his sword to deflect the arrow, only just missing it to the throat.

More figures emerge—four, maybe five rebels. Panic breaks out in the marketplace as civilians scatter, dragging children and goods out of the way. Another soldier falls, clutching his knee where an arrowhead has buried itself deep. The nearby patrolling troops respond quickly, their training overcoming their shock. Swords flash as they search the rooftops and alleyways.

Ah Fei curses as he takes in the unfolding ambush.

The rebel leader throws something—a handful of crushed powder into the air. A heartbeat later, smoke explodes around her, dense and suffocating. The Imperial men surge forward, but the rebels move first.

Their figures glide through the fog like ghosts. Fragments of blades catching the light are the only thing that's visible from where we stand.

Despite the rebel's skill, though, the Imperial soldiers rally as the smoke clears. There are now only three soldiers left, but they outnumber the two remaining rebels. It is evident that the former have been trained for combat in a capacity that far exceeds the latter. It is just the woman, and one younger man left.

One soldier swings at the woman, and she barely ducks in time, the sword slicing a thin line across her shoulder. She hisses but does not stop. Another soldier aims for her with a spear, but before he can charge, an explosion rocks the square—a firecracker, loud and bright, shattering what little order remained.

Ah Fei, now out of his stupor, tugs me back the way we came. However, I can't help but resist as I watch the woman take the distraction and bolt. She leaps onto a stack of crates and pulls herself onto the rooftop. The last rebel hesitates, looking to her for direction, but she shakes her head. "Leave!" she commands.

The rebel obeys, vanishing into the alley using the panicked crowd as a cloak. The soldiers, coughing and cursing, struggle to pursue them.

I watch as the leader pauses for just a moment. Our eyes meet across the mayhem—hers glowing with intrigue, mine wide with shock.

Then, she is gone, vaulting across the rooftops and vanishing beyond the smoke.

"That was reckless," Ah Fei huffs, fully turning me back now. Though he tries to mask it, underneath, I sense a hint of admiration, maybe even… recognition?

But never mind him. My heart is still pounding, not just from the battle but from the sight of her.

Another pair of golden eyes that the proves I might not be alone.

21

THAT EVENING

FORMOSA PORT, 1800

As the sun tilts westward, the morning's frenzy of confrontation bleeds into the evening. There is no doubt that this port has seen its fair share of civil unrest. Droves of Imperial guards show up to line the streets in no time.

Sensing that this would be a good time to head back to the dock, Ah Fei and I walk back that direction with a new sense of urgency, our steps falling in sync. We stop occasionally at stalls to pick up provisions, but we don't linger.

I hope whomever Zhèng brought me here to meet is worth the trouble.

As we near the edge of town, more and more Bloomers emerge, eyes hallow and glassy from their chronic addiction. The worst of them is a girl laid out on the side of the path, limbs strewn about haphazardly.

Her bronzed skin suggests that she might be native to the island. Or maybe even from a nomadic clan like Ah Fei and me. But the answer doesn't matter. Flies swarm around her and I don't see her chest rise or fall.

A nauseating ache anchors deep in my chest.

"Do you ever think about it?" Ah Fei interrupts, voice uncharacteristically subdued.

"Think about what?" I ask.

I try to push the sorrow out of my voice. I don't think it's working.

"How different things might have been if we weren't born under the Pingshen empire."

The question almost stops me in my tracks.

Of course I do. But I'm not sure what he wants out of a conversation that depressing.

I let out a breath that I find tastes of bitterness. My response is meticulous. "What would be the point of doing that?"

He shakes his head. "It's just…I think about it often."

He stops by a closing stall selling dried cuttlefish. His fingers run absently over the remaining hanging strands before thumbing a silver coin to the vendor and taking three.

He continues without missing a beat. "I think about what would've happened if all of us Wave Kin had abstained from the war. If the Weiman had chosen loyalty to the ways of before rather than the demands of the future."

I watch him as we walk, unsure of how to respond.

It seems like this is something he needs to get off his chest.

"I don't know about your clan," he resumes, "but with mine, everything is temporary. Homes. Family. Especially alliances. If the seasons change, so do we. We're survivalists. No matter the cost."

Growing up, Hokan adults called the Weiman and Humic "traitors". People who had traded their ways for power. People not to be trusted nor depended on. Hearing this now—his account of their ethos—only confirms a bias I hadn't even realized I'd absorbed.

"Our Elders called it freedom," he intones.

I regard him carefully. "Was it not?"

He scoffs, a humorless sound. "That's what they told us when we were children." He gestures loosely toward the city around us. "That the mortals' win was certain, and that we needed to be on the side that would be victorious. After that, it was indoctrinated into us that the empire's *generosity* is the only entity worth obeying." His face is littered with disgust. "But we were never given a choice—to decide if we want to live this new kind of life or embrace our traditions."

Ah Fei stops talking abruptly as two Imperial guards pass by us. I tuck my head deeper into the hood.

When they're out of earshot, he pushes on. "Every child in my clan gets their first dose of aetherbloom after they greet their twelfth summer."

I blink, stunned. "I—" My tongue feels swollen. I lick my dry lips. "—I'm so sorry." It's all I can manage.

He shrugs, but the motion is brittle. "The Elders say our abandonment of the Gods can only be justified if we make something of it. If we ensure every Wielder in the clan is found. The Wielders were the clan's gateway to honorary citizenry." His voice hardens into something fierce. "But that was a lie. We're *not* Pingshens. We never will be. The Wave Kin still alive today were exiled as 'untouchables' long before we were ever born. *No* amount of Wielding will change that."

His words settle between us.

I hadn't expected him to carry the same fury as me.

He does such a good job at hiding it.

I'm woefully unprepared for the small seed of *real* companionship that takes root in my chest.

"I asked the question because the focus shouldn't be about just surviving anymore. It should be about making sure there is still a place for us at all," he rushes earnestly. "They have already destroyed our livelihoods. And with this war on the horizon, they are willing to destroy the land that was ours first. Put *our* bodies on the front lines. We can't let them do that, Shi Yang."

I stop walking, turning to him fully. I think about my sea village. I think about my quest to avenge their suffering. But I haven't considered that same suffering might be reaching other shores. Other nomads.

Who would fight for them? As selfish as it may seem, I'm not sure I would volunteer for it to be me.

"But what do you suggest we do?" I counter. "Overthrow the Emperor? You saw what they did to those rebels back there. And that was just with a handful of Imperials. Imagine an army."

Ah Fei sighs, "I know, I know." Suddenly, his expression becomes serious, more than I've ever seen it. "But don't think we don't have an army of our own."

Confusion laces through my brows. He says the words so frivolously.

I stare at him for a moment, then pull my hood lower and turn toward the docks. "Come on," I say. "We should get back to the ship before Zhèng and Luo return."

Ah Fei falls into step beside me, and for once, we walk mutely no longer lost in the market, but in the undercurrent of something far more complex.

In the evening, I help Ah Fei prepare supper for the crew. We don't revisit our conversation from earlier in town, nor do we speak of the rebels we saw. I try to ask—casually—if he knows anything about them, especially the woman who seemed to be their leader. He only brushes away the question with a guarded *Yeah, I've seen her around once or twice.*

I know it's a lie. I can see it in the way his hands grip around the chopping knife. But I don't press. That's a thread to pull on another day.

Later, I spend the night playing mahjong with Hé, Ah Fei, and Huò. The men drink until their laughter turns sluggish and the tiles clatter carelessly on the board. It isn't until the early hours that we finally call it a night.

But sleep doesn't come for me.

I lie awake, staring at the underside of the deck above me. Zhèng and Luo still haven't returned, though no one else seems troubled by their absence.

They did say that it may take a day or two.

I sigh and shift in my hammock.

I should sleep. Gods know I need it. But the unease I've been carrying all day sits heavy in my chest, refusing to settle. I sway restlessly, catching every creak of timber, every soft exhale of slumber, and every whisper of wind through the seams of the hull.

Then, I hear it. A low sound, just above deck. A voice, humming under its breath.

I know that there's two people stationed on night watch tonight. And one of them is Kāng.

Unable to help myself, I slip from my hammock, making sure my movements are noiseless. Bare feet against the cool planks, I make my way toward the whispering voice. The few lanterns that remain rock gently, casting pools of weak light that I avoid smoothly. As I ascend the narrow stairs, the words clarify.

"…Too long. He grows careless. Weak!"

I frown.

It's Kāng's voice. There is no mistaking the grated sneer for anyone else—the bitterness that drips from every syllable is a giveaway.

As I creep onto the main deck, I brace myself to find both men hunched together, grumbling in hushed tones. Instead, I see only Kāng's partner slumped against a barrel of wine left over from supper, snoring like he hadn't a care in the world.

So much for a night watch.

I scan the deck, but Kāng is nowhere in sight. Again, I hear it. More mumbling comes from the side of the ship furthest away from the dock. The side cloaked in complete darkness.

My heart picks up as my feet carry me closer.

Kāng's voice drops further, shaded with submission. "I've given you my word. The compass will be yours even if I must pry it from his cold, dead hands. All I ask in return is that when the time comes, you'll grant me… what was promised."

A shiver crawls down my spine.

I need to tell Zhèng. But first—I have to know who Kāng's speaking to. Who embedded a traitor in his crew?

I hesitate, torn between fleeing back to my hammock and risking a closer look. Then I take a single step closer, edging along the deck, until I can peer around the curve of the ship's hull into the shadows beyond.

For a moment, I see nothing but Kāng's silhouette, but wait—

It's a figure, amorphous. Larger than the average man, darker than the surrounding night. Almost a void. My breath catches, but when I blink, it's gone.

Another voice comes in a language I don't understand and abruptly Kāng's shadow moves, his posture rigid. He glances over his shoulder right at me.

"You," he growls.

My pulse ricochets as I turn on my heel racing back across the deck. I hear Kāng's footsteps thundering behind me. My eyes scan the boat for a quick weapon, but find none.

Maybe I can make it to the armory.

I'm nearly at the stairs, ready to dive into the hull, when I collide with someone. Solid arms catch me before I go sprawling.

It's Ah Fei—bleary-eyed, just waking to prepare the morning rations.

"Hey," he mumbles. "What're you running fr—"

He cuts off.

Kāng stops just a pace behind me.

Ah Fei's gaze shifts from me to Kāng for only a second. In a heartbeat, the fog of sleep vanishes, replaced by razor-edged awareness.

"What's going on here?" he demands.

Kāng says nothing.

I don't hesitate. "I heard him," I blurt. "He was plotting to betray the captain. To steal the compass."

Kāng surges forward, face twisted with fury. "You eavesdropping whore!"

I brace to meet him head-on, but Ah Fei steps between us before I can move. His fist connects with a crack, sending Kāng flying across the deck.

"I suggest you leave," Ah Fei says coolly, as if commenting on the weather. "Before the captain returns and cuts you down himself." Then his arms lift subtly, and water from the harbor rises behind him, curling over the rail like a serpent waiting to strike. "And if he doesn't… I will."

Kāng groans, staggering to his feet. His scowl burns hot through the swelling already blooming across his jaw. He stumbles toward the gangplank, seething.

"You'll all be dead soon!" he spits. "Dead!"

We watch in silence as he disappears into the growing onslaught of dockside traffic—sailors, fishermen, merchants all starting their day.

Only once Kāng escapes into the crowd does Ah Fei release the water, letting it crash harmlessly back into the port. I heave out a deep breath before gathering his attention.

"I need to tell Zhèng and Luo," I say. "I have a bad feeling about whomever put Kāng up to this."

Ah Fei nods in agreement. "They should be back today. They never stay away more than a night." He concentrates on my face for a moment. "You okay?"

"I'm fine," I say, forcing a breath. "Thanks. Really. Feels like the whole boat just got lighter with him gone."

Ah Fei shrugs, lips tugging into a tired half-smile. "Long overdue."

I don't doubt it. I've only dealt with Kāng for a couple moons, and that was more than enough. I can't imagine having to put up with him for whole cycles.

"Come on," he says, gesturing me along. "You can wait for the captain with me. I've got a mountain of sweet potatoes that need peeling."

As we head toward the galley, Ah Fei veers off and gives a harsh kick to the other mate who'd been assigned night watch.

"Ey! Wake up, you sorry excuse of a pirate!"

The man jerks awake like he's been yanked from a dream. "Wha—?"

"Sleep well?" Ah Fei drawls. "Hope it was worth it. Because when the captain hears about this, you'll be scrubbing barnacles till next monsoon."

"W-wait! Please—!"

But Ah Fei's already walking off. I glance back at the man, offering only a shrug before following the cook below deck.

Zhèng and Luo don't return to the vessel until the evening. The last slivers of daylight have bled from the sky, leaving only a bruised purple haze over the harbor. By the time they climb aboard, I've worn a path into the wooden planks near the railing, pacing back and forth, thoughts churning with the weight of what's been laid at my feet.

I don't hear them approach—not until a deliberate cough cuts through my preoccupation.

I stop mid-step and turn. Zhèng stands there, poised to speak, but I cut in first.

"I have to tell you something," I rush.

His brows rise at the interruption, but he must see the urgency in my face. He gives a slight nod that says, *Go on.*

So, I do. I recount everything I heard. When I'm finished, both men look murderous.

"Where is he?" Luo says lethally.

"Ah Fei ran him off," I say. "After knocking him on his ass."

Zhèng processes the information. When he speaks, his voice is clipped, focused.

"Forget Kāng for now. We came here for a reason. No distractions." Then, he looks at me. "Well done, Shi Yang." He turns and strides toward the gangplank. "Let's go," he calls back. "I want to be out of this Gods-awful port by sunrise."

Without another word, I gather my robe from yesterday and fall in step behind him.

Once we step off the dock, the underbelly of the port city swallows us whole. Stray dogs skulk between overturned carts, sniffing for scraps. Torches burn, casting jittery shapes against the crumbling walls of aetherbloom dens and teahouses plastered with handbills. Signs advertising Imperial edicts, the upcoming Festival, and—

"I'd say the portrait's rather flattering, wouldn't you?" Luo drawls, tone dripping with mirth.

My face, painted with lazy ink lines, stares back at me.

Not terrible work—though the artist clearly had strong feelings about the size of my ears.

I shoot Luo a murderous glare and tug my hood further forward.

"I hate you," I remark.

The man shrugs unbothered.

"Come on," Zhèng shouts from ahead.

When we enter a larger body of people, Luo leans in beside me.

"So, we heard about a big disturbance in the market yesterday…" His expressions is equal parts exasperated and expectant.

I lift a hand to cut him off. "It wasn't me."

Luo's brow arches, his skepticism evident. His gaze sweeps over me, assessing. "Mhm." He doesn't sound convinced. "I suppose you made it back in one piece."

"Yes. Ah Fei did his job," I reply, careful to keep my tone even.

Hopefully, that's enough to sidestep any further interrogation about yesterday's events.

My skin prickles as we pass a brothel where a scuffle spills onto the street, its entrance glowing red from the screens and light inside. Laughter and curses tangle in the night, but my scowl deepens as two naked drunks stagger out, their bodies slick with sweat and excess.

One slings an arm around the other's shoulder, barely holding himself upright, while both men flaunt their nudity without shame, flashing passersby with the kind of reckless abandon only found at the bottom of a bottle.

Behind them, the brothel's boys linger in the doorway, arms crossed, lips curled in distaste. One spits on the ground as the drunks hurl a few half-hearted insults back at them, but their anger fizzles out beneath their own slurred giggles. They are too far gone to care.

One of them stumbles straight into me.

My fingers flex, instinctively curling into fists. His body lingers for a breath too long, and I shove him off with enough force to send him staggering.

"Watch where you're going, asshole," I sneer.

He reels, blinking, his mind slow to catch up. Then, his bloodshot eyes rake over me, widening slightly as realization dawns. His lips stretch into a sloppy grin.

"Hey… how—" he hiccups, "—how much for a night?"

Revulsion rolls hot in my stomach. I'm already tensing, my fist drawing back to break his nose, when a figure moves beside me.

Luo stands there with an arrow that glints in his grip, the pointed tip leveled at the man's genitals. "Think *very* carefully about your next action," he says, voice as cool and void of emotion as his face.

A *shing* sound cuts through the air. I turn in time to see Zhèng's swords, unsheathed in a blink, crossed and pressing against the throat of the other drunk. The man stiffens, the lump in his throat bobbing as he shakes against the cold steel.

For a long moment, no one moves. Then, the first man takes a step backward, his mouth opening and closing. He promptly spins and bolts, tripping over his own feet as he disappears down the street. The other lets out a pitiful whimper, and Zhèng releases him with a flick of his wrists.

The drunkard doesn't hesitate, just scrambles away, vanishing into the crowd like a rat.

I glance between the two men at my side, chewing the inside of my cheek. "I was going to handle that," I mutter. *Thank you.*

Zhèng sheathes his swords in a fluid motion. "We'd expect nothing less of you." *You're welcome.* His voice carries no mockery, only certainty.

We press on. As we venture deeper into town, I catch two more wanted posters nailed to wooden posts. It makes the looming possibility of being caught and executed even more real. So, I distract myself instead by counting all the different languages I can hear being spoken.

"Where are we going?" I ask eventually.

"We did some digging yesterday. There's a place where whispers gather," Zhèng replies without looking back. "If anyone knows where to find who we're looking for, we'll hear it there."

The din of the main path dulls as we turn down a narrow alley. Ahead, a weathered sign hangs precariously above an open door covered by a tattered cloth.

The Happy Valley.

How quaint.

The faded lettering, the cracked wood—everything about it warns away those who value their lives.

Zhèng pushes through, and the moment we step inside, the hum of conversation arrests. Eyes snap toward us in assessment. The patrons are a mix of what seems to be sailors, pirates, and other outlaws. The wild look in their eyes is exacerbated by lives spent on the edge.

The space reeks of aetherbloom smoke, sweat, and something fouler that lingers beneath.

However, Zhèng pays the stares no mind. He strides forward with the same confidence as before, heading toward a corner table as if he already owns the place.

"Stay close," Luo warns from behind.

I hadn't planned on doing anything other than that honestly.

At the main cart in front of the room, a keep "cleans" a cup with a filthy rag. His expression is as nasty as the liquor he serves.

Zhèng signals for drinks and leans against the table as he sweeps the room like a predator assessing its prey. "I'll ask around," he says. "You two keep a low profile."

But I barely hear him.

A strange, prickling sensation runs down my spine, a feeling I can't shake. My eyes wander the room again—

There's a man leaning against the wall across the room. I squint. The scar across his forehead comes into focus. My heart plummets to my stomach.

It's him.

The man who set this all in motion. The pirate that took *everything* from me.

22

MIDNIGHT

FORMOSA COUNTRYSIDE, 1800

As if sensing the daggers I send his way, the scarred man lifts his head.

He freezes.

My blood begins to burn, hot and furious, as recognition flares in his expression. His lips gradually twists into a menacing smirk.

"Shi Yang, what's wrong?" Luo questions, concern evident.

I regard the co-captain sharply, having forgotten his presence. My vision blurs into light at the corners. I focus back on the wall, but the pirate is gone. Disappearing in an instant, as if he were never there to begin with.

"I just saw someone we should be worried about. I'll tell you once we're back on the boat, but we need to get out of here. Now." I pull my hood lower over my face, forcing my breathing to steady, and wait for the light in my eyes to subside. Luo grasps the severity immediately.

"Okay," he agrees.

Zhèng returns to the table just then, three cups in hand and an irritated frown on his face. "No one here knows anything useful," he grumbles. He perceives the alertness in both of us immediately. "What's happened?"

"We need to hurry this up and go," Luo demands.

Zhèng doesn't take offense to being told what to do and instead nods resolutely.

"Understood," he says, rising from the table.

As we step back into the crowded streets, I keep my hood secured as my thoughts race.

I swore the next time I saw that man I would slaughter him where he stood. Instead, I froze, letting him steal another day of life he doesn't deserve.

A tightness in my chest begins to take over. Hatred bubbles in the back of my throat, making the skin on my face hot with shame.

Letting him slip away is an affront to everything I've endured.

Abruptly, I stop in my tracks allowing both men to stride ahead. The crowd parts and flows around me, but I remain rooted. Zhèng notices my absence first, and spins around, confused. "What are you doing?"

"You brought me here to meet someone," I remind. "If I'm going to kill the man responsible for my past, I need to understand my present. That's the only way I can ensure my future." I extend my hand toward him, palm up. "I know you wouldn't leave the compass on the ship in a place like this. Give it to me. We have no more time to waste."

Zhèng casts a considering look to my outstretched hand and back to my face. He hesitates—only for a heartbeat—but then he reaches into his tunic.

The compass gleams in the glow of the night life around us as he places it in my hand. The moment it touches my skin, the needle spins. Huddled together in the middle of the road, we watch it finally settle, pointing east.

When we turn to look in that direction, the road that greets us leads out of town, into the dark unknown.

"Where the compass leads, I follow," I recite.

Zhèng chuckles ruefully at having his words thrown back at him.

I spare them a twitch of a smile before I turn and stride toward the path.

I do not check to see if either man is behind me. Whether they follow or not doesn't matter in the slightest.

The compass tugs at my hand, guiding me through dark. I can hear the crunch of both Zhèng and Luo's footprints on the dirt road after me.

It's a good thing they didn't decide to run back to the boat. I would've made sure the crew never let them live it down if they had.

No sound accompanies our journey other than the decibels of crickets hiding in the tall grass. The only source of light we have is the beamlillies reflecting the rays of moonlight. Their dim luminescence allows me to make out the rolling plains and rice fields. I can only imagine the image of mountains that kiss the Heavens in the distance. All things I have only ever heard about during Hokan fire gatherings—tales of the land before Pingshen rule.

The trek remains a quiet journey until we reach a modest temple at the edge of the city. The structure's paint has weathered significant damage. It's doors and shingles are caked in dirt, and invasive weeds grow up its frame. It looks to be abandoned, but the air around it radiates a strange energy.

When I am close enough that the columns tower above me, I stop in my tracks. The other men eventually come up beside me.

The compass is vibrating aggressively now, the same way it did the night I snuck aboard the trade boat.

"This is it," I murmur, stepping forward.

The compass grows hot in my hand as I ascend the stone stairs. My foot falls on the final step and the doors creak open as if summoned by my presence.

Okay…

I enter cautiously. Behind me, I can hear two pairs of swords, and a bow unsheathe from their holders. Just like me, the captains are preparing themselves for a fight.

Inside, the temple is dimly lit by rows of flickering candles. The scent of incense is almost overpowering. There's a singular altar, and before it kneels a lone figure with their back to me. The entity is draped in obsidian flowing robes, their hair silver as the moon.

Suddenly, the figure speaks, their voice carrying throughout the closed space. "Shi Yang, you've come." The statement resonates as if housing more than one voice inside it. It unsettles me in a way I cannot explain.

They rise and turn, revealing a face hidden behind a mask carved to resemble a fox. "I'm Huli."

My breath catches.

A fox.

The face of the girl from the flowerboat materializes front and center in my mind's eye.

"A fox spoke to me. Told me to come find you—to make sure you see me… It said that this would help you make the right choice…"

It can't be.

The compass in my hand ceases its pulsing. Abruptly, it glows in concert with the flames of the candles growing brighter.

My wide eyes bore into the mask. "You…you were the one who sent her to me?"

Huli nods shortly, the only indication it is not a figment of my imagination. "I was."

My mouth opens, but no words tumble out. I do not understand who or *what* this is.

Was I always meant to come here? How could this… fox… know that I would? How does it even know me?

My thoughts are interrupted by a hand placed on my shoulder.

Luo's eyes are stricken with awe. "This is who we wanted to take you to," he breathes. "*You* found *them*."

The implication of his comment makes my stomach twist.

They have ties to this enigmatic figure. What is going on?

Before I can respond, Huli gestures toward the altar behind them. "Come. There is something you must see."

I glance back to Zhèng. I'm not sure what I'm looking for; protest, caution, fear. However, I only find encouragement that comes in the form of a subtle nod.

He and Luo take Huli's summons as their cue to give us privacy. Without further preamble, they step back out into the cold, dark night to wait.

Once it is just me and Huli, I move cautiously toward them. Above the altar, the signage reads: *For the Mother of the Sea and Ocean.*

It's a shrine to Mazu.

The altar is adorned with offerings: fruits, flowers, and a polished bronze mirror with a decorated handle. Huli lifts the mirror and holds it out to me.

"Look."

I waver, gripping it slowly. Then, I gaze into the reflecting glass. However, it becomes quickly evident that this is no ordinary mirror. The surface ripples like water before an image emerges.

In it, I see a scene as if watching from afar. There's a figure, cloaked in a shawl that gleams in the daylight as if threaded with fibers embedded with silver. There is a hood covering their face, but from the black void of the cloak, glowing eyes as bright as the sun shine through. They are standing atop a mountain, in front of a gigantic, looming temple. Their hands are hidden within the robe, but a blade rests at their side. It sings with an energy that is louder than the howling winds.

As the figure approaches the doors of this temple, a hand reaches up to lower their hood.

It is me.

My breath stutters as my mind reels. This feels like both a vision and a memory simultaneously. Before I can contemplate it further, something else emerges from the temple.

In a hulking form, a figure taller than the temple it came from, stops in front of me. Its form is a void, shadows bending deviously all around it.

It can be nothing other than a God.

But not just any God. It must be Yán Luó, the King of Death.

In the vision, I can't hear sound, but there are words exchanged before Yán Luó moves. His hand, large, but sickly looking, rises before me. The air pops as rays of power burst out from my eyes, mouth, and hands. Similarly, shadow pours out from his figure. The world is split in two, one half of it pulsing a blinding light, the other swallowing everything in darkness. Both sides clash at our meeting, neither breaching the other. The forces of each power begin to shake the ground and the Heavens violently, until everything explodes into nothingness.

Then, the image shifts.

I'm floating. My vision is obscure, dusted with a screen of yellow light as my body levitates in the air, the wind rushing against my form. I can feel heat rising from beneath me. The type that is only birthed by fire. There is screaming, and an acrid scent of burning flesh that pollutes the atmosphere around me. I know that I'm in the middle of a battlefield.

The same one from my vision before. Except, *I'm* now the dragon of smoke and shadow.

I let out a deafening roar, and dive straight down. My mouth is agape, teeth bared, as I clamp my jaws down.

Then the vision fades.

I stagger back, breathless and heart pounding.

I don't even know where to begin.

"What is this?" I demand, thrusting the mirror back into Huli's direction.

They take the object out of my hands. "It is a galeglass. A portal for one to look through that stretches across time, Worlds, and infinite possibilities."

Worlds? Infinite possibilities?

"What… even are you?"

Huli places the mirror back on the altar. "I'm a spirit. But different than the others. I voluntarily act as an intermediate between the Worlds when I feel so inclined."

I can only blink absentmindedly, my mind fraying. Huli just presses on.

"I was asked to give you a message," the spirit says indulgently. "One I found rather… intriguing. Would you like to hear it?"

The knots already in my stomach tighten even further. "Do I have a choice?"

"We all have choices," Huli responds cryptically.

Gods. Let me just be done with this.

My face contorts into a grimace. "Fine. Tell me."

"Your path is set, but the outcome is not. You have the power necessary to reshape destiny, not just for yourself, but for the world as you know it," Huli tilts their head minutely, "but only if you master the balance between your mortal desires… and what you have inherited."

Inherited?

I frown. "What are you talking about?"

They take a step closer. "You are the daughter of Mazu."

My mind blanks. Then, I break into hysterical laughter.

"Daughter?" I heave between cackles. "Please!"

This is Godsdamned absurd.

"Others might show gratitude for such a revelation," Huli says coolly.

I wipe a tear from the corner of my eye, still breathless. "I'm sure they would. But me? I'll pass on being hollowed out like a gourd and worn like a costume by a deity."

I turn my back to them, done with riddles and theatrics.

I'll find answers another way.

I'm almost at the entrance when Huli calls out.

"You speak of a Jítóng. I do not. Your existence is far more complicated. However, that is for you to find out later."

I clench my fists.

More of these non-answers. I'm genuinely reaching my limit.

"There is mentor who will find you," Huli continues. "Be ready to learn when they do."

They drift toward the wall flanking the altar. A row of swords hangs there, each one exquisitely forged. Huli's hand hovers over the first two, then settles on the second. With reverence, they wrap it in cloth and return to me.

I don't reach for it immediately. Just stare.

Accepting it feels like stepping across a threshold I can't return from. A submission to whatever path has been carved out for me.

But… I want answers. I want to know what really happened to my clan. I want to know what the head of the Lo family knew, what he feared.

If the power I'm in the position to gain is the only way to get that information… I should take it.

Tucking the compass into my tunic, I reach for the sword. Huli retracts it momentarily.

"Be warned," they caution. "The closer you come to your true power, the more adversaries will seek to destroy you. And if you aren't careful, you may become your own biggest adversary yet."

This gives me pause.

Do I have the fortitude to fight off my own power?

A sudden crash echoes from outside, followed by shouts and the clang of metal. Luo bursts into the temple, his bow drawn. "Imperial soldiers are here!"

Huli thrusts the sword into my hands. "Take it. Protect the compass and this blade at *all* costs!"

The weapon glows faintly as it touches my skin. When I look up from it, Huli is gone. The flames of the candles around me swipe out as a gust of wind sweeps the space.

"Shi Yang! We must go now!" Luo shouts desperately.

That snaps me back to reality. I race out towards the fight.

Outside is mayhem. The Imperial guards swarm the temple's courtyard. As Zhèng and Luo proceed to lay waste to most of them, I sprint out towards the dirt road we came from.

I've got to get the compass and sword out of here.

I'm darting through the melee when a solider approaches me, sword raised high. I lift my own above my head just in time to block it. When the metals clash, the sound reverberates throughout the yard. A bright glowing emits from my sword as it rebounds the guard away from me violently. I stare at the weapon in disbelief.

Well, that's convenient.

A *bang* and a sharp whistle pierces the air. I turn to see another solider leveling a musket at me. Before I can react, Luo sends an arrow into the man's chest.

Then, Zhèng comes right behind, slashing the man's head off in one swoop. "Keep moving!" he barks.

I nod my head at his command, striding down the road. I can distantly hear thundering footsteps behind me, but I don't stop. I can only hope that they belong to the captains.

By the time I can hear the bustling of the port town, I am sure I've rid of perusers. I stop just on the outskirts, lungs heaving and heart hammering. A couple of minutes pass before Zhèng and Luo appear, smeared with blood. Not their own most likely.

"How did… they… find… us?" Luo asks between pants.

"Someone must have recognized you, and reported it" Zhèng responds, eyes on me.

"Yeah, I'm pretty sure I know who," I concur. "Let's just get to the ship. We can talk there."

They both nod, following as I led us through a narrow alley, and back into the belly of the city.

Above us, the first light of dawn breaks across the horizon, casting the town in shades of gold.

23

EARLY MORNING

DEPARTING FORMOSA PORT, 1800

The port becomes smaller and smaller as the seconds pass.

I lean against the main mast, my knuckles aching as I clutch the compass and the handle of the sword given to me by Huli.

In the daylight, I can make out some of its intricacies and decor. The hilt is iron, carved delicately into the head of a dragon. It's tongue curls and scales bristle as the blade extrudes from its mouth. The metal itself is made of steel. And engraved on the flat edge, is swirls and billows of an element. I'm not sure whether it is supposed to represent fire or water.

Perhaps it's both.

"So, who was it you saw back there?" Zhèng interrogates.

We've all barely spoken since our return to the ship an hour ago. Each of us are too lost in our own thoughts.

"At the liquor house," I start, "there was someone from my past." I swallow down the fury that sits at the back of my throat. "A pirate who sold me to a flowerboat—the same one who raided my village and clan cycles ago. The man who was our ruin." The heat is building in my chest now, bubbling up from my stomach. "The man who sought to be *my* ruin." I spit the words like venom, my gaze fixed on the compass as my fist clenches around it. My eyes begin to cloud at the corners. The grip I have on the device produces a hairline crack on its glass surface.

"Shi Yang!" Zhèng calls.

I'm shaken out of my daze. I register the breakage in a stupor.

I hadn't realized I was even squeezing that hard.

I loosen my hold on the device. "That was not intended."

Luo only fixes me with a weighted look. "It's okay."

Zhèng steps closer. "Your eyes… they were beginning to glow again."

This takes me aback, but I have no clue how to respond. So, I continue with my confession instead. "I'm pretty sure he recognized me and tipped off the Imperial guards."

"It could've also been those drunkards," Luo suggests, as if trying to take my mind off the pirate. It doesn't work.

Zhèng's eyes narrow. "Do you know his name?"

My lips twist into a bitter smile. "If I did, he would be dead by now." I straighten, attempting to suppress the rage. "All I know is that he bears a mark across his forehead, and his ship flies the flag of the Southern Sea Raiders." I turn to stare straight into the captains' eyes. "Similar to the one you wave."

Zhèng doesn't cower at the accusation, but his reply is defensive. "I'm in alliance with a Confederation of pirates. We all fly similar flags. My fleet is vast, at least hundreds of sailors. There are bound to be factions of it that engage in operations and dealings I'm not privy to."

"Then, perhaps," I say, stepping closer into his space, "You 'ought to tighten the lash in which you keep these pirates tied. Lest someone else does it for you."

He doesn't respond, but his eyes are a storm of indignation, guilt, and reproach.

Backing away to lean against the mast once more, I carry on. "The next time our paths intersect, he will atone for what he has done." My eyes slide to Luo, "And so will everyone who aided him in any way."

I still know nothing about the co-captain. Once a man I thought immature and unserious, has become more elusive and reserved than the captain. Something has changed with him, and I intend to find out.

Luo meets me head on. "Revenge may satisfy your pride, but it will draw more attention to us. We can't afford that right now."

"Easy for you to say," I snap, rounding on him. "You haven't spent cycles being treated like less than a dog, beaten and starved for another's profit."

Luo bristles. "You want to bet on that claim?"

Zhèng steps between us, raising a hand. "Enough. Both of you." He looks at me, commanding. "We'll deal with that pirate when the time is right. But right now, I need to know what happened in that temple. What did Huli show you?"

I hesitate. I turn away from the men toward the horizon, contemplating whether I want to tell them the truth. But, then it occurs to me—I *was* the one who demanded that we trust each other.

My fingers tighten around the blade's hilt. "Fragments. My dream that may manifest itself into a prophecy," I close my eyes to focus on the feel of the wind brushing against my face, "If I permit it to become so. Something no one is prepared for." My voice wavers. "Especially me."

I only feel a little guilty at omitting parts of what I learned. Despite the spoken truce days ago, I know I'm not the only one to still withholds vital information.

Luo's brows furrow like he's thinking deeply about what to say next. "Huli is a fickle spirit. They rarely show their visions without purpose." He hesitates for a beat. "But I didn't expect them to reveal so much to you."

At that, my suspicion flares. "You seem to know *a lot* about them. How?"

He responds, tone careful. "Huli is… an ally. Of sorts. They present themselves in times of need and uncertainty. We've sought their guidance before on matters of importance to our…*business*. They've helped us navigate many dangers, but the price is always high."

"What kind of price?" I press, stepping closer.

Zhèng sighs, running a hand through his hair. "They don't take coin or goods. They take secrets, memories, and sometimes… futures. They're dangerous, but often you have no choice but to entertain their dealings."

"And you brought me there knowing this?" I question.

"You needed answers," the captain appeases. "And Huli could provide them. We didn't force you to accept their vision." His face falls slightly. "If it makes you feel any better, we've both had to give them something."

"And so, what?" I say bitterly, "You think that because you've sacrificed, that I must too?" I turn away seething, staring out at the sea. Its waves becoming choppier as my chest rises and falls. "Men are all the same. Poisonous, selfish beings."

"You're right." Zhèng cuts in. "I'm sorry that we did not consider your agency in all this," he steps up beside me at the railing. "But you must understand, we wouldn't have been able to get you the answers you seek without them."

That may be true, but still my forehead puckers. "They know my destiny better than I do. And now I have to figure out how to survive it."

"Whatever Huli showed you, we will help you face it."

I glance at them, my expression conflicted. After a few moments of silence, I nod slowly.

"Fine. But don't think this means I trust you completely. Not yet."

"Fair enough," Zhèng says with a faint twitch of the lips. He nods, "Trust is earned, not given."

With that anecdote, I exit the conversation. As I walk away, I half expect for Zhèng to demand I return the compass to his possession. But he doesn't. Which is good, because I hadn't planned on giving back regardless.

The compass will stay on my person for the foreseeable future. Maybe I can find some spare tweed to fashion a necklace…

As the ship sails on into the evening, the captain's declaration sits at the front of my thoughts, tittering with the same rhythm as my hammock.

They'll "help" me, huh?

I snort softly to myself, turning on my side. A part of doesn't believe it, but the other part—one that has grown since stepping foot on this ship—naively does. Because, for the first time in a long time, I suppose I don't feel so *completely* alone.

Later that night, the ship is quiet, except the gentle creak of the hull. Instead of gaining the slumber I desperately need, I spend hours counting the planks encasing the quarters, until my head throbs. I take that as a sign to seek solitude in the open air.

As I ascend the steps to the deck, the crisp scent of seaweed and salt greet me. The light of daybreak paints the worn wooden planks with a soft glow.

I amble tiredly to the nearest railing, leaning my elbows on it. Below, my eyes catch on the sight of the pulsing waves. Suddenly, I hear a faint humming sound. A lullaby sung by the water.

It whispers.

Shi Yang… come home.

My brows crease, and I lean farther, mesmerized. "Who's there?" I call out.

Shi Yang, you are home.

It feels like a summons. One I almost cannot fight.

"Shi Yang? What are you doing up so early, child?"

I snap out of my trance. My entire upper body is over the ledge. One more second, and I would've joined the fish.

I sweep my head around in the direction of the voice at the top of the sterncastle.

There, Old Chou stands alone, his thin frame outlined against the rising sun.

Tossing one final glance to the waves, I pull away from the railing. By the time I have reached the bottom of the stairs, Old Chou has started back up whatever activity he was doing before I came out here. When I come to the top, he looks to be in some sort of martial practice. Perhaps, the one he offered to teach me.

His movements are slow and deliberate, his arms tracing gentle arcs through the air. There is something calming about the way he moves, as if he is a part of the ocean itself—steady, unshaken, always flowing.

It is the opposite of how I feel inside.

My powers, my anger, and the calling of my destiny… my mind and body are fracturing.

I take a breath, steeling myself, and step forward. "Old Chou."

He doesn't stop moving. A small smile tugs at his weathered face as his gray eyes blink peacefully. "Ah, the Little Fighter comes to greet the day." His hands glide through the air in the same way of his manner; kind and attentive. "What brings you out so early? Couldn't sleep?"

He has no idea that he just saved me from possibly diving to my death. My heart aches. I feel a fondness welling up in the corners of my eyes.

"No," I admit, stopping a few footsteps away. "I didn't expect you to be up here." I pause, fighting the urge to bite my lip and twist my hands. "But I'm glad you are. You told me to let you know when I'm ready. And well…" I say, softly. "The way you move… like you're in control of everything around you. I would like to learn."

Old Chou's movements slow to a stop, expression softening. "It's not what you think, child. Tai Chi is not for showing power. It's about balance—between body, mind, and spirit. It teaches you to flow with the forces around you, not fight against them."

"I don't care if it's not for displaying power," I say quickly, though my voice wavers. "I just... I need balance and control. My body, my powers—" I throw my hands out exasperatedly, "—they don't feel like mine. I don't know what I'm doing or how to control them."

Old Chou lets out a deep hum.

I hesitate only a breath before quietly adding, "I don't know if I trust myself to follow through on the path I have set myself on."

It is a secret between us, meant for his ears only.

"Ah, I see," he says tenderly. "You carry the weight of the world on your shoulders, but you don't know how to carry your own heart. That's a heavy burden, child." He takes a step backward, gesturing toward the open space in front of him. "Come. Let me help you lighten it."

A single tear lines the bottom lashes of my eye. As I let my eyelids shut—releasing a breath I didn't know I was holding in—I allow the water to dampen my cheek. I quickly wipe it dry before following him.

As we reach the clear deck, Old Chou stands beside me, his posture relaxed and grounded. He raises his arms, curving them gently as if cradling an invisible sphere.

"We'll start with something simple," he says. "This is called 'Holding the Moon.' It's the foundation of balance. It is the source that pulls and pushes the waves that carry us. Let it carry you."

I try to mimic his stance for a couple of moments, but my arms feel awkward, my shoulders too stiff. "It feels... unnatural."

Old Chou chuckles, stepping closer. "That's because you're forcing it. Relax your shoulders. Let them sink, like a pebble." He places his hands gently on the base of my neck, guiding the muscles down. His touch is light, like a father helping his child. I'm instantly teleported to the cycles on the sampan, watching the boy and his father train.

I adjust, and the tension begins to ease. "Better," Old Chou says warmly. "Now, think of the moon in your hands—not heavy, but full of life. Let it float."

I close my eyes, breathing deeply. I imagine the moon resting lightly in my hands, its cool glow spreading through my fingertips, dampening the heat that simmers constantly in my chest. The sway of the ship beneath my feet seems to match my movements, and for a moment, I feel… in sync with myself.

"Good," Old Chou says. "Now distribute your weight evenly. Feel the ground beneath you—even if it moves, it supports you. Let the cadence of the sea guide you."

I move slowly, moving my weight from one foot to the other, my arms flowing in a smooth curve. It is clumsy at first, my balance unsteady, but Old Chou's patient voice anchors me. "Don't fight the sway," he says. "The ocean isn't your enemy—it's your partner. Dance with it."

We continue for what feels like hours, the sun climbing higher in the sky. When our practice comes to an end, Old Chou speaks. "You know, strength doesn't always come from force. Sometimes, it's in how you let go."

Letting go. I don't know if I could ever do that.

I bow my head to Old Chou, a small smile tugging at my lips. "Thank you," I say quietly.

Old Chou places a reassuring hand on my shoulder. "You've done well," he says. "You're stronger than you know. Trust yourself."

I nod, my chest feeling lighter than it has in days. My muscles ache, but it is a good ache, the kind that comes from effort well spent.

The other crew members arrive to the main deck with breakfast in hand.

"Now off to breakfast, you. I have plenty of tasks lined up for all of you today," he says, shooing me away with a playful hand.

Later in the afternoon, I'm moving deftly among the barrels and sacks of the galley, when a deckhand finds me.

"Shi Yang," the wiry man gestures impatiently for me to follow, "the captain wants you."

I roll my eyes in mild irritation, though I'm secretly grateful for the excuse. The earthy scent of damp wood and fermentation has become increasingly suffocating.

Wiping the dirt on my hands on the rough linen tucked in the waist of my tunic, I follow him up the narrow stairs, hardly able to keep up with his hurried steps. The sun beats down mercilessly, its heat pressing against my back as I weave through the bustling crew.

What do they want to lie about now?

When we reach the quarterdeck, I spot Zhèng standing with his back to me, arms folded as he speaks to Luo. The co-captain stands slightly taller than him, even when leaned against the railing.

Planting my feet firmly, my hands at my sides, I call up to them. "You wanted me?"

"My quarters," Zhèng voices back. Then, both men sweep out of sight.

My eyebrows scrunch, but I begrudgingly follow the two men. When I close the door, they are standing by the desk, arms crossed.

"So, last night taught us three things," Zheng starts. "One: someone planted a mole on my ship. I intend to figure out who. Personally. Two: the man that you want is somewhere within my fleet. I've already started combing through my crew lists and ship rosters to narrow it down."

My brows lift.

Well, he works fast.

"And what's the third?" I inquire.

"You need training," the captain replies. "Pirates and Imperial soldiers alike, are ruthless. Especially when you have something they want."

"So, you need to be ready," Luo cuts in. "We know you're clever. Observant. That won't be enough. An entranced sword can only protect you so much if you don't know how to use it properly. As of right now, you're sloppy with a real blade."

"Sloppy?" I repeat. "You've barely seen me fight with one!"

It's not that I think either man is wrong. My training from childhood *is* dull. However, my pride won't let me take an insult laying down.

Luo's mouth curls. "I've seen enough. You're quick, and you have some skill, but you're reckless."

"And I suppose *you're* offering to teach me?" I shoot back. "You don't even use a blade!"

"Not offering," Zhèng interjects, tone leaving no room for argument. "I'm ordering it. Luo will train you, starting now. If you're going to survive whatever fights we encounter ahead, you'll need more than quick reflexes. At least until you understand how to hone your Wielding."

I bite back the retort on the tip of my tongue. "Surely someone else could—"

"Just," Luo exhales, "listen. I don't use a blade because when I *Wield* it, it always lands true to my victims' demise."

I freeze.

He's a Godsdamned Wielder?

My mind scrambles, and nostrils flare. "You didn't think this would be something you'd want to share *earlier*?"

"You never asked," he responds pragmatically.

I'm pretty sure that my teeth clench hard enough to break glass. I advance on him with my hand raised, palm opened, but Zhèng catches it mid-swing.

"No one else knows," he placates. "Not even Ah Fei."

I wretch the limb from him, ignoring the warmth of his touch lingering a second too long. I send a scowl to both men before storming out of the space. I hear their footsteps patter behind me.

"Learning swordsmanship from anyone else on this boat, against threats like *these*, will get you killed," Luo calls after me. He looks out unto the crew fulfilling their tasks and pretending not to eavesdrop in on our disagreement. "No offense, that is."

They all shout back "*None taken!*" in unison.

I level him with an unimpressed look.

Something in me wants to argue, but I know—after the conversation we had yesterday—they *are* trying to help. Whether it's to help themselves, or me, is another conversation all together.

I chew on the inside of my gum.

Despite what I've been preaching, I haven't been fully honest either…

"Fine," I say, finally. "When do we start?"

Luo's face relaxes subtly. "We'll start tomorrow morning. You'll need all the energy you can muster."

"Okay." My eyes dart to Zhèng, who has been watching the exchange with amusement. "Is that all?"

The captain huffs at my brazenness. "Yes. You may return to your work now."

They only receive my departure as a response.

24

THE NEXT DAY

CRIMSON OCEAN, 1800

It's when the sun sits high in the sky, its heat sweltering the deck whilst everyone else eats their midday meal, that Luo insists our lessons begin.

"Do I not deserve a bit of sustenance before being subjected to your antics?" I complain as I drag my new sword behind me toward the center of the main deck.

Honestly, the fact I get to forgo *another* helping of pickled vegetables and wild fish is an upside to the lesson. However, I would *never* let him know that he's done me any favors.

"Your stance, Shi Yang," he chides, ignoring my whining. He circles me with the might of a hawk. His wooden sword taps lightly against the flooring, the sound a tempo to his critique. "It's far too wide. If your foundation is weak, your blade will be, too."

I inhale deeply, narrowing the gap between my feet as he instructs, though his discerning gaze suggests I've yet to meet his expectations.

"Better," he concedes with a teasing lilt, "but, not ideal. Observe."

Stepping before me, he assumes a stance of perfect poise. He's naked again, of course. His sun-bathed shoulders rest easy, his weight balanced. The sweat slick muscles move gracefully in giant arcs, slicing the air. When he raises the practice sword, it is with such fluidity that it seems less a tool and more an extension of himself.

"Like so," he murmurs, casting a sidelong glance at me. His brow arches, daring me to match his skill.

I square my shoulders, mimicking his posture as best I can. My muscles protest the arrangement, but I suppress the discomfort, determined to hold the form.

"A decent attempt," he remarks, voice considering.

Before I can retort, he steps behind me, his presence a warm shadow. His hands, calloused yet gentle, find my arms and coax them into relaxation.

"Too rigid."

His words blow against the loose ringlets of my hair. This close, I register the faintest scent of something distinct lingering on his skin.

The smell of rain…

A memory in the back of my mind stirs.

"If you learn to brandish your sword as you do your stubbornness," he banters, "perhaps you might become the best swordsman to ever exist."

I'm knocked back into the moment, the thought gone as soon as it came.

"I would appreciate the guidance *without* the theatrics," I mutter, though I comply, letting my arms drop beneath his touch. His hands linger for a heartbeat before he withdraws.

"Shall we, then?" he asks, lifting his sword with a flourish that borders on ostentatious.

I nod, gripping the sword Huli gave me.

He lunges without warning, a sudden, calculated strike that forces me to react on instinct alone. Steel crashes against steel with a jarring shriek. The impact vibrates through my arms, rattling my bones. I brace for the eruption of energy I'd felt at the temple to send Luo flying across the deck, but nothing comes. He doesn't budge. Instead, it's *me* who absorbs the full force of the blow, my slippers skidding on the deck as I grit my teeth against the shock of it. His attacks are delivered with a strength that belies his lean frame.

His Wielding must be more powerful than I think.

With a rapid twist, he breaks the lock and knocks my sword out my hands. It skids across the floorboards with a loud scrape.

Before I can gather my wits, the tip of his blade rests lightly against my throat. "A lapse in concentration," he chides with a small grin that borders on roguish, "can cost you everything."

He lowers the sword, before returning to his starting position, movements almost lazy. The flat of his blade tilts toward my fallen weapon.

"Again," he says, voice tinged with playfulness. "We keep going until you win."

I don't win.

Not that day, or the next. Not for two weeks straight.

Each morning begins before the sun has fully broken the horizon, with dew still clinging to the sails. The sea is blanketed in a low haze as I spend the early hours with Old Chou, who teaches me more movements of Tai Chi.

After that, I spend my afternoons being defeated effortlessly by Luo.

Evenings, however, are reserved for lighter company. I spend hours watching Ah Fei Wield water and trying to mimic the skill. It doesn't help me get any closer to understanding my own Wielding, but it's… nice. Then, there's nights spent with Hé, who takes it upon himself to instruct me in the less honorable arts.

He shows me how to stack dice, count dominos, and hide them both in places I'd rather not mention. He teaches me how to keep a straight face when bluffing, and how to cheat so convincingly that it feels like skill. We laugh too much. Drink more than we should.

It's all wonderfully, achingly mundane.

For a while, I forget I'm supposed to be something more. That my blood carries prophecy. That the compass, resting against my collarbone, doesn't mean to lead me to something I never wanted.

For a while, I'm at peace.

But that doesn't last for long.

Chaos finds me, thirteen days from my first lesson with Luo. The day starts like the ones before it—drenched in sweat and repetition.

We're taking a break, seated on a low crate near the stern. The co-captain passes me the waterskin, and I take a long swig before handing it back.

He drinks, wipes his mouth with the back of his hand. His cheeks are pink from the sun. As we sit in silence, I remember that there's something I've been meaning to ask. And now feels like the right time.

"So…" I drawl.

He mirrors my tone immediately, eyes narrowing with suspicion. "Yes…?"

I elbow his arm, but it's more playful than pointed. He only laughs.

In the time we've spent together, we've grown rather… comfortable. No longer apprehensive of the other, we've found a fragile companionship while besting each other in combat.

Pretty fitting, if you ask me.

"Tell me about your Wielding," I poke. "You said that when you Wield a blade you never miss. That's why you use a wooden one with me, right?"

"Yeah," he replies slowly, like it's obvious. "And?"

"Well, when we fight," I push, "I can feel the strength of your energy… within the wood."

I pause, waiting for him to confirm what I've already suspected is true.

For a beat, he says nothing. Then a wry smile tugs at his lips—though his eyes don't share in the humor. "You are… very observant," he says carefully. He shifts, a little too casually. Then, he adds, "Yes. I've mastered earth. But I've also… learned to Wield wood."

I try not to let my awe show, but something must flash across my face because he looks away quickly, as if that might stop me from asking the next question.

I remember Ah Fei saying that Wielders mastering more than one element was unheard of. Nearly impossible. That it would take a high-level Wielder to do it. And yet, here one is.

On a pirate ship in the middle of the Ocean.

I try to keep my words casual. "How did you learn t—"

His mood switches abruptly, tension gone and replaced with a too-bright grin as he rises and rolls his shoulders. "Enough about me," he announces. "We've wasted enough time."

The wooden sword spins once in his hand before he points it toward me in challenge.

"One more round?"

I am thrown off by the change of subject, but I decide to leave it be. I can recognize a retreat when I see one.

If he doesn't want to talk about it, I'll respect that. Even if curiosity burns me.

A small smile finds its way to my lips, and I rise to meet him again. When I'm back at my starting position, my fingers curl tight around the hilt of my sword. My arms are tired. My legs ache. But something in me burns hotter than exhaustion.

Because I just *know* I can win this round.

This time, I take the initiative, lunging toward his side. He deflects with infuriating ease, his smirk deepening. The rhythm of our sparring intensifies, each exchange quicker, more precise. My breath comes fast, my skin soaked with exertion, but still, I press forward, driven by the singular goal of landing a blow.

After weeks of mapping his movements, memorizing his attacks, my body reacts before thought can intervene. It mirrors his hits and counters with an instinct that feels innate. We're locked in a dance, steps and strokes guided by some unspoken choreography. His actions suddenly awaken some buried recollection.

I know him.

I stop all movement, dropping the sword. "Where did you learn to fight like this?" I demand between breaths.

His face freezes and his eyes spark with despair, before shuttering with resignation. "Long ago," he says, voice dipped in a painful cadence, "I was tutored by someone who believed a blade would save me."

Though his words are cryptic, they plant a seed of curiosity. My mind scrambles for the origin of this familiarity, and then it all clashes together.

Luo and… Lo.

The smile melts from my face.

"You're the boy," I whisper mouth dry. My heart beats furiously in my chest. "You're the first boy that went missing." I take a step back as if scorched by his presence—by his betrayal. "You're a Hokan."

He doesn't speak for several moments, nor try to bridge the chasm growing between us.

His eyes slide downcast. Shame laces his next words.

"We… should talk."

PART FOUR: QUAIL

25

TWELEVE CYCLES AGO

KWANGCHOW PORT, 1788

Taunts ring in my ears as I'm shoved into the muck of the tidal flats, wet earth plastering to my legs. I scramble to my feet, but one of the village kids grabs the collar of my tunic, yanking me back down. Another pulls at my hem, forcing me to flail helplessly to keep them at bay.

I kick at their shins and kneecaps with everything I have in me, but they don't stop. Not until they've bored of it. When their arms grow tired from striking me, and their laughter dies down, they scatter, leaving me curled on the shore. I press my forehead to the coarse sand.

But I don't cry.

I've learned not to give them that satisfaction.

Instead, I let my anger simmer, a burn that feels hotter with each passing day.

They may have the best of me now, but I swear to myself there will come a time when I won't cower. A time when I'll fight back, my fists will meet their skin with the kind of force they won't forget.

When I'm sure they're gone, I sit up, brushing the dirt from my arms. The bruise forming on my elbow is tender, but I ignore it. Pain is something I've grown used to, something I've learned to swallow.

I pull myself to my feet and glance toward the floating village. The adults there know of the cruelty I endure. They often witness it; they just don't particularly care enough to interfere.

The chatter of evening chores drifts across the water, wax candles and lanterns already lit.

Before the confrontation, I was supposed to be fetching water and bringing it back to Ba for his evening bathing. However, the thought of returning to the sampan now, where I'll be met with silence or worse, makes me hesitate. The water laps against the shore, urging me to make a decision.

Without thinking, I collect the old clay jug, and head inland, away from the boats and the village. I won't go past the shore, but I need a moment to be alone.

The object feels heavy in my hands—even without being full—as I wonder down the coast, avoiding the eyes of anyone lingering outside their boats. No one acknowledges me, and for once, I'm grateful.

I don't want to be seen.

Once I stop farther away from the hive of junks, I bend to dip the curve of the ware into the water. As it quickly begins to fill, I stare into the rippling surface of the ocean for a long moment. My reflection is distorted in the fading light of early evening. I hate the way I look—small, weak, powerless.

My jaw tightens as I straighten, gripping the jug tightly.

I still don't favor the idea of returning just yet, so I continue walking. The land feels foreign under my feet—packed solid, unmoving. Though I risk potentially being caught and punished by the Imperial soldiers for wondering this far, I cannot help but venture on. The farther I go, the quieter it becomes. I find myself drawn to a cluster of bamboo trees that move gently in the breeze.

As I step into them, the faint hum of insects replaces the familiar cries of gulls. The thin stalks creak softly, a sound that blends with the rustling of their leaves. I journey deeper, the ground cool beneath my bare feet, when I hear it—a faint *thwack, thwack* cutting through the stillness.

Curious, I follow the sound, weaving between the trees. As I get closer, it turns into a controlled beating. My heart quickens. It isn't the sound of something natural; it's the sound of effort, of practice. The sound grows louder as I approach until I reach the edge of a small clearing.

Peering through the density of the trees, I see him—a boy, slightly older than me, wielding a wooden sword. His movements are lethal, his posture solid despite his thin frame. He swings the sword again, the force of the motion sending a racking shiver through the bamboo leaves above him. He hits the trees, each blow landing hard enough to scratch the green from the stalks. Pale brown wounds are left behind as his calling card. Looking around, I notice that there are similar marks on a lot of the trees.

I stay hidden, watching, studying, as he repeats the same sequence over and over.

I recognize him. The Lo boy. His family's boat is docked at the far end of the village.

On days when Ba deems me too unimportant to interact with, I watch the boy and his father practice from our egg boat.

It's often that families come and go from the village, hopping from port to port, so I do not know any of their names, but this Lo family is different. They do not blend into the background of the decaying tapestry of the area.

His father is one of the few men bold enough to openly speak against the Emperor and the Pingshens. He often tries to appeal to the other adults in the clan about us being stronger than them. That we can reclaim the land they once pushed us off of.

But they never listen to him.

The rest of the clan are content to cower away on these boats so long as we are left alone. Happy to accept the scraps we are given. They fear the retribution of the Emperor too much to demand anything more.

The boy takes another swing at the trees, sweat dripping down his temple.

It occurs to me, then, how much he resembles his father. On the surface level, they share the same features: their noses tall, and brows low. But deeper, much like his father, he doesn't care what anyone thinks of him. He doesn't conform to group activities.

He's an outsider like me.

The only reason the other children don't torment *him*, though, is because of his training.

Every other day, he and his father spend hours and hours upon their deck practicing different forms of defense. It's as if they are preparing for something—privy to a looming threat that rest of us do not know of.

As I continue to watch the boy, the way he moves stirs something in me.

Admiration?

No, I don't think anyone has earned that from me. But, perhaps, an understanding?

There is a connection I cannot place.

I step forward without meaning to, my inquisitiveness drawing me closer. A dried leaf crinkles underfoot. The boy freezes mid-swing, his cutting eyes darting toward the trees where I'm hiding.

"Who's there?" he calls out. Not scared, nor angry—just attentive.

I stall, debating whether to run or reveal myself. However, a warmth in my chest I cannot name, decides for me.

Slowly, I step out from behind the trees. The water jug has become unbearably heavy, so, I lower it to the ground before standing upright again.

As he looks me over, I can see his eyes catching on the bruises on my arms and the split at the corner of my lip.

"They did that to you, didn't they?"

He doesn't expect a response. Everyone knows I'm the girl who doesn't speak.

"Cowards," he mutters, shaking his head. "Always picking on someone who won't fight back. Makes them no better than the Pingshens."

I drop my gaze, gripping the hem of my oversized tunic.

I suppose he's right. They beat on the weak to just to feel like they have some semblance of control. Punching down on whoever is below them because they cannot reach up to the man they really want to punish. They *aren't* any better than the Pingshens.

At least not to me.

So, then why does a part of me still want to be accepted by them?

The boy sighs then, the sound almost exasperated, and tosses the wooden sword at my feet. It clatters against the ground, making me flinch.

"Pick it up," he says.

I blink at him, confused.

"Pick it up," he repeats, more firmly. "You want them to stop, don't you?"

I hesitate, staring at the sword as if it might bite me. Finally, I bend down and grasp it, my fingers fumbling against the worn wood.

"Not like that," he reprimands, stepping forward. He grabs the sword from me, adjusting my grip, and shoves it back into my hands. "Tighter. You'll lose it if you hold it like that. Once that happens, your own weapon will could be turned against you. Then, you're dead."

I tighten my grip, my hands trembling slightly. His words terrify me but also set alight a sting of defiance at the thought of someone using what's mine to condemn me.

"Stand like this." He plants his feet shoulder-width apart and motions for me to copy him. I mirror his stance awkwardly, feeling like a fool.

"At least you're not falling over," he mutters. "Now, don't swing all crazy. Keep it steady, controlled." He demonstrates, the sword moving in a slow, precise arc. "Like that. Now you try."

I swing, clumsy and hesitant.

"Too slow," he says flatly. "Again."

I try again, frustration simmering in my chest.

"Still too slow. Tighten your wrist." He taps the wooden sword in my hands. "It's not just a stick. It's part of you."

I adjust my grip once more, steady my stance, and swing again. This time, it is cleaner, sharper.

He nods once. "Better. But don't think that'll scare them. They'll only stop if they know you're serious. If you hesitate, you're done. Understand?"

I meet his gaze, my resolve hardening.

"Good," he says. "Now, again."

We practice until my arms ache. When he finally lets me stop, he smirks faintly. "You're tougher than you look. Keep at it, and they'll think twice before crossing you." He looks down to the sword in my hands, gesturing at it with a tilt of his head, "It's yours. Practice with it whenever you can."

I nod, my grip still firm on the sword as I turn to leave.

"Hey," he calls after me, voice softer now. "Don't just fight to stop them. Fight to win. If it's between you or them, do not hesitate. Choose yourself. Again and again."

I level him with a small nod of my head, before I turn for the village. His words stay with me long after I leave the clearing. On the walk back, the sky opens, and rain begins to pour.

However, I don't mind getting drenched. Instead, the natural smell lodges into my brain, attached to this day.

The day I felt a spark of something new for the first time: power.

After that, the boy and I meet every other day. He never tells me his name, and I never tell him mine, but our friendship grows all the same.

He teaches me whatever his dad teaches *him* earlier in the day. I take to the dagger and knife more than the sword, and I spend a lot of time laid out on the ground from our hand-to-hand sparring, but I enjoy it.

Just earlier today, three moons since I first started learning with the Lo boy, I managed to punch back at the older children. I'm even sporting bruised knuckles to prove it. It'd made me feel larger than life.

It won't be long until *they're* running from *me.*

That's exactly what I expect the Lo boy to say when I show him today except—

He's not in the clearing.

I frown, my head whipping side to side.

This is the time we agreed to. The time he never misses.

Perhaps, his training with his father ran longer than usual. Yeah, that's got to be it. I'll just wait here until he's done.

I plop down on the flattened grass and wait. And wait. And wait.

I wait until the stars return to their positions in the night sky.

It is only then, that I leave. But I can't shake the feeling that I must check to see if he's alright. So, instead of returning immediately to Ba's sampan, I tiptoe along the shore, peering through the night for the Lo boat. When I find it, it floats there, dark.

But the nerves in my stomach don't settle. Something tells me to keep searching. My eyes are gliding around the floating village when I notice the Council's boat has light coming from it.

What are they still doing up?

My legs carry me over before sense can talk me out of it.

When I reach the boat, I press my ear to the wooden side that towers above me. I can just barely make out their voices. The soft lapping of waves nearly drowns them out, but their anger cuts through regardless.

"...You *gave* it to him?" the Eldermother's gravelly voice whips. It rises to a level that betrays the meeting's discreetness. "To your son!"

Son?

I peek my head over the edge of the boat. And there they are. The Lo family—the father standing before the Council, and the mother holding the son off to the side behind him. Their backs are to me, but as if sensing my presence, the boy looks over his shoulder.

I duck down, heart racing.

I shouldn't be here.

I am about to flee—escape back to Ba's boat and let sleep drag away any curiosity I have left when—

"You doubt the Goddess?" the Eldermother says, quieter now, but more dangerous for it. "You claim your son's life as justification to lead our people into darkness?"

"No," the Lo father says, a thread of desperation slipping through. "I claim his life as proof that we must *change*. You sit in this boat, clinging to tradition while the rest of the world begins to burn. There is a war coming. You think we'll be spared, just because we keep our heads bowed?"

"We know that you have shared aetherbloom with others," another Elder claims.

"You've corrupted our people," the Eldermother cuts in. "Do you understand what you've set in motion?"

"I've given them a chance," the Lo father says. "I have been told what is coming. An army builds in the shadows of this empire. One that does not adhere to the reality we know. And you want to meet it with silence and song? Our people deserve to fight. We deserve to survive!"

"Enough!" one of the Elder men snaps.

The Lo father stands quietly in defiance for a beat. "You don't have to believe me, but it won't stop it from coming."

I shift too hard, pebbles skittering beneath me. A voice inside shouts. "Who's there?!"

As soon as feet begin to shuffle in my direction, I sprint back down the shore.

The very next day, the boy, and his family's boat are gone.

For eight weeks, I wait for Lo family to return, but they never do. Early in the mornings, I practice what he taught me in the bamboo clearing, hoping to suddenly hear his admonishing tone pointing out a flaw in my stance.

But it's only ever silence.

The Lo family's leave was not initially felt by anyone else but me until three weeks ago when two more family boats had gone in the night. One day, their boats bobbing here, a few days later, nothing but still water in their wake.

Where did they go? What did the Lo father know?

26

LATE AFTERNOON

CRIMSON OCEAN, 1800

The silence in the captain's quarters is suffocating.

Its oppression is broken only by the groaning creaks of the ship's wooden frame as it cuts through the waves. Even through the closed doors, the notes of a pending rainstorm linger in the air. And with the scent comes a memory, rushing in with relentless clarity.

I shut my eyes tightly.

A boy who taught me to sidestep a blade, to stand my ground even when my legs trembled with fatigue. A day that revealed to me a version of myself I hadn't known existed. The feeling I once had of belonging, of being seen, comes back to me like one falls to sleep, slowly then all at once.

But then, I let my eyes drift open.

And here he is, decades later.

The boy is still there, but time has taken its dues. The sight of him now is a strange collision of past and present, a reminder of who we were and who we've become.

Luo exhales sharply, running a hand through his hair. "Shi Yang—"

"I looked for you everywhere," I say, cutting him off. My words tumble out, shaky and too fast. "I thought maybe you'd been banished or—"

"Shi Yang—"

"You can't even imagine how long I waited for you. Moons!" My voice is bordering hysterical now. "So many of the clan disappeared after you. We dwindled to almost nothing!"

The betrayal is too much. Two side of my emotions are at war with each other.

He is the only other member I have.

I hate him.

I'm no longer alone.

"Shi Yang!" he snaps, pulling me back. He takes a step closer, his eyes locked on mine. "Stop."

I clamp my mouth shut, but my fists are trembling at my sides.

"I need to know," I whisper. "What happened to you? Where did you go?"

He doesn't answer right away. Instead, he leans against Zhèng's desk, staring at the floor. His jaw is tight, his expression distant. "It's not a short story," he says at last.

"I'm not going anywhere," I respond flatly.

He gives a faint, humorless chuckle. "No, I suppose you're not."

I don't find *any* of this humorous.

In absence of a response from me, the silence stretches, broken only by the pitter patter of rain drops beginning to fall outside. Finally, he turns to me, his face shadowed, but his eyes burning with something I can't quite name.

"I didn't leave, Shi Yang," he confesses. "I was taken. We all were."

The words don't shock me, but for a moment, I can't breathe.

What I'd feared most was confirmed.

He straightens. "You know that though, don't you?"

I stay mute.

He gestures towards two vacant barrels in the corner of the room. "Sit," his tone softening, "I'll tell you everything."

I stare blankly at him. Glancing at Zhèng, I recognize that the man has been oddly quiet the duration of this spat.

Obviously, he knows.

And for that, I hate him too.

Reluctantly, I move over to the barrel, but I do not sit. If Luo has a comment to make about my defiance, he does not share it. Instead, he walks past me and sits on one himself.

From above, the light in the room contours his face differently than I'm accustomed to. The shadows reveal bags under his eyes in a way that makes him seem decades older than he is. He looks beaten, in more ways than one.

"Shi Yang," he begins, "I should've told you this earlier—and I'm sorry for the deceit—but I thought if you knew, you'd see me differently." He swallows hard, pulling at the neckline of his tunic. Just as the rain beyond this room begins to pick up, sweat accumulates on his temple. "That night I was taken… My parents," he chokes, "they were slaughtered trying to protect me. My father's throat slit, and my mother ravaged to death by the men carrying out the deed. I see it in fragments. Slashes of terror; of grief."

He looks out into space as if he were experiencing the memories vividly.

"I tried to fight back using the knowledge my Baba taught me. Although the power awakened by the aetherbloom my father had given me was strong, I didn't know how to control it. The next thing I remember was waking up in a cold, dark cell." He rubs at his wrists absentmindedly, "I can still feel the chains some nights," he breathes. "Day after day, I would be tormented and beat. One night, when they had finally broken my spirit, I was dragged through the halls of what looked like an underground city. A labyrinth of opulence, with golden filigree and jade inlays… nobles and cultists bustling about. There was no mistake about where I was." When he looks up, his tragic eyes arrest mine. "I was in the Serpent Emperor's palace."

My mind blanks, paralyzed with fear, with loathing, with grief.

Luo continues on, "I-I was taken to a chamber of an alchemist. He never showed his face; a man shrouded in darkness. The guards referred to him as 'The Master'."

Heat rises, molten and fierce deep inside my chest.

"He tasked himself with studying me. My response to pain, and most importantly, my tolerance to aetherbloom." He closes his eyes tightly. "He conducted tests routinely on me. Observing how I would react to increased dosages. At first, the symptoms were what one would expect. My mind wondered in a twilight space for what felt like eternity. More than once, I felt like my skin was being peeled off me. Aching pinpricks all over." He shifts his hand to hover over his legs. "I would scratch at my thighs until I bled. I thought The Master would tire of me…that he would bore of watching me die a slow death. But he never did."

I tuck my hands underneath my armpits to hide their shaking. The moaning of the ship against the rising hostile waters falls into concert with the sounds of our breathing. I glance over at Zhèng. His jaw twitches roughly as he broods in silence. He looks furious enough to tear the world a part. When I turn back to Luo, his eyes are glossy in the candlelight.

"Until one day, they gave me *too much* aetherbloom." He breathes shakily, the sound weighted with the memory. "That time, my body didn't shut down, and my mind did not wander aimlessly in the abyss. Instead, when the guards beat me, I took their weapons from them. And when I struck with them, they fell and did not get back up. Every aim I made for a vital spot landed true. The muscles in my body had corded and hardened as if the aetherbloom had rewritten the very fabric of my being. That is how my Entropic Wielding presented itself to me. The drug had induced a beast from the shadows somewhere within me. One I couldn't tame."

Like I can't.

"I thought I could escape. I thought I could tear my way out of that dungeon. But my rampage didn't last long. The Master himself is a Wielder. One more powerful than any I'd ever seen before. That is," he says, his voice dropping to a whisper, "until you."

My palms are slick with sweat. He licks his dry lips, as if prepping himself for what comes next.

"The Master… when he saw what I could do, what the aetherbloom could trigger, became obsessed. My body, my power—it wasn't just a curiosity anymore. It was a weapon. One the Emperor desperately needs."

His lips tremble, and for a moment, he looks away.

My mind races, and in the flurry of thoughts, I think about the edict.

So, Merchant Fang was partially right. The Serpent Emperor is keeping aetherbloom all to himself, not for indulgence, but for domination across the world.

The edict's real purpose was so that the Emperor could monopolize the production of, and experimentation with aetherbloom. Foreign rulers must deem it too great of a threat if Pingshen is the only nation producing Wielders—weapons beyond other mortal nations' capabilities. It's only a matter of time before they unite against the empire.

The thought makes the hair on the back of my neck stand on end. I'm brought out of my contemplation when Luo speaks again, his voice barely audible.

"After that, the tests only got more severe. More invasive. Sometimes my power would activate, and sometimes it wouldn't. But The Master learned one crucial thing: it was triggered by survival. That's all he needed to know. He started capturing others. I don't know how he found our clan, but he'd been searching for a being of immense power. Someone like you." He chokes, before letting out a dry sob. "And because I wasn't strong enough to kill any of them, or even myself, he—"

I want to reach out, to offer comfort, but before I can uncurl my hand, Zhèng is kneeling down before him. His hand is gentle as he brushes away the tears, his thumb caressing Luo's high cheekbone.

I feel like an intruder, yet somehow, not unwelcome.

Maybe, in time, I'll understand what they share.

Luo takes a moment to collect himself, his breath shuddering as he wipes at his face. He gives Zhèng's hand a nuzzle, a gesture so small I almost miss it. Then, with a deep breath, he continues.

"My very existence gave him the incentive to find more of us—or wipe us out trying. Every night, others were dragged in. And I watched what he did to them. I saw the bodies, barely clinging to life. I heard the screams as their minds and bodies were torn apart. The Master's chambers reeked of aetherbloom and rotting flesh. Hokans were subjected to his tests, forced to endure the terror of the drug. Some ended up like me. Weapons of mass destruction being held captive in the bowels of the Emperor's palace with no one to save them."

At this, my arms unfurl and my hands flex at my sides.

I was a child. There's nothing I could've done back then.

I repeat this mantra in my head until the words begin to jumble together. It does nothing to quell the guilt that attempts to consume me.

"But most of them did not survive. And the guards, they spoke about it as if it was nothing. Like we weren't people at all."

I shift on my feet, my head feeling light from the abundance of hatred taking root in it. "How did you manage to escape?" I ask.

"I spent every night trying to harness my powers and my strength. Until the very last night, a figure appeared in my cell. It was Huli."

The ship begins to rock even rougher now. I plant my feet to find balance as my stomach twists. I recall Luo's words from weeks ago. I wonder what Huli required of him. I wonder how he even had anything left to give.

"I struck a deal with Huli for my escape—for the escape of anyone else who was still alive. And they granted it. For a price."

He doesn't elaborate.

"Some made it out. Many more didn't. For cycles, all that haunted me was the knowledge that I wasn't strong enough. *I* wasn't enough." He stands then, stepping closer to me. His hand reaches out, trembling slightly as he grasps mine. There's a vulnerability in the gesture, a fear that I might pull away.

I almost do.

"But now, standing here, looking at you—I know what I didn't know then: I was never meant to be the one to stop this. *You* were."

I swallow harshly. "Why are you so sure of this? Of me?"

"The Emperor fears our people because of the potential of what we can be—because of *you.* You are something greater than him, greater than The Master. And they know that. He spent cycles trying to break the Hokan, to twist our lineage into something he could control, but he couldn't. And now, the power he fears is standing right in front of me."

"You think I'm supposed to fix *everything*?" I retort, though the heat in my voice feels hallow.

Deep down, of course I want to make the Emperor pay. I want to make The Master grovel for his life. I want to burn this entire empire to ash. But, amid the anger, I can't help but feel an inkling of reservation.

I wanted to find out what happened to the clan. And now I know, but I didn't think it'd include having to defeat an empire.

Luo tightens the grip he has on my hand. "No, Shi Yang. I think you're the only one strong enough to end it. And if you let me, not only will we fight beside you, we *will* kill for you."

My heart thunders in my chest. I feel a blush rise to my cheeks but immediately let lose a sharp counter as a distraction. "And if I tell you I don't want your help?"

"Then we will still keep that promise." Zhèng replies.

"I was too late to save them," Luo says quietly, "But I will *not* be too late to save you."

The room feels smaller now. I can't bring myself to look at Luo, not when his eyes hold so much hope—so much faith in me. Faith I'm not sure I want.

My gaze drops to the floor, tracing the cracks in the wood as if they might offer some escape from the storm brewing inside me.

"You don't understand," I say finally, voice brittle as I pull my hand away and step back. The distance between us feels necessary, like a shield against the vulnerability his words have unleashed. "I've spent my entire life running, hiding, surviving. I'm not a hero, and I'm certainly not anyone's savior. I'm just someone who's good at not dying."

"You don't believe that," Zhèng cuts in.

I open my mouth to argue, to push back against the certainty in his tone, but the words catch in my throat. There's something in the way he looks at me, something that feels like understanding. Like he sees the cracks in my armor, the fractures in my resolve, and still looks to me anyways. For a moment, I almost let myself believe him.

Almost.

But then I remember. The barrels below deck. The Aether. My stomach twists, and I take another step back, my eyes narrowing as I glare at them both.

"If you've seen with your own eyes the truth of aetherbloom's terror," I accuse, "why do you carry the flower on your ship?"

Luo's face pales, and for a moment, he looks as though I've struck him. Zhèng's jaw sets.

Luo opens his mouth to respond, but Zhèng cuts him off. "Because it's the only leverage we have."

I blink, caught off guard by his bluntness. "Leverage?"

Zhèng steps closer. "The Emperor has the help of a being—unbeknownst to the rest of the world—that is capable of incomparable shadow Wielding. A potency so strong that he can impart his power onto men who do his bidding. If we're going to fight him, we need to understand the drug and its potential for chaos. We need to know how it works, how to counter it. And yes, sometimes that means carrying it with us until we can get in the hands of someone who can render its powers for good."

His words make a twisted kind of sense, but they do little to ease the knot of apprehension tightening in my chest.

"And what happens if *those* hands are the wrong ones?" I press. "What happens when that *someone* decides to use it, just like The Master does? How many more lives will be destroyed because of it?"

Luo flinches. "We are *not* like him," he says, voice trembling with barely restrained emotion. "We would never—"

"*You* may not be," I interrupt, "but what's to say that this other Wielder is not? Mortals are greedy, insatiable, untrustworthy fiends."

The crescendo of the storm outside makes up the remaining sound in the room.

For a moment, I think the captain's going to argue, to defend their risky plan, but then he speaks, and his words send a chill down my spine.

"What if…" he begins, "the *someone*… isn't mortal at all?"

The world seems to freeze.

The atmosphere grows still, the creaking of the ship fades into silence. The compass, on my person as a necklace, begins to hum. However, I ignore it as my mind stumbles, trying to make sense of his words.

Isn't mortal at all? What is he suggesting?

Do they somehow have *another* spirit acquaintance on standby?

My brow furrows and my eyes slide back and forth between both men for a moment before it clicks.

They're in communication with… a God?

The thought is both terrifying and absurd, and yet the look in Zhèng's eyes tells me he's deadly serious.

However, before I can respond—before I can even begin to process the implications of his words further—the ship lurches violently. I stumble, grabbing onto the edge of the table to steady myself. Luo crashes into the wall, his eyes wide with panic, and even Zhèng stumbles, his demeanor cracking.

Then it comes—a deafening roar that shakes the very bones of the ship. It's a sound unlike anything I've ever heard, deep and primal, reverberating through the air like thunder. My blood runs cold as the realization hits me. That roar… it's something ancient, something mythical.

It's the cry of a dragon.

The ship jostles again, harder this time, and I hear the splintering of wood somewhere above deck. Shouts and screams echo through the hull, and the sound of rushing water fills my ears. Zhèng's face is pale now, his earlier confidence shattered. Luo looks like he's about to be sick.

"What," I whisper, gripping the now vibrating compass hanging at my chest, "is happening?" My voice is barely audible over the chaos. But Zhèng doesn't answer. He's already moving, shoving past me toward the door, his hand gripping the hilt of his sword.

The dragon's roar comes again, closer this time, and I feel it in my chest, a deep vibration that makes my heart pound.

And I know there's no escaping it.

27

DUSK

THE CELESTIAL TRENCH, 1800

Luo and I burst out of the captain's cabin. The door slams against the wood with a resounding crack as we follow Zhèng onto the deck. My feet skid against the rain-slick planks, barely finding traction as I sprint toward the sterncastle. My calloused hands latch onto the ornately carved balustrade, steadying me as I take in the scene.

The sky has soured into an eerie, unnatural green, a sickly pallor stretched across the Heavens. The sun has been swallowed by a mass of storm clouds. The sea churns violently beneath us, its surface fractured by sheets of rain that distort the horizon, turning the world into a blur of ghostly haze.

"Eye's up!" Zhèng's voice cuts through the storm. The wind and thunder nearly devour his command.

Another roar churns the air as panic flares in my chest.

My sword—Huli's gift—is still in my hammock. Useless. Out of reach. I pivot toward the stairway leading to the main deck, my pulse hammering. But the downpour is blinding, reducing everything not within arm's reach to vague shapes. I nearly overshoot the stairwell entirely—until Luo's hand clamps onto my arm, yanking me back from the brink of a deadly fall.

I open my mouth to give a quick thanks, but before I can, the ship lurches again. The water beneath us convulses, an unseen force wrenching the junk boat upward before slamming it down again. The violent motion tears us both from our footing.

We hit the stairs hard.

Pain explodes across my back, my skull ringing like a struck gong. My vision swims, and the world tilts dangerously. Distantly, I hear the sound of bodies hitting the deck—sailors tossed like dolls by the force of the impact.

Then, I realize I didn't hit the deck alone. Luo broke my most of my fall. I turn to check on him but…

He isn't moving.

My stomach lurches.

I push myself up, ignoring the screaming protest of my limbs, and grasp his shoulders. His face is slack, eyes shut. A trickle of blood slips from his temple, lost in the rain.

"Luo?" My voice is hoarse, barely audible over the storm. I shake him once. Twice. "Luo, wake up! Please, not now!"

I snap my head up as another bellow splits the sky, closer this time, crackling with raw fury.

I need my sword. Now.

With a deep breath, I turn toward the sterncastle and holler over the raging wind, "Zhèng! Luo's down!"

Zhèng's response is immediate, and ruthless. "Leave him! Go prepare yourself!"

My chest tightens, my gaze darting back to Luo's still form. But there's no time to hesitate. Zhèng's voice isn't a command—

it's an order for survival. I scramble to my feet, swallowing the sick feeling rising in my throat.

As I rush down the ladder toward the crew's quarters, I hear Zhèng barking another command, his words lost in the tempest. But there are footsteps pounding overhead toward the direction I came from.

Someone must be going to retrieve Luo.

I let out a small, shaky breath of relief, and then force myself to refocus.

The sword.

I find it easily. Its familiar weight grounds me as I wrap my fingers around the hilt. I waste no time racing back up to the deck. But as I reach the final step, an inexplicable shiver races down my spine.

Something is very wrong.

The sea erupts.

An enormous serpentine form bursts from the depths, shattering the surface with a deafening crash. A wall of water spews around it, drenching the deck anew. The dragon's iridescent blue scales shimmer with an unnatural luminescence as it surges skyward. It moves with an impossible grace, its long, sinuous body slicing through the storm-choked air, disappearing into the dense, roiling clouds.

For a breathless moment, nothing. Then, only the sound of rain hammering against the ship and the ragged breathing of sailors who dare not move remains.

We cannot see it.

We can only hear the wind shift, feel the change in pressure, sense something colossal circling above. Time stretches like a drawn bowstring, every man gripping his weapon with white-knuckled hands, waiting for the inevitable.

"Battle stations!" Zhèng roars.

His words set the crew into a frenzy of motion. There is no hesitation, no questioning what they face—only grim determination. Small, brass cannons are hastily loaded, the hiss of powder igniting lost beneath the crashing waves. Harpoons are readied, barbed tips glinting in the sparse light, and sailors arm themselves with daos, spears, and bows strung taut with sinew.

None of it will be enough. We are no match for this dragon. But at least we will die fighting.

I wipe the rain from my eyes, peering into the churning sky. I jerk my head left, then right, searching—

A bolt of lightning rips across the sky.

For a heartbeat, the world is saturated in stark white brilliance. And in that instant, I see it.

The shadowed outline of the beast sits above the junk midair. Only its eyes—burning of molten gold—are visible through the mist.

The breath catches in my throat.

Then the dragon descends.

It plummets toward us with terrifying speed, a streak of darkness slicing through the storm, its massive jaws yawning open to reveal row upon row of ivory daggers.

"FIRE!"

The command is drowned by the barrage of cannon fire. A volley of brass balls hurtles skyward, red sparks and gunpowder smoke trailing in their wake. Some shots miss, swallowed by the storm, but at least one finds its mark—slamming into the dragon's side with a dull, sickening thud.

The beast lets out an ear-splitting screech. It coils mid-air, twisting to evade the next onslaught, then retaliates with a force that makes my stomach drop.

The dragon's tail—thick as a ship's mast—whips through the air and crashes into the port side of the junk. The impact is cataclysmic. The ship groans in protest as the hull splinters, wooden shards exploding like shrapnel. The force sends men flying—some straight overboard into the ravenous sea. Others, less fortunate, are impaled by jagged debris. Their screams are lost in the wind.

The shockwave throws me sprawling across the deck. My vision reels, the world a blur of rain and chaos. I barely manage to roll to my feet before the dragon attacks again—this time, targeting me.

Its head barrels toward the bow, its cavernous maw gaping wide.

I move on instinct.

Seizing a nearby rope of rigging, I kick off the deck, swinging high into the air just as the dragon's jaws snap shut behind me. I land hard against the foremast, the impact rattling through my bones, but I manage to steady myself despite the ship's wild motions. My heart slams against my ribs.

A memory floods my mind—one born of cycles spent hunting fish in the open waters.

A spear through the eye. That's the quickest way to stop a sea creature.

I can only pray the same rule applies here.

"Aim for the eyes!" I yell, voice piercing through madness.

Because if we don't blind it, we die.

The battered cannons belch fire and smoke, as a final volley streaks toward the dragon's head. The creature twists its body with impossible agility, dodging most of the projectiles. One cannonball strikes its jaw, ricocheting harmlessly off its shimmering scales. Another grazes its left eye, drawing a cry of pain that causes the rigging to shudder.

Then the dragon retaliates.

It rears back, throat bulging, and with a deep, guttural exhalation, spews forth a scalding torrent of water.

Boiling deluge floods the deck. Men caught in its path drop their weapons, their bodies writhing in agony as skin blisters and peels away in gruesome ribbons. The acrid scent of burning flesh mixing with the salt and rain, turning my stomach.

Fury burrows deep in my chest, molding into resolve.

The dragon must be brought down before the crew is decimated to nothing but carrion for the sea.

I seize the sword at my waist. A deep, shuddering breath steadies me—then I leap.

The world rushes around me as I plummet through the rain-slick air, the cold sea wind slashing through my soaked clothes like a thousand knives. I land hard against the dragon's form, my ankle twisting beneath me. A sharp pain lances up my leg, but I bite my lip to keep from crying out. My only comfort is that the beast, too consumed in its wrath, does not notice my arrival.

I exhale sharply and begin to climb.

The dragon's scales are vast, each one larger than my palm and slippery with rain, but I dig my fingers into its ridges, hauling myself upward. Every powerful undulation of its body threatens to throw me off. The storm rages around us, yet I keep moving, each pull bringing me closer to the beast's head.

Lightning arcs through the sky, illuminating the scene in flashes. Zhèng and the crew are a flurry of motion beneath me, harpoons and grappling hooks at the ready, waiting for the moment to attack.

I reach the dragon's crown and steady myself on its skull, favoring my uninjured leg. The ship is nothing but a speck beneath us now, the sea an endless, roiling abyss. My fingers tighten around the sword's hilt.

Then, something unexpected occurs.

The blade shimmers. A ghostly light pulses along its edge. The compass against my chest thrums, vibrating as if awakened.

But I push the distraction aside—there is no time for questions.

With a scream, I raise the weapon high and drive it down into a gap between the scales, right in the wound left by the cannon's blow.

The dragon shrieks, its body convulsing in agony. Below, the captain seizes the moment.

"Harpoon the damn thing!" Zhèng commands, voice carrying high, above the storm's howl. "Pin it down!"

The order is followed instantly.

Spears sail through the rain, ropes tightening around the dragon's limbs. The beast thrashes against its new restraints, but the men move with ruthless precision, locking the lines in place. The junk moans under the strain, but the crew does not err.

I clutch onto the dragon's ridged brow, but the violent struggle sends me tumbling forward. My hands shoot out on instinct, catching onto a part of the horn above the beast's eye. The heat radiating from its scales sears my body, but I grit my teeth and hold on.

Its eye finds mine.

A vast, molten gaze, burning gold like a bleeding sun. I'm nothing in comparison, smaller than the breadth of its pupil, yet its attention traps me.

The world fades.

The screams of men, the crash of waves, the wind's howl—everything vanishes into a silence so absolute it feels as though time itself has stopped.

And in the reflection of the dragon's eye, I see—

Myself. But not as I am in this moment. In the mirrored glow, my own eyes blaze with the same golden fire.

The dragon stills as if trying to communicate.

Below, the battle rages on, oblivious to the exchange.

Zhèng's voice carries over the storm. "Shi Yang! Don't let go!"

"I hadn't planned on it!" I shout back, but my voice feels distant, as though I'm speaking from somewhere far away.

I swallow, my heart thundering in my chest as I remember Huli and their prophecy.

"A mentor will find you. Be prepared to learn when they do."

Everything connects now. The compass. The sword.

A sentence claws its way up my throat, escaping before I can stop it. "You're here for me."

The dragon rumbles, a low, vibrating growl. Then, as if roused from a trance, it thrashes violently, twisting against its restraints. The ropes break.

I lurch forward as the beast rises, its powerful body maneuvering through the air. My sword slips from my grasp, falling uselessly to the deck below. I barely manage to secure my grip with both hands as the dragon soars higher.

And it dives.

A piercing shriek is the only warning before we plunge.

The sea rushes up to meet us, a yawning abyss of black, churning waves. Cold dread seizes my gut.

Then—impact.

The ocean envelops us.

The frigid water shocks my system, the pressure squeezing the breath from my lungs. Darkness engulfs everything. I fight the instinct to inhale, but my body is spent, the exhaustion from battle sinking into my bones.

My limbs grow heavy, and my hands fall from the dragon's body. I'm floating, weightless in the water watching as the beast circles me. Its body closes around me into a makeshift cocoon drawing nearer and nearer.

As the world fades into endless, inky black, a single thought forms in my mind, quiet and certain.

This is it.

This is how I die.

28

UNKNOWN

UNKNOWN, 1800

The depths are alive.

That is the first thing that comes to mind when consciousness claws its way back to me.

I'm no longer sinking. No longer tangled in the chaos of the dragon's wake. Instead, I'm lying on cold, uneven stone. My body aches—my lungs raw from nearly drowning. I cough, each breath tasting like metal. But it is air. Blessed, aching air.

My fingers curl against the damp floor as I push up to my elbows, taking in my surroundings.

I'm in a cave.

The walls rise high, shimmering with an ethereal glow. The ceiling is lost in darkness, but tiny specks of blue and green light twinkle above like fallen stars. They're glimmering creatures hovering, casting a dim light across the cavern's heart.

One of the tiny creatures falls onto my forearm. It slugs slowly down the length of my arm as I bring it closer to my face to observe. Its movement elicits a tingling sensation—one I want to itch. I'm both disgusted and fascinated.

Then, my eyes shift past my arm, my brows furrowing.

The mouth of the cave is sealed not by stone, but by water.

There is a wall of it, holding firm against logic itself. The ocean beyond whirls, but it does not breach this unseen threshold. It is a barrier, a boundary between this cave—this world?—and whatever lies outside. My pulse hammers as I rise, muscles protesting. I quickly shake the glowing bug off me, and step toward the barrier.

As I approach, the surface ripples, as if disturbed by the impact of a rock. Something compels me to touch it, so I reach out a single finger.

When my skin meets the water, my reflection emerges in its depths as a wavering, ghostly thing. But even through the distortion, something is wrong.

The shape in the water is not mine.

I freeze.

From beyond the barrier, darkness unfurls.

Tendrils of black ink spiral outward, blooming until my reflection is engulfed entirely. And then, within that abyss, two golden eyes ignite.

A familiar horror grips my chest.

The shadowed dragon swims through the water like a wraith, its inky form curling against the liquid barrier, poisoning it with its presence.

I stumble back, my breath coming sharp and uneven. My heart races against my ribs, the cavern walls closing in.

The nightmare has followed me.

It's here, and it's real.

A voice from behind cuts through my terror.

"There are many things to fear, child. Your own reflection should not be one of them."

The voice echoes through the cavern, pressing against my ears and into my skull. I turn around.

Huli.

They step from the shadows, their form neither fully solid nor entirely incorporeal. Unlike the last time we met, their face is revealed.

A young woman's face.

The features are delicate, almost painfully so, sculpted with a perfection that does not belong to anything human. Their skin glows faintly in the dim cavern light, like polished pearl, and their robes—blinding white—flow unnaturally behind them, as if caught in an unseen current. Their eyes, though… those are wrong. Entirely black, endless and unfathomable, yet still decipherable in their expression.

Knowing. Not unkind.

I swallow hard. "*You*," I say tightly.

I should feel relieved that I'm not alone, that I have not been abandoned in this alien place. But I know better now. I remember what I have learned about Huli since we last met.

They aren't a foe, but I would not call them an ally.

Huli tilts their head slightly, as if plucking my thoughts from the air. "You are unhappy with me."

I let out a short, humorless breath. "Let's just say I know now what being involved with you entails."

Huli hums at this, as if weighing my words. "Zhèng and Luo have told you about my deals, then."

They step lightly around the perimeter of the cave, their bare feet making no sound against the stone. Huli's gaze lifts briefly to the creatures drifting along the cavern ceiling before they stop near the water barrier, looking back at me.

"They were not supposed to disclose that," Huli says, voice carrying displeasure.

My breath catches. There is no anger in their tone. No warning. But something worse.

Offense.

A sick pulse of worry clenches in my gut. Zhèng and Luo—*Gods willing, Luo is still alive*—might find themselves in trouble because of my blunder.

"They only told me there is a price to pay," I say quickly, rushing to placate.

Huli makes a sound of acknowledgment, something amused yet unbothered. "Of course there is." Their voice dips, as if addressing an impatient child. "I'm a spirit that answers to no one. I help because I *want* to. And I *want* to because there is something in it for me."

The casual arrogance grates against me. My hands curl tighter at my sides as they continue.

"For as long as I have existed, no good deed has ever been done without the expectation of something in return. You of all people should know that."

Heat rises up my neck at the accusation. "And what is that supposed to mean?" I ask tightly.

Huli turns back to the rippling water barrier. The inked darkness still hovers there, waiting. They study it as if seeing something deeper within its depths. When they speak again, it is almost conversational.

"When the pirates boarded your ship, you saved that Rabbit boy and his mates. Not because you are a *good* person, though that is likely what you have told yourself."

I stiffen, my stomach turning to lead.

Huli continues as if recounting a simple fact. "You helped because you received satisfaction from ending a life you deemed *unworthy.*"

My mouth goes dry as I think back to that night.

Had I expected something in return for saving their lives? A feeling of righteousness? The power to arbitrate justice in a world where it rarely prevails?

Huli keeps assessing me. "Even your quest now, though admirable, is selfish in nature. Your care for your clan was an excuse to find Luo. And *he* is an excuse to demand atonement from the empire for ruining your life." Their voice drops. "And to punish it. Rightfully so."

No. I don't feel that way. I wanted to find Luo because I cared about him. Because I wanted figure out what his father knew.

I don't.

I...

They step closer, mist curling at their feet. My body tenses as a wisped hand lifts to my face, gently positioning it back toward the water barrier. My skin prickles at the touch—not quite cold, not quite warm. Not quite *real.*

"*If* punishment is your sole objective, I can introduce you to many forms of power that would enable you to achieve that," Huli murmurs.

I feel myself being drawn in, my pulse slowing. The darkness beyond the barrier calls. The golden eyes watch, unblinking.

I wrench myself free from Huli's grasp, shaking my head, breaking whatever strange pull was trying to settle over me. My breath comes uneven.

"That thing," I manage, forcing the words out, gesturing toward the barrier, where the shadows still writhe. "That is *not* my reflection."

Huli's lips curl into something that is almost—almost—a smile. "Are you so sure?"

I stagger back, horror crawling up my throat, my back colliding with the cold stone wall.

No.

Huli does not press forward. They merely observe, patient and expectant, as though watching something inevitable unfold.

"It is time you *truly* understand what you are," they say. "And what you are meant to become."

I shake my head. "What I am?" My voice cracks slightly. "I don't even know *where* I am."

Huli studies me for a long moment. Then, they gesture toward the cavern beyond. Where the stone gives way to something deeper. "There is someone who has been waiting a long time for you."

They turn, their form shifting as they step toward the tunnel beyond. It is clear they expect me to follow.

My feet remain planted. I *don't* want to go. After a beat, I move with reluctance, into the unknown.

Stumbling through the darkness is unnerving. Each time my shoulder clips the jagged rock lining the narrow tunnel, pain flares. However, it is a fleeting sensation compared to the storm in my mind. I let myself drift, unmoored in contemplation.

What is the crew doing now? Has Zhèng recovered from the attack? Did the dragon return for seconds after dragging me into the depths?

How long has it been? Hours? Days? Have they already considered me lost to the sea, another name to whisper over cups of wine before moving on?

The idea shouldn't sting. But it does.

I press forward, through the haze of blue light that waits at the end of the tunnel, where an opening takes shape. It is covered by long, wilted vines of deep-sea kelp. Huli stands at its threshold.

Beyond the seaweed curtain, there's movement. The ground trembles beneath my feet. The presence lurking behind the curtain must be vast. I know it's another dragon.

Huli turns toward the glow, parting the kelp. The light spills outward, washing over them in hues of blue. They do not look back at me, nor do they need to.

"Come, Shi Yang."

My pulse quickens. My feet remain anchored.

I have exceeded my dragon quota for a lifetime, thank you. Perhaps the wall of water outside isn't as solid as it seems. Perhaps, if I try hard enough, I can push through it and swim back to the surface.

My lungs would burn, my limbs would ache, but it would be better than this. Better than stepping toward whatever power lies beyond that veil.

But just as I prepare to retreat, to run—

Heat burns against my chest.

Slowly, I glance down. The compass.

In the chaos, in the terror of my descent into the deep, I'd forgotten it was even there. Yet it here remains, nestled against my skin. Its silver surface shines, as if forcing me to stay.

I clutch it tightly, the sensation grounding me. It pulls in one undeniable direction: toward the opening.

"Fine," I exhale, shoving my fear down deep where it cannot reach me.

Steeling my nerves, I step forward, pushing past the curtain of seaweed as the compass tugs me onward. The strands caress my arms like grasping fingers before slipping away.

In the center of an abyss lined with blue crystals sits a mountain-like creature.

Redish gold scales shimmer like the sky during sunset scattered across a restless sea, each one gleaming with an otherworldly radiance.

It is the Dragon King—sovereign of the seas, guardian of the boundless depths, a God made of flesh and scale. Awe paralyzes me. I have heard his name whispered in reverence, woven into stories meant to command both fear and respect. Yet no tale could've prepared me for the reality before me.

A sudden prickle of unease sends me searching for Huli, but when I look to my side, the spirit is gone.

Wonderful.

A deep exhalation rumbles through the air. My breath catches as I snap my attention back toward the dragon. As if sensing my discomfort, one massive eye eases open.

The color transitions between the deepest blues of the ocean's trenches and the searing brightness of gold. It peers not just at me, but through me, into me.

When the God speaks, his voice vibrates through my body, a sound that is less spoken and more felt.

Old friend, the dragon's voice echoes in my mind, bouncing off my skull left and right. ***What brings you here to me?***

My heart hammers violently in my chest, and my brows furrow at the implication. But before he continues, I remember how I was abducted.

"You—or one of your dragons—attacked our ship" I rasp, trying to find my footing though the seabed beneath me is nothing but sand. "Why did you do that?"

The Dragon King does not blink. ***I did no such thing. The creature who brought you here was not one of mine.***

I freeze. My mind stutters. "What?"

My dragons do not harm unless told to, he states plainly. ***What you encountered was a beast that serves a different power.***

This makes no sense. I shake my head violently, jumping back to respond to being considered his "friend".

"Okay… But how could we be "friends"? I think I would know if I'd met a being such as yourself before now."

The Dragon King only hums. The great coils of his body unwind, sending currents of wind swirling through the chamber. My hair whips around my face harshly as I stare in disbelief. I instinctively step back, heart lurching as the sheer size of him becomes clear.

When he rises to his full, terrible height, a white mist begins to swirl around him, wrapping around his enormous form like silk spun. It gathers, twisting in a slow dance, obscuring his towering figure entirely.

When the mist finally thins, the dragon is gone.

And in its place stands a man.

A giant of a man—taller than Zhèng, broader than any Imperial Solider I've seen. He exudes an aura so majestic that it makes the very air feel heavier. His skin is an irritated shade of red, a remnant of the scales that once adorned his dragon form. His beard is long and thick, curling past his chest, each strand silvered with time. His face is worn, lined with a permanent scowl.

He's clothed in a heavy red robe, embroidered with intricate golden patterns. Around him, a faint glow lingers, a quiet reminder that he is no mere man, that he has only taken this form for my sake. Not that the small, curved white horns protruding from his forehead leave much doubt of his true nature.

He steps toward me. I swallow hard, bracing myself against the unnatural burden of his gaze.

Finally, he actually speaks. "You do not remember me, then."

It is not a question, but an observation. He seems intrigued.

Before I can answer, he nods, as if understanding something I do not. His expression changes—not disappointment, or satisfaction.

"Not to worry, my friend," he says. He turns on his heel, moving toward the far side of the chamber, where a crystalline wall shimmers like the surface of a still tide lake. "I will help you remember."

With a wave of his hand, the wall fractures, splitting apart like breaking ice. Light spills forth from the chasm beyond, too bright and expansive to be contained by the cavern's depths.

Gods. What is going on?

A rush of dizziness overtakes me. I feel like I'm losing my mind. Or maybe—I'm still trapped in a nightmare.

Yes. That must be it.

If I close my eyes and retrace my steps, if I lie back down in the cavern's cold embrace, maybe I'll wake up on the junk, another morning of grunt work ahead of me, another day closer to the treasure I sought in the beginning. That would make more sense than standing here, at the threshold of a Founding God's realm.

However, before I can make a move back towards the tunnel, the fractured wall reveals something else—something that makes my breath catch and my blood run cold.

Through the chasm of light, I see a throne room.

It's a throne of gold and pearls, of intricately carved armrests and silk-draped walls. One I have only merely heard through the descriptions of the magistrates that passed through the flowerboat. It's the seat of the Emperor of Pingshen in The Forbidden Palace.

However, some part of me—deep within the labyrinth of my mind—knows this is not a mere vision.

This is a memory.

But whose?

29

UNKNOWN
DRAGON KING'S REALM, 1800

I step forward despite myself, my heart hammering, my mind reeling. "Is this another galeglass?"

The Dragon King nods in my periphery. "Yes," he waits a beat, "this is your past."

My head snaps back up towards him. I let out a nervous chuckle that sounds too grating to be considered polite. "Surely, you don't think lying in a moment like this is beneficial."

I know my past. It looked nothing like this.

The Dragon King, as if having expected my disbelief, closes the chasm. "Would you like to know who you were?"

The seriousness in his voice drains whatever calmness I had left from my being. I absolutely *do not* want to know, but the man pushes on without waiting for my response.

"At first, you lived as Lin Mo Niang. A fisherman's daughter who dwelled on Meizhou Island in the mortal realm. It's said that when you were born, you didn't cry nor a shed a single tear. Even past your adolescence you never gained the ability to talk, therefore earning the epithet."

My breath catches. "Silent Girl," I whisper the name. Memories rush back unbidden of my childhood spent in quiet.

The God agrees in acknowledgment before continuing. "Despite being mute, Lin Mo Niang was bestowed the gift of knowing—of divine sight. You could see distant shores as though standing upon them and dream of events yet to pass."

I stand before him, spine rigid. I'm unsure of what to say or do as his gaze pierces me.

"You lived simply," he continues. There is a small note of affection attached to the beginning of his next statement. "You refused to marry, choosing instead to spend the rest of your days guiding fishermen and tradeships from afar, speaking through the wind, the water, and the tide."

I swallow hard, my throat raw.

"You were so revered in your province, that you earned the attention of your dear great leader," he explains. "You were a member of his war council for some time, bringing good fortune and prosperity to Pingshen." His eyes dance around my face for a beat. "Especially, in the war room. So much so, that he had promised to entrust his power to you. But he didn't obviously."

I know who he's referring to, even though it's known as a different name: Mazu.

He makes a small incline of his head. "The one who dared defy the order of Gods and fate alike."

"What did she do?"

"She ascended," he states. "She did not stand in judgment before one of the ten Magistrates of Hell. Lin Mo Niang escaped the Underworld—a feat that proved herself worthier than the Heavenly Court's chosen ones. Her spirit did not travel to the afterlife; instead, it joined the ocean. And the ocean—" he inhales deeply, his massive ribcage rising like the swell of a wave, "—crowned her."

My thoughts swim as the God continues his tale.

"The other Gods did not wish for a mortal to ascend without their blessing. The Jade Emperor, the highest of the Founding Gods, refused to accept her. She was never welcome in his Court. Lin Mo Niang was… an affront to them. A reminder that the Heavens did not decide fate alone." His gaze pins me to the spot. "And they still hate her for it."

I try to take everything in, but I can't help but acknowledge the twinge in his voice. "What was she to you?"

A heavy silence hangs between us before he finally speaks. "She was… my best friend in our first life," he says. "We had meant to be together for eternity until…" he cuts off.

My hands tremble. "Until what?"

"Until she committed a forbidden act," he says solemnly.

My head feels like it's going to explode. "Forbidden?"

"She split a part of her own divinity and wove it into human flesh—a mortal vessel far more powerful than a Jítóng. She did this not out of benevolence, but as a contingency plan. If ever her power were threatened or the balance of the sea jeopardized, she would have a mortal she could shape—mold—into a duplicate deity who would almost possess the entirety of her true power."

I find myself in a state of limbo, tittering back and forth between vindication and fury. My throat is dry, but I force my voice steady. "So, I'm what? A consequence of her greed? Her arrogance?"

"Power is a temptation, Shi Yang, even for Gods," the Dragon King rebukes. "As the living fragment of Mazu's power, hidden beneath human skin, you were not meant to live a mortal life. You were meant to Ascend, to carry out her will when the time came." The Dragon King regards me carefully. "Gods are born from exemplary mortal lives, not created from the manipulation of a single deity. Your very existence incites challenge to the natural order, which, in turn, begets conflict."

My mouth dries. "What do you mean?"

"Others seek to claim you. You know this. Yán Luó. The Emperor. Even those who aim to hold sway in the Jade Emperor's Court. You aren't just a mortal. You are a Godling. And that makes you both a prize and a threat."

My knees buckle, and I have to grasp my thigh to keep upright. "What?"

"The Gods are not as absent as you think, Shi Yang," he says. He clasps his hands behind his back. "Yán Luó and the Serpent Emperor have struck a bargain. One which involves Yán Luó producing a formidable army for Emperor to conquer the world. In return, Yán Luó collects all the souls who will die in the conflicts that follow. And I fear," his face twists with worry, "when Yán Luó accumulates enough death, his power will rival that of the Celestial Court."

My mind races through the outcome of what has been said. All end in war and carnage. However, there is a part of me that resents having all of this being laid at my feet as if it were my problem to solve.

"I understand the severity of the situation, so do not mistake this as apathy, but…why are you telling me this? What do you hope for my response to be? I'm not the world's hero, and I never wanted to be."

The Dragon King watches me for a moment before he proceeds. "The aetherbloom, the suffering, the slow, methodical decay of your people—it was not mere cruelty. It was both an exchange and preparation. Yán Luó informed the Serpent Emperor of your creation before you were even born."

I stare at him, my heart a riot in my chest.

"The Serpent Emperor," he continues, "did what any man does when threatened with something he cannot control. He tried to control you, and when he couldn't do that, he destroyed all Hokans to punish you."

The words slam into me like a broadside cannon.

A calculated attempt to purge my existence. An eradication of an entire peoples. Over a fate I didn't ask for.

A hatred so intense, begins to fill my stomach. It threatens to bubble up my throat and spill out. Similar to the way that boiling water erupted from the maw of the dragon that brought me down here. But, through the fury, my mind refocuses and my goals shift. There is one that must answer to me before and above all. "And Mazu? Where is she while I'm expected to bear all of this?"

The Dragon King's expression mirrors something akin to pity. "She resides in the deep now—off the shores at Soul Singer's Cove."

At this, a chill snakes through my veins. The compass had shown a course that journeyed straight through there.

Was it always guiding me to her?

"But make no mistake, Shi Yang," The Dragon King interrupts my thoughts, "She still watches you. Still waits for the moment you Ascend to claim your place."

"I'm sure she does." I say spitefully.

So many people have tried to rid me of my birthright: free will.

But they failed.

I'm still here. Still alive.

And they will *all* answer.

The Dragon King studies me with satisfaction.

I'm not sure whether I can trust him, but so far, he's been the only one to tell me the greatest amount of truth.

I suppose he is waiting to see whether I will rise or be buried. I straighten my spine, forcing my breath to steady and my hands to relax.

"Huli said that I needed to be ready to learn." I watch his features closely. "What are you able to teach me, and what do you want in return?"

He smirks without saying a word.

Let him think that he has the upper hand in this situation. He is just as much of a God as the rest of them.

"I can teach you only *some things* about the power you inherit from Mazu—powers that me and her share." He paces closer to me. "However, there are also things only I know. Like how to call your dragon. I will show you." He inclines his head slightly. "But the imperative question is: what are you willing to sacrifice to learn?"

I stare him down, a new purpose forging in my mind and heart. "Everything."

PART FIVE:
EAGLE

30

UNKNOWN

DRAGON KING'S REALM, 1800

The deal is struck, and the weight of my fate settles heavily on my shoulders. Without another word, The Dragon King turns, and I follow. The space around us grows colder as we venture deeper into the labyrinthine depths of his realm…domain?

Or is it his prison? I can't tell. I don't know what this place is, nor what it will make of me.

The absence of a sky above me makes time feel like a river without banks, flowing endlessly in every direction. How long have I been here? Minutes? Hours? Days? The thought sends a shiver down my spine.

The scent of moss and damp earth fills my nostrils, pulling me from my spiraling thoughts. At the end of the tunnel, the Dragon King steps into a rocky chasm. A shard of white light slices through the darkness from above, spilling into a circular clearing.

We are far beneath the surface. There should be no light. But I guess the mortal rules of nature do not exist here. This is a

God's realm, a place where reality bends to the will of its master. I could be anywhere. Or worse, I could be nowhere at all.

"I have more than enough time to waste, but you do not. Perhaps you would like to join me so that we may begin?"

His tone ignites a spark of irritation in me, but I swallow it down.

I step forward, my slippers crunching against the uneven stone. The clearing is unlike anything I've ever seen. The Dragon King stands on a raised platform surrounded by a moat of opaque water. The thin stone walkway leading to it looks fragile, as though it might crumble under the slightest pressure. The water on either side of the walkway is impossibly deep, its surface reflecting nothing but darkness. I quicken my pace, my heart pounding as I reach the platform.

The Dragon King folds his arms in front of his stomach. He places his forearms parallel to each other as he raises them to chest height.

His movements are almost ceremonial. I squint, trying to decipher their purpose, but his voice cuts through my thoughts before I can.

"A mortal's ability to *Wield* is nothing more than a reflection of their mastery over their own qì." His voice is slow, just as his movements. "Yours is tainted. Erratic. Shaped in a crucible of suffering. And that makes you dangerous. You must learn to control it. Those with darker intentions wish you to embrace your powers recklessly, for once you do, you will no longer be bound to the will of Mazu."

I glance down at the black water beneath us, its surface still and perfect like polished obsidian. "I fail to see the downside,"

I retort, voice clipped. "I don't want to be bound to anyone's will but my own."

My eyes narrow as I focus on the water, and suddenly, my stomach spasms. Something is beneath the surface.

"That may be true," he says, unmoved, "but this is not about what *you* want."

"And why not?" I counter. "It's *my* Godsdamned life."

The Dragon King says nothing as he lifts his top forearm above his head. "Huli told me about the shadowed dragon you became in your vision. You know a war is coming," he continues. "You've been given a path that will see you at the helm of the very universe as you know it. Do not allow self-wallowing pity to forsake your duty." Then, in one swift motion, he brings his forearm down perpendicularly to the other, creating a sharp angle.

The movement is accompanied by a deafening stomp that shakes the ground beneath us. The force is unimaginable, far greater than anything a being of his size should possess. It's the might of a dragon. The platform splits in two with a thunderous crack, separating me from him. I stumble, my arms flailing as I fight to keep my balance on the trembling stone. He twirls his arms in a fluid motion, once more, first to the right, then to the left, before thrusting them downward, palms open. Instantly, the water around us surges, defying nature and rushing up around us. It arches until it becomes a cocoon of marbled light from above and shadow from below.

Mist weaves around me, threading through the matted spirals of my hair like spectral fingers. For the briefest moment, there is an odd sense of comfort—as if the water itself cradles me, like a child held close to a mother's bosom.

But the moment is ephemeral.

The current thrashes. I snap my head toward the Dragon King. "Then tell me," I shout over the roar of water. "*How* do I unleash my power? How do I call the dragon within me?"

"Dragons are creatures bred from power," he says. "In order to call yours, you first need to understand what fuels your power. What breaks you. What sets you ablaze from within. Only when you finally know the answer, will the beast claw its way out from within you. And if you are not ready… it will tear through more than just your skin."

Before I can respond, he spreads his arms wide.

The water encases him. But it does not drown him—it *transforms* him. His body elongates, twisting, warping into a divine creature. Scales erupt from his skin, his limbs stretch, his spine extends. It is mesmerizing.

Once he is done transforming, the God, in his new form, breaks through the surface of the water to hover before me.

What is the common thread that binds each moment your power has surfaced? His question reverberates through my mind.

I hesitate. My mouth parts, but the words are slow to come.

"Survival," I finally say, but the words feel wrong. "I've always just tried to survive."

Before I can react, his tail lashes out, striking the cracked platform and sending me flying backward.

I hit the wall of water with a force that knocks the air from my lungs. I struggle against the current, my limbs flailing wildly. My vision blurs as I fight to stay focused. Through the warped surface of the water, I can see the dragon watching me. He's waiting, testing me. Pushing me to my limits. He's not coming to help.

My body is demanding air. I reach into the depths of myself, searching for the familiar heat in my chest to rise, to burn, to save me.

Nothing comes.

The darkness closes in, a cold and merciless abyss.

I want to survive. I do.

My vision is going black.

I don't believe you. The Dragon King's voice pierces my mind. ***What is it that honestly fuels your power?***

My heart pounds in my ears. Thoughts of the raid night rush forward. Memories of flowerboat plague me. The possible loss of the crew.

As my vision finally fades, I hear his final command: ***Find your answer or die.***

My eyes snap open.

My hands clutch at my tunic, pressing against my chest as if to confirm that I still exist—that I'm still intact. My lungs heave, but no air soothes them. Every inhale is thin as though I'm breathing in something lighter than air.

I glance around. Nothing. A void stretches endlessly in every direction, swallowing all light and sound.

Where am I?

Panic claws at my throat, but I swallow it down. This isn't death—I see no Silver Bridge, no heavenly magistrate weighing my sins.

The darkness begins to alter. It doesn't recede so much as it folds. And then, there is shape.

Distant outlines emerge as I shuffle forward cautiously, disrupting the stillness of the ankle-high water that stretches through the void. With each step, the scene grows more lucid. The formless dark gives way to lacquered pillars, draped silks, and the cloying clouds of smoke of incense curling toward the rafters. The scene is like an ink painting still drying at the edges, bleeding back into the background. At its center stands a chair—no, a throne.

And beside it, a shadowed figure.

As I amble nearer, two voices fade in. Their conversation is already in motion.

"This was not part of our deal," the hooded figure argues.

I inch closer, careful, silent.

The throne sits high, gilded and monstrous, its gold sheen almost blinding. I move around its edge, my gaze sweeping over the figures before me.

The hooded one strolls nearer, and as the shadows slant across his face I see a violent red complexion, darker than The Dragon King's. Ashen hollows carve deep into his features, outlining them in thick black lines. His face is too lifeless, like a painted mask come to life. But I know better.

It can only be Yán Luó.

And seated upon the throne is the Serpent Emperor. He reclines, draped in robes of imperial gold and obsidian blue, embroidered with dragons that shimmer. The silks ripple with his slightest movement, the threads enchanted to mimic the sinuous grace of the beasts they depict. A crown of sculptured gold and pearls rests upon his head. His face is sharp—high cheekbones, a strong jaw, and eyes like polished onyx. His long, lacquered nails tap idly against the armrest, the only sign of his irritation.

A sharp breath catches in my throat, and I take a reflexive step back, water rippling at my feet.

I freeze.

But… nothing happens. Neither man turns. Neither man reacts.

They don't see me. Or they *can't* see me.

I should not be here.

The Dragon King's words ring in my mind: "*Find your answer or die.*"

Yán Luó saunters from the emperors' side to before him. Looming over the man like the reaper he is. His form is unsettling; a void wrapped in the shape of a man.

The Serpent Emperor's jaw tightens. "I have given you prisoners, Bloomers, and bodies after bodies from my conquests. And yet you speak as if I'm some ignorant prince still suckling at his mother's breast!" He leans forward. "I have even sacrificed two of my ports. There's no way for me to know where she is before she's there!"

Yán Luó obviously does not take kindly to the tone. As with just a raise of his hand the Emperor lets out a choked cough. He struggles, scratching at the golden arms of the chair. He strangles out a thin wisp of a "Please" before the God of Death drops his hand.

The Emperor hacks and coughs violently as breath rushes back into his lungs. After a moment, hand still rubbing his throat, he utters a bitter, raspy, "Apologies, your divinity."

Yán Luó hums before continuing as if the conversation had never been stilted. "You grasp on the situation slips with an unperturbed ease. Those rebels remain. Those pirates remain. The Hokan girl *remains.* Your throne, and the wars you promised me, are under threat on all fronts."

The skin on my arm begins to pebble, as if prickled by a gust of chilling wind. However, I know it to be slinking dread that is the culprit.

The Emperor, now having retrieved his composure, waves a dismissive hand. "She is a speck of dust. She will be dealt with, as will the rest."

A presence stirs at the far end of the materialized chamber. The doors creak open, and footsteps echo closer.

My teeth clench. It is the scarred pirate.

His gait is slow as he makes his way to the throne. The fear he hides beneath his impassive persona is palpable as he stands in front of the duo. He kneels before the Emperor. Then, turning to Yán Luó, he presses his forehead to the seemingly polished floor before standing once more.

"Your Majesty," he says, voice dripping with feigned reverence. "I bring news from Base 3."

"Speak."

"Survivors of a wreck reached its shores a moon ago," the pirate answers. He lifts his head slightly, his grin widening. "I was told that it was Zhèng and his men. They crawled their way to land like rats only to be met with Imperial forces. As of two days ago, they've been transported to Ningbao. Just for you."

My heart hammers at the mention of the crew, relief flooding my system.

Some of them survived. Thank the Gods. Or…maybe not? I don't even know right now.

Wait…

A moon? I'm sure when the dragon attacked the ship, we had at least two moons left. I have only been in the Dragon King's presence for a couple of hours. There's no way I have been gone for that long… right?

The Emperor's fingers pause against the armrest. "And?"

"The girl was not with them, but there is a way we can draw her out." The pirate's eyes gleam. "The Festival of Heavenly Liberation."

I blink at a lost.

"Me and my men will raid the shores the night before, and you can have the Imperial soldiers pin it on Zhèng. The people will be celebrating freedom. No one will question hangings in the name of the empire—in the name of their *freedom*—if they believe the perpetrator has impeded on it." The scarred captain shrugs, letting out a smirk. "A common enemy always unifies a collective."

I want to move. I want to scream, to reach through the veil of this place and tear the beating heart from his chest. But I'm trapped, a ghost tethered between worlds.

"Yes," the Emperor agrees. "That is a good idea. And when my guards stop you, you will be imprisoned for the rest of your miserable life, of course."

At this the scarred pirate stutters. But the Emperor cuts him off with a scathing look.

"You didn't think that your *insolence* would go unpunished, did you?" the Emperor demands. His tone is deadly. "It is *your* fault the girl is somewhere out there galivanting around instead of here in my possession! With *my* compass!"

The pirate says nothing, only clenching his jaw before slowly bowing his head.

Yán Luó only watches the conversation with disdain. Then, as if sensing me, he jerks directly toward me.

My stomach lurches.

He *can* see me.

No. Impossible. I'm not even *there*. I'm—

His lips curl. "Do it," he says smoothly, eyes not leaving the space where I linger unseen. "The girl will come."

I stumble backwards, rushing to get away from him. But, in my hurry I trip over my own feet, and I fall.

I plummet.

Back into the water. At first it was shallow, but now my body sinks. Further and further. From below, the chamber vanishes into ripples of white, black, and crimson. My mind reels, fragments of words still echoing in my skull.

The festival. Ningbao. Hangings.

The crew. Zhèng. Luo.

They will all die. And I'm the only one who can stop it.

More importantly, that scarred pirate will be there. And he will die at my hands.

Heat raises from within, bubbles appearing in the water surrounding me as if boiling. A bright light takes over my eyes, and then I'm out of body once more. Looking at my mysterious power take control of my empty shell. As if on instinct my arms begin to twist and spin pulling ropes of water around my person until it is swirling around me in a sphere. The next thing I know, I'm back inside myself, yellow vision fading, as I burst from the wall of water. My body is thrown from the abyss and flung unceremoniously back into the Dragon King's realm. The moment my body collides with the stone platform, pain explodes through me. My limbs crumple beneath me, my lungs heave, saltwater and air warring in my throat as I choke and cough.

The world spins.

My heart slams against my ribs, wild and frantic, making up for lost time. It recklessly tries to keep pace with the power still coursing through me. I tremble as I press myself up from the damp surface.

A shadow looms over me.

"You found your answer. Good," the Dragon King's voice is calm.

I barely have time to gasp before he speaks.

"Now—again."

31

UNKNOWN

DRAGON KING'S REALM, 1800

I don't tell the Dragon King what I experienced in that void. Partially, I do not think I would be able to find the right words to describe it if I could, but mostly, because he does not ask.

Instead, we spend what feels like hours—which I'm sure is much longer—training. He sends me back into the water, and out I come with only one thing on my mind: Getting to Ningbao before the Festival.

Again and again, I'm thrust into the wall until I return sooner and sooner. On the final round, my consciousness stays intact. No out of body possession. My powers, and the water, respond to my command. It doesn't just surge from my skin—it answers me. Not always. And certainly not perfectly. But enough.

The progress prompts the Dragon King to push my power further in the next trial.

"You're a quick learner," he comments. "Now, you need to learn how to call a dragon. We will start with teaching you how to communicate with one that is not your own."

The wall of water surrounding the domain peels back in a spiral. A serpentine current threads through the air, and from it, a colossal shape begins to form. Blue-gold scales glittering with a sheen of abalone and pearl.

The beast hovers above the Dragon King's head, suspended in silence.

"Though my dragons are not fueled by aggression," he says calmly, "I have instructed it to attack you."

My blood turns cold.

"It will not cease until you've convinced it otherwise."

"Wait—!"

He speaks a single word—one that sounds like it belongs to an ancient language—and the dragon *dives.*

I throw myself to the side, water cascading in a wave that buffers the blast. The sheer force of the dragon's passage cracks the platform beneath me, fracturing into pieces. A shriek thunders through the water-chamber.

I thrust my arms forward, willing the current to answer—and it does, but sluggishly.

Shoūsh!

I lash out with a tendril of water, hitting the dragon across the flank. It barely flinches.

"You'll never best it with force," the Dragon King calls out, utterly unconcerned. "Speak to it."

"Speak to it—?!" I snarl, ducking as the dragon loops back and whips its tail toward me like a battering ram. I throw up a shield of water just in time.

Speak to it.

My heart pounds, my mind races. I don't know the language. I don't know the *words.*

Another pass. The dragon plunges again, maw open. Rows of translucent teeth like sculpted glass. I roll, reach into the well of my power—and push.

"Stop!" I cry.

The water surges around the dragon, forming a barrier. But it tears through, unfazed.

The shockwave alone hurls me backward, off the platform and into the ink-black depths of the moat. As I plunge beneath the surface, a searing burn blossoms across my skin. I can still hear the dragon's roar above, muted and distorted, but the rest of my senses begin to fail. My eyes see nothing, I gag on the taste of sludge. This is nothing like the water from before. Fighting against the heaviness of the liquid around me is futile. My chest is retching on my last strings of consciousness, when I feel a slithering sensation curling around my limbs. The next breath, my skull explodes in agony as its unraveled and breached. In the space that follows, I am no longer in my body.

In my mind's eye, I am face to face with darkness. But from that darkness emerges more and more dragons. Their eyes watch for only a moment before they merge into one great entity. One consciousness. A consciousness that shows me the truth.

Of how they were once free as the guardians of the Astir World, spiritual guides to the others. Beings of peaceful qì. Until the Great Ascent. It was then that the Gods culled them and their might into servitude for their regimen. Creatures of will and wisdom debased into monsters of ruin going against their very nature. And when the dust settled—when the Astir World had closed them out, and the Corporal World saw them as nothing but something to fear—there was nowhere left for them but with the Gods.

I feel their grief. I feel their sorrow.

And then it's gone.

I'm wrenched violently from the vision, expelled from the water with no warning. Air scorches my lungs as I crash back onto the platform, coughing, shivering, reborn into pain.

The Dragon King simply stands with his arms folded. Watching.

Bastard.

The dragon roars again, dragging my attention back to the fight. I throw myself under the dragon's body, twisting the current to propel my body upward, over its spine. Water crackles around my arms. I wrap it into a pointed spear and hurl it—the point strikes the dragon's shoulder. It shudders, turns, eyes gleaming.

In them I see no hatred. And I remember: it's not fighting me because it wants to. It's following a command.

Like I did, for so many years. As a girl with no choices, forced to obey.

When I land back on the ground, I stop all assaults. The dragon whorls in front of me, rearing back. Ready to charge.

But I don't dodge. Instead, I close my eyes.

Show me how to speak to you, I think. Not in words. In feeling. *Show me how to reach you.*

A thrum echoes in my chest. I remember the dream-void. The pressure of drowning. I listen to my qì just like Ah Fei had told me to. In it, I find chaos. And when I extend it to the dragon, it takes it. When I've opened my eyes, our consciousnesses become one.

The dragon halts mid-lunge. Its body vibrates.

I hold my arms out wide. I open myself—every wound, every fear, every ache.

The dragon slows. It circles, eyes locked on mine.

As I hold its gaze, I am transported through centuries of existence these spiritual beasts have lived. An existence spent looking for the same thing as me: freedom.

We are the same. I say to it. *Help me, and I will not use my power to exploit you. Not like the Gods have.*

The chamber stands still as I await the dragon's response.

Unexpectedly, the serpent leans forward, brushing its snout against my hand as it lets out a soft rumble.

I release a breath I hadn't known I was holding. My forehead gently touches the rough skin. Then, the dragon begins to dissolve, its form unwinding. It returns to the water, to the wall, to whatever place it came from. But something lingers in its absence. A whisper in my blood.

We heard you.

I stagger back, my legs nearly giving out.

The Dragon King does not praise me. He doesn't need to. I know what comes next. "I'm going to try," I say.

The Dragon King regards me for a long beat. "I don't think you are. It may reject you if you try to merge with your dragon spirit now."

"I know, but I don't have time."

He turns and steps aside, leaving me alone at the center of the bedrock disc. The walls of the chamber still tower around me, curved like the inside of a shell, water threading down them in lines.

I kneel. I let the water touch my skin, seeping through my pores, curling around my wrists. I close my eyes, and I listen.

Come to me. Show me where you are.

A deep, thrumming warmth spreads through my limbs, my veins, wrapping around my ribs.

For one fragile moment, a larger presence within awakens. I can sense a great body rising from slumber. Somehow, I can feel the barest hint of molten breath against my consciousness. Feel two blazing golden eyes with vertically slit pupils looking back at me.

But the moment doesn't last.

A searing pain lances through my chest, and suddenly, I'm falling again. Not into water, but into myself; into a hollowness where something vital should've been.

The connection severs in an instant, slipping through my grasp. The presence withdraws, retreating into the depths of my being, distant and untouchable.

I gasp back to reality, my body curling in on itself.

A bitter ache radiates from my sternum, as though something inside has cracked further instead of healing.

No—no, no, no. I'd been so close.

I clench my teeth against the wave of frustration and disappointment. Somewhere above, the Dragon King observes in silence.

"You are still unbalanced," he says at last. "Your qì remains fractured. Without harmony, there can be no bond."

Unbalanced? Fractured? My qì was solid enough to start controlling my powers. Good enough to communicate with the other dragons. Why not my own?

I force myself upright, though my limbs feel worn out. "Then I will fight without it."

I've spent more than enough time here.

The Dragon King regards me. "Even knowing that you are incomplete?"

My lips press into a thin line.

Incomplete. Yes. I know that better than anyone.

I'd come here seeking answers. Instead, I found only more proof of my own limitations.

But, I no longer have the luxury of time. The Corporal World won't pause for me to find balance. And Yán Luó certainly won't either. Someplace far above—too far—the Festival will likely soon commence. Zhèng and the crew are probably already in chains. Or worse.

I straighten, ignoring the way my body aches. "Send me back."

"Send yourself back," he responds.

Another test.

I close my eyes and call for the beast. At first, nothing. And then, it answers.

From beneath the swirling depths around us, the dragon returns, its body coalescing from ocean mist. It soars through the space before finally laying before me. This time, I don't hesitate. I rush forward and mount its rounded back, steadying myself on the curve of its spine as it arches like a tidal wave ready to fall.

"And Shi Yang," the deity calls. "Do remember that the Celestial Court *is* watching you."

I don't stutter. "Good. They should be."

I lean down, pressing my hands softly onto the dragon's skin. "Take me to Ningbao," I whisper.

The realm opens a portal before me—a path of water parting through the wall, a gateway to the world beyond. And the dragon flies, carrying me with it through a whirl of light, mist, and pressure. The world blurs until—

We breach.

Water gushes around us as we rocket back into the mortal realm. Wind howls. The stars above are real now—pinpricks of clarity in a night sky that tastes of salt. Beneath me, the dragon twists and swims through the air just above the water's surface. Spray fans from its sides like wings. The surface gleams silver-white in the moonlight.

We are far from land, but I can feel the compass around my neck already pulsing as we fly higher and further through the night pulling me exactly where I need to go.

Hours slip past in a blur of cold wind and aching limbs. I try to sleep, curling into myself to escape the high-altitude chill, but it creeps in anyway. However, I can't say that I mind it too much.

We pass over the mainland as the sun dawns. And the way its golden light reflects off the mountainsides… I blink against the brilliance, and to my surprise, tears prick the corners of my eyes.

This view—it's unlike anything I've ever known.

Despite the uncertainty of what's coming, I think I finally understand what it means to be a bird, suspended between earth and sky. Unfettered by walls or chains or the judgments of those who live with their feet rooted to the ground.

A grunt from the dragon beneath me pulls me out of my reverie.

Ningbao is just over the horizon.

I press a hand to the creature's scaled hide, offering silent thanks—whether for the flight, the clarity, or the companionship, I'm not quite sure. Perhaps all three. I brace myself for the gradual descent.

In the remaining time, I intend to develop a plan.

Zhèng. The crew. If they're anywhere in the city, it won't be in the open.

I force myself to think.

Where do secrets linger longest? Where does knowledge seep through the cracks?

My mind turns, and turns, and turns. Then, it clicks.

I reach Ningbao in the early evening. The city on the small island rises like a fever dream, a mirage made real on the edge of the South Pingshen Sea. Fireworks burst in the sky, painting dragons in light above the city. Boats crowd the harbor, covered in red silk and flower offerings. The entire shoreline sings with drums, flutes, the rousing of thousands of people in celebration.

The Heavenly Liberation Festival has begun.

As we near the port, the dragon dips low, gliding just above the waves to avoid drawing too many eyes. I rise carefully to my feet. The shoreline races forward.

"Go," I whisper to the dragon. "Melt into the tide." Then, I leap. The sea closes above my head, sound vanishing. As I descend, the dragon dives behind me dissolving on impact.

As I'm floating underwater, the serpentine silhouette of the creature forms before me a final time.

Thank you, I say.

It nods once, before falling away into the depths.

Now, I'm alone.

I swim underwater, my resolve solidifying with every tread of my limbs. When I finally reach the island, behind a line of rocks near the south docks, no one notices. Especially not in the madness of celebration.

The streets are ablaze with color and motion.

Crimson banners ripple in the wind, bearing the Emperor's sigil. Children race between stalls with sparklers in hand and mouths sticky with tanghulu, laughing through clouds of fried meats and dumplings. Women in embroidered robes carry offerings to the temple, their footsteps in time with the beating of ceremonial drums.

My heart races—not from awe, but from urgency.

I crawl from the shallows, water sheeting off my clothes, and disappear into the flowing crowd of bodies before anyone can properly see me. The heat of the crowd begins to dry my soaked tunic as I weave through market lanes and down narrow alleys.

I press deeper into the city's center, slipping behind vendor carts and ducking under awnings. When I spot the largest brothel, I know I've found the place.

Its entrance is wide and gold-lit, with velvet curtains. And outside of it, Imperial guards.

Dozens, flanking the entrance that leads to the upper levels of the brothel—the part reserved just for the Imperial magistrates.

Their boots are clean, which means they haven't been stationed long on the ground here. These aren't common city guards. These are ceremonial enforcers, brought in for the Emperor's appearance at the Festival—and likely to keep order during the executions.

One of the guards leans down to speak to a robed official who gestures toward the eastern tower behind the temple complex.

A firework blooms overhead, and for a moment, the sky burns purple. The crowd roars in delight.

I slip back into the shadows, my body pressed to the cool stone of a nearby wall. I exhale slowly, steadying my pulse.

The next part of the plan begins.

32

LATE EVENING
NINGBAO, 1800

While waiting for the streets to thin of commonfolk, I manage to snag a few skewers of roasted meat left too long on an abandoned vendor's cart, and a bolt of silk pilfered from a distracted washerwoman's line. The fabric is dandelion yellow and slightly frayed at the hem. It's long enough to fashion into something resembling a concubine's robe. I braid and force my hair into an updo, twist the silk across my chest, and bind the ends with a cord torn from the same laundry line.

My old tunic gets stuffed deep into a mound of alley trash, buried beneath rotting fruit peels and the stink of piss.

The compass I keep tight to my waist, bound beneath the sash. I have no sword, no dagger. So, I need to make this quick.

Get in and get out. My presence does not need to be known by Yán Luó.

I roll my shoulders back, and force softness into my steps as I make my way over to the building. My gaze is lowered as I approach the soldiers. It only takes a total of ten heartbeats before they begin to jeer.

"Now, where did *you* come from?" one of them calls, eyeing my hips.

"Lost?" another asks, stepping closer, fingers already twitching near his sash.

"Blessed be the Emperor," I breathe. "I was told to come here for the commander."

They laugh.

One of them throws a chicken bone into the pathway. "*Which* commander?" he leers, accent heavy.

My heart picks up subtly, as I scramble for an answer. One vague enough to evade direct naming, but specific enough to distinguish a fetish.

Several eyes wait expectantly.

"The one… who demanded someone who doesn't ask questions," I state finally.

I wait with bated breath, preparing myself to run if the answer doesn't suffice.

But to my luck, one of the soldiers chuckles, "Definitely Commander Wáng."

I let out a discreet, shuttering sigh.

"He's up top toward the back rooms," comes a voice from the side of the group. My eyes flick to the younger guard. He's less drunk than the others, more eager to prove himself. Maybe nineteen summers. His armor too big at the shoulders.

Him.

I walk past the rest. "Will *you* take me to him?"

He straightens a little, chest puffed. "Me?" he asks, suspicious but intrigued.

I nod. "I was told not to come through the front." I lean into whisper, "He doesn't want too many eyes."

His eyes scan my skin, considering. Hesitation lasts only for a moment before his pride wins.

"Come with me," he says.

The other drunken soldiers resume prattling as we step away from the entrance.

We move quickly, down the side alleys veined through the back of the pleasure house. I make sure we stay just ahead of the brothel's noise, away from the street torches.

As soon as the last echo of laughter fades behind us, I strike.

Elbow to his throat. He stumbles, choking, and I slam him into the wall before he can draw breath to scream.

He's stronger than I expect. He lashes out, catching the edge of my jaw with his fist.

He goes to reach for his sword, but I catch his wrist, twist it hard, and drive my knee into his gut. When he doubles over, I slam his head against the wall.

Once.

Twice.

He crumples, dazed, but still conscious. Blood dribbles from his temple.

"Zhèng Yī?" I hiss, gripping the collar of his uniform. "The pirate and his crew—the prisoners from the ship. Where are they being kept?"

He grits his teeth.

I jab my thumb into the base of his throat with as much force as I can muster.

"They—" he gasps. "In the tower. Past the temple. Shackled. They're set for execution with the third day's Imperial Procession gong."

I hold until his face goes pale. Then, I let go.

The tower. How am I supposed to get in there in less than a day?

Shouts come from behind me. The clatter of boots.

I bolt, darting back into the street with the silk robe flying behind me, feet slapping stone.

An arrow skims my arm, grazing flesh. I scream—but it's more instinct than pain. Another arrow. I duck behind a barrel, roll into the alley mouth, before stumbling back onto my feet. I pivot down a narrow pass, but it ends in a stone wall. I skid to a stop, trapped.

I turn, heart wild in my chest, compass burning against my skin. It thrums faster and faster.

There had been a well of water in the main plaza in front of the temple. If I run back in that direction before they get here I can—

"There she is!"

Three of the soldiers rush toward me their swords glinting.

So be it. At least they aren't the ones with the arrows.

The first one attacks, blade already half-drawn, but I don't meet him with force—I turn. I pivot on my heel and step into the flow. The soldier's weight works against him. I catch his wrist, redirecting the arc of his strike, and shift my hips, letting his momentum roll across my back. He stumbles forward—off-balance—just long enough for me to plant my elbow hard in his spine. A crack sounds as he crumples with a yelp of pain.

The second soldier is already on me.

I duck low. His blade whistles just above my head.

I rise into him like a wave from beneath, slipping under his guard. My palm strikes his sternum in a snapping motion—*fajin*, Old Chou called it. Energy released in a single, focused burst. He gasps and staggers back, mouth open but breath stolen. I land a sickening kick at his kneecap. It juts awkwardly out of his leg as he falls in agony.

The third sends his shoulder slamming into my ribs. I hit the wall hard enough to rattle my teeth.

Pain explodes through my side. I try to pivot, but I'm slower now, winded. He grabs my hair, trying to slam my head back against the brick, grabbing me from behind.

A chunk of hair rips from my scalp—I bite back a cry and stomp down on his foot. Elbow his ribs.

He grunts, but doesn't let go.

The first soldier is crawling back up.

I thrash, trying to shift my center, trying to find the softness in the motion, the yielding. But there's no space. His arm locks around my throat. My vision pulses.

I can feel myself slipping away—my limbs going sluggish, my thoughts scattering like dropped coins.

There's a thud behind the soldier and I, as if something has dropped down into the alley from above.

The soldier doesn't have a single second to react before he gurgles, his arm around my neck falling away with a jerk.

I fall forward on my knees, gasping for air. I focus on the dirt path as my breathing evens out. But then, a pair of feet step into my vision. When my eyes follow them upward, I'm met with a woman. But not just any woman—a woman with golden eyes.

The rebel leader from Formosa.

She offers her hand. I take it, letting her pull me to my feet.

"Come," she blurts, taking off toward the mouth of the pass.

I follow immediately without question. We run and run until the sound of the soldiers' spiked boots are a distant hum. I stagger behind her through the alleyways, breath shallow and feet dragging, the pain in my ribs dull beneath the haze of adrenaline.

The rebel woman barely glances back, but she slows enough to let me keep pace. She doesn't speak—not until we reach an old gate at an abandoned local bathhouse.

We round to the backside of the house. The woman kicks open a hidden panel and shoves me through. We run in pitch-black, the confined air heavy with moss and mold. When we reach a rotting door, I see light coming from behind it. Without ceremony, she pushes it open and twenty pairs of eyes greet us.

Rebels in armor stitched from fishing net and scrap iron, others in brigandine, faces hidden behind painted masks. One hammers out nails from a crate of black powder barrels. Another scrapes dried blood from a set of knives. From the outside, it's a ruin. Inside, it's vibrant with breath and purpose.

The woman doesn't address the questioning eyes of her comrades, just waltzes over to the one with knives handing him her own. Most of the others in the space take the hint and go back to their work or conversations. I just stand there dumbfounded.

"Umm…" I say slowly. "Hello?"

The woman turns to me as if she had already forgotten I was there. "Yes?"

Her nonchalant attitude is off-putting. But I find myself slightly amused.

This must be how it feels to speak with me.

"Uh, thanks for saving me…" I follow up. My hand reaches up to cover my sluggishly bleeding arm.

She eyes the gesture, but doesn't acknowledge it further. "Don't worry about it."

Several questions are running through my mind. There's so much I want to know about her. I blurt out the first that comes to mind.

"What were you even doing there? What you're *all* doing here?" I ask. "Don't get me wrong, I am very grateful, but Formosa is quite far from here."

That makes the other people in the room return their attention to us.

For a beat, it looks as though she is contemplating whether to respond or kick me out. But then, she decides on the former.

"I was there," she starts, "because I've been following some of those Imperial *pigs* around, familiarizing myself with their patrol routes and routines, for days now." Her words are short, and to the point. "That's how I know that The Emperor arrived a day ago. He's been holed up in the temple like a rat since he got here."

I like her.

"I saved you," she continues, "because Ah Fei would've wanted me to." Her eyes rake over me. "Having seen you with him in Formosa is the only reason I intervened," she says bluntly.

Okay. Maybe I don't like her.

However, the mention of Ah Fei makes my stomach twist.

Of course. That's what Ah Fei had been talking about. "Don't think we don't have an army of our own."

She presses on. "He's the only reason I'm about to show you something very important."

She doesn't wait for me to inquire further. Instead, she gestures for me to follow her into a room farther in, where a painted map of Ningbao stretches across the wall. Colored thread marks the Imperial Procession route. Red tags cluster around the final plaza like a slow bleed.

"What's this?" I probe cautiously.

"The reason we're here. We're going to kill the Emperor."

She says it so simply as if it's inevitable.

Then, my mind floats back to Merchant Fang and his slip of tongue.

"This plan of yours," I breathe, "I heard someone allude to it moons ago…" My eyes zero-in on her features looking for a tell.

She only shifts her weight slightly.

"It was a Merchant. Fang. You know him?" I press.

She weighs her options for several moments. "He's a…" she pauses, choosing her words carefully, "benefactor of sorts."

Before I can wrap my head around the information, she pushes the conversation past the topic quickly.

"We plan to end it at the Procession tomorrow. The Emperor will be there, in person, surrounded by dancers, tributes, guards, distracted. Too busy lauding in the praise of the sheep that follow him," she almost spits.

I inhale slowly. "End what?"

"Their occupation of the archipelagos. Their hands choking our islands. He uses us as a buffer against the West knowing that he's inciting a war. They will leave our islands to burn while their warships cower behind our homes," she explains. "With his death comes the liberation of the western islands."

They're real people who've lost cultures, names, entire bloodlines. Just like me. But…

My eyes wander to the corners of the room where several barrels of gun powder sit with purpose. "You're going to kill civilians in the process."

Images of the children running through the streets with sparklers come back to mind.

The rebel leader—she still hasn't told me her name—glances at me sideways. "These Pingshens will not shed a single tear when The Untamed or The Others annihilate my people first." Her next words are firm. "Causalities are indivisible from the realities of war. I rather it be them, than us."

And, honestly, I can't say that I disagree.

Killing the Emperor is enticing. Almost distractingly so. But… the crew needs me. Zhèng and Luo need me. And more importantly, I still have scores they could help me settle.

"I need to get into the temple at the Festival's center without being seen."

She quirks an eyebrow as if wondering what that fact has to do with her plans.

I rush out an anecdote that I'm sure will make her reconsider. "There are prisoners behind it that I need to get out. And I think Ah Fei is among them."

An unreadable look flashes across her face. The leader uncrosses her arms before responding. "I saw them being dragged in a couple nights ago. There weren't many of them," she comments apologetically.

My stomach drops, but I push through.

"I know they're being held in the tower behind the temple, but I will need—"

"A distraction?" she cuts in.

"Time," I correct. "Mayhem that I can use as a cover. I'm not here to stop you."

She studies me. Not just my face, but deeper.

A long pause.

Then, to my surprise, she smiles. It's not warm, but there's something in it that feels close to understanding.

"You'll get your distraction," she says at last. "But once the Imperial soldiers take arms, we won't be waiting. We strike at the heart. You'll only have a couple of minutes after the first bomb goes off."

I level her with a stare. "That's all I'll need."

She nods. "Then it's settled. You can sleep here tonight. We set out to plant the barrels and take our positions at dawn."

The rebel leader finally tells me her name, Mei, before sending me to be fixed up by their in-house medic. They give me a bowl of porridge, and a small blanket sprawled across the dirt in the corner. After that, she—along with the rest of the rebels—all finalize their parts in the siege tomorrow and call it a night.

However, I can't help but twist and turn anxiously.

What if the bombs don't go off tomorrow? What if the rebels fail? They're woefully outnumbered. What if we all die tomorrow?

I heave a sigh, trying to shut my mind off for just a moment.

Screams render the air.

I snap upright with the rest of the room. Bodies jolt into motion, half-clothed rebels stumbling toward the weapon crates. A blade clatters to the floor.

"Is it the guards?" someone breathes.

But the door of the bathhouse doesn't burst open.

Instead, in the distance there are more shouts and sounds of wood cracking, of torches hitting a dry stall. Then, women's panicked shrieks.

My blood goes cold.

I forgot. In the blur of the day, in the heat of planning, I forgot what tonight was. The scarred pirate's plan.

My hand shoots to the sword rack.

"Shi Yang!" Mei shouts behind me as I wrench a blade from the wall. "Where are you going?!"

I don't answer. I'm already out the door, feet pounding over dirt, the compass thumping like heartbeats against my breastbone.

The scarred pirate is here. It's time I end him.

The glow of fire climbs through the early morning sky. Lanterns swing, their tassels catching flame. People run in every direction, dressed in their festival best, their sleeves soaked in blood and ash.

And standing at the end of the street, as if it were all his stage—*him.*

His ruined face splits into a smile when he sees me.

I break into a run.

He pulls his sword slowly from his sheath, like he's been waiting for this moment, and then darts away from the main fight into the nearby alleys back toward the south dock. I race after him.

The fires fade behind me, but the air here is pungent with smoke. The area is closer to the sea, full of half-burnt empty shacks where people have since fled. Their broken doors swing in the wind.

I venture deeper, turning in a slow circle, sword gripped tight in my hand. My head snaps left and right. "Coward," I mutter under my breath. "Come out and face me."

A sudden *slice* flashes across my right shoulder.

Pain blooms hot. I gasp, swinging my blade in a wide arc.

But there's *no one there.*

My breath comes fast.

"You should've stayed on your back, girl," comes a snarl from the shadows. "You had your chance."

"Where are you?!" I scream.

There's another swipe from the other side, this time at my side. I cry out, stumbling back into a pile of broken crates. My free hand presses against the wound. Blood seeps through my fingers.

My eyes flit frantically around me. "Face me!" I shout, voice hoarse. Still nothing.

But I remember what Ah Fei said.

Listen to the qì of the world around you, and then listen to your own.

I stabilize my breath. Everything fades. The blood, the sting, the spinning fear. I push them all away.

I can feel the buzzing energy in me, in the dirt beneath my feet, in the wood of the stalls behind me, in the waves from afar, and—

There you are.

I duck under the next shadowy blur that rushes me and drive my sword up in one sharp thrust.

Metal meets flesh.

A grunt. He stumbles back.

Now I see him—fully. The scarred pirate, stepping from the veil of darkness, blood running from a fresh wound along his ribs.

He charges again. We clash—steel on steel. My wrists rattle from the impact of the blow. I let out a growl and lunge. Our blades lock again—shoulder to shoulder.

With every strike, flashes of the flowerboat plague my mind. The beatings. The ghastly men. All because of this *animal.*

I let out a roar, swinging the rusty blade in my hand at his head.

He dips. The sword gets stuck in the wooden beam of the building behind him. It takes me too long to pull it out. He shoves me back. I skid and pivot on instinct, catching his next swing with the flat of my blade. Sparks fly. I strike back with short, fast cuts—aiming for his legs, his side, his neck. He parries all of them.

Fury surges through me.

This sword is not enough. But I know what will be.

I spin away from him, toward the sound of the body of water. Only a few paces away.

I sprint toward it. But then, my legs are arrested, the familiar dark feeling taking over my limbs.

"Oh, don't you think about running," the pirate shouts almost hysterically. "I was supposed to live a long life fat off riches and domination. But because you just couldn't stay in your Godsdamned place, I'll be in prison until I rot!" His shadowed grip grows tighter. "You should've died with the rest of those barbarians!"

My feet slide across the dirt as I'm dragged back to him by his shadow. He expects me to give up.

But, I'm not the same person I was all that time ago.

With a yell, I pull my arm, fighting against his hold. It's slow and painful. Pulling at the very joints of my shoulder, but I lift it in the direction of the dock and—

Water slams up from beyond like a geyser. I snap my wrist back, and the stream speeds through the air. It lands true on his chest, sending him staggering backward. The attack shocks him and his shadow weakens.

That's more than enough.

I spin, slashing down my arm. The water slices through the wooden frames of the stalls, knocking him to the ground.

My attacks don't stop. The air around me is humming.

He deflects my assaults with his shadows, but I give him no time to counter. Finally, I raise both hands. The water splits into four streams. Like tentacles, they writhe, lashing out to wrap around his wrists and ankles.

I flick my hands up and each strand pulls taut, hanging him up above the ground.

He groans in agony as they pull farther and farther apart.

My breathing is ragged. A heat from within swelters and builds in my chest. Golden light begins to accumulate in my eyes until it is all I can see.

More water from the dock flows around me now. Small serpentine rivulets wrapping around my body as I walk. The water creates a vortex at my feet, propelling me to his height.

"Go on then," he heaves brokenly as his limbs are stretched to their limits. "Kill me. It makes no difference." A lazy smirk crosses his face. "Even *you* can't stop what's coming."

"Maybe not," I concur. "But I *can* end you."

The water forms a spear—long and clear.

I thrust it forward.

It pierces his chest with a wet crunch. He gasps—chokes—but I don't stop. I force more water into the shaft, expanding it inside him, ripping through bone, tendon, and lung. His scream breaks apart in his throat. Ribs crack. Flesh tears. The squelch of ruined organs is the only sound I hear. The only sound I *care* to hear.

Then, nothing.

I release the water holding him, and his body slams to the earth with a dull, final thud. I sink to my knees, the strength draining from my limbs. The light fades. All the rage, the purpose that carried me here evaporates.

I stare at him. The hollow shell. The bloodied ruin of a man who caused so much pain.

And I feel… nothing.

Only a cold, cavernous emptiness yawning open inside me.

Is this what vengeance tastes like?

I search for the fury I once clung to like a lifeline. The grief. But there's only silence now, echoing back inside a body that no longer knows what it's supposed to carry.

I'm unable to dwell any further on the thought, because in the next second, a deafening explosion rolls through the city with a *boom*. People scream in terror.

In the distance, at the temple, a larger column of smoke billows in the air.

The rebels must have changed their plans. The rescue isn't later. It's now.

33

DAWN

NINGBAO, 1800

Mei warned me: after the first bomb detonates, I'll have mere minutes to reach the tower. Minutes before the Imperial forces bear down upon the city like an iron fist.

I'm entirely too far from the temple's plaza now. I'll never make it there in time. Unless…

I exhale sharply and shut my eyes, tuning myself to the water's hum like a struck bell. I call…

A large splash spills from the water at the dock. Moments later, a colossal form flies overhead. I look up at the dragon, its mass silhouetted by the brightening sky.

The dragon's vast body gleams with rivulets of water sliding down its blue-green scales. It descends toward me.

"I didn't mean to call you back so soon" I say. "But I need your help."

It lowers its body in front of me. ***Climb on.***

I waste no time.

In one motion, I vault onto its back. A hand latches onto a twisting horn, as my legs brace against the curve of its neck.

Then we're gone, lifting in a vertical climb that presses my spine to the sky.

Below us, Ningbao is a scorching battlefield.

It's utter chaos as civilians flee for the harbor, clutching bundles of belongings and screaming names over the roar of destruction. The pirates have vanished, leaving the rebels behind to clash with the advancing Imperial guard. Through the ruin of the pleasure quarter, just beyond a collapsed archway, someone darts across the wreckage with too much agility to be anyone other than Mei.

Before I can think, I murmur, "Down."

The dragon obeys. It plunges fast into a death-spiral that rips the air around us. The scream of wind drowns everything.

We slam into the earth with a quake that fractures the stone beneath, sending dust floating into the sweltering air. The dragon coils protectively around the perimeter as I leap off its back and run toward her.

Mei is laying waste to one guard when I draw close. Her face is smeared with soot and blood, her dark hair a mess. She flinches when I call her name.

"Mei!"

Her head jerks. Her golden eyes widen at the sight of me—and the dragon behind me.

"What have you done?" I exclaim, chest heaving. "I thought you were supposed to wait for the Procession!"

Her mouth presses into a hard line. "That pirate ambush? It gave the Serpent Emperor the perfect pretext to run. If we hadn't moved now, we'd have lost our only chance," she quips, voice is ragged with hatred. "And I wasn't going to let that happen."

I swallow a spike of guilt.

I should've told her—should've warned her about the scarred pirate, about the Emperor's plan.

But the confession withers on my tongue as the ground suddenly lurches. Another distant blast, from the temple this time. The dragon's head turns sharply toward the noise, its body rising.

My stomach lurches. I can only hope that the tower behind it is still standing.

I send Mei a censuring look.

She tightens her jaw, meeting me head on. "I told you that you would only have a couple of minutes," she says unapologetically.

Despite my irritation, I want to stay and help her and the rebels. I want to ask her about her eyes. But I can't. Not right now. And if this attack goes to shit, likely not ever.

My lips pucker as I make peace with having to leave her, and whatever answers she holds, behind, before sprinting back toward the dragon. I swing onto its back, gripping the spine ridge with raw fingers. Then we're airborne—cutting through the rising smoke and ash, heading straight for the temple's broken silhouette.

Toward the Emperor and Yán Luó.

Toward the crew.

The temple is no longer whole. Its once-elegant ceramic roof has collapsed inward, reduced to fractured beams and shattered tiles strewn across the scorched plaza. What remains is a blackened skeleton—ruins.

I count at least a dozen guarding the blackened steps of the sanctum, their blades and bows drawn, muskets shouldered. Others dig frantically through the rubble, searching for survivors or perhaps corpses.

I guide the dragon lower, angling for the tower beyond. That's when they spot us.

Shouts erupt. Arrows whistle upward—some already set ablaze. The dragon jerks midair, twisting and banking to avoid the barrage. We dive, skim, circle the perimeter of the plaza. Through the smoke, I glimpse the tower—half-collapsed, charred, but still standing behind the temple.

Then the dragon screams.

A flaming arrow pierces the side of its neck. It twists in pain, dropping in altitude abruptly. I lose my grip. My body slips, slides—then falls, plummeting to the ground below. A scream rips from my throat.

Then I remember.

The well at the center of the plaza.

I wind my arms around, trying to mimic what I learned in The Dragon King's realm.

I'm falling closer and closer—

Water shoots up high from the well, curling until it finds my body. Just before I hit the dirt, it cradles me, breaking my fall. I slide down its crescent shape, my feet skim across the plaza atop a wave that carries me. I veer left—then right—channeling water into long ribbons that lash outward, cutting through the soldiers. The water shields me from both sides as arrows fly and bullets sing.

Behind me, the dragon recovers enough to unleash a sweep of its tail. The last of the guards are hurled backward, their bodies slamming into broken pillars with bone-snapping finality.

Once the opposition is quelled, I spare a quick glance at the mess of a temple.

Yán Luó… he's too powerful to die from something as mortal as falling stone. But the Emperor…

I shake my head.

They are not the priority. Not right now.

I race back to the tower. the splintered remains of a stone wall, now little more than rubble. I vault over the broken slabs, scraping my palms, scrambling with torn fingers over sharp rock until I reach the soot-blackened entrance.

With a sharp motion of my arm, the last of the water from the plaza rushes after me. It hisses as it snakes across scorched ground, then surges up the stone tower walls, soaking it to the bone.

I don't wait for the steam to clear.

Inside, it's dark and rank. Chains rattle in the gloom. I smell the iron before I see it—and rot and sweat.

"Zhèng?" I call. "Ah Fei? *Anyone*?"

I'm losing hope when—

A cough answers. Followed by a voice like rust scraping metal from somewhere far above: "Took you long enough."

I bolt for the narrow staircase, taking the steps three at a time. My slippers pound the stone, resounding up the shaft. At the top floor, I come to a sudden halt—and the sight steals the air from my lungs.

Ah Fei is slumped against the far wall, face a mess of bruises, one eye swollen shut like a rotten plum. Huò lies beside him in a pool of drying blood, his chest rising only shallowly. Rabbit hobbles toward me on a mangled leg, missing two fingers, his face streaked with grime and disbelief.

"Shi Yang," he breathes. His voice breaks on the first syllable. "G-Gods, ya' came."

Old Chou sits propped in the corner, a grotesque bruise spreading across his cheekbone, eyes sunken with exhaustion. He smiles faintly, despite it all. "Told them…" he murmurs, barely audible. "Told them you'd come."

The burn in my throat reaches my eyes. I have to bite the inside of my cheek hard enough to taste blood to keep from falling apart.

No time. No time.

I drop to my knees and press dampened fingers to the corroded lock. Water flows into the mechanism, and I saw back and forth until it snaps.

I rush forward, tearing at ropes and rusted cuffs, helping one man up after the next, hands trembling as I move from face to face. Huò can barely stand without help. Rabbit leans against me with a ragged breath. But it's Zhèng—

I freeze when I reach him.

He's barely recognizable. His face is a grotesque map of swelling, blood, and bruises. His skin has taken on a grey-green pallor, and for a terrible moment, I think he's already gone.

My breath catches.

But there's the faintest rise and fall of his chest.

"What did they do to him," I whisper hoarsely, voice cracking.

"They beat him," Huò answers, voice like gravel, "for days. And…" he swallows, unable to look at me. "almost drugged him to death with aetherbloom. He's been unconscious for over a week."

My fist clenches so tight I hear a knuckle pop. I drag in a breath, trying to center myself, trying to remember what comes next—where we need to go, what we need to do—but something's wrong.

One person is missing.

"Where's Luo," I ask slowly.

No one answers.

I whip around. "*Where is he?*"

It's Ah Fei who responds this time. "H-he's not here," his voice cracks. "He survived the dragon attack. He made to Base 3 with us. But… he never left. He's still there."

At that, the world begins to shutter.

No. No, no, no, no.

"Shi Yang?"

I'm going to be sick.

"Shi Yang!"

They are going to tear him apart there. He's going to be nothing more than shell of himself when they're done.

"Shi Ya—"

Old Chou's voice barely reaches me before the tower shudders violently beneath our feet. The wooden floor lurches sideways, throwing us all against the walls. Dust rains from the ceiling. The sound of gun powder fills the air. Another blast shakes the entire structure.

The rebels are going to blow the entire plaza up.

I refocus.

"Grab Zhèng and follow me," I announce urgently.

I rush to Old Chou's side, draping his arm around my shoulders and guiding him through the spiraling hall. The stairs crack beneath our weight. Smoke curls in from a lower floor. Somewhere below, a fire has started.

I don't look back.

We reach a window. One of the few not yet blown apart. Wind howls through the narrow arch as we step onto the slim landing.

"We're going to have to jump," I say breathlessly, scanning the smoky skyline.

"Come again?" Hé sputters behind me, dragging Zhèng's limp weight in his arms. "You want us to what?!"

There's no arguing. No room for doubt. The tower is groaning. With a sharp whistle through my teeth, I call to the sky.

Come on. Come on. Come on—

The dragon tears through the smoke. It lowers itself by the opening and they jump onto it one at a time. I'm the last to go.

Behind me, the wood groans again—longer this time. The floor beneath my feet trembles. Then the entire wall behind me collapses inward with a roar of fire and ceramic.

I jump.

Wind claws at my skin. I'm weightless for a heartbeat—

I slam into the dragon's side, slipping down the curve of its scales. My fingers scrabble for purchase, but I'm sliding—fast.

A hand catches mine.

Ah Fei's face appears above, teeth gritted. "I've got you!" he yells over the wind.

He pulls hard. I scramble up, panting and wide-eyed, heart thundering.

Go! I tell the dragon.

Then, we're off toward the port of the island.

When we reach the docks, it's pandemonium. Smashed crates and burning skiffs litter the shoreline. Civilians scream and scatter. Bodies with injuries from the bombs lie in pools of blood. The remnants of boats drift in shattered pieces, masts broken.

The dragon drops low, hovering long enough for us to dismount. Then, it retreats back into the sea for the last time.

Thank you.

My gut clenches at the goodbye I don't have time to give.

We begin scouring the docks, eyes darting, hearts racing. We need a junk—anything seaworthy—to escape.

Suddenly. a coldness slips inside my lungs, beneath my skin, behind my ribs. I stop, turning.

Behind us, the burning island groans and spits embers into the sky. And down the charred planks of the dock, his robes untouched by flame, comes a figure heading toward us with steady, unhurried steps.

Yán Luó.

"You," I snarl.

"Ah." His voice is smooth. "You recognize me. That saves time." He takes another step toward me.

I raise my voice, eyes never leaving him. "Get to a boat! Do not wait for me!"

Behind me, there's a scramble.

"But—" Hé starts, desperation coating his tone.

"I said go!"

My voice thunders with something not entirely human. It silences all argument. I hear their feet pounding the dock as they flee.

Now it's just us.

"You have him," I seethe.

I don't have to tell him who I'm talking about.

Yán Luó's smile twists. "He will be… a great asset of mine," he murmurs, as if speaking of a game piece. "If you try hard enough… perhaps you'll see him again. Eventually."

My body reacts before my mind does. My scream is wordless.

A wall of water rises behind me as I throw everything I have at him—daggers of water, tidal waves, spears and blades sharp enough to flay bone.

But Yán Luó barely moves. He steps through it all like mist. He raises a hand. Just one. Then slashes it horizontally. Darkness explodes from him, slamming into me like a battering ram. My back hits a dock pillar with a sickening *crack*. Pain sears through my ribs. I gasp—but before I can suck in breath, another blast of shadow strikes me, knocking me into the sea.

The world goes silent.

Salt stings my eyes as the sea closes over me like a tomb.

I sink.

Deeper. And deeper

Golden light blooms inside my skull, and my eyes flare open.

A whirlpool begins to churn around my body, violent and wide. The ocean spirals in maddened hunger, dragging nearby vessels into its maw. Ships collide. Wood splinters. Because something has stirred. A dark entity rearing its head.

It feeds off the anger. The rage.

It says, ***Yes. Use me.***

And, I do.

My mind splits open, falling inward and downward, and my body follows. My form twists, expands, warps. Bones stretch and skin thickens. Horns curl from my skull, massive and jagged. Claws lengthen into obsidian blades. I let the shadow dragon take over.

I storm out of the water, a massive, dark beast of wrath. The few civilians who remain at the dock drop to their knees in awe or terror, their minds barely grasping what they see.

Yán Luó simply watches—arms folded behind his back, head tilted in detached curiosity.

I dive straight toward the God of Death with an otherworldly howl. Just as my claws are about to rend him from existence—he lifts a single hand.

And *stops* me.

My entire body halts mid-air, frozen in place by an invisible force. I flail, twisting violently, my tail lashing out.

"You cannot fight death," Yán Luó says, voice still calm. "Not yet."

With a casual flick of his wrist, he slams me down. *Hard.* The dock shatters beneath me like glass. My roar is ripped from my throat as my gigantic body convulses from the force. Even in this divine form, I feel my power fracture.

I quiver in pain, watching uselessly as he walks up slowly. When he stops before my trembling mass, I brace for death.

But it never comes.

Instead, he just looks at me calculated. "I underestimated your potential," he says at last. He leans in slightly, his eyes gleaming with cruel promise. "You are too useful to kill. Yet." He straightens. "We *will* meet again, Shi Yang."

Without flourish or drama, he turns. His body disintegrates into wind and ash, vanishing in a swirl of smoke that's swallowed by the wind.

One day, I'll kill you.

The golden light that once surged in my veins and eyes begins to fade. My ribs rise and fall in labored heaves.

I try to fight it, but… darkness claims me.

There's soft wood beneath my cheek. The pitch of the floor beneath me makes my stomach tilt slightly. But my eyes remain shut.

Why won't they open?

My brow furrows. My skin feels tight, bruised. Every inch of me aches with exhaustion.

Come on. One, two, three… open.

I still see nothing. I move my toes just to rule out the possibility of me being dead.

Still alive. Okay, one more time. One, two, three…

My eyes peel open and I am immediately greeted by light that is too bright.

My eyes peel open—and immediately I regret it. The light is far too bright, white-hot and stabbing. My eyelids slam shut with a hiss of breath.

I try again, *slower* this time. Blinking past the haze.

Wooden beams blur into focus above me. The scent of salt air and musk lingers in my nostrils. Canvas flaps in the wind. Ropes groan against masts. I blink a few more times, and then it all becomes clearer: I'm in a cabin. Small, cramped, swaying gently. A ship cabin.

And this ship is sailing.

But how…?

Beyond the thin wooden door, voices rise in muted conversation. Familiar ones.

"—she'll wake," Huò mutters. "She's too damn stubborn to die."

"Honestly, I wouldn't expect her to wake up any time soon," Hé says. "Not after what she did."

"Well, someone needs to take the helm," Huò counters. "Zhèng's out for at least a couple moons."

A laugh from Ah Fei. "We've already decided, didn't we?"

There's a pause.

My eyebrows twitch.

Decided?

The bed creaks as I force myself up onto my elbows. I groan as lightning stabs through my ribs. My body feels like it's been trampled by war horses.

Before I can utter a word, the cabin door crashes open.

Four faces spill in—bruised, burned, bloodied, but… smiling.

"Shi Yang!" Hé throws himself forward before I can brace. His arms wrap around my shoulders as he mutters a stream of curses and thanks, his voice shaking. I wheeze a breath, barely able to lift mine in return.

Ah Fei saunters up to the bed with a proud smirk. "Well look who decided to stop napping," he says.

Huò and Old Chou lean against the doorframe with arms crossed.

"We saved Zhèng," Huò adds quickly. "He's below deck. Alive. *Barely*. But alive. Don't worry, I stitched him myself. The herbs are holding."

"You scared the hell out of us," Ah Fei mutters. "But then again, when haven't you?"

I try to crack a smile at the comment, but even my lips hurt.

"You're alive," Old Chou murmurs softly. "That's all that matters."

My chest pulls tight. I want to speak, to say a thousand things. But all I manage is, "Where are we?"

"Sailing west," Ah Fei replies. "Just off the coast of the mainland. We're still being hunted by the Imperial Navy, but we've got distance. For now."

"And Pingshen?" I ask. "The Emperor?"

They all exchange looks.

"Well," Huò starts, "it's rumored that the Serpent Emperor was killed in the bombings. No one has seen him since, but the rubble's deep. They're still searching."

"As for everything else," Ah Fei shrugs, "Chaos. Revolution in some cities. Celebration in others. It's hard to say which is which. There's a power vacuum warlords are eager to fill."

I sigh. "The Untamed will advance for sure. The Other too. They'll certainty see this as an ample opportunity to invade."

The thought brings an uncomfortable chill through me.

My head tips back against the creaking wood of the headboard. The ceiling swims above me.

So many dead. A war on the horizon. We gave Yán Luó exactly what he wanted. And Luo… is still gone.

I am halfway into that spiral when Hé's voice cuts in again.

"Sure, the world's going to shit," he says, "but at least we have our new captain to show us the way."

My head snaps to him, then drifts to the rest of the crew. No one contests.

The compass around my neck thrums once. Then, it spins. And spins. And spins.

THE END

SHI YANG'S STORY WILL CONTINUE IN

THE DECENT

COMING 2027.

ACKNOWLEDGMENTS

First and foremost, I need to thank my family.

Thank to my mother (and my first supporter) for being one of the biggest inspirations for Shi Yang as a character and a woman. A black woman. You have shaped my perception of what it means to be a giver, a hero, and a good person. I hope throughout this book, as you read, you found that you—your bravery, elegance, and intelligence—were reflected. Your drive and dedication to what you love astounds me, and I cannot wait to take on this writing journey with you in the future.

Thank you to my sister Rae for helping me discover my affinity for sociology and understanding the human condition. It led me to poetry, which led me straight to writing fiction. You have been a consistent source of light and laughter in my life, and I cannot imagine living without you. We share the same mind, so, I knew when you told me that this book was "something I should be proud of", that it was indeed my calling. I appreciate every shoulder and ear you've lent me, and I plan on continuing to do so for you forever.

And to my lovely, darling husband—thank you for being my rock. For pushing me to not only better myself and take care of myself, but most importantly, to make space for myself. Since the moment I told you of this goal you have done nothing but support me in every way you can. I cannot confess enough gratitude for that. You have had a hand in this project every step of the way. From flying me out to China and Hong Kong to do in-field research, to providing cultural anecdotes and information that made this story so incredibly rich, to helping me do my final (final and actual final) edits. You are a dream. You are an angel. And you are mine. Thank you for carrying me and my passion project in the palm of your hand so that it may bloom as safely as it has.

To my older sisters Jen and Ness, thank you both for being some of my earliest supporters of my love for the arts. Ness, I still remember watching you draw on the stairs and copying it. That love is what got me into art school which led me to the professor who encouraged me to become a writer. And Jen, going to concerts with you when I was a teenager, been exposed to how art can touch one's soul changed the way I looked at life. It made me believe in the power of creativity—something completely intangible, yet it makes the world go round. I will forever be grateful for those experiences.

I love you all more than words could ever explain.

As for non-family members, I would like to thank all of my friends, both online and in real life, that have supported me through this process. I am glad to have you in my life.

I would also like to thank the researchers that informed so much of the world and character building within this story. I will now list the authors and their projects/articles/etc. so that others may learn what they have spent a great deal of their livelihoods discovering:

"Culture Summary: Taiwan Hokkien" – Ian Skoggard. 1995.

"Medium of the Margins" – BiblioAsia, 2020.

"Technical Choice and Social Practice of Sampan Boats" – Yan Zhang, 2019.

"Examining Pre-Colonial Southeast Asian Boatbuilding" – J. Malig, 2016.

"Tangka Floating Life Dissolves" – Modern Chinese Literature and Culture Resource Center, 2017.

"The Uncertain Origins of Hong Kong's Tanka People" – Louisa Lim, 2016.

"Junk Trade, Business Networks and Sojourning Communities: Hokkien Merchants in Early Maritime Asia" – James K. Chin, 2010.

ABOUT THE AUTHOR

Y. Hu received degrees in Sociology and Art from the University of California. She is currently pursuing a law degree, whilst living peacefully in the mid-west with her husband. The Ascent is her debut novel in any genre.

Printed in Dunstable, United Kingdom